The Gift
That Time Forgot

T M Dewfall

This book is a work of fiction: Names, characters places and incidents are either the product of the author's imagination or, if real, are used fictitiously. All statements, activities, descriptions and information of any kind contained herein are included for the reader's pleasure and enjoyment and cannot be relied upon for accuracy.

ISBN: 978-0-244-95663-9

First published as an eBook in December 2017

The right of T M Dewfall to be identified as author of this work has been asserted by him in accordance with the Copyright, Designs and Patents Act 1988
All rights reserved. No part of this book may be reproduced, transmitted or stored in an information retrieval system in any form by any means without the prior permission from the author.

For Sarah

Your love of the environment and its beautiful green and blue spaces is the only reason this book exists today. Perhaps we can only hope that one day the world might be so much safer, so much fairer, a kind and loving place for all humans and every one of the planet's wonderful creatures.

Prologue

Twenty Thousand Years Ago, Maybe More

It was a beautiful summer's morning, or at least the signs suggested it was going to be. The sun had not long risen to give this part of the world a glorious yellow glow. Gentle waves lapped at the shore, carving tiny ripples in the sand, and out to sea lingered the remains of a hazy mist.

Cutting through the air, a strange whooshing sound could be heard, faint at first, but growing with each passing second. Anyone watching would never have been able to recognize the noise, let alone believe their eyes as the spectacle unfolded.

Luckily no one was watching. There was no one around, and there would not be because no soul existed in this place back then. There was just a beautiful sandy shoreline with magnificent trees growing to within a hundred yards of the beach. A river flowed nearby, cutting through the sandy mounds, its waters disappearing into the sea after a pleasant meandering journey.

Appearing as if out of nowhere, the prow of a boat nudged its way into view; piercing the receding mist as it did so. It was a vessel the design of which had never been seen before. It was shaped like a shell, mimicking a giant clam, its upper surface almost transparent but with a sparkle reflecting the sun in myriad angles. A second boat appeared, then a third, and another, then more, until ten of these strange looking craft emerged, each heading for the shore.

Around the boats appeared the source of the strange noise that now echoed throughout the area. Great whale-like sea beasts were gently rising and falling, breathing and blowing, their hot air dispersing the mist or perhaps even causing it. Lines or ropes connecting these magnificent animals to the clam-like craft were disconnected, coiled up and safely stored. As each whale was released, it gave a great bellow and moved gently alongside its boat.

Then many hands reached over to pat and caress it in a visible show of gratitude and affection.

The creatures gradually formed a long line and began to sing out together, a beautiful harmonic sound calling to the world as if offering a greeting. They swam out further for a few hundred yards, searching for slightly deeper, more comfortable water, then turned around and waited. Moments later they were joined by hundreds of dolphins, also part of the great trek north, all jumping and spinning and plunging playfully back into the sea. They too had played a significant role, swimming and surfing at the prow of every boat, dramatically reducing the drag of the water, keeping the journey at a fast and steady pace.

Each craft inched forward until it ground upon the sand, the bow precisely designed to fit the slight incline of the beach, two ramps appearing moments later. As the boats lined up together, close to the river's exit, at least a hundred people from each one jumped ashore. Uncertain of the next move, they began to confer, seemingly discussing the best way forward.

Eventually, these people stood, facing the trees, and waited. Standing there, still and hardly breathing, they were an impressive vision. Some were tall, some shorter, with a wide variety of skin and hair colours. Everyone was strong, fit and healthy, prepared for what had been a long and testing voyage. Their clothes were simple; all wore trousers and tops, men and women both, each in gently varying colours. On their feet were thin almost invisible shoes of a stunning design, closely following the contours of their feet, offering protection without constraint.

Thousands of birds of nearly every variety soon emerged and broke the silence, their song bringing alive every tree along the beach. Three of the boat people, one man and two women, stepped forward, their smiles beaming on their kindly faces. They exchanged glances, then the woman with auburn red hair now glowing in the early morning sun held out her hand. As if a communication had somehow passed between them, the birds fell silent. Moments later, many could be seen flying off in different directions, each seemingly with purpose and intent. A group of larger birds, almost eagle-like but bigger and stronger, soared upwards and began circling and spreading out, moving further inland. Then the birdsong resumed, their effortless harmonies a joy to hear.

Apparently taking the renewed birdsong as a cue for action, the visitors began moving back and forth between their boats and the shore, executing each step with a quiet and calm sense of focus. They started unloading containers that looked like mini versions of the clam-like vessels, but these had a flatter bottom, a deeper inside and a lid hinged at the back.

Within a few hours, all the containers were unloaded and lined up along the side of the nearby river where they displayed an incredible variety of contents. There was an impressive range of dried fruits, berries and nuts, box upon box of neatly packaged seeds, clothes, materials, tools and spares. More surprising was their collection of musical instruments, both string and wind, and a keyboard of striking innovation. In other containers, exotic plants were growing with peculiarly shaped leaves and bright, colourful flowers, some emitting an enchanting pale blue glow. Nearly everything was carefully wrapped and protected from seawater and dampness.

Two people from each boat eagerly volunteered for the final task. Once aboard, the craft gently reversed from the beach, and manoeuvred to face the sea, before departing smoothly and calmly, with no visible sign of power or propulsion, and no agitation in the water. When they reached the point where the whales and dolphins were waiting, pinpointing the perfect position, the craft stopped and began to revolve, gathering speed and spiralling down beneath the waves. As they approached the seafloor, they continued to rotate and grind and displace the sand underneath. In a few minutes, the boats were hidden, secured in the seabed. The two crewmen from each boat were met by their dolphins as they surfaced from the water and carried quickly back to shore.

Only then did the whales gather in an arrow-like formation. In a final flurry of rising steamy breath, they began to leave, surrounded by the dolphins, all finally heading home, wherever that might be. As they gently drifted away, a wondrous whale song resounded through the ether. A tantalising rhythmic beat filled the airwaves, caused by the regular slapping of their tales and blowing of their breath, all resonating back to the beach.

Having stood to watch their craft safely moored below sea level, the newcomers now joined in. They sang in beautiful harmony with the whales and danced to the captivating rhythm, obviously a favourite melody performed many times before. Once again, the air was filled with the swishing of wings as thousands more birds joined in the celebration, each one chirping its part in the chorus. As they flew out to wish farewell to their departing friends, many could be seen landing on the backs of the whales, hopping from one leg to the other, simply dancing for joy.

Not to be outdone and desperate to be part of the day's proceedings, a cloud of the most brilliant and highly painted butterflies surrounded the people still dancing on the beach, their movements choreographed to perfection with the music as they flitted to and fro, flying in circles, energising the air around them.

When the song ended, the new arrivals cheered and clapped in a show of friendship and love, watching as the whales gradually disappeared from view. Silence reigned but only briefly, a sign of respect and gratitude. The birds had all returned, their mission completed; news of "the arrival" had been passed on.

Slowly at first, then growing in volume, a rustling noise came from behind the trees, and ghostly ripples appeared in the river. Showing no surprise or concern, the boat people grew ever happier and more delighted. Animals, hundreds and thousands of them, nearly every shape and size, began emerging from the forest. Otters and beavers were bursting from the banks of the river, and in their wake, fish were leaping playfully from the water and flapping their fins. The boat people clapped and cheered once more as the animals jumped all around them, seemingly overjoyed to meet their visitors.

At that moment something almost unimaginable occurred. Without saying a word, one of the boat people, the same female with piercing green eyes whose auburn red hair was now adorned with brightly coloured butterflies, made eye contact with a beaver, sending each other into uncontrollable laughter. Of course, it was contagious, and soon all the boat people were in fits of giggles. Incredibly, the animals and birds were making their own laughing noises too, and the fish were gurgling with pleasure. These were sounds that had never been heard before, at least not on these shores.

What took place next would have astounded anyone else there to witness it. The animals gathered together, teams of rabbits, rats, mice, squirrels, otters, beavers, dogs, hogs, and many others too.

Each team headed for a shell container selected by its size and weight. Some containers were lifted and dragged over rough animal tracks alongside the river or through the forest, the tiny creatures hiding underneath acting like wheels, the larger ones pushing and nudging, providing momentum and guidance. Other containers were gently pushed into the river where they floated and were paddled and propelled upstream, the fish below providing lift in the shallower waters, allowing the containers to skid along their slippery scales. As soon as one animal tired there was always a queue of others there in support, offering to take its place.

Where they could, they followed the river, as the terrain was as level and gentle as could be. There were, of course, areas where the river was partially blocked. Here, the otters and beavers had to carve a way through, letting friends in their wake repair any damage as the last container passed by. Occasionally they had to leave the river and find another route, recruiting more suitable animal helpers, especially over the remaining five miles or so.

The people followed closely, taking diversions where necessary, guided by the eagle-like birds flying high above. They were clearly in good spirits, singing, joking and laughing along the way, but still with a steely determination that exuded confidence and lack of fear. They too were organized into teams to carry and share the task of transporting their containers.

How they knew where they were going or why is a puzzle. It seems the destination had been part of a global search that had started many years previously. The search had been carried out, not by humans, but by birds all around the world, each with a shared understanding of what was needed and an area to discover. As the search narrowed to a mere handful of places, squirrels and other small creatures had taken on the task of a final evaluation. Somehow pictures had been relayed and, between them all, the final choice of location had been made. It was a home suitable for tens of thousands of people, well away from rising sea levels and ferocious storms, a place of safety, a place to develop and thrive and continue their most demanding journey.

The birds and animals had been only too delighted to take up this challenge. Just why this incredible accord existed between these particular people and these creatures is hard to understand. It was based on trust, based on a shared respect and love for each other, and a desire for freedom, simply an astonishing sense of togethering.

By the middle of the following day, they had all arrived at their destination. As the crow flies, it was little more than twenty-five miles. In reality, of course, it was far further as the river meandered this way and that, carving routes around hills and across the countryside. Despite the distance, the journey had been undertaken without a single accident. There were no broken bones, no strained backs, twisted ankles, torn scales or damaged fins. As the last of the animal teams arrived, the final container was nudged into position with the others, now all neatly lined up outside their final resting place.

Finding a way in had not been easy but the rats had first discovered and then enlarged the entry point and guided them to it. Almost immediately they found the old dried up waterway that had previously been identified, providing a smooth but undulating path directly into their new home.

Those carrying the small transparent plant containers went first, lighting the way with the plants' pale blue glow. As they entered the darkness, the blue light of the plants began to grow in intensity, almost as if the leaves were feeding on the darkness itself, eventually creating a sense of daylight. At the end of the path, they could hardly believe their eyes as they emerged into the most magnificent cavern you could ever imagine. It was huge by any standard and full of incredible translucent stalagmites and stalactites, formed over thousands, maybe millions of years.

They stood there for quite some time, struck by the sheer wonder of it all. Feeling invigorated by the sight around them, they began to carry all their containers up into the cavern and stack them neatly together. Despite their strange shell-like shape and various sizes, they all managed to fit together perfectly.

Making their way back outside, the boat people climbed up and stood on the rocks high above the cavern. They called out to thank all the animals that had helped transfer them to this incredible location, creating a chorus of joy and pleasure with their harmonious voices that would never be forgotten. The animals, in turn, waved or shook their tails or barked or tweeted in reply, before simply vanishing from sight, perhaps heading home. One moment they were there, the next they were gone.

The boat people returned to the cavern and some started to unpack the critical containers. Others began assessing the cavern's internal and external structure and quickly confirmed their plan to enlarge the inside. Their first task was to identify those stalagmites and stalactites that could be safely removed. In fewer than two days, the cavern began its rebirth, taking the form of a magnificent circular dome-like building, creating a vision of astonishing beauty. The overall plan and all the fine detail had been part of a meticulous design process started several years before and carried out by teams of their architects and artists all working closely together with a single objective.

Even now, panels around the edge of the cavern were being created and carved with inscriptions that were designed to be remembered forever. Some of these inscriptions described their epic journey to this wonderful place, and all the preparations required to make it a success. Others told of the whales and dolphins and their tireless undertaking. More spoke of their arrival at the beach and the joyous activities of the birds, animals, and butterflies. Later panels would record their beautiful homeland now left behind, their history, their achievements, the difficult decisions taken, and everything else about them.

On their third evening, however, something happened, something almost too awful to describe. Many of the boat people were outside assessing the immediate landscape, planning its future use, doing calculations, making drawings, laughing, happy and enjoying life. The sky overhead began to cloud over, darkness setting in. Wondering what was happening, they looked up to see the sky full of birds flying north. More and more animals began to appear, each travelling as fast as their legs could carry them, a few entering the cavern but most climbing up and over it to the rocks high above. The air was alive with warnings and urgent glances that could not be ignored. Without hesitation, everyone retreated inside the cavern, sealing it with a large rock positioned by the entryway.

Hardly a minute later, a terrible destructive power unleashed itself somewhere in the world, leaving only unbearable pain, sorrow and sadness. The very event that had terrified them and triggered their expedition to this new land had occurred. The earth beneath their feet shook and continued to vibrate. For more than an hour they waited, hoping the cavern would hold, worried they might all be buried alive but fearing far more for the lives of those outside.

Many hours later they ventured out, their hearts heavy, fearful of what they might find. Not only had they felt the world shake and tremble, but, deep inside themselves, they had known the piercing pain of their animal friends.

As they rolled back the entryway rock to assess the damage, everything seemed normal, as if nothing had changed since the day before, except a lingering smell of sulphur in the air around them. They sent their scouts out in all directions. The eagles were back, high in the sky providing support and guidance. When the scouts returned, it was clear that life was far from normal. Beyond the cavern and its immediate vicinity, a disaster of untold magnitude had occurred. The beautiful woodland they had recently travelled through close to their landing beach was terribly damaged, with thousands of trees uprooted and toppled. The land within many miles of the coast had been severely flooded.

Their divers discovered their craft still intact, safely buried under the surface of the sea where they had been secured. What they did not know, however, was whether their follow-up boat people would ever arrive. The abrupt end to their communications suggested the worst.

They were not to know, but it was a disaster of unimaginable suffering. Their whole population was lost, and their beautiful homeland was destroyed, now resting hundreds of feet below sea level. A huge earthquake had occurred, almost directly below it, creating a massive fracture in the earth, wrenching continents apart with unbelievable force, causing a massive tsunami and triggering eruptions of many previously dormant volcanoes. It was an untold disaster in the world as they knew it. Millions had died, and a thousand times more animals and birds had been wiped out.

Only then did they realize, with a terrible sadness, what had become of some of the creatures that had so willingly given their time and energy to help them just a few days earlier. Those living near the sea had tragically perished in the floods caused by the tsunami. Even the survivors now had new homes to build, new lives to create.

The predictions made by their scientists had become reality, but far sooner than expected. They knew how lucky they were to be alive, to have survived at all, but struggled to shake the sense of loss for those who had died. Their new home inside the cavern had been well chosen, far away from the source of the earthquake. It was strong enough and high enough and far enough away from the turbulent waters. Though shaken, it had survived undamaged except for a few broken stalactites. They hoped the messages and warnings given months before to old neighbours near and far had been taken seriously. They desperately hoped that others had survived too. Their new accommodation was intended to be home for a hundred thousand; now little more than a thousand would live there.

Such losses made the future more challenging than ever. They needed to carry on what others had started a long time ago; the most important work mankind had ever been entrusted with. This task rested with them alone now. With complete trust in each other and all their animal friends, they still believed they could do it. Despite everything, they had no choice. They would not look back. They had to get started. Now. Together.

Chapter 1

Today

'Where are you? You're late.' Fred's mobile phone vibrated. 'Those shifty looking guys are back, come quickly.'

'Agh, look at the time,' Fred shouted to himself as he threw down the spade and dashed into the house.

He washed his hands, grabbed his wallet and keys, then rushed for the front door, slamming it behind him. Careering down the front path he skidded hard right. Thirty paces and another right turn around the corner, he narrowly missed the postman. Fred's cries of 'so sorry' hit the back of the poor flustered man who was now scrabbling around on the ground gathering up his scattered postbag.

He raced the eighty yards to the end of the street, took a left turn, sped across the road, then almost stumbled over the moss-covered rickety brick pavement. He swerved sharply right into Cumberland Walk, narrowly missing some fresh piles of dog mess. 'Honestly, does no one use those dog litter bags, shameful!'

Four minutes later he arrived and threw himself into the waiting seat, gasping for breath, his fair hair all over the place.

'Where have you been? We've been sitting here for ages,' said Jo. 'And just what are you wearing?'

'Sorry,' muttered Fred, hardly able to get his breath back after his mad dash to get there. 'Old gardening clothes. I've been preparing the ground for Dad's new shed. It's arriving soon, and I promised I'd help. Anyway, what's happening with our four crooks?'

Jo, Fred, Bill and Sally were sitting at a table outside Ye Olde Chocolate Shoppe in the Pantiles in Tunbridge Wells. It was a perfect place as it was traffic free so there were no noisy vehicles constantly revving their engines and no diabolical diesel fumes spewing into the atmosphere. It had always been a popular place to stroll and be seen, and that was still the case today. It had a charming historical feel, with foundations and buildings dating back to the

1600s and the Chalybeate Spring was famed in the past for its healing waters. But there was far more to it than just an attractive and welcoming place to meet. There was always a murmur or muttering of history that was hard to identify but impossible to ignore. It was as if the place was desperate to reveal a secret from its long forgotten past, gently nudging those present and urging them to return when the truth might finally be told.

Jo and her three pals were all thirteen years old, with birthdays just a couple of months apart. They had been friends since primary school, which seemed like eons ago now. They were all in the school orchestra, various clubs and societies, with Jo and Fred in several sports teams too. Bill was a technology wizard always playing with computers and other electronic bits and bobs. Sally was mad about chess but not yet good enough to get into the school team.

'They're over there,' said Sally, 'in the next café, huddled together. They keep arguing, obviously up to no good.'

'Are you sure?' laughed Bill, slightly sceptical. 'They could just be discussing finance or politics for all you know.'

'Don't be daft,' replied Sally. 'Just look at how they're dressed, all in black, plus it's all in the body language. They've been behaving oddly, you know they have. They're most unpleasant.'

'You can't judge a book by its cover,' said Jo, 'but I do agree they have been acting strangely for several days now. Just as well we've been keeping an eye on them. They're constantly tapping away on those iPhones, checking them all the time.'

'Hmm,' muttered a jealous-sounding Sally, 'It would be great to have one of those, they're so cool but just silly money.'

'Ah well, you'll have to get a part-time job,' laughed Bill. 'A newspaper round would be perfect. That I would love to see, you getting up early and peddling off on your old granny bike.'

'That's not fair. I could if I had to, you know that.'

'Come on guys, let's be serious. Somehow we must find out what they're up to,' said Fred. 'If only we could hear what they're saying.'

'We could attempt to plant a bug on their table,' said Bill. 'That's what James Bond would do, surely?'

'Or better still get Harry Potter to cast a spell to broadcast their entire conversation out of this teapot spout,' added Sally.

'Let's move and take the table next to them,' suggested Fred.

'No way, we'd be far too close,' said Sally. 'Those guys are positively evil. I'm staying right here.'

Jo suddenly sneezed several times, grabbing a paper tissue from her pocket to wipe her nose and dab her watering eyes.

'Your hay fever is bad today,' said Fred sympathetically.

'Yes, it's the bright sunlight this morning. Dusty rooms set me off too. It's particularly bad this year, I don't know why.'

'Seriously, we have nothing to worry about,' said Bill. 'Those guys have no idea we exist, even though we've been following them nearly all week. They're too absorbed in their own devious business.'

'Right,' said Fred, 'I'm going to stroll over there and see if I can get any clues about what they're up to. I'll walk past, under the colonnades, as if I'm going along to the newsagents at the far end.'

'Don't you dare, that could be dangerous,' said a worried Sally.

But Fred was up and off. They held their breath as they watched him close in on his target, linger briefly behind them to look in the café window at the menu, and then walk on. Three minutes later he was back. As he took his seat, a cloud of butterflies swooped in on him then fluttered away and began to circulate around Jo's head.

'Wow,' said Sally, 'look how brightly coloured they are, there's a whole swarm of them. They seemed to be following you, Fred, although now they appear to have adopted Jo instead.'

'Yea, perhaps they prefer your shampoo, Jo,' laughed Fred, 'or more likely they're just attracted to your red hair. There was one flying around me when I was digging in the garden earlier.'

'I've never seen anything like it,' said Jo, gazing up. 'There must be ten or more, and so many different colours. They are absolutely beautiful. Anyway, my hair's not just red, it's auburn red, so there!'

'Their movements seem to be coordinated,' added Bill, 'as if they're dancing to a tune we cannot hear, painting delightful circles in the air. One's landed on your hair, Jo, and another. Oh, now they're off, lifted gently away by the pleasant summer breeze.'

'Bill, what's happened to you? That was almost poetic,' smiled Sally, winking at the others. 'Anyway, come on Fred, what did you overhear? Spill the beans. I'm desperate for gossip.'

'Sadly, nothing. They were just muttering to themselves. Then two of them started speaking in a language I couldn't understand. Jo, it's a pity you weren't there to help me out,' teased Fred.

'Ha ha,' laughed Jo. 'We've all got our weaknesses, and I admit my French and Mandarin leave a lot to be desired. So, what next?'

'I could walk past them, trip up, and slide my phone into that pot plant next to where they're sitting,' suggested Bill.

'No, that's crazy,' said Sally, 'that's asking for trouble.'

'Too late,' said Fred. 'Look, our crooks are getting up to go.'

'And they're heading this way too. Oh no, this could be really nasty,' said Sally. 'Quick, change the subject.'

'Er... Sally, how's the double bass going, are you improving?' asked Bill rather loudly, hoping that everyone nearby could hear.

'Not good. I have trouble keeping up with the rhythm. Just can't get the timing right. How's your violin, Jo, still on the squeaky side?' asked Sally, fiddling with her glasses to steady her nerves.

'Yes,' said Jo, 'I'm not sure I'll ever get the hang of it.'

'And I'm struggling with my saxophone, too many dud notes,' interrupted Fred. 'I think I'm improving a bit, though the neighbours would probably disagree. What about you Bill?'

'Oh, well, I've nearly finished building my electronic keyboard. Just got to add in the chip that simulates all the different instrument sounds then I can start practising and...'

The four men in black walked past, the tallest and ugliest one pausing briefly right next to them to look at his phone. Jo, Fred, Bill and Sally simultaneously froze thinking they'd been rumbled.

'And, it was the best bacon butty I've ever tasted,' threw in Fred in a desperate attempt to break the silence. 'But the guy sitting opposite had ketchup trickling down his chin and onto his smart looking shirt and tie. It was hilarious, though he didn't think so.'

Jo and Sally just looked at each other, lost for words. They burst out laughing. It was such a ridiculous conversation and entirely out of context. Of course, seeing such a reaction, Bill and Fred's nerves could stand it no longer, and they doubled up too. Bill fell off his seat and was only saved by Fred's rapid reactions in grabbing his arm and hauling him back to safety.

The man looked up from his phone and turned towards Fred and Bill, giving them a withering look while muttering something under his breath, then walked off with his gang.

Chapter 2

What Is It?

'Whew, that was close,' said Fred, once safely out of earshot.

'Yes, a ghastly few seconds, but what was all that nonsense about bacon butties? Where did you dredge that up from?' asked Sally.

'Don't honestly know,' replied Fred, 'but I couldn't think of anything else to say. My brain went blank. For a terrible moment, I thought they were on to us. That was a nasty evil look he gave us.'

'Yes, very scary,' said Jo, still recovering from her fit of nervous giggles. 'But who's going to follow them? We mustn't lose them.'

There was complete silence, no one really wanting to take on the challenge. 'We don't have to,' said Jo. 'We've had a bit of fun, and we could stop now. On the other hand, another day or two wouldn't hurt.' For some reason, Jo desperately wanted to carry on though she would have to admit that she didn't really know why.

'Er, well, I suppose Bill and I could, couldn't we Bill? We are heading that way after all. It just makes me feel jittery in case they spot us,' said Sally, pushing her glasses further up her nose.

'Yes, it was fun to begin with,' said Bill, 'but it's getting a bit boring now. I hope we're not going to waste our entire holiday chasing around after those idiots. Anyway, I need to go to the library, and Sally needs to get some shopping for her mum, so we might as well follow and see what they get up to.'

'We'll be very careful, keep our distance,' said Sally. 'We can always do a runner if we need to. Not that I can move very quickly at the moment with my sore leg.'

'No, you're really limping. It still looks painful. You should get it looked at as you've had it for a couple of weeks now,' said Fred.

'The physio actually said it was a small tear in the calf muscle that hasn't healed properly,' replied Sally. 'She gave it a deep, thorough massage but said it needs to be carefully stretched and exercised. That was two weeks ago, and it's still no better. Anyway, we'd better go before we lose them.'

'Look, we obviously can't carry on as we are,' said Jo. 'There aren't enough of us to keep tabs on these guys properly. I have a nasty feeling that huge fellow won't forget our faces in a hurry. We definitely need some extra help. We could recruit Anna and her friends. What do you think? They're spot on in the right parts of town selling their Big Issue magazines, and we often stop to chat with them, so they know us well. They might enjoy the excitement of acting as spies. Also, they won't raise much suspicion as people are used to them being around.'

'Good thinking,' agreed Bill. 'We'll have a chat with them and see if they're happy to help. That might release us and give us our holiday back. See you guys here again at about eleven tomorrow?'

'Great, sounds good. Right, I've got an hour or two spare, so I'm helping Fred with the shed work. I bring the brains and he brings the muscle,' said Jo, winking.

'Oh no you don't,' insisted Fred. 'You may only be a feeble female and a vegetarian, but there is hefty digging to be done.'

'How does being a vegetarian come into it?' smiled Jo, letting the "feeble" comment go and flexing her biceps to demonstrate more of a muscle than Fred was expecting. 'You're almost a vegetarian yourself apart from all those bacon butties you can't resist. They're not healthy you know, they're far too salty and fatty. You really ought to give them up. And I'm not a vegetarian, I'm a vegan. I don't eat any animal derived products, thank you very much.'

'Let us know what happens and where they go. Text if you make any startling discoveries,' called Fred, ignoring Jo's comment.

Bill and Sally set off in pursuit of the four dangerous convicts, or just ordinary honest citizens, whatever they might be. They made an interesting pair. Bill was tall for his age but skinny while Sally was the opposite, slightly shorter than average and well-rounded though not overly so. Bill had long black hair, and Sally had short blond hair and blue eyes. Despite their physical differences, they were great friends and were never short of conversation.

Meanwhile, Jo and Fred headed back to Fred's house in Madeira Park. Jo and Fred had been friends since, well, forever. Their parents had lived in the same street for over fifteen years. As they made their way back along Cumberland Walk, thankfully at normal walking speed this time, Jo was keen to know how much progress Fred had made with the shed preparation.

'Not a lot to be honest. I have partially cleared the area. Annoyingly, there's a hard lump of ground in the middle that I need to level off. It's what I was trying to do when I got your text earlier.'

'At least we've got a decent break now from school, even if we do have quite a lot on before we go back in September.'

'I suppose you've already started on your school project, have you?' asked Fred. 'I'm giving myself at least a couple of weeks off to get this shed preparation done. It's interesting that we've both been given the job of organizing the charity activities next term.'

'Yea, I'm certainly looking forward to that, and I've got the parks and wildlife project too, which is exciting. We've been so busy lately, what with the running and cycling clubs and everything else. I haven't even had much time to do my violin practice recently. How's your saxophone coming along, truthfully?'

'Not too bad, though going through the scales is pretty dull if I'm honest. I'll be ready for the music competition somehow, even if I have to ting it out on a triangle.'

A few minutes later they were in the back garden, spades in hand, ice-cold drinks at the ready.

'You've made tremendous progress since I was here a week ago,' said Jo. 'Now it's all marked out, you've moved those beautiful blue plants, and leveled most it off. You don't hang about, do you?'

'Well, Dad loved your suggestion and agreed it was the perfect position for the shed, though Mum wasn't happy to lose that ring of tiny bright blue flowers even though they were obviously weeds. She said they had an enchanting blue glow each evening as the sun went down, though to be honest, we could never see it. Anyway, I replanted them, but they obviously didn't like their new location as they seemed to die and vanish almost overnight,' said Fred.

'I remember the discussion well 'cos I felt guilty about suggesting that this was the best spot in the garden. Then your mum and dad started arguing about it, so we made a hasty retreat to the Pantiles to avoid any further embarrassment.'

'Yes, and that was the first time we saw our four men in black and decided to follow them. We were desperate for something exciting to do. It seemed a good idea at the time. How sad is that?'

Anyway, I see what you mean, it's quite a lump,' said Jo looking carefully at the ground. 'What happens if you can't dig it out?'

'I'm not giving up yet. Stand back, and I'll whack it with the sledgehammer. Oh, hang on, the butterfly is back. It's landed on the rock. Jo, see if you can encourage it to leave.'

Jo knelt down and gently moved towards it. To her surprise and delight, the gentle creature flapped its tiny wings and jumped onto her outstretched hand. She slowly stood up and lifted her hand watching the butterfly fly off into the nearby bushes. 'Did you see that? It really tickled. Anyway, it's safe to carry on.'

Fred nodded, raised the sledgehammer above his head, took a deep breath and brought it down with all the force he could muster. Unfortunately, it bounced off, out of his grip and hurtled right past where Jo was standing. She looked petrified.

'Hells teeth,' shouted Fred. 'Sorry, I didn't mean to aim it at you. I'm not doing that again. It really hurt. My arm is still vibrating.'

Fred stood back, and Jo came to stand next to him, her heart rate slowly getting back to normal. 'Phew, that was close. But it didn't sound like it was made of rock, more like iron or something.' They both bent down to examine it more carefully, trying to wipe the soil away with their fingers.

'We need a broom,' said Fred.

'Or we could turn the hose on it,' suggested Jo.

Fred went back to the garage to get the hose and connected it to the outside tap.

'Let me try. Stand back or be drenched,' Jo said with an impish smile on her face.

The hose washed the mud from an area about three feet in diameter. What it revealed was quite a surprise.

'What is it?' asked Jo, puzzled. 'Perhaps it's a giant dustbin lid or maybe a Roman gladiator's circular shield?'

'No, don't think so. You're letting your imagination run away with you,' smiled Fred. 'It could be a fragment of a wartime bomb, or more likely just a long-forgotten manhole cover.'

'But what are these peculiar marks all over the surface? It's most unusual; loads of lines and dots and squiggles.'

'Who knows. I don't suppose my hitting it repeatedly with the spade or attacking it with the sledgehammer has helped. Why don't we take a picture of it and then we can look it up on the Internet?'

'My phone at least takes decent pictures, so I'll do that,' said Jo.

'And I'll dig down and look for the outer edge of this thing, whatever it is. Perhaps if I can get underneath it, I could lever it out.'

Jo took a few close-up snaps from different positions while Fred started digging. He soon discovered there was no obvious edge that he could find. Instead, every few inches down it just spread out another couple of inches or so. After digging furiously for half an hour, he had excavated only twelve inches down. The "thing" was still circular, but the diameter had increased too.

'I'm giving up,' said Fred. 'I'm getting nowhere, and it's exhausting. Maybe take a few more photos and then I'll cover it up again. Let's keep it to ourselves until we can investigate a bit further. I'll pretend I've been too busy to do much work out here if Dad asks. I've got another week or so yet before the shed arrives.'

'I don't suppose there's any chance of a piece of your mum's fantastic chocolate cake, is there? Only I'm feeling a bit weak and wobbly after all this hard work, watching you dig and scrabble in the dirt. Oh, hang on, my phone's bleeping.'

Jo checked her phone message. It was from Bill and Sally. It seemed that the four guys had gone to the same cash machine they had been seen at the previous day. Then three went off to the old 'grot spot' cinema demolition site, and the fourth drove off in what looked like a brand-new Porsche.

'They're clearly not as stupid as they are mean looking,' said Jo.

'Do you want to come back tomorrow morning and do a bit more exploration before we meet the others?' asked Fred.

'I was going for a run, but this is much more fun. I'll do some research tonight and see what I can find. Now, how about that cake?'

Chapter 3

Optical Illusion

At precisely 10 o'clock the following morning, the door bell rang.

'She's like clockwork that girl,' thought Fred.

'Well,' reported Jo, 'I found nothing on the web that matched what we discovered in your garden. There are no records of plane crashes or air raid shelters anywhere nearby. I found many ancient hieroglyphics going back to the Mayans of South America, the ancient Egyptians, and the peoples of Greece, but nothing resembling what we found yesterday. Did you know there was a lake here once upon a time, so maybe this is just a manhole cover for a drain to take away excess water?'

'Suppose it could be,' replied Fred. 'I've got the high-pressure hose out today to see if that can shine it up a bit more.'

They found five drill-like holes laid out in a semi-circle, about an inch from the edge. 'Let me give them a good squirt to get all the dirt out,' said Fred. Ten minutes later, the rock or metal surface looked much clearer once it had been thoroughly dried and polished. It looked like a mass of scratches, incredibly thin lines, dots and dashes, and Jo snapped away once more to record everything.

'Let's stuff some tissues into the holes to dry them out,' said Jo.

A few minutes later, on closer inspection, they saw that the holes were about two inches deep and appeared to taper and narrow. They were not quite vertical but slightly angled, gently curving. 'I wonder if something else was once fixed to it,' said Fred. 'I can't quite imagine what fitting would have been used, though. There's no thread of any kind that I can feel. Also, if you look closely, they are not a consistent shape. They are all slightly different in size and not equally spaced. The hole on the left is a bit further out and larger too.'

'Ooh,' said Jo, 'this makes me feel quite dizzy. Have you noticed that when you gaze closely at the pattern of dots and dashes, they seem to jiggle around?'

'No, not really. It's just a load of marks and scratches.'

'Try changing your focus as if you're looking straight through them.'

Fred peered intently, 'Nope, it's not doing anything for me.'

'Well, it's making me feel really wobbly,' sighed Jo, trying to stand up. 'Oh, hang on. If you peer at it from this angle, all the lines and marks form a large circle and inside it are hundreds of overlapping circles and groups of circles within circles. How odd. You can't see it from anywhere else.'

'Must be some form of optical illusion. These marks are all incredibly delicate, finely engraved. It's very hard to feel anything. Maybe it's the manufacturer's logo or trademark, though it seems much too complicated for that.'

'Oooh, strange,' said Jo. If you put your nose about six inches above it and try to look through all these dots and squiggles, you definitely get a sensation of movement. It's even more noticeable if you nod your head slowly up and down. You try it.'

Fred moved in, lowering his face to the object's surface, and tried his hardest to change his focus. 'Nope, I still can't see anything, certainly no movement.'

'But you always had trouble with those 3D images from the school computer lab whereas I could see them straight away. Let me have a closer look.' Jo peered in once more and yelled out, 'Can you grab a pen and paper, quickly?'

Fred rushed off and was back in a couple of minutes, 'What have you seen?'

'The dots and dashes seem to join up into continually changing patterns like little groups or blobs. See, have a look from here. Hope your Mum can't see us, she'll think we've gone mad.'

'No, she's out meeting friends for coffee and won't be back for ages. They think they've discovered some errors in the Council's spending. The budgets aren't adding up correctly. They're determined to track it down and expose what's going on.'

'Hmm, that's good, gives us more time for this... Oh no, the movement has stopped... no, it hasn't, it's started again.'

'Hang on a sec, don't move,' whispered Fred.

Jo looked up very slowly and brushed her bright auburn hair away from her face. Millie, the cat, was crouched there, looking straight back into Jo's very green eyes as if trying to tell her something.

If that was not strange enough, several robins and a couple of greenfinches suddenly flew down right next to Millie, and she ignored them completely. To Jo's continuing surprise, the brightly coloured butterfly returned and gently fluttered down once more, landing on Millie's head, with Millie again taking no notice. One of the robins then hopped right up onto the metal plate, took a few tiny steps forward to peer directly into Jo's face, and then dived back next to Millie. By this time, the rest of the greenfinch family had arrived and were standing in a group watching every move intently.

Jo was even more astounded when a squirrel scampered along the top of the fence and leapt down to join the other spectators. 'Well, I've never seen anything like this before,' said Jo, 'but what a great start to my first article for the wildlife newsletter – squirrel, cat, birds and butterflies in friendship pact.'

'OK, back to business,' said Fred, gazing back down at the squiggles again. 'What do you want me to write down?'

'I don't know. It's the way the blobs are moving. They seem to float about, almost changing every few seconds. It seems like the fewer the blobs, the bigger they are. I'll call out the number of blobs that I can see,' said Jo, hesitantly.

Five minutes later they had a list of almost a hundred items. Jo paused, 'Let's stop there, I can't crouch like this any longer, and my brain is hurting. We need to look at the numbers and see if any of it makes sense.'

Jo stood up and walked away, stretching her legs. At which point, Millie leapt onto the plate as if she owned it. Then the birds started hopping on and off it as if it was covered with their favourite nuts and seeds.

After another ten minutes of looking at the numbers, it remained a series of gobbledygook.

'This is pointless,' said Jo. 'I know my maths isn't fantastic and I'm useless at Sudoku, so it's hardly surprising we're getting nowhere.'

'Why don't we get Bill and Sally to come here instead of meeting in the Pantiles and we can make some sandwiches for lunch. Let's see if their fresh minds can figure out what is going on,' suggested

Fred. He knew he might possibly get some help with the digging and leveling that way if nothing else.

Half an hour later, Bill and Sally arrived through the side gate.

'Over here,' called Fred, 'come and take a look.'

It was not long before they'd been brought up to speed. They did the touchy feely thing with the rock or manhole cover, barely able to stop laughing, but they could not see what Jo had seen and were exceedingly sceptical. They were now huddled around the patio table looking at Jo's list of numbers.

Bill was doing his impression of a monkey, scratching his head while deep in concentration. 'Well, at least this is more fun than chasing around after those four idiots and certainly far less tiring.'

It was aspiring chess player Sally who worked out the first clue. 'We seem to have several groups of numbers, or at least I presume that is what your squiggle represents?'

'Yes,' said Jo, 'there were longer periods of time, about five or six seconds when nothing happened at all.'

'So look, the first number of each set is always in the range of 1 to 5. All the other numbers go from 2 to 10. The sequences with a lower first number all have lower numbers in the rest of the series. What happens if you subtract the first number in the sequence from all the rest of its numbers? Give me the pen and paper.'

Sally peered at the new numbers for a moment and continued, 'So, the numbers are all reduced to within a range of 1 to 5. What is so special about the number 5?'

'Dunno,' said Bill, beginning to get a bit bored and impatient. 'Oh, er, hang on, well, yes, that's it, it's obvious, that's how many holes there are along the edge of the plate. It could be just a coincidence of course.'

Fred stood up, 'There's only one way to find out, let's have a closer look.'

Chapter 4

All Fingers and Thumbs

As they gathered around the plate, down on their knees, Sally said, 'As finger pulls they seem well designed, so let's see if we can lift it somehow though it looks far too heavy to me. What do you think?'

They put their hands out with Fred taking two holes and the rest one each. Sally counted down, 'three, two, one, lift.' With one massive heave, they tugged as hard as they could, but their fingers came straight out, sending them falling backwards, all laughing with embarrassment. Bill even managed a complete backward somersault, probably his most athletic achievement for a very long time.

'Well that was a waste of effort,' laughed Bill, secretly admiring his gymnastic prowess. 'Hope no-one is around with a camera 'cos if that ever got onto YouTube we'd be a laughing stock.'

It was then that Jo had a brainwave, 'Let's try sticking our fingers in these holes in the same order as the numbers appear. For all we know they might act like push button switches.'

'Good idea,' agreed Sally, willing to try anything. 'But how are we supposed to know which hole is which? We don't know where to start from or which way to go, do we?'

Fred bent closer to examine the plate in more detail. After a few moments, he said, 'This hole, the wider one on the left, is further apart. The other holes are all angled slightly towards it. Let's assume that this is the first hole and the rest follow clockwise from there.'

After much debate about how to proceed, they decided that Jo would need to do the readings as only she could see them. She would count the blobs and call them out. Bill would do the subtraction and call out the result. Sally would put her fingers in the holes numbered 1 to 3 and Fred would do the same with holes 4 and 5.

They concentrated hard. Jo let her focus drift into the squiggles and dots and waited for the starting point. She yelled out '3', and Bill put three fingers up to remind himself.

Jo yelled, '8.' Bill said '5.' Fred stuck his finger in Hole 5.
Jo called, '5.' Bill cried '2.' Sally put her finger in Hole 2.
Jo said, '7.' Bill shouted '3, sorry, 4.' Fred tried Hole 4.
Jo yelled, '4.' Bill replied '1.' Sally put her finger in Hole 1.

And so it went on. Two minutes later all was quiet. Nothing happened. They stood up, all disappointed. The birds had stopped chirping, and Millie was losing interest.

'I hate to mention it,' said Bill, 'but I'm starving. This is clearly a waste of time. I can't believe I'm saying it, but I think that tracking those four lunatics would be more fun after all. We might still be able to find them if we hurry. Let's eat our sandwiches and go.'

'Do we have to?' said Sally, 'I'd much rather carry on here. I really don't like all that chasing about and getting so close to those ghastly men. It's all very stressful.'

'We're quite safe, honestly Sally, it's just a bit of fun to liven up the holiday. But I agree with Bill, let's make our sandwiches, leave this, and go hunting,' said Jo. 'I'm really sorry to have wasted your time with this. I don't know what I was thinking.'

The friends headed off to the kitchen and made their cheese and tomato sandwiches though Jo had a delicious salad concoction with hummus. They sat on the patio, munching away and pondering what the four convicts might be up to.

'I'm just going to try one more thing,' said Jo, licking her lips to remove the last remnants of hummus. The others chuckled, always amused at Jo's refusal to let things go, even when the odds were stacked against her.

She wandered over to the plate, knelt down and put her face close to the grid of dots and dashes. She let her focus drift out through the centre of the plate. Almost immediately a single blob came into view and she knew she only had to subtract 1 from the next blob counts.

The plate showed 3, so she put her finger into the second hole.

The plate showed 6, so she put her finger into the fifth hole.

Eight numbers later she could not work out what she was seeing at all. It was a number of overlapping blobs. What should she do? She had no idea. She had not seen this combination before.

Her concentration intensified as her brain focused on the image below. If she'd looked around she would have noticed that nothing was moving, even the birds were completely motionless as if holding their breath. She looked up at the trees as they seemed to gently urge her on, their leaves faintly rustling despite there being almost no breeze. She looked down and slammed her hand on the plate.

'We're off Jo, are you coming?' yelled Bill.

'I'll be right with you,' said a dejected Jo as she stood up slowly and stretched her tightening muscles.

Suddenly there was a gentle rumble from somewhere underground. Jo watched in total disbelief as the centre of the circular plate began to slowly rotate and move downwards. She leapt back, amazed and shocked at what was happening, desperately trying to stifle her surprised yell in the process. The plate revolved until it disappeared from sight altogether, leaving a gaping hole in its place.

Fred and the others heard Jo's muffled cry, stopped and turned, then dashed over to see what was up. Jo was just standing there, fearfully pointing at the plate. Fred got there first and stood next to her, then slowly, tentatively, they bent down to look. Bill peered over Fred's shoulder while Sally kept her distance.

Below they could see what appeared to be a dark old well, with steps carved into the wall, curving away into the blackness.

For a moment, they were utterly speechless, Fred being the first to find his tongue. 'How did you do that?'

Jo mumbled an explanation of sorts. 'Well, I saw this peculiar combination of blobs. I suddenly realized they looked a bit like a hand, so I just put my hand over them. There was a strange vibration, and the centre of the plate started to revolve and, there you are.'

'Incredible. So that's what the five holes were all about,' pointed out Bill. 'Four fingers and a thumb. It's so obvious now. Why make it so difficult? What kind of graphical user interface is that?'

'This is no time to joke,' said Sally. 'What's down there? I really don't like it. It's horrible, whatever it is. I think you should close it.'

'Oh come on. We can't possibly stop now,' said Fred. 'We need to investigate. Who wants to go first? Jo, it's your call.'

'Me? No, it's in your garden, I'm happy to follow you, Fred.'

'Oh, well, er, I don't really like these enclosed spaces very much, but I suppose I could give it a try.'

'We should at least have a look shouldn't we?' encouraged Bill, hanging back a bit. 'I mean it would be silly not to, wouldn't it?'

'Do we have to?' added Sally. 'I mean it could be a trap. There could be something ghastly down there, just waiting for us. I really think we should close it. We might be letting something terrible out. You're not really going down there are you, Bill, surely?'

'Er, possibly, probably, well maybe, not sure,' said Bill, with some trepidation, 'but if I am, I'd better pay a visit to the loo first, you know what my stomach is like at the best of times.'

Fred went to find some torches and Bill headed off too, saying, 'Sorry about this girls, but I won't be long.'

As Jo and Sally waited for the boys to return, Sally whispered, 'Jo, if you are all going down there, then I suppose I'd better come too. The boys will think I'm useless if I don't join in, won't they?'

'No they won't, but sometimes I guess we just need to face up to our fears otherwise we can never get rid of them. But there's no pressure. You could wait here and stand guard instead.'

'Maybe, I'll see how I feel,' said Sally. 'Er, Jo, now, while we're waiting, I know this might not be the best moment, but I've finally got you alone. I'm worried about Bill. He's so skinny and doesn't look at all well. His diet is terrible, and he never eats his five fruit and veg a day. If his parents didn't call him down from his bedroom with all his computers, I don't think he'd eat at all. Also, he never gets any exercise, not that I can talk as I'm not much fitter. Can you think of something we can do to get him to snap out of it?'

'Hmm, you're right, he really isn't taking proper care of himself. He's obsessed with his technical bits and bobs, whatever they are. His skin is pale, and he's got more pimples than he used to have. His black hair has got really quite out of hand too. Let's have a chat about it later. And I'm a bit worried about Fred now too. He really does hate small enclosed spaces. I'm feeling a bit guilty. Wish I'd just jumped down this hole first now.'

'I know what you mean, but Fred never lets anyone down. I'm sure he'll just control his nerves and step up to the challenge like he always does. Anyway, please don't mention this conversation to Bill. I'd hate him to know I was worried about him.'

'I wouldn't dream of it. But I'll have a quiet word with Fred as he'll know the best way to approach this. It'll be better coming from him, and he'll find the right words too, he always does.'

Back in the kitchen Fred finally located some torches and waited for Bill to reappear.

'Hang on a sec Fred, er, before we join the girls, can I just talk to you about something? I'm a bit worried about Sally. She seems to have put on a bit of weight recently. I don't mean that she's fat, she's not at all. I mean she's not sporty, and she's never been big on exercise, not that I'm one to speak, but I've always been a bit like a beanpole. I'm just worried that with her calf strain she might be really struggling.'

'Well, to be honest, you could both do with getting some more exercise. Why don't you join Jo and me next time we go for a cycle ride? At least it might be a start. Anyway, let's chat about it later. The girls will be wondering where we've got to.'

'Come on then, let's go, but please don't say anything to Sally. The last thing I want to do is to stir up a hornets' nest.'

A few moments later Fred handed two of the torches he'd found to Sally and Bill, keeping one for himself. Taking a deep breath, he climbed through the hatchway and inched his way in. Reaching the floor, he flashed his torch around.

'What can you see? Not worth coming down, is it?' yelled Sally.

'Well, the floor seems to be almost circular, about fifteen feet in diameter with curved walls. There's nothing here, it's completely empty, but guess what? I've just seen an area of wall with more lines, squiggles and dots. Come down and look.'

'This is sure to set me sneezing again,' said Jo, checking her pockets for a supply of tissues. 'It's bound to be dusty down there.'

'Very likely,' replied Sally. 'It looks horrible. My leg is going to be painful. I'm really not keen but I suppose I'd better give it a try.'

One after the other they shuffled down, passing the large screw mechanism and plate that had now swung away to fit neatly into the side of the wall. Sally was the last one down, taking it very slowly and carefully, ready to climb back up again if things got nasty. Her blond hair was blowing in a slight breeze caused by starlings that had started swooping and circling just above. Millie stood peering over the edge, meowing, but not quite brave enough to jump down. They looked around, shining their torches everywhere.

'Well, one thing's for sure,' said Fred, 'this is definitely not a run-off or overflow for any lake that might once have been here. Have you noticed how spotlessly clean it all is? There's no dirt, dust, or watermarks of any sort. It's as pristine as if it had just been built.'

Jo added, 'Fred, shine your torch back on markings you saw.'

As Fred adjusted the light, Jo moved closer to examine the new puzzle, allowing her focus to drift away.

'What can you see this time, anything?' asked Sally, secretly hoping this might be the end of the adventure.

Jo was interrupted, and they were all aware of a faint rumbling noise, growing louder, overhead. With a horrified look upwards they saw that the screw device had reactivated.

'No!' yelled Sally. 'The plate, look, it's swinging back into place, rapidly closing shut. Quick. Stop it!'

Fred reacted first and rushed to the steps. Sadly, before he could reach the top, their exit was sealed. Sitting down on the steps in defeat, he looked up. 'Wow, what is this stuff?' he exclaimed. 'It's like metal on the outside but glass or a lens on the inside. I can see the whole garden as if it were a 360-degree photo.'

Suddenly, another gentle rumble took place. A whole section of the wall, right where Jo had been standing a few seconds earlier, rotated outwards to reveal a tunnel, gently sloping downwards.

All four of them jumped around then stood frozen like statues, shocked at what was happening, terrified at what might come out. After some moments Jo took a deep breath, 'Come on, we can't just stand here like petrified idiots. We may as well follow this through now, though goodness knows where it might lead.'

'But we might get trapped. How will we get out? Shouldn't we go back?' muttered Sally, hoping her friends wouldn't think she was being utterly pathetic. Bill grabbed Sally's hand in a desperate attempt to calm her down, or maybe just to steady his own nerves.

'Uh oh, good job I paid a visit to the loo just now,' said Bill, nervously. 'Fred, are you happy with this as it all looks a bit "undergroundish" if you know what I mean?'

'I think I'm all right. We can only hope that whatever let us in, will also let us out,' said Fred, trying to reassure himself by putting a positive spin on things. Luckily no-one could hear his heart pounding or see how tightly his fingers were crossed behind his back.

Chapter 5

Underground

They inched forward into the tunnel. 'Amazing, look at that!' said Fred as he shone his torch ahead. 'The walls are made from stuff that seems to project the light ahead like a million cats' eyes.' He put his hand on the wall to feel the rough protruding rocks. 'How incredible is that? Feel the wall. It's completely smooth, yet it looks as if it's all been hacked out in a hurry.'

Five yards into their walk, the rumbling sound warned them that yet another wall had closed behind them. They spun round and dashed back shining their torches all over the closed passageway. There was just a completely blank wall with no indication whatsoever of a doorway or how they might open it.

Sally burst into tears. 'I can't do this. I just want to go home. We might never get out. Just leave me. You go on.'

'Come on Sally,' said Fred calmly, 'we'll be fine. If they wanted to hurt us, they would have done it by now. There must be something special here. Whatever it is we must find it. We can't give in now.'

Bill put his arm around Sally's shoulders as he gently persuaded her to carry on through the tunnel, which continued to weave left and right, following a steady downward route.

'The air seems fine. None of us has fainted so far, and although it's a bit musty, it's not as bad as you might expect,' said Jo, 'given that no one has been down here for a very long time.'

'What's that faint rustling noise?' asked Bill. 'Sounds a bit like traffic noise or wind in the trees, perhaps a noisy computer fan.'

No one answered, all listening out for it. They continued in silence, each wondering what they had got themselves into.

They had not walked more than a few hundred yards when Sally cried out, 'No! My torch has gone out.'

'It's no problem, we've got two others,' replied Fred, 'so no need to panic yet.'

'No. It's panic time,' yelled Bill. 'Mine has gone out too.'

Sally let out a deep moan and Jo, Fred and Bill felt decidedly uneasy, frightened indeed as they imagined being trapped underground forever.

'Sorry, my fault, I should have checked the batteries back at the house,' said Fred, 'but I had no idea we were going to be doing anything like this. It's odd, though, look, the light doesn't seem to have diminished much, does it? Wait a minute. I'm going to try something. I'm going to turn my torch off just for a second.'

The four friends stood there looking at each other in trepidation as the last torch went out at the click of a button. Incredibly the illumination in the tunnel stayed on.

'How is that possible?' asked Bill. 'We can still see ourselves, and the tunnel is still lit. It's almost like daylight now, getting brighter, yet there are no light bulbs anywhere. It's as if the wall has absorbed some of the earlier torch light and is now bouncing it all back. This is just ridiculous. It's against the laws of physics, surely.'

'Well, let's not worry about it now,' urged Sally, feeling very slightly more positive. 'If we're not going back, I think we should keep moving. Leave the photons to sort themselves out?'

'Ooh, so you have been paying attention in your science lessons after all,' teased Bill, trying desperately to lighten the mood.

After fifteen minutes or so, the passage turned then opened out into a larger area, a bit like a small cavern. Oddly the path stopped abruptly, though the roof continued for another twenty feet or so.

'Woah, stand back,' shouted Fred as he moved gingerly forward, turning his torch back on and looking carefully over the edge. 'There seems to be an underground river flowing down there, but it's a good twenty feet or so below. This must be the noise we heard earlier.'

'I don't much like the sound of it,' whispered Sally. 'If that water suddenly surged up here we'd be in terrible trouble, wouldn't we?'

'True, but it's not wet or damp where we're standing,' said Jo, 'so I hope there's not too much danger of an immediate flood.'

'Over here, look,' shouted Bill, 'there's a small archway, almost hidden.'

They made their way forward, following Bill. Soon they reached a circular alcove. Inside it was a spiral staircase cut out of the rock.

'We can either go back the way we came or see where this leads,' suggested Bill, as he took the first steps upward. 'Take care, it all looks quite worn. We're not the first people to tread this path.'

'Hang on,' said Fred, 'don't dash off just yet. There's another of those panels with lines and dots and squiggles just here. Let's see if Jo can make any sense of it.'

Jo looked as hard as she could but try as she might, she was not able to repeat the previous trick of changing her focus, and no hidden movement was revealed. Eventually, they decided to follow Bill and see where the steps went.

They seemed to go on forever, and they had to stop and rest several times to ease their aching legs. After a good ten minutes of climbing, the stairs opened out into another small area with a further ten or so steep steps carved into the wall, leading up to what appeared to be another screw plate. Fred climbed the steps and shone his torch upward. Surprisingly, the light permeated through it to reveal what looked like the inside of a stone built room.

'How do we open it?' asked Fred. 'There's no visible handle.'

'We had the same problem back where we came in. We don't know how to open the damn thing to get back out again, do we?' pointed out Sally, feeling increasingly uneasy once more. 'I knew it was a mistake coming down here.'

'Let me come up and have a look,' said Jo, edging past.

Jo took Fred's torch and shone it directly upward at the glass plate, then at the surrounding area. She could see nothing that might give a clue as to how it would open. She tried pulling on the supporting screw structure, but it was rock solid, with no give at all.

'Try putting your hand on the glass,' suggested Fred. 'That made the entrance open before, perhaps it will work again.'

'But there are no holes on the underside, and I can't see any blobs that might represent a hand,' said Jo, frustrated.

Trying anyway, Jo felt a recognizable vibration and the plate began to rotate. She quickly dropped down a few steps as this new screw undid itself and the mechanism swung back into the side of the wall. Tentatively, Jo climbed up the steps and out, closely followed by the others, though into what, they had no idea.

'Yuk, this is horrible,' declared Sally, 'it's dark, cobwebby and it smells so musty. There's none of that special lighting here either. I really don't like it. Where are we?'

'No idea,' said Bill, 'we could be anywhere, even still underground, though it doesn't feel damp. It's hard to estimate how far we've come, with all the twists and turns. I guess we must be somewhere near the Common, at least in that general direction.'

'Jo, shine the torch around, see if there are any more circular plates or any kind of exit for that matter,' said Fred. 'And quickly Bill, put something into the plate to stop it from closing or we could be marooned here forever. Use your shoe if you have to.'

'I'm not gonna ruin my...'

But it was too late. The increasingly familiar rumbling sound indicated that their only way back was already cutting them off. Bill swung around following the beam from the torch Jo was holding, hoping to find something else to prevent the screw from closing, but as he did so his flailing arm gave Jo quite a whack. She staggered and fell painfully against the side wall. Jo threw her arms out to try to protect her head, dropping the torch as she did so. Slowly, she pulled herself up using the wall as a prop. The part of the wall she was now pressing against started to move, slowly swinging in towards her. Jo yelped and jumped back, right into Fred's arms, as a section of the wall gradually opened and light streamed in.

Fred looked out, somewhat surprised to catch a glimpse of what appeared to be a bookshelf on the wall outside. Whatever Jo had touched to make the wall open clearly had a life of its own. It took less than ten seconds to open, but no sooner had it done so when it began to reverse direction and close again.

'Quick, everybody out,' yelled Fred, releasing Jo and pushing her out through the narrowing gap. As he followed Jo through, Fred caught Sally's arm and tugged her in his direction too. As Sally stumbled out, she grabbed Bill who was bent over trying to scoop up the torch that Jo had dropped and yanked him after her. Much like a set of violent dominos tied together, they appeared one after the other on the other side of what might easily have been life imprisonment.

The four of them were somewhat shaken by their desperate attempt to escape the confines of the stone room. They were breathing heavily and wondering where they were as the wall closed almost silently behind them, leaving no sign that a doorway had ever existed. They found themselves in a long narrow corridor lined on one side with bookshelves. They edged forward, dusting themselves off, trying to get the cobwebs off their clothes and out of their hair.

'We're out!' yelled Sally with an enormous grin on her face. 'What a relief. But where are we? Looks like some old archive, a whole load of exceedingly tatty books. What is this place?'

'Are you all right Jo?' asked Bill. 'I gave you a nasty thump in there, I'm really sorry. I didn't mean to bash you.'

'Don't worry. It was an accident. Good job you did, though, otherwise we might never have got out. Other than a bruised hand and a graze on my elbow, I'm completely fine, honestly.'

'I know where we are,' said Bill excitedly, looking around. 'We're back in the Pantiles, the second-hand bookshop, overlooking the Chalybeate Spring. It's where I come to help the owner of this place, identifying and classifying all his old books. I usually work in the storeroom through that flimsy wooden door at the far end there.'

Without warning, a face appeared out of nowhere, giving them quite a fright. 'Who are you and what are you up to?' said an elderly grey-haired gentleman in a gruff and somewhat agitated voice.

'Oh, er, hi Ben,' stuttered Bill. 'I, er, just, er, brought my friends in to show them your magnificent collection of rare books, but if we're in the way, we can always come back another time.'

'Oh, sorry Bill, is that you? I didn't see you standing there. Didn't notice you come in,' replied Ben. 'Brought your friends to help with the sorting, have you? Very kind I must say. It's a never-ending job. Sorry, it's still a bit of a state in there. I know I said I'd clean it up, but I just haven't found the time. Shout if you find any valuable gems. I could certainly use some, the way business is going just now. If we don't find something soon, I may well have to sell the place.'

'It's no problem. I enjoy going through them. I'll soon have them all classified. Let me introduce Jo, Sally and Fred, my best mates.'

There was a lot of handshaking and 'how do you dos' while Bill tried to hide the torch surreptitiously behind his back. Ben excused himself as the shop door chimed and he retreated back to the counter to greet a customer.

'Phew, that was close,' muttered Fred. 'Let's get out of here and grab a drink from the café. We have a lot to talk about!'

Chapter 6

Silent Sounds

They tumbled out of the bookshop, Bill tripping over the doorstep, and wandered over to what they called the "Choco Shop", their preferred café. As luck would have it, a table became free as a couple of elderly ladies paid their bill and left. Jo waved to Vera, their favourite waitress, and a family friend. She knew their order well and soon came over with a pot of tea for Jo and Fred and two cold fizzy drinks for Sally and Bill. Of course, she did not dare forget their usual packet of double-layered chocolate wafer biscuits either.

'I can't believe what just happened,' said Sally. 'Sorry if I was a bit negative back there, but I hate it when I can't see ahead. I like to plan my moves, as you know. Anyway, who do you think built those tunnels, and when, and what was it all for? What materials is it made of, you know, the entrance plate and the tunnels with that wonderful light reflection? How come only Jo can operate it and …?'

'Whoa, slow down!' exclaimed Fred. 'We've only just discovered it. We were lucky to get out of there alive quite frankly. Without Jo, we could have been stuck in there forever, but then again we couldn't have got in there without her.'

'If it's any consolation, I don't understand what's been happening either,' said Jo, 'and I've no idea why none of you can see what I can see with the moving blobs. I reckon you just need more practice.'

'Sally, how you managed to climb all those steps in that narrow spiral stairway, with your bad leg, I'll never know. Are you sure you haven't been kidding us, trying to get a sympathy vote?' asked Fred.

'No, of course I haven't,' snapped Sally. 'I had a few painful twinges to begin with, but then it seemed to ease completely. At the moment, it doesn't hurt at all. Look, I can balance on it and even do a hop. Perhaps the physio was right, it just needed a thorough workout. How about you Jo, I don't think we heard you sneeze once, did we?'

'No, I didn't, despite the slightly musty air which usually sets me off. In fact, this is the first time in ages my eyes haven't been itchy and red. Fred, you didn't seem fazed by the nasty enclosed space.'

'No, it wasn't a problem at all. I felt completely comfortable, no sense of the walls closing in on me. Must have been the adrenaline and all the excitement. It didn't even cross my mind.'

'We're just in time,' muttered Bill, distracted. 'They're back, those four ghastly blokes we've been following. They've sat down at the next café again, the same table as before. No, don't all turn around, it will look too obvious.'

'Well,' said Fred, 'another chance to find out what they're up to.'

'Oh, yes, it must be my turn. I could pretend to be their waitress, get close and listen in,' said Sally, 'that would be great fun.'

Her three friends looked at her in amazement. 'Wow,' said Bill, 'what's happened? You're suddenly confident and almost fearless. You'll be wanting to go straight back down into those tunnels next.'

'I definitely do,' replied Sally, smiling broadly but not quite understanding what was happening to her. 'It was so exciting, I can't wait ... stop looking at me like that, I'm serious.'

For a few brief moments, three disbelieving wide eyed faces just stared at her wondering how their previously terrified friend could have been so completely transformed.

'Let's not be hasty, guys. We need a plan,' said Fred.

'Oh, no!' muttered Sally. 'Look, it's that nasty girl from school, Gertrude, you know, the one with the spiky black hair, the bully from the year above. She's vicious. She's always picking on girls smaller than her. She's always on at Sandra in our class, just because she's small and wears glasses like me, and has freckles all over her face. Oh no, she's heading this way. Who's that guy she's with?'

'That's Grant, he's from our school,' replied Bill. 'He's revolting, a really nasty piece of work, always terrifying the new lads. I can't stand him. He's a bully too, and he certainly doesn't like me. He's got three or four mates who are always creating trouble, causing havoc. Nasty little gang. I reckon these two must be related. Look at them both, they're almost identical and dressed the same. Could even be twins. There could be trouble ahead, perhaps we'd better go.'

'No, we most certainly won't,' said Jo. 'There are four of us, and they won't bother us here, not with all these people around. We need to stand our ground. They're cowards at heart, too stupid by far and they only get their way using brute force.'

'They won't see us, they've got their noses in their phones,' said Bill. 'And they nearly walked right into that little kid. What idiots!'

It was a testing few seconds as they watched Gertrude and Grant walking closer and closer, heading towards them. Fred was getting ready for a confrontation, but at the last moment, they veered away.

'Ha, why am I not surprised?' said Fred. 'Look where they've gone. They must know the four blokes we've been following. They've butted into their conversation. Yes, all smiles, friends apparently, partners in crime. Look, all six are wearing black'

They looked away, briefly interrupted by Vera as she popped over to check they were enjoying their drinks, bringing an extra pack of biscuits as a treat. Fred winked and took care of the cookies, though not without a bit of a tussle.

'Why do they make it so difficult to open these packets?' After handing the biscuits around, he started fiddling with the wrapping.

Sally was intrigued, 'Fred, why do you always tie knots in everything, you do it with crisp packets too I've noticed?'

'Sorry, it's become a habit. We all do it in our family. It's a challenge to see how small and tight we can make the knot. Of course, the original reason was to stop the stuff blowing away and adding to the litter problem.'

'Uh-oh, Grant and Gertrude have seen us,' said Jo. 'They're pointing at us. They're all looking this way and laughing. Now they're on the move again.

Grant and Gertrude walked right past them without a sideways glance but with big grins on their faces. 'Phew, that's a relief, they've gone. What do you think they're up to?' asked Sally. 'We daren't follow those two as well.'

'Ooooh, look, the birds are back,' said Bill. 'A mass of starlings just swooped into that tree.'

'And look at the robins, pecking crumbs off the tables,' said Jo. 'One has landed over there on their table. Those guys won't appreciate that.'

'Now we've got one too,' said Fred, gently placing his last few biscuit crumbs near the bird while trying not to scare it away. 'Anyway, how are we going to tap into their conversation? Maybe I should go for another stroll or better still, send waitress Sally.

Seriously, we need to get this right, can't afford another failure.'

They quietly pondered what to do next, watching the birds jumping and flying close by. The robin in front of them was strutting around as if it owned the place. Having finished off the crumbs, it suddenly stopped right in front of Jo, looking her straight in the eye. Jo bent forward, making steady eye contact back, neither of them blinking for several moments. As the robin flew off up into the tree above, Jo peered over at the four crooks in the next café, then beckoned her three pals to lean in closer.

'We don't need to eavesdrop. I know what they're talking about.'

'You're so funny sometimes, Jo,' said Bill, sitting forward, 'but don't be silly, we're too far away, there's no way you could possibly hear from this distance.'

'Honestly, I'm not joking,' replied Jo. 'They're talking about police, banks, cash machines, money, CCTV cameras, mobile phones, diversions and JCB diggers. We know that at least three of them are in the building trade, so some of it makes sense. Oh, and something about a fire at the old derelict cinema site. They've just said they'll meet tonight as planned. The ugly one with curly hair is talking about playing golf tomorrow. Now they're arguing about whose turn it is to pay the bill. They're going to leave some cash on the table and go.'

'Good story, great imagination, I love it,' laughed Sally. 'Have you ever thought of writing a novel?'

The smile was quickly wiped from Sally's face when a few seconds later one of the four guys chucked some money on the table, and they all got up to leave. The last one took a swipe at the robin on his table as he stood up and kicked viciously at another one pecking at his feet, leaving Jo fuming.

'That was entirely uncalled for,' muttered Jo, ready to rush over and confront them for their appalling behaviour.

Fred put a restraining hand gently on her arm just as a pigeon dive-bombed the guy doing the kicking, targeting a deposit right on his forehead, which dribbled down his face and onto his jacket.

'That's justice if ever I saw it,' said Jo as she sat down laughing.

The man was cussing and swearing as he grabbed a serviette from the table and mopped his brow, face, and jacket before rushing to catch up with his mates.

As the four guys walked past, the oldest one looked their way and paused slightly. He muttered something to his buddies who all turned to look in their direction, smirked and then moved on.

'Did you hear that?' said Fred. 'It was the same strange language they were speaking yesterday. I have a nasty feeling they were swearing at us.'

'They almost were,' replied Jo. 'He said, "It's those damn pesky kids again and the girl with the weird red hair. This is becoming too much of a coincidence. We may have to do something serious about them if this continues." Guys, I hate to say it, but this is now extremely worrying. They finally seem to have noticed us.'

'Jo, don't be silly,' said Fred, 'there's no way you could have understood that. We all know your language skills are almost non-existent. You're just imagining things.'

'No, I'm sure they were speaking English. That's what I heard anyway. You certain you don't need hearing aids, Fred?'

Fred's mind was racing. He could not understand what he'd just seen and heard. He did not know how to put it into words. The last thing he wanted to do was upset Jo or make her appear stupid in front of her friends, but he had to find out. He framed the question carefully in his mind. He had to get it right before actually asking her. He thought something along the lines of, *'Jo, suddenly you are fluent in an impossible language when we know that your French is terrible, let alone your Mandarin. But even more astonishing was how you managed to get the gist of their conversation when we were nowhere near them. We could hear absolutely nothing and were too far away to even lip-read. How did you do it?'* Fred was happy with his question and was just about to open his mouth when...

'I don't know, Fred,' replied Jo. 'It's as much a mystery to me as it is to you.'

'Pardon, what don't you know?' asked Bill. 'And what has Fred got to do with it? What's a mystery?'

'Well, Fred just asked me how I knew what they were discussing, when they were so far away,' replied Jo, 'so I answered him that I hadn't a clue how I managed it.'

'Well I didn't hear Fred say anything,' said Bill. 'Did you Sally?'

'No,' said Sally looking confused. 'Did you, Fred?'

'Well, no, I don't think so,' pondered Fred, beginning to doubt himself. 'But that was certainly what I was thinking.'

'What the hell is this, Jo?' said Bill, standing up. 'First, you can see things that we can't, and then you can hear things that we can't. Then you can translate a silly foreign language, and now you can read minds too. I give up. This is too much. I'm going. I need to catch the library again before it closes. You coming Sally? Shall we all meet back here tomorrow afternoon? And please, stop playing these silly games.'

With plans for the next day agreed, Bill and Sally left, excited but confused, unable to understand any of what had just happened. They took their time walking as the last thing they wanted was to catch up with Gertrude and Grant, or the four gruesome guys in black.

'Oh dear, that was embarrassing wasn't it?' said Jo, rubbing her arm and examining it carefully.

'Just a bit. How's your arm? Bill gave it quite a knock just now.'

'Well, it was sore, but it seems fine now. That bruise on my hand must have been just a smudgy mark because there's no sign of it, and the graze on my elbow must have been grit because that's gone too.'

Fred and Jo waved to Vera and asked for some water. They sat facing each other across the table, somewhat bemused. Fred could just about grasp the reality of opening the manhole cover in his garden, but had no idea what powered it, or why Jo's hand could work it. Finding the tunnel with the lighting was fascinating. Discovering the underground river made sense because he now knew where the source was for the famous local spring. Yet how Jo had been able to hear what was going on, on a table thirty feet away, with all the surrounding noise, was inexplicable. As for her becoming a linguist, well, he was lost for words. Just how she was able to answer his question when he had not even asked it, was utterly baffling.

Fred took a deep breath. He had to ask Jo what was going on. He fired off his first question, then another and another. The pair of them faced each other over the table, deep in discussion, oblivious to everything around them, desperately trying to make some sense of things. It had certainly been the strangest day they'd ever had.

Vera arrived with a jug of water and two glasses, ten minutes later, apologising as she did so. 'Really sorry it took so long.'

Fred and Jo continued to focus on each other, completely ignoring Vera, who was attempting to grab their attention. She coughed politely, but it had no effect.

'Hello, hello, is anybody in there?' she called, smiling and making a noisy play of putting the tray down right between them.

'Oh sorry,' said Jo, 'we were a bit wrapped up in our conversation, lots of challenging things to talk about.'

'That's all right. Sorry to interrupt you and apologies for taking so long to get the water, but as you can see we are incredibly busy. So many orders and messy tables to clear, and the kitchen's a nightmare. You wouldn't like a summer holiday job helping out, would you, only we could really do with some help?'

'That's a very kind offer, Vera' replied Jo, 'but I'm afraid we're kind of busy just now.'

'I thought I'd ask anyway. You've both been strangely quiet which seems very unusual for you two. Suppose it's difficult to hold a useful conversation with these noisy neighbours at the next table. You're usually so chatty. Not in love are you?' Vera winked, perfectly aware that she was stirring things.

'What? Of course we're not. You know us better than that. Don't be so silly. Whatever made you think that? We're just good friends!' exclaimed Jo, going slightly pink. 'And anyway, we've just been discussing the unusual events of our very peculiar day.'

'Oh, I see,' said Vera, trying hard not to laugh, 'I was only joking, but the elderly couple on the table behind you were smiling and pointing at you. When I asked them what was up they said you'd spent the last ten minutes just sitting and staring at each other, silently gazing into each others' eyes, very romantic, they thought.'

Fred and Jo looked at each other, somewhat horrified and more than a little embarrassed. It slowly dawned on them that they'd had a long conversation about everything that had happened, yet seemingly had not uttered a single word.

Chapter 7

Robbery

It was 9:15 the following morning. Fred had been up since 8am. He had not been able to sleep. All night long he had tossed and turned as his mind wrestled with the events of the previous day. Now, to make matters worse, he was somewhat annoyed as the local BBC news had interrupted the replay of last night's Premier League football match with a breaking announcement...

... **Bank robbers raid Tunbridge Wells ... JCB ram-raid ... fire ... cinema ...**

'I don't believe it,' exclaimed Fred jumping up. 'That is almost exactly what Jo overheard in the café yesterday afternoon.'

At that moment, there was a ring on the doorbell. Fred ran over to the front door, opening it to Jo who stormed in yelling, 'Have you seen the local papers? It's just what I told you. Look, here, it's on the front page of the Daily Post,' she said throwing it in front of Fred's nose.

Daring Dawn Robbery
[Abby Newsome]

In the early hours of this morning, raiders robbed a branch of NatWest Bank in Tunbridge Wells. It is believed that this daring and carefully planned robbery took place at about 3am when a JCB ram-raided the branch opposite the Town Hall, completely demolishing the brickwork and removing not one but two cash machines believed to contain more than a hundred thousand pounds.

This was done under the noses of Police and Fire Service representatives who had been called at 2am to tackle a blaze at the Odeon Cinema site where demolition work had recently commenced. The fire was finally brought under control at about 4am, at which point the police discovered the damage and robbery at the bank.

It would appear that the JCB had been stolen from the old cinema site some time before and had presumably been parked in a side street close to the bank branch. According to the police, the CCTV cameras overlooking the bank and its cash machines had been forcibly twisted in a direction to prevent identification of those involved in the robbery.

Apparently, the police were informed of the outbreak of the cinema fire by a concerned passerby who ended the call before his details could be obtained. Police are requesting information from anyone who might have seen or heard suspicious goings on at the time in question and have also asked the person who made the emergency call to come forward as his mobile number appears to be untraceable.

This is the third of these break-ins within a twenty-mile radius in the last two months, and the police need all the help they can get to put a stop to them.

Jo carried on, 'So, what are we going to do? There it all is in black and white. I didn't make it up. And we'd seen those four guys visiting the very same cash machines several times. They were apparently checking out the site, getting their plans prepared. They obviously started the fire as a distraction, designed to keep the police involved further down the street. We must go and see the police now and tell them everything. Perhaps we should also call Abby Newsome, the reporter, the one who wrote the article.'

'Hold on,' said Fred. 'What exactly are you going to say?'

'Well, the truth, of course, about those four crooks. We need to tell the police what we overheard them discussing yesterday.'

'Hang on a mo, you can't do that,' pointed out Fred, 'cos only you heard them, and you were thirty feet away, and nobody else heard anything. To put it bluntly, they ain't gonna believe you.'

'Oh, I see,' sighed Jo, somewhat deflated, 'but I could lie and say that we all heard them?'

'But you never tell lies, they always backfire. Anyway, the police will interview everyone who was there, and they will all confirm that they heard nothing and that from where you were sitting you couldn't possibly have heard them either. Then no one will believe anything we say, ever again. Plus the crooks might get wind of it, and they'll be after our blood too,' warned Fred.

'But we can't just let them get away with it. What do we do?'

'Well, not much at the moment,' said Fred. 'We're just going to have to follow them more closely and get some real evidence, assuming they're still about. We know they are away playing golf. Presumably, they can't just disappear because they work on the derelict cinema building site and it would be obvious to the police that they had something to do with the robbery if they were to just vanish off the face of the earth.'

'Mmm, I take your point. So, really, all we can do is bide our time and see what they do next. At least we know for certain now that they are crooks, we're not just imagining it. Plus we have a real cast iron reason for following them too. And I bet this is just the tip of the iceberg. There's no telling what other dubious stuff they're involved in.'

'Suddenly it's much more exciting, but probably dangerous too.'

'It is disappointing, though, particularly since I knew it was going to happen.'

Jo was silent for a moment, wondering what to do next. *'OK,'* she thought, *'but there is something else I need to do. I really want to examine those walls in the entrance to the tunnel more closely. Those squiggles and lines must be there for a reason. I need to persuade Fred that this is more important than watching last night's silly football game.'* They looked at each other, smiled and agreed to go back down into the tunnel.

'You were doing it again,' muttered Fred, 'we both were, communicating without speaking. How and why are we doing it? How is it possible?'

'I don't know. It's mystifying and very worrying. And why us? And why now?'

'Your guess is as good as mine. But you must admit, it is fun,' said Fred.

'It is, but I think we ought to make an effort not to do it unless we really have to. Otherwise, everyone is going to notice, and that could get embarrassing, like yesterday in the café,' said Jo with a fleeting shy smile. 'And anyway, we don't know how long it's likely to last, do we? It might vanish as quickly as it came. It would be a shame to lose it now, wouldn't it?'

Fred nodded, a broad grin appearing on his face. He was loving every moment of it. They went out to the garden, grabbing the torch on the way.

'I can't believe this, Jo. Every time we come out here and go anywhere near the "plate", out comes Millie, as well as the birds in the neighbourhood, all chirping, almost in harmony.'

'What are you going to tell your dad about this plate thing?' asked Jo.

'I already have, last night when he came home from work. He was exhausted, and I thought that was a good time to broach the subject. I told him that we had unearthed a manhole cover, something to do with an old lake which, surprisingly, he already knew about. He's gone out now to order the cement and concrete patio slabs for the shed base and has agreed that we just need to make a simple trap door in the shed floor when it arrives. That way, if anyone from the Water Company ever wants access, there'll be no problem.'

'That's great,' said Jo. 'You'll just have to make sure that nothing substantial is put over the trap door so we can easily get in and out.'

They both bent down, peering at the plate and Jo began searching for the blob formations. 'It's quite laborious having to do this every time,' said Fred. 'What happens if you just put your hand flat on the plate?'

'Well, the blobs aren't forming a hand print yet,' replied Jo, 'but I'll give it a go.'

No sooner had Jo put her hand on it than the screw plate began to open. They looked at each other in utter amazement, somewhat shocked and confused that such a mechanism could exist, let alone one that recognized and remembered the characteristics and touch of her hand. Without questioning it any further, they both scrambled in, the screw mechanism again closing rapidly behind them.

Chapter 8

Togethering

'Fred, we don't need the torch,' said Jo. 'Incredibly, the lighting system is working here now. It came on as the hatchway closed. And look, in the stronger light, you can see that these walls all seem to be made up of vertical panels, four or five feet wide.'

'You're not suggesting there might be tunnels behind each one are you?' asked Fred. 'Can you see any movement anywhere, blobs floating around or any more hand symbols?'

'No, not yet, I need to get closer.'

Jo walked over and put her nose close to the panel she'd seen the previous day but saw nothing. She stepped back and saw a flicker of movement. As she moved closer once more, the image disappeared. She stopped. She moved back, and the image returned.

'Well,' she said, 'these panels are different. I need to be further back to spot what's happening. I guess that makes sense as it's a much larger area. Oh! Most peculiar. As I let my focus drift slowly out, I can see what looks like thousands of layers of those strange markings. I'm skimming through them, layer after layer. It's weird, it's like a three-dimensional world of lines, circles, and squiggles, as if I'm travelling fast through pictures of space and time, passing stars and going through galaxies. If I bring my focus back to the front, the marks join up into strings of unintelligible characters scrolling upwards. Now it's changing again, to flickering images.'

'What do you mean?' asked Fred.

'Well, like those very early TV pictures. I can see the rough outline of a strange looking boat and a giant sea creature, possibly a whale. Now maybe a beach and some trees. I can see a few people, and they seem to be jumping up and down or dancing perhaps. Oh, it's not quite as fuzzy as it was. There are birds in the sky, and a butterfly just floated by. And there are animals, maybe a beaver or two and they're joining in and they all seem to be laughing together.

How silly. Now they're pushing a strange box through the trees, and another into a river. It's all a bit blurry and grey. Wow, it's changed again, now it's all in colour, and far more detailed, more like a modern TV movie. Are you sure you can't see it, Fred?'

'I am trying, believe me, but it really doesn't work, I wish it did.'

'Oh my goodness, more strange symbols, but... I can read it, or I think I'm reading it. The lines and squiggles are forming words... they're flying all around... now they're settling down... WOW!'

'What's it saying? What's happening?' Fred asked, desperate to know what was going on.

'I'll read it, oh no, wait,' said Jo staggered by what she was now seeing. 'It's not words any longer, it's... a...'

Jo suddenly stepped back a pace shocked by what she had seen. How this could possibly be happening. She moved forward again.

'It's... a person, a female. She's looking at me. She has beautiful green eyes and... auburn red hair... just like me. She's introducing a man and another woman, and they're dressed in simple light coloured clothes. Now she's starting to speak... strange words...'

Fred moved nearer, just behind Jo. He could sense she was apprehensive, wondering what was about to happen. He put his hands on her shoulders to steady her. He was looking past her, peering at the panel, seeing nothing but lines and dots and squiggles. He felt her relax. Suddenly Fred felt an intense tingling sensation surging through his fingers and the panel lit up before his eyes. He slowly removed his hands from Jo's shoulders and moved to the side to watch Jo's face more carefully. He saw her begin to smile.

Jo took a deep breath fighting to understand the flow of emotion running through her. Before she could begin to make sense of the spoken words surging through her brain, they miraculously seemed to translate themselves into English. She turned, smiled at Fred, and they both looked back at the panel ready to share what was to follow.

(O) Welcome, Joanna, or Jo as you prefer to be called, and welcome Fred.

'B...u...t how does she know who we are?' stammered Fred.
'I've no idea,' exclaimed Jo, 'but I think we're about to find out.'

(O) You may be wondering how we know who you are and how we are able to communicate with you in this way. What you see on the wall are not just "squiggles and lines and dots" as you describe them, but brain patterns. Brain patterns are common across many life forms, and these are integrated into the images before you.

'Why don't they just communicate in English?' pondered Fred. 'It would be much easier and far less complicated, surely.'

(O) These brain patterns are entirely independent of language so while we all might speak in different tongues and find it hard sometimes to understand each other, we can all communicate through brain patterns, but, only if we know how. The picture you see before you appears as a jumble of lines, dots, and squiggles to the uninitiated. It is, in fact, a highly complex three-dimensional image rich in multi-media information that your subconscious absorbs as you change your focus and your viewing angle. As your brain processes these patterns it interjects information from your own memory, and you see a complete message as we intended it. We may not know precisely who you are, but we already know a vast amount about you, about the kind of person you are, because only someone like you could be having this conversation with us today.

'Wow, that's smart isn't it?' said Fred. 'We can't even do that with today's technology. Just who are these guys?'

(O) You probably would like to know who we are and why we have chosen you, because, that is what we have done. We are the "Ancients". You may not know it but in your memory you have the star positions for your time indelibly recorded from staring up into the night sky. You can compare them to those from our age and, without realizing it, make a calculation. It is enough to say that we have been around for hundreds of thousands of years, far longer than your experts believe that mankind has been truly intelligent.

'Is that a polite way of saying that we're a bit thick?' asked Fred.
'No, I don't think so,' answered Jo. 'It's just their way of saying that they, the "Ancients", were just as bright if not cleverer than we

are now, even if they were, or are, er… ancient.'

(O) We need to tell you a little more about ourselves. We are very different now from how we once were. In our long and distant past, we had some terrible times. The details need not concern you yet, but it's enough to say that we were torn apart by internal strife, argument, greed, inequality, and mistrust. We were unbelievably selfish and bullies too, always fighting each other and our neighbours, never willing to see the good in anyone. It's easy with hindsight to see how dreadful we had become.

After many more centuries than we care to remember, something happened, very gradually, though it is fair to say that we didn't notice it or understand it at the time. Somehow our minds were opened and we found we were on the road to a whole new way of life. We began to trust and appreciate each other, and laughter could be heard once again. We shared our chores and our knowledge, and we were all completely equal, men and women both.

The greatest thing was that we came to recognize nature, discovered its purpose, and the importance of preserving the wonderful environment we had turned our backs on for so long. It was a new dawn, and a new caring and sharing attitude spread through us. It was a magic ingredient, a new light to follow. We were so lucky as we very nearly destroyed everything, including ourselves.

We now live side by side, harmoniously, with ourselves, our neighbours and all the magnificent creatures that are lucky enough to inhabit this incredible world. We have made surprising new friends that have enriched our lives, as you will very soon discover.

'Whew!' said Fred. 'What an incredible transformation. If we could repeat that process today, then our world would be so much…'

(O) We arrived on these shores some twenty thousand years ago desperate to find a place of safety when our own beautiful homeland was destined for destruction from unimaginable planetary forces. We had a vital mission to accomplish, the greatest and most challenging ever devised. This conversation we are having today suggests that, despite our best efforts, the task has yet to be finalized. We always knew this was a possibility given the magnitude of the assignment

and the nature of our adversaries, so we left signs around the world, desperately hoping that the right individual might one day find them.

Only one person in the world today could have opened our "entryway". It is linked once again to brain waves and brain patterns. Only those with certain exceptional qualities are able to manipulate it. Now that you are here we can begin to explain why. We wish to share with you something quite remarkable, a gift, something that will change your lives, in many wonderful ways.

Our gift, life's magic ingredient, has many facets. All will become apparent as you learn about them and adapt to them. Parts of this gift will gradually transfer to your trusted friends, those who possess similar special qualities, often without them realizing it. In time, it is our hope that your circle of trust will grow significantly, creating an inordinate number of overlapping trust circles, and that millions, even billions, might eventually benefit from our gift to you today.

'So, it's beginning to make sense,' said Fred. 'The squiggles you saw on the entryway surface that then became a series of overlapping circles ties in perfectly. It must be the Ancient's signature for this magic ingredient, you know, the trust circle thingy.'

(O) The first change that you might already be noticing and worrying about is what we call "togethering". You might initially understand it better as a kind of "messaging" though it is very much more than that. It allows people with the right values to exchange thoughts, ideas and images without actually communicating verbally.

'That's what happened yesterday, and this morning. That explain things... so you do trust me,' said Fred, a small grin appearing.

(O) It can be quite disturbing when it first happens, but it is immensely powerful as you will soon discover. You will find that you can turn this "messaging" on and off to suit yourself, and you can decide who to include and who to exclude, at any moment in time. You don't need to be with someone for messaging to work, as messages will always be passed on until they reach their destination. The ability to forward messages in this way exists in all human and animal brains including birds and many insects, though these

messengers are completely unaware of their involvement.

'It's a bit like sending texts on a mobile phone,' said Fred.

'It is,' responded Jo, 'but the beauty of it is that you don't need a phone and you don't need to "pay as you go" or commit to a monthly contract. It's all free. Isn't that terrific?'

'The trouble is, perhaps you can't communicate with someone you don't know, and, therefore, you might not be able to order a pizza, or pay for it,' pointed out Fred, 'for example.'

Jo raised her eyebrows and the communication continued.

(O) The most remarkable and rewarding aspect of "togethering" is an ability to share information and knowledge quite freely. After all, it is what people do with information, how they transform it into knowledge and how they use that knowledge, that is important. With "togethering" you have only to ask a question in your mind, and the answer will be sought, found and returned, no matter how many participants might be involved. And it happens in the blink of an eye.

'Wow,' said Fred, 'that's fantastic. It's a bit like Google but a thousand times better. You don't need broadband or wifi or the Internet, and there are no annoying adverts to get in the way either.'

(O) Don't be surprised if you appear to get help from birds and other wonderful creatures too. As they begin to get to know you better, there is little they won't do to assist you. You will be surprised at how adept they'll become at tuning into your "togethering" world.

'I bet that's what happened yesterday in the café, when you could hear the conversation between the men in black,' said Fred.

'It's hard to believe,' replied Jo, 'but there were birds on both tables. Is it possible that the robin on their table passed the chat over to our robin and on to me? It's too incredible to be true, surely.'

(O) You will almost certainly be wondering why you are here and, more importantly, why we have chosen you. We have been searching for someone rather special, and very soon we will reveal the unique qualities we have been looking for.

We could go on, but this is enough for now. Your subconscious needs a short time to process the information we have given you and allow your mind to unlock paths that have remained lost, forgotten and unused since the early days of mankind. This interaction and even your previous communication with the entryway have already enriched the inner workings of your brain, as you are discovering.

We have given you a vast amount of knowledge from this first meeting, but you will have only recognized and understood a tiny part of it. More will gradually be revealed to you when you are ready or when you need it. Sometimes you might think we have interrupted you or are talking to you directly, which, in a way, we will be. Don't be frightened, we are always here to help you and to care for you.

It would appear we have waited a very long time for your arrival, far longer than we ever imagined, but better late than never. Return soon, Jo and Fred, we have so much more to share with you. You may not know it yet, but you need us, almost as much as we need you.

The three smiling faces faded and vanished altogether leaving Fred and Jo standing facing a blank squiggly wall.

'Oh... My... Gosh,' said Jo. 'What do you make of all of that?'

'Well, it's fantastic, but crazy. How can it possibly work? We know the messaging bit does though because we've tried it.'

'But all that stuff about a mission, why us, why me? How can we possibly help, we're just teenagers. They've got the wrong people. Their entryway and all the rest of it has clearly malfunctioned.'

'I think we need a break to get our heads around it. Let's get out of here before Dad gets back,' replied Fred, jumping up the steps. 'Hang on, there's a face peering at the entryway. It's Dad, he's back already. He's looking at the entryway, bemused, just as we were. OK, he's walking back. He's gone inside. Let's go.'

Fred put his hand up on the entryway, and it immediately started to unwind. They waited until the screw mechanism had moved to one side, and leapt out, the entryway closing behind them.

'How did you do that?' said Jo. 'I thought it needed my hand?'

'Well, you obviously trust me even more because you've just shared another skill,' teased Fred.

Chapter 9

Information

'Oh, hi kids,' called Fred's dad, 'where have you been? I've just been out taking a closer look at that manhole cover you discovered. It certainly is very strange. You're quite right that we must ensure the Water Company has access to it whether they need to or not. I've ordered all the slabs and bags of ready mixed concrete for the shed base. It should all be delivered here in the next few days.'

'We've just got back from Jo's,' replied Fred, wincing at his little white lie. Seeing his mum engrossed in a mass of papers on the table, he was curious as to what she was up to.

'You're not still trying to solve that difficult Sudoku puzzle are you, Mum,' teased Fred, knowing how many days she'd spent on it.

'Not really, though I do keep looking at it. It's impossible. None of our friends can do it either. We think it's been wrongly printed. You're welcome to try it, though.' Fred's mum smiled and pushed it towards them. Jo took the pencil being offered but laughed and shook her head at the same time.

'Anyway, we're actually working on something with Jo's parents. There's something fishy going on with the Council's plans and budgets. It all seems to relate to the sale, demolition and regeneration of what was once the Odeon cinema site in town, you know, the "grot spot" we've had to put up with all these years.'

Fred's mum continued with her tale, but Jo was slightly distracted by the Sudoku puzzle. As she looked closely, it seemed to blur, repeatedly going in and out of focus. Then numbers appeared to float around in front of her eyes, zooming haphazardly through all the little boxes. Slowly they began to settle down, just a few numbers swapping places, then all was still. Jo absentmindedly pencilled in the numbers, put the paper down, and looked back up.

Fred's mum was still talking. 'You see, the sale a few weeks ago, according to this report, was made to, well, it doesn't actually say. It seems there's a trail of companies involved. It's all very suspicious.'

'That's right, Global Property Investments, Acquisitions & Takeovers Corp,' said Jo, 'known simply as "Global" in the trade. It's the holding company, based in Washington DC in the USA.'

Fred's mum gave her a quizzical look, 'How do you know that?'

'Oh, I think it was in the local paper last week, wasn't it, or maybe a Google alert I set up for the old cinema site,' responded Jo.

'Well, that's good because I couldn't find it anywhere, thanks.' Jo's mum grabbed the pencil, scribbled a note and continued. 'Anyway, again the amount involved isn't precise because…'

'£10 million,' added Jo.

'Well, how do you know that? I can't find any published figures anywhere,' said Fred's mum, a little bemused by Jo's outburst.

'I've seen the figures somewhere, though to be honest, I can't remember exactly where. I'll have to check on my laptop,' said Jo, quite matter of fact all of a sudden. 'I remember because the whole situation was quite strange. I might be wrong, but I think Global put in a bid for £10 million and the Council actually bid £12 million. Strangely though the Council then, later that day, withdrew its bid saying they really couldn't afford it. It was all very peculiar.'

'Well, that's very odd. There's no way the Council has hidden reserves like that. It doesn't make sense. They'd have to borrow the money and increase taxes and that wouldn't go down well at all,' said Fred's mum. 'Something is not right here, very suspicious.'

'Now, as far as we can make out,' said Fred's dad, 'there's also a shortfall of nearly £100,000 in the accounts, but without seeing all the individual transactions, we can't be certain.'

'Oh yes, that involves Jeremy Moreless, and his company Moreless Consultants. Now, the Council's accounts suggest that Moreless Consultants has been paid £25,000 for doing a feasibility study concerning a new rebuild of the site. But the truth is they've actually been paid £125,000, and the exercise was completed in just two weeks, not ten as they stated. They shouldn't be allowed to get away with it,' sighed Jo. 'To be honest, this seems to be just the tip of a very messy financial iceberg.'

All went quiet for a few moments, everyone bemused by Jo's sudden confidence. Eventually, Fred's mother got her voice back, 'Good heavens, who is this girl? Where did you dig out all that information from? I've spent days searching the net for this stuff and not only have you already found it, but you've got it right at your fingertips. Your parents didn't tell us that they'd made so much progress. I appear to have been wasting my time.'

'No, no,' said Jo. 'Those consultancy fees were in a blog I was reading, maybe a discussion group online, sorry, I can't remember. My parents were talking about it and they were getting a bit frustrated too, so I offered to help. They've been very busy since and we haven't had a chance to chat about it, let alone get back to you.'

'Oh, I see,' said Fred's mum. 'Well your Googling skills must be infinitely better than ours. Perhaps you could send us the links when you get a moment. That would be incredibly helpful.'

Fred's mum gave Jo a long quizzical look, wondering what was going on. Then she noticed the Sudoku puzzle and grabbed it. She could not quite believe her eyes and held it up for her husband to see.

Taking the opportunity to intervene before the exchange between Jo and his mum got any more bizarre, Fred nudged Jo towards the door, 'Sorry Mum but we've got to go, we're late meeting Bill and Sally. I'm sure Jo will get back to you on it very soon. Byee.'

Fred grabbed Jo, pushing her out through the front door. 'What just happened, Jo? Where did you get that information from? Mum is usually excellent at finding stuff on the web. How did you make the time to do all that research with everything else we've got going on?'

'To be quite honest, I can't remember exactly. It's not that I've been particularly interested with the financial arrangements of the cinema site. I've mainly been investigating the footfall in the town centre relating to my school project on the possible health benefits obtained by frequent visits to lovely parks. But somehow the info just seemed to leap into my mind. I did overhear my parents the other evening discussing the cinema site, and I offered to help. I haven't actually given them any feedback yet. Wherever does the time go?'

'I think we'd better check your Internet search history pretty quickly. What do we do if we can't find anything relevant?'

'Don't be silly, it's bound to be there.'

'Are you sure because I have a feeling that there is a good reason why you don't remember doing it... because you probably didn't.'

'Oh come on Fred, that's nonsense, how's that vaguely... oh!'

'Precisely. What were those Ancient guys talking about? You

only had to think of a question, and the answer would be found in the blink of an eye. The way you responded just now was an exact fit to their description of what could happen.'

'But that would mean that my brain has been altered, sorry enhanced, already, in less than twenty minutes.'

'Exactly.'

'But how can that be possible? It's totally mind boggling, terrifying. I don't even want to think about it.'

'And what did you scribble on that Sudoku puzzle while my mum was talking to me?' asked Fred.

'Not sure. I saw all these numbers flying around and filling those boxes, so I jotted them down, probably absolute rubbish. You know how useless I am with that sort of thing.'

'Well, I'm willing to bet you solved their impossible puzzle too. How on earth am I going to explain that to my mum?'

They walked the last two hundred yards in silence, chatting rapidly and strolled into the Pantiles.

'While we're waiting for the others, let's watch the boule competition over there under the trees,' suggested Fred.

'Good idea,' said Jo. 'It's a great game, like huge marbles, very popular in France, but they call it Pétanque. The sign suggests it's the final of the summer knock-out challenge, should be fun.'

They wandered over, surprised to see so many teams and spectators enjoying the final match. No sooner had they arrived when a flock of starlings swooped in and settled into the trees, causing quite a racket as if cheering on the players too.

'Look at all those birds up there,' said Jo, 'and see how many squirrels have appeared. There must be four or five of them up in the trees quietly watching, peeping through the branches. Unusual, I'm surprised they haven't scarpered with this number of people around.'

Jo and Fred sat down on a nearby bench, trying to decide which team was likely to win. The final game was reaching its end, and it was a close call. Suddenly, with just three boule left, the crowd hushed and looked incredulously at the ground. A squirrel that had been edging its way down the nearest tree suddenly rushed across the court to the cluster of boule that had already been thrown and grabbed the small jack, holding it between its teeth like a large nut.

The players yelled in an attempt to frighten it off, sending the crowd into hysterical laughter. The squirrel, however, was not to be deterred and seemed to gain in confidence. It looked all around, before running straight over to Jo, jumped up onto the bench where she was sitting, dropped the jack into her lap and winked at her.

If this was not a big enough surprise, it seemed to speak to her, *'Hi Jo, my name's Squidge, it's great to meet you at last. We've waited so long.'* It then proceeded to put its right paw up waiting for Jo to gently "high five", before leaping up into the tree behind.

Jo was shocked at the words she'd heard and as bemused as everyone by the squirrel's actions but delighted at this wonderful interaction with such a friendly and apparently intelligent creature. She grabbed the jack, stood up, held it out in the palm of her hand and shouted, 'The burglar has decided to go straight and return his ill-gotten gains. Who wants it?'

At the sight of the squirrel's antics and Jo's retort, everyone roared with laughter once more, except the referee who stood scratching his head, not entirely sure whether to replace the jack roughly where it had been before the squirrel snatched it, or declare a replay. He knew that in this very competitive sport, with bottles of bubbly at stake for the winning team, he was on a hiding to nothing. 'Young lady, please throw it back where it came from.'

Jo never much liked being in the spotlight, let alone being put under pressure like this. She looked around and saw that she was the focus of everyone's attention, waiting to see what she might do.

(O) You can do it, Jo. The crowd and the players are waiting. Just concentrate on the target and believe in yourself. Throw it.

Without another hesitation, she took aim and hurled the jack with some force, probably more than was required. It went higher than she had intended and landed quite short and completely wide of its target. It bounced once then hit a stone which sent it in another direction altogether, before it finally zigzagged and rolled on, ending up in exactly the spot it had been in before the squirrel had stolen it.

The crowd clapped and roared their approval, and the tournament final got under way once more.

Chapter 10

Sharing Skills

As Jo and Fred walked away from the boule court, they saw that Bill and Sally had arrived and witnessed the whole commotion.

'Wow, that was crazy,' said Bill. 'Trust you, Jo, to be at the centre of it. I saw several people recording it with their mobile phones. You'll be on breakfast TV tomorrow with a bit of luck.'

'That squirrel almost seemed to pick you out on purpose,' laughed Sally. 'Why do things like that never happen to me?'

'Fred, you are not going to believe this, but, first of all, that squirrel actually spoke to me, and, then I got a message from the Ancients telling me to throw the jack back.'

'I believe you, Jo,' replied Fred, silently. *'I don't think anything will ever surprise me again, not after you know what.'*

'Guys, let's grab a table and chat about what happened yesterday and earlier today,' said Fred. 'There's lots you need to know.'

Fred and Jo covered the events between them, butting in on each other as they thought of something to add or something they'd missed out. Sally and Bill had also seen the news earlier and were amazed that Jo really had overheard the conversation between the crooks about the robbery and had not invented it as they'd suspected.

They were intrigued by the visit back through the entryway in Fred's garden. When Jo summarized what they had seen on the wall panel, they slumped back in their seats, open-mouthed. As Jo paused to take a breather, Sally muttered, 'But what was all that stuff about "trust circles" and "togethering". It's a lovely word, but I don't think it's in the dictionary. And "sharing the gift", I don't understand that, it makes no sense. I don't see how it can possibly happen, do you?'

'No, I don't understand it either. It's too silly for words, too sort of futuristic. The whole thing is, well, nonsensical. It's as if we are in a dream, or we've gone through a portal into a parallel universe. As for the robins passing on human conversations, no way that's possible. Not even Facebook can do that, though Twitter might be more appropriate I suppose.' Bill's attempt at a joke went completely unnoticed and several minutes passed by as they tried to take it all in.

Meanwhile, the sun came out, and the temperature rose. It was turning into a beautiful day. Luckily they were sitting under a huge umbrella and were nicely in the shade. The waitress, Vera, came over to greet them. 'Hi guys, is it the usual? Oh, by the way, you may not have heard, but I've decided to open a vegetarian restaurant next door. After the long chat I had with you, your mum and grandmother the other day, Jo, we did some market research and concluded that there was definitely quite a demand. So, we open in a couple of weeks' time. Why don't you all come along and test out the menu?'

'Oh, that's fantastic, we'd love to, thanks, that'll be great,' replied Jo, though the look on Fred and Bill's faces was a picture. The thought of a meal without meat was not filling them with enthusiasm.

'So, is it the usual then?' asked Vera again.

'No,' said Sally, 'We'd all like ice-creams today; vanilla for me, chocolate for Bill, pistachio for Fred, and lemon for Jo, please.'

As Vera left, the other three looked at Sally in amazement.

'Bbbut,' stuttered Bill, 'you could at least have asked us first.'

'Oh, sorry, I thought I had,' said Sally apologetically. 'I'll call Vera back. What would you like instead?'

'Well, that is exactly what I want,' said Jo.

'Me too,' said Fred.

'And me,' said Bill, 'but, how did you know?'

'Well,' said Sally, 'I knew that I desperately wanted an ice cream, and I was imagining it, in a world of my own, sort of. Then I thought I'd asked you all, and you answered, but obviously I didn't, and you didn't, or so you say. Sorry, I'm very confused.'

'I hate to say this,' pointed out Fred, 'but I think that has just clarified everything. Sally knew what we were all thinking. She obviously sent us a "togethering" question, and we all answered without realising it. So, it looks like we've all become part of Jo's trust circle, or whatever you'd like to call it.'

'That's amazing,' exclaimed Bill. 'How did you do it, Sally?'

'I have absolutely no idea. Jo, you'd better explain.'

'You don't have to do anything,' said Jo. 'Just relax, think of something sensible, and pretend you're asking it. Hear the words in your head, and think of us. You don't need to look at us either.'

'I'll try it. I'll write down my question and then see if your answers match,' said Bill, as he pulled out a small pencil and a piece of scrap paper from the depths of his trouser pocket. Before he had written even the second word, his three friends answered, 'Hummus and Falafel, Spaghetti Bolognese, Burger & Chips.'

Bill was shocked. 'But I didn't finish writing my question. It was going to be, what are your favourite meals? How does that work?'

'Well,' said Fred. 'Jo's brain was enhanced in some way by looking at the entryway or by interacting with the panel, and that enabled her to do it. Now, somehow, she has shared this skill or whatever it is, with us, and our brains have been, er, enabled too. We are now all part of the same trust circle. So, Jo trusts us, and we trust each other, and that's all there is to it, maybe.'

A moment later, Sally said, 'I don't think so. I've just asked Bill a silent question, and I didn't get an answer?'

'Oh, what did you ask me?'

'I asked you what time we should meet up tomorrow.'

'No,' replied Bill, 'sorry, I didn't receive it.'

'So,' said Fred, 'it seems that Jo needs to be one of the participants and it doesn't work without her involvement. That's a shame. Can't you let us use it, Jo, without you being included?'

'Well, I'm not sure I can. I would if I could, but I don't honestly know how to control it. I have a feeling that it's all up to you. You'll be able to use it when you are ready, whatever "ready" means.'

'Perhaps we just have to practise some more. It will be fun trying anyway. Now, what are all you guys doing tomorrow?' asked Sally.

'We're off down to Hastings visiting my aunt,' said Jo. 'She's not been well, so we're going to try and cheer her up and take her out for a fish and chip lunch, though I'll probably have a delicious salad.'

'And we're meeting family friends for lunch in a pub in Sevenoaks,' replied Fred. 'What about you, Bill?'

'Well, I was due to be at the model aircraft competition on the Common. It's the annual event, but I probably won't go now.'

'Why not?' queried Fred. 'You've been planning it for months.'

'I have, yes, but three weeks ago there was a major disaster.'

'He's right,' said Sally, 'I went to watch. Bill's planes were fantastic. He had a larger one, a Tiger Moth model, and two smaller ones, Spitfires, though truth be told I suppose the scales were all wrong. Anyway, he had done something terribly clever with them, he, er, sorry Bill, I interrupted, you'd better explain.'

'Well, I had programmed the three to fly together using one controller. The three planes communicate using a short distance radio signal of about forty feet. I control the Tiger Moth and it passes a slightly modified signal to the two Spitfires so that whatever the Moth does, they copy it, making sure they always keep within communication distance. This means that they effectively fly in formation doing loops and dives and twists and turns.'

'Oh yes,' interrupted Fred, 'you showed us the early version when all three planes went off in different directions, hilarious.'

'Yes, well, it wasn't that funny. Can't expect to get things working perfectly the first time,' replied Bill. 'Anyway, everything was going well and the people watching it had never seen anything quite like it. It was the third or fourth time I'd demonstrated it. I'd been improving it a lot over the past few months. After about ten minutes, I completely lost control, and the planes vanished over the trees. We hunted around for ages, but we never found them.'

'I remember you telling us now,' said Jo. 'We just thought it was another failed test. Sorry, we should have helped you look for them.'

'We're not giving up, though, are we Bill?' said Sally, sounding fiercely determined for once. 'We are going to the Common tomorrow, and we're going to ask around and see if anyone saw anything or managed to locate your planes, aren't we Bill?'

At that moment, Vera arrived with their ice creams, and Bill immediately offered to pay for them. It was technically his turn, though he did not know if it really was or if the others were now ganging up on him, subconsciously, using "togethering".

They sat almost in silence, immersed in their ice creams until Sally pointed over to the kitchenware shop. 'Isn't that Sandra over there, the girl with the little dog?'

'I think it is,' said Jo, 'I'll wave and see if she'd like to join us... yes, she's seen us, she's heading this way.'

'Hi Sandra,' said Sally, 'what a lovely puppy. It's a spaniel isn't it? What's her name? How old is she?'

'Oh, hi guys. She's called Chaser. She's three months old and full of beans and just wants to chase anything that moves. She's incredibly friendly and can't stop licking all my friends, so beware. Better gobble up those ice creams, or she'll have a go at those too.'

'Can we get you one?' asked Bill.

'No thanks. That's very kind, but I need to get Chaser home. Anyway, it's good to see you all enjoying your hols. See you soon.'

Jo managed a quick pat on Chaser's head and ruffled her ears before Sandra headed off.

Just at that moment, who should come round the corner but Gertrude, with a huge chocolate brown labrador in tow. It was all she could do just to hold on as it was behaving very aggressively, more like a rattled bull terrier. Grant appeared too, whistling and kicking a ball into the huge dog, aggravating him and clearly winding him up.

Unfortunately, they were heading directly for Sandra. The angry labrador caught one glimpse of Chaser and off he went, pulling the lead out of Gertrude's hand and barking furiously. Sandra pulled Chaser behind her for protection but the little puppy was squealing like mad. Grant and Gertrude ran over, shouting, 'Can't you keep that damn pathetic specimen of a dog quiet?'

'Can't you keep your animal on a lead? It's dangerous,' squeaked back a somewhat terrified Sandra. 'He's the one who's creating mayhem, and he's ten times bigger than my dog.'

'Your scrawny dog is as pathetic and useless as you are,' said Gertrude. 'My dog will make mincemeat of it, you just watch.'

Jo and her pals could hardly believe their eyes, all four screaming, *'Heellpp'* at the same moment, though no sound actually left their lips. They reacted instantly, almost dropping their ice creams on the table as they ran to help, with no idea of what they might usefully do.

Now there were lots of dogs in the Pantiles at that particular time, and most were sitting quietly beside their owners, but not for long. Seven or eight of them suddenly pricked up their ears, escaped their owners and dashed over, determined to see what was going on.

It was not clear precisely what happened next, but two tiny dogs started nipping at Grant's feet causing him to back off, and the rest confronted the wild Labrador. Sadly, they were no match for him, and by the time Jo got there, several little dogs had been bitten, Grant was gone, and Gertrude was hiding in a shop doorway. Sandra and Chaser were too shocked to know what to do next.

(O) Gently does it, Jo. This dog has been specially trained to be a fierce and ferocious bully, much like its owners. But we know you love all creatures, and if you're gentle and patient, this dog will recognize you, calm down and like you too.

As Jo arrived on the scene, the other dogs surprisingly all stood back, appearing to form a circle around the unfolding confrontation. Jo edged closer and closer and was now almost face to face with the ferocious labrador. It was still snarling with the taste of blood in its mouth, pawing the ground like something out of a Spanish bullring.

They stared directly at each other and then Jo spoke gently but firmly, although no-one could hear the words she uttered or see her lips move. Slowly the growling grew quieter, eventually stopping altogether. The Labrador took a tentative step slowly towards Jo as she put out her hand. Then to Jo's surprise and relief he let her first pat his head, then tickle his chin and finally started to lick her hand. Jo gently took hold of his collar and calmly led the labrador over to its owner, Gertrude, who was still cowering in the shop doorway.

As Jo attempted to hand the dog back, Gertrude snarled, 'Give me my dog. What have you done to him? Zorog, come here, NOW. How dare you try and befriend him? You haven't heard the last of this. I wouldn't want to be in your shoes. Get out of my way.'

With that, Gertrude grabbed the lead and stormed off, Zorog digging his heels in. Grant was still nowhere to be seen.

'Well,' exclaimed Bill, 'I've never seen anything like that before. Labradors are always such gentle, kind and friendly dogs; it's in their DNA you know. Usually they can be trusted, even with babies. That one was really wild. My heart is still thumping. You OK, Sandra?'

'Think so,' replied Sandra, 'but that was really frightening. What a shame, though, he's such a beautiful animal. Thank you all for coming to help us. Jo, how did you do that? You really managed to quieten that beast down. Thanks again. See you soon guys.'

With that, the four friends picked their dripping ice creams up and wandered home. Fred called out, 'Good luck tomorrow Bill, hopefully see you on the Common, later on in the afternoon.'

Chapter 11

Trouble Above

'Hi Bill,' shouted Sally, arriving on the Common the following day. 'Sorry I'm a bit late. Any sign of your planes?'

'No, not yet, but I've only just arrived myself.'

'Has the competition already started, only I can see two or three planes flying at the moment? It's a beautiful day for it.'

'Some teams are just giving their planes a final test flight, but that's crazy. I mean it's so easy to crash these things.'

Bill and Sally wandered around, interrupting picnics with their questions. While a few individuals remembered seeing his fantastic flying display, they knew nothing about his lost aircraft.

Walking over to the competitors' area, Sally was surprised to see so many entrants. 'Won't some of these planes collide with so many racing each other, especially when they are all close at the start?'

'No, don't be daft, they don't race together,' explained Bill, 'just one at a time. It's a time trial you see. Those five markers, out in the distance, outline the circuit. There will be a marshal standing by each one. The planes have to pass by on the outside. Otherwise, they are disqualified. They do seven laps each.'

'Oh, I see. What's happening over there?' asked Sally, pointing to a screened-off area with crowds of people. 'Let's go and take a look.'

'Not sure,' replied Bill, squinting to get a better view. 'There's a gold painted Range Rover parked up. It says "MIGHT" on the side of it, and "Military Flight Research Ltd, Intelligent Drone Division" below it. Wow, that's exciting. I'm surprised they're allowed to compete, but I guess they have to test things out somewhere.'

Their conversation was interrupted by the loudspeakers. 'Welcome everyone to today's model aeroplane competition on our fiftieth anniversary. We seem to have a record number of entrants today. We also have MIGHT here this year, and they have kindly agreed to sponsor the event and provide the prize money too. The first competitor is ready to go, so let me pass the microphone over to the MIGHT Managing Director, here in person, to start the ball rolling. Please welcome Mr. Harry Hopter.'

'Hi Everyone. Let's take to skies, guys, three, two, one, lift off!'

With a roar from its tiny petrol engine, the first plane took off. The applause from the excited crowd was immense. Over the next three hours, the competitors sped noisily around the course.

'It's been quite exciting, hasn't it?' said Sally, 'though I know you desperately wanted to participate.'

'Well, perhaps next year,' replied Bill. 'It's been a great show. The mini electric powered drone with the four rotor blades was very maneuverable, quite fast and extremely versatile. It's clearly the shape of things to come. That American Mustang is still in the lead. It's well ahead of its challengers with a time of five minutes and twenty-five seconds. Still, I don't think that's an unbeatable time, as long as the aero aspects are properly engineered.'

Bill and Sally were standing close to the take-off area when the person standing close by turned towards them. 'Hi guys, I'm Abby, Abby Newsome, a reporter from the Daily Post. I've just been overhearing you and you seem to know a lot about what's going on here. I wonder if you could spare a minute to help me write tomorrow's article? It's very technical, and I'd hate to get it wrong.'

'Oh, hello, of course, we'd love to help. I'm Sally, and this is my friend Bill. He's the one to advise you. He'd be flying today too, but his planes were stolen a few weeks ago now.'

'That's rotten luck, Bill, but pleased to meet you,' said Abby. 'What do you think I should include in my report then?'

After ten minutes of constant scribble, Abby had pages of notes but did not quite know how to stop Bill's enthusiasm. Then the announcer's voice interrupted them. 'It's been a fabulous competition once again. The final entry is from Grunt Technology Solutions, and Jake Grunt is piloting their latest design. They're hoping to obtain significant development funding from MIGHT if they can win today. Seven laps to go. Good luck.'

Bill, Sally, and Abby watched as the guy with the controller jumped up onto the podium, with an ugly giant of a man standing behind him helping to start the plane's engine. 'Look, that's two of the four crooks we've been following,' pointed out Sally.

'It is,' agreed Bill, 'and that's Grant and Gertrude helping with the launch. The pilot must be must be their father. No wonder they were so friendly in the Pantiles the other day.'

'Are you saying you know these guys?' asked Abby.

'Well,' said Bill, 'we don't actually know them, we've been sort of following them for several days. You see they...'

'Erm... Bill?' asked Sally, not knowing quite how to put it into words. 'Have you noticed they have just launched not one but three rather familiar-looking planes? They might not be white, but still.'

'They are, they're m... m... m... mine,' stammered Bill, 'my Tiger Moth, and my two Spitfires, and they've painted them blue. So they stole them. What are we going to do? And look at that radio controller he's holding? It's the latest model, incredibly powerful and extremely expensive. They must have used that to tune into my frequency and steer my planes off course three weeks ago.'

'So,' said Abby, keen to get the full picture, 'are you certain that those are your planes and this guy Jake stole them from you?'

Sally butted in. 'If not, it's a massive coincidence. The planes look identical to Bill's, apart from their colour. What's more, we're pretty sure these guys were involved in that bank robbery the other night.' Suddenly realizing she might have said too much, she quickly added, 'Though we don't have any definite proof of that either.'

'Well,' commented Abby, 'I've had my doubts about Jake Grunt and his business activities for some time. I've been watching him closely. Let's meet up and swap notes. You could be a great help to me, and I might be able to assist you too. Here's my business card.'

Abby excused herself, thanking them profusely. 'You've been superb, but I'd better go as I need to snap a few more photos and get some more gossip from the competitors. Please call me soon.'

As Abby walked away, the three planes took off, circled and flew close together, just as they had been programmed to do by Bill.

Bill looked around, desperately hoping to find the police somewhere nearby. Sally sighed, 'We desperately need *help,* but the police are too busy, never here when you need them.'

Jake's three planes were zooming around the course. They completed one lap, then the second, the third, and the fourth, so far in less than half the time of the American Mustang that was currently in the lead. At this rate, they were almost guaranteed to take the prize.

The planes were halfway through the sixth lap, flying beautifully together, with the crowd cheering each time a marshal raised his flag, when a very odd thing happened. Three rooks appeared high above the circling planes. To begin with, no-one took much notice. Nobody really likes rooks; they can seem like frightening birds at the best of times. These three were especially irritated by the sound of little petrol engines buzzing around and fouling their air space.

If the public below could have seen their little faces, they might have been forewarned, but the rooks were smart and just like fighter pilots they came from out of the sun to avoid being seen. They dived, one after the other, gaining speed as they did so. By this point, the planes had started their final lap and had already passed the second marker, the marshal having raised his flag to signify all was well.

As the planes reached the third marker, the marshal was just raising his flag when the three rooks attacked the blue Tiger Moth. They flew alongside and lunged and pecked and flapped and kicked. The Tiger Moth was defenceless, completely unable to protect itself.

Grant's dad, Jake, standing on the podium, was desperately, trying to get the planes back on track as their flight became increasingly erratic. Had he had a modicum of aviation intelligence he would have known that a loop-the-loop would have solved the problem and his planes might have escaped their attackers.

'What the hell?' he exclaimed. 'What's going on? Where did those damn birds come from? Get them out of it, quick.'

'How exactly are we supposed to do that?' sneered Grant. 'Shall I get your shotgun from the car?'

'Don't be an idiot, Grant,' cursed his dad, 'you'll end up killing someone. That's the last thing we need right now, drawing more attention to ourselves.'

Bill and Sally looked on with astonishment, unable to believe what was happening.

The Tiger Moth staggered past the fourth marshal who raised his flag, then lowered it, then lifted it again, muttering, 'That was too close to call, better give it the benefit of the doubt.'

Between the fourth and final checkpoint, marked by a man with a chequered flag, everything escalated. The rooks launched a final attack and smashed the tail fin of the Tiger Moth. The plane was now uncontrollable. It zigzagged, did a loop-the-loop, and flew off towards the woods with the rooks in close pursuit. The two Spitfires were still flying in formation but were performing incredible acrobatics that mimicked the Moth's fatal wounding.

The crowd cheered at the magnificent display, marvelling at the skill of the pilot, completely unaware that it was entirely out of his hands. It was a good five minutes before the little petrol engines spluttered and died, but by then the planes were nowhere to be seen.

Over the loudspeaker, the competition organizer made a final announcement. 'The last entry, from Grunt Technology Solutions, has unfortunately failed to pass the final marker on the last lap and, according to the competition rules, has been disqualified. It's a great shame as it looked like a certain winner, but rules are rules. The winning entry, therefore, is the American Mustang. Congratulations. Come forward and collect your trophy and winner's prize of £5,000 from MIGHT's Mr. Harry Hopter.'

The crowd cheered with delight, but Jake was furious. He threw down the radio controller and very nearly crushed it into the dirt as he jumped off the podium, spitting and cursing. A string of expletives followed, all picked up by the announcer's microphone as Jake stomped backwards and forwards. A little while later, still fuming, he spotted Harry Hopter leaving and caught him up just as Harry climbed into his Range Rover and started its engine.

Jake put his head through the window and a brief chat quickly erupted into a heated argument. Leaping back, Jake cursed as the golden vehicle accelerated, all four wheels spinning, the promise of a million pounds of funding vanishing in a cloud of dust and gravel.

At that moment, Jo came pounding over to Bill and Sally, followed a few minutes later by Fred. 'What was that all about, what just happened?' asked Jo. 'I thought I heard a cry for help and then I listened to a mixture of cheering from the crowd, and moaning and groaning over the public address system.'

'And I saw Jo in the distance and was already rushing to catch her up,' said Fred. 'Then she took off like a scalded cat, heading here.'

'If we told you, you'd never believe us,' replied Sally, 'but first let's retrieve Bill's stolen planes, before Jake and his gang get there.'

They were suddenly interrupted as a family of blue tits circled them several times before tweeting like mad, almost urging them on.

'Come on guys,' said Jo, 'this way apparently, no time to lose.'

The birds proceeded to flit from tree to tree, then across the cricket pitch, past the pavilion, over Major Yorks Road, and into the woods on the west side of the Common. Sally brought Fred and Jo up to date with everything that had happened while they chased after the birds who seemed to be getting more and more agitated.

After a ten minute speedy trek, they arrived to find the three planes wrecked at the foot of a vast oak tree, surrounded by six elderly walkers. The birds chattered loudly and then flew off.

'Completely smashed up,' said Bill, bending down to rummage through the bits, 'but at least they all stayed together.'

'Are they yours?' asked one of the walkers. 'Only there were two young guys here a minute ago, both dressed in black, riding what looked like small cross-country motorbikes. They seemed intent on destroying the planes even more, then grabbed some bits and screeched off in a cloud of dirt. They've made a real mess of the path here with their wheel-spin. It distinctly says "No Cycling" too. Some people have no respect for anything. Disgusting behaviour.'

As Bill looked closely at the wreckage, he could feel his despair rising. 'They've gone, the three small processors and memory cards, the vital components. I have to get them back. There are all sorts of extra features that I'd built in for the future but hadn't been able to test. Jake mustn't get his filthy hands back on them, whatever happens. At least I have copies of all my hard work safe and sound at home. Hopefully, Grant's dad and his buddies are too stupid to fully understand what they've got their grubby mitts on.'

'Oh, by the way, we met Abby, the Daily Post reporter,' said Sally. 'She's great, very chatty, in her early twenties I think. She gave us her business card. Bill helped her with an article about today's competition due for publication tomorrow. Abby has her eyes on Jake too, really doesn't trust him. She'd like to meet up again and she's offered to help us if she can.'

'Well that's brilliant. And don't worry Bill,' Jo said, trying to reassure him, 'we will get your electronics back, somehow. At least we know what our crooks are up to this time. We're not going to let them get away with it. Let's meet up tomorrow and come up with a plan. Meet at say 10am, usual spot in the park?'

Chapter 12

Update in the Park

The next morning, Bill, Fred and Jo were chatting excitedly in their usual spot in the Grove, their local park. As they waited for Sally to appear, they were smiling at Abby's article in the local paper.

Model Aircraft Display Drones on all Day
[Abby Newsome]
An incredible display of radio controlled model aircraft took part in the annual competition yesterday on the Common. Over thirty aircraft battled it out for the £5,000 prize, which was eventually won by the American Mustang Team in five minutes and twenty-five seconds, a new record time. (See the centre pages for pictures and all the technical details.)

However, there was much commotion when the Grunt Technology entry was disqualified as it failed to pass the final lap marker. It would easily have achieved a winning time had it not been attacked by birds. Jake Grunt stormed off when...

They hastily put the newspaper to one side when they saw Sally striding rapidly towards them from the far end of the park.

'I've just bumped into Anna, selling Big Issues outside M&S. She recognized Jake immediately from my description and told me she'd seen him meeting someone outside the Council Chambers before going off to lunch together. She wasn't sure, but she thought it might be the same guy who is responsible for the Tunbridge Wells regeneration schemes, including the old cinema site. Interesting eh?'

'You bet,' said Jo, 'but what devious plan is he up to now?'

'That's not all,' exclaimed Sally. 'Apparently, in the Farmers Market last week, outside the library, there was a huge row between Jake and the farmer who was selling his locally made wine. Jake purposely smashed several bottles. Then he bullied the poor farmer before storming off. Sadly no one heard what it was all about.'

'This guy Jake is a real thug,' muttered Bill. 'He's causing mayhem wherever he goes. Following him has turned out to be anything but boring and I'm almost beginning to enjoy it.'

At this point, several squirrels had halted their acorn collection to gather close by. They were standing on their hind legs, their front paws pulling their ears forward as if to hear more of the discussion.

'I'm afraid there's more,' added Sally. 'There's a new environmental power company that has recently opened in the Victoria Centre, called SunRayPower. Well, it has submitted a bid to provide cheap solar electricity for the upgraded Civic Centre and Jake was seen deep in discussion with their owners. Anna was too far away to catch the chat, but it can't be good news if Jake's involved.'

Then it was Fred's turn to break some news. 'Bill, I don't suppose you heard the local news this morning?' As Bill shook his head, Fred carried on, 'Well, Jake and his gang have been given a second chance by MIGHT to demonstrate their model aircraft, but in a much more challenging mini-drone competition. The prize money will be £2million, to be used to develop the demonstration prototype into a full product to be delivered within twelve months. The central part of the test has to include a minimum of thirty small electric powered drones, flying over an area of one square mile, which must be capable of identifying and reporting any moving object in that area for a sixty minute period. MIGHT are hoping there'll be three, maximum four competitors. The date for the demonstration has been set for a month's time, an incredibly tight timescale. Is it possible that your stolen designs could be used to provide what's required?'

'Well, there's no limit to the number of planes that can fly together as they automatically register themselves with each other and the central controller. You can also control how far apart the planes fly by specifying the area of ground to be covered. I must admit that I haven't been able to test out those aspects thoroughly because I only had three planes. At the moment, they wouldn't stay aloft for sixty minutes without some kind of refuelling capability, but my design allows for that too. Changing to electric engines makes little difference as in-flight refuelling is almost impossible with these miniature planes. They'd also need to add the cameras and process the images to locate things that might have moved on the ground but

I've recently been experimenting with something very similar with my latest prototype. So all in all, yes, I think my designs might well be a good base to satisfy many of the test requirements.'

'Right,' sighed Jo, 'we either have to stop Jake somehow or steal back Bill's components. Or, we need an even better solution to the problem, Bill's Version Two. Though I guess that'll be a tremendous amount of work for Bill and probably for us too, and I've no idea how we'd find the money to construct thirty planes, have you?'

'And don't forget, somehow we need to get an invite into this mini-drone competition,' added Fred. 'That could be even trickier.'

Unusually for them, they were somewhat deflated, seemingly faced with insurmountable problems. Not to be deterred, this did not last long. Looking at each other, cheeky grins began to appear, and their usual positive approach to life's difficulties re-emerged. They knew what they had to do, and they loved a challenge.

'Maybe stealing Bill's computer chips back is the best answer. That would be daring and exciting, but very high risk,' said Sally.

'I think it's time to have a brainstorming session like we usually do at difficult times like this,' said Jo.

'We need to put a real spanner in their works,' mused Fred. 'Something that will unravel everything Jake is up to and bring it all to light. If we can get the police onto them before the competition, we might be able to disqualify their submission.'

Sally interrupted, 'Fred, I hate to say this, but I think that's your mum heading this way so we'd best change the subject. Bill, create a diversion, do something silly, quickly!'

'Why me, er, what can I do?' Bill scrabbled around for a couple of pieces of paper from his bag, quickly folding them into paper darts. Giving one to Fred he shouted, 'GO.' The darts flew across the path, one landed in a bush, the other nose-dived into the ground.

'Hi kids,' called Fred's mum. 'Pleased to see you're making the most of your holiday. Still playing with paper planes, I see. I thought you might have grown out of that by now. I'm off to meet Jo's mum and a few others to prepare for tonight's open Council Meeting. We're due to discuss the Council funds fiasco now that we have more info to go on – don't forget to give us those web links Jo, when you get a moment. By the way, have you heard about the missing items at Scotney Castle, you know, the National Trust property out near Lamberhurst? The police are baffled. Jo, your grandmother is due there tomorrow for her volunteering day, and she thought you might like to join her to take a look. We know how you like to be involved in these types of investigations. Anyway, see you all later. Fred, I probably won't be back until around three.'

As Fred's mother walked off into town, several nearby squirrels grabbed acorns and started cracking them together to make a sound like maracas. About ten seconds later, four or five rooks landed on the ground on the other side of the path, making a series of strange croaking cries. Then a small gathering of pigeons flew into the tree, only to be joined by a flock of starlings settling next door.

'I see we've attracted more company,' laughed Bill. 'Why is it that wherever we go these days, we seem to attract the animal life?'

'Hmmm,' said Jo, getting back to their previous conversation, 'we need some extra help to monitor what those crooks are up to and where they go but I don't see who else we can ask. Bill, you're the whizzo electronics guy, so what's a good techy solution to this?'

'Well, it's tricky. If we knew their mobile numbers it might be possible to put a tracking mechanism in place, though I don't really want to try that unless we have to. I could put my latest prototype plane up, but it would be noticeable, so it's not a practical proposition just yet. I could hack into one of Google's mapping satellites and redirect it overhead, but they might get the hump if they find it lingering here for too long.'

'Not to worry,' said Jo, not quite certain if Bill was serious or joking once more. 'On another note, if Fred's house is going to be empty, shall we take another trip down the tunnel?'

'Ooh, yes please. It was so exciting last time. Come on, let's go,' said Sally, jumping to her feet and tugging at Bill to get a move on.

Bill, Fred, and Jo just looked at each other, and no words were required to comment on Sally's unbelievable transformation from frightened girl to intrepid investigator.

As they got up to leave, the squirrels, rooks and pigeons huddled closer together briefly, before the birds flew off and the squirrels scampered away to continue playing and gathering acorns. Jo was the only one to witness this peculiar behaviour. Walking away with the others, the seed of an idea was beginning to take root in her mind.

Chapter 13

A Password

In no time at all, the four were back at Fred's house. They opened the entryway and disappeared from sight. Once inside, they quickly opened the next doorway and again walked down the uniquely lit tunnel and approached the spiral staircase, where they stopped.

'Right,' said Jo, 'let me try again and see if I can read what's on this panel; the one that did nothing last time we were here.'

Jo stood in front of the panel of dots and squiggles and tried changing her focus as she had before. Nothing happened.

'Perhaps it needs a password of some sort,' said Sally, smiling.

'Don't be daft,' said Bill, 'there's no way...'

Suddenly twirls and swirls appeared, all moving at a rapid rate in various directions. Gradually, and then accelerating, they remodelled and slowed, and a familiar shape of a large hand appeared in the midst of the lines and squiggles. Jo quickly placed her hand on the wall to overlap the image, but that was it. Just as Jo was about to give up and move her hand, words sounded in her brain.

(O) Hello, Jo, we're glad you have returned. What you are about to see will amaze you and your friends. You will never be able to speak or write about it, but you will always remember it. We just need a password. Thank you. See you inside.

'Wow, Sally you were right. Bill, you shouldn't have laughed,' said Jo. 'The Ancients have told me we need a password.'

She looked back at the panel and shook her head. 'You're not going to believe it, but the image of a hand has changed to a picture of a padlock, just like a secure web page. How do they know about that? Now there's an egg timer. Quickly we need a password.'

'Well, there's only one that comes to mind,' said Fred, 'but I cannot believe that the Ancients would have used it.' The other three looked at him, knowingly, as he muttered, 'Open sesame.'

Jo was about to repeat the very same phrase when the panel and the section of the wall rumbled and opened.

(O) Well done Jo, Fred, Sally, and Bill. You may not have realized it but you were all thinking the same thing, and that was good enough for us. Come on in, we have so much to show you and a lot to explain. By the way, you know we would have let you in without a password, but that was too good a joke to miss, haha.

'Wow,' exclaimed Sally. 'We can all hear them now. Fantastic!'

'And I do believe they have a sense of humour,' chuckled Fred.

The four of them entered another well-lit tunnel which curved round to reveal the most incredible sight they had ever seen. The area was vast, a huge dome-shaped cavern rising in the centre to well over 200 feet. It was circular and its diameter must have been at least 250 yards. Around the outside were slim archways, each about 30 feet wide. From there, a series of massive arches spread out to a wide central column. The whole structure was beautifully bright with a translucent appearance, apparently constructed naturally from interconnecting stalagmites and stalactites. All around the edge were hundreds of panels all covered in yet more lines and squiggles. The four friends stood there in shock, hardly able to breathe.

'How can this possibly be here?' asked Sally.

(O) Turn to the first panel, guys, just to your left. It is time to tell you more about who we are and why we came here.

Moments later the panel flickered into life, and the show began. 'They're back, the three of them, just as you described, Jo. And her hair and her eyes, just like yours,' said Bill, with Sally nodding, 'and now we can see and hear them too. Absolutely brilliant.'

'And background pictures too,' added Sally. 'I love it.'

(O) What you see before you is our second home. Our first one was destroyed by a tumultuous earthquake and resulting tsunami. Luckily our scientists were wise, and we were ready, almost, and we were led here. This was one of only a few safe places on the planet. It

was absolutely perfect for us, but we knew we would have to prepare it carefully, ready for our occupation, and those who would follow.

Our original home was in the Atlantic, a mere hundred miles to the west of the Mediterranean Sea. Ours was a beautiful island 1000 miles long and 600 wide, shaped like a diamond. Its most easterly point was rocky and dangerous, and the weather played constant tricks as the moisture from the Atlantic met the heat of the Mediterranean, often resulting in thick mists and dangerous sea currents. This kept it hidden from fearful sailors, though none were brave or skilled enough in boat building back then.

It had an ideal climate, superb sunny weather with rain almost only at night, and wonderfully rich and varied vegetation. The geography was perfection with mountains and valleys, plains, inland lakes, forests and white sandy beaches. We shared it with the island's animal life, and they were our partners and best friends, with a bond and level of trust stronger than you could ever imagine.

'Sounds like a beautiful place to live doesn't it,' said Fred, 'but not sure they'd have liked cruise ships and holidaymakers galore.'

As Sally nudged Fred to shut him up, the programme continued, no one noticing the pause while they completed their conversation.

(O) The Mediterranean was much smaller then, narrow and shallow, more a great river than a large sea. The lands around it were lightly populated with many small groups, most struggling to survive, nothing like the numbers living there today. We periodically sent our sailors through into this river to check out the population and assess their development. On our very first trip, we caused one small group to flee, terrified by what they had seen. After that, we adopted more appropriate forms of dress, and used much smaller boats disguised with wooden construction and, on the face of it, using oars and sails for power. We completely hid our capabilities and purpose from these people, not wishing them to fear or envy us. We were seen as passably normal and somewhat approachable.

What we discovered was surprising. A few groups were gathered into small communities, some looked after their people, cared for the injured or those unwell. Any who could no longer hunt or fish were given gentler tasks, things that still needed to be done. A job of some sort was found for all, making them feel useful and part of the family. They would often get together, especially in the evenings when work was done for the day and they would chat and laugh and even dance and sing. It was a delight to see them enjoying life, encouraging each other, regardless of whether the day had been successful or not.

Sadly, we found too many other places where the people were aggressive and war-like, caring little for those who were aged or infirm, making everyone pull their weight or be discarded. Some were just left to themselves in the hills where wild animals roamed. By far the worst were those groups that were male dominated, with females having no rights and rarely listened to. In some places, women were treated like slaves, tied to the home and not able to walk out on their own. Some had rarely felt the sun on their arms or legs or enjoyed the delight of a gentle breeze blowing through their hair. There was no equality of life whatsoever, and the women were downtrodden. They were given no opportunity to enjoy the freedom of life or make choices or take responsibility for their actions.

For us, it was hard to comprehend the thinking behind such behaviour. We saw no joy in the lives of these people. There was no evidence of kindness, consideration, learning or sharing, no fun or humour, and indeed no real love to be found anywhere. We were hugely saddened and dismayed at this discovery recognizing that this was how we once were, many thousands of years before.

We were also shocked and disgusted by the treatment of animals by these groups. So much cruelty, with some animals hunted for food or clothing, yet others revered and protected for no apparent reason.

For many years we had tried to encourage friendship, peaceful behaviour, equality, trade, support and knowledge flow between these people, and sought to improve their lives, at least amongst those whose actions suggested they might be interested.

Over time, we found a few wise and intelligent people that we could trust and on one or two occasions even brought them to our land as visitors. They were amazed by what they saw of our culture, our health, fitness, openness, our love of all creatures, the care we showed for the environment and our determination to protect it. We sent them home with new visions and a desire to cultivate new aspirations and lifestyles for their own people. Some even documented their visits, though they never really understood exactly *where they had been or who we really were. Some of those early texts have been copied and modified many times over the ages, but we can see that they still exist in your writings today and remain a source of intrigue and discussion, sometimes even conflict, sadly.*

Back then the gap between the coasts of Africa and Europe, between Spain and Morocco, was only a few hundred yards and it was rocky and dangerous in places. The flow of water was fast causing strong eddies and currents, making it passable only to those with sound knowledge and strong navigational experience. When the earthquake occurred, this gap widened at an unbelievable pace, and the earth cracked along the line of this ancient river. As Africa was wrenched asunder from Europe, the Atlantic waters poured into the area, and a massive tsunami spread in two directions, first into the Mediterranean then back out across the Atlantic.

Millions of humans and many more animals and creatures were annihilated. Most died from flooding, but many died from asphyxiation due to so many dormant volcanoes that were triggered into eruption. Our own land vanished in seconds, disappearing far under the sea, leaving no trace that it had ever existed.

For well over a year prior to the earthquake, we had given warnings far and wide, not just to neighbours and friends but also to those who looked on us with distrust and menace. Many failed to take heed, sceptical of our sincerity and our understanding of the situation. Others took our warnings to heart, making preparations to save themselves from the massive floods to come, one or two to save their animals as well. We can tell from your memories, Jo, that stories of these events have survived history in some form, perhaps more in the words of folk law passed down through the ages.

We were so happy when we later discovered that people in more than a dozen important locations had listened to our warnings and had been reasonably well prepared. We had asked our bird and animal friends if they would be kind enough to take on another challenge of significant magnitude. We were delighted when they agreed to carry out a surveillance mission of all the locations on the planet that really mattered to us. These were all places where humanity was taking root, green shoots appearing, where civilisation was springing forth through intelligent discussion, cooperation and consideration for others. They reported back that nearly all had suffered significantly during the upheaval, but the "light", as we liked to call it, was still burning and hope was high for the future.

Several of these were especially important to us. They were sources of sound human endeavour with strong feelings of how they believed civilisation should be, though at extremely early stages in their communal development. We have since been back to these places offering assistance and guidance. Not everything has worked out as we had hoped, not everyone appreciated our efforts to help.

Some communities were keen to hear what we had to say and began to follow the path we were proposing. But other groups opposed nearly everything we believed in, such that we could not intervene. Some became aggressive and hostile while others adopted the mantle of superstition, somehow thinking that by sacrificing animals and humans their own lives and conditions would somehow be miraculously protected and improved. These actions were totally against our own belief in the importance of life, all life, and we had no option but to leave them to their own devices, hoping for a second opportunity at a later date.

At least we tried, but maybe we could have done more. We were saddened by our failure. We had so much to offer, yet these people refused to listen or understand, refused to open their minds and see a different and vastly more positive future. But that was then, and this is now. And "togethering" has evolved slowly and surely over the passing centuries, getting stronger, wiser, preparing itself for the ultimate challenge.

'But that's terrible,' said Fred. 'How could people possibly ignore such advice and guidance? What did they have to lose?'

'A great deal,' suggested Jo. 'Life back then was tribal with dominant clans refusing to give up power. They were probably not open-minded or interested in new ideas. Remember, it was less than 500 years ago that early scientists proposed that the Sun rather than Earth was at the centre of the Universe. Look at the trouble that caused! And don't forget how long it has taken for women to get the vote here. There is still huge inequality and unfairness even in today's society. Getting people to change habits and beliefs is hugely difficult. Anyway, let's see what else the Ancients have to say.'

Chapter 14

Discovery

(O) Our real surprise was to discover other sites in this new country of ours that we had no idea about. Some five thousand years ago, our bird friends had identified a location that was surprisingly close by. It was at the centre of an area with a radius of some twenty miles at the time. It was made up of many small communities, and they seemed friendly and generally pleased to meet us, though fiercely independent and sometimes confrontational with their neighbours.

We paid frequent visits, not only because they were so close, less than one hundred miles due west of us, but also because they were reasonably open minded and honest. We would spend days on end discussing everything imaginable. They apparently enjoyed our visits and the knowledge we were able to impart. We shared some of our plants and seedlings with them and carefully explained how to farm and take care of the produce and how various meals might be made. Our greatest joy was being able to improve their diet and their health in general. In just a few years, no more than ten, we managed to bring these separate communities together, sharing their strengths and dramatically improving their chances of survival.

They soon recognized that their lives had flourished since meeting us, and they began to listen carefully to our words and take our advice on many things. Their numbers were steadily growing, and they were collaborating and progressing in a whole range of areas. With survival no longer a threat to their existence they realized that they could start to tackle the harder challenges in life, not just the easy things. They became more positive and more confident in themselves, both individually and as a larger community.

We would celebrate our friendship every year on the longest day, always in the same place, sitting on the ground together, in a circle. One year we arrived to find that they had decided to celebrate the kindness we had shown them, something they wanted their people to remember forever. They had honoured us by rolling small rocks into a circle for us all to sit on and made mats of straw to make them more comfortable. This spot became known as The Circle.

We thanked them profusely, but we were adamant that we had no need of such symbols and that it was the sharing of knowledge and kindness that was the thing of importance as far as we were concerned. They replied that this was just the beginning and that we had shown them that almost anything could be achieved by working together, fairly and equally, and by having purposeful objectives that everyone believed in. They said they would create a lasting monument and that one day the whole world would know about it and be part of it. These small rocks would be replaced with larger versions and become a beacon to the Circle of Knowledge and Trust.

In truth, this was all part of our search for people ready to join our circles of trust. Sadly it was all too soon in the development cycle of these people and, although we felt the seeds had been sown, "togethering" failed to take hold. We had no option but to carry on our search for others.

'That's incredible,' said Fred, 'a monument to knowledge and trust, created all those years ago. Are you all thinking what I'm thinking? Are they talking about Stonehenge?'

'Well, it's the right distance from here,' added Jo. 'Can that really be what the stones are all about? Did those people actually honour the Ancients by building the gargantuan stone circle we see today, or what's left of it? It's a fantastic idea, but can it possibly be true?'

(O) Sadly the earthquake that destroyed our homeland came too early and the vast majority of our incredible people perished. Our advance party did arrive here safely and survived. They were our brightest and strongest and were deeply trusted. They brought with them all of our history, our inventions, values and hopes, and examples of everything we knew.

'But this place is remarkable,' mumbled Bill, his thoughts straying from the Ancients' story to their immediate surroundings. 'I think we must be right under the Common. I cannot think of anywhere else where a cavern this shape could exist.'

'You could well be right,' said Fred, 'and, you know what, given all the problems with the old cinema site, it's a good job the Council know nothing of it otherwise I'm sure they would try to convert it into an underground car park or something equally unimaginative. You can bet that horrible Jake would wheedle his way into it too.'

(O) This location, our new home, was initially formed by an ice age millions of years ago. The leading edge of a glacier carved out this dome, and as it did so, rocks were piled up on all sides and above it. With the end of this particular ice age, the glacier gradually melted and withdrew. As luck would have it, the rocks were perfectly positioned to form a roofed dome. Over the intervening years, millions of stalagmites and stalactites formed, millimetre by millimetre. Just how the limestone outcrops were created here in the middle of a sandstone area is a mystery that only the past can reveal.

When we were led here by our animal friends, our engineers had little to do after assessing the stability of the structure, shifting only those features necessary to divert the drips and flows of water to the sides. Much more effort was required to create the beautiful circular shape you see today. In fact, there are three of these dome-like structures, and all three are interlinked. How we arrived here and found this place is fascinating, involving many amazing creatures, but we'll reserve that story for another time.

You may not have noticed it but at the centre there is a wide spiral staircase leading up to another surface access point, though it can only be opened by yourselves. The entrance is well-known to you as Wellington Rocks. A similar construction exists in the other domes, and you know these as High Rocks and Toad Rocks.

'Bill, it seems you were dead right about this being below the Common,' said Fred. 'Sorry, carry on, didn't mean to interrupt.'

(O) These domes formed the centre of our community. We survived, lived, multiplied, and our scientific efforts continued. From here we tried to help thousands of others to recover and survive too. Gradually we travelled and spread out across the globe, helping where we could, only sharing our secrets with those few whom we believed to be trustworthy and ready to take on such responsibilities.

That is enough history for now, but each panel around the walls will give you information about everything we have done and all we have ever learnt. Behind the panels are examples of all that we have created or protected but they cannot be opened yet. They will reveal themselves when you and the rest of the world are deemed ready. They cannot be opened by force, only by thoughts, words, and kindness. "Togethering" will know when that time has come.

Today, Jo, you have acquired new capabilities, and we need to explain a bit more about them so that you are not shocked when you realize what is happening. Take a trip around this beautiful dome, explore for a while, then come back and we'll reveal a little more.

The four friends spent almost an hour exploring the cavern.

'But there's no sign of life anywhere,' pointed out Fred. 'No living quarters, bedrooms, kitchens, or bathrooms. It's just a massive open space. And it is all spotless. What exactly did they do here? Where did they all go? Why did they leave?'

'And where are they now?' added Jo. 'It's all very strange, but I guess we'll hear soon enough, when we're ready to be told.'

'This is staggering,' gasped Bill, as they approached the fabulous spiral staircase. 'It must be forty feet wide, and it goes up and up forever. It seems to be made out of that stalagmite stuff, but how did they carve it out like this? Let's go up and see where it leads.'

'Whoa, hang on, that might not be such a good idea,' warned Jo. 'It's a fine day, during school holidays, and if it really does come out at the top of Wellington Rocks, we're bound to be noticed – there'll be loads of little children and parents milling about up there.'

'Yeah, you're probably right,' said Bill. 'And we'd better get back if the Ancients have more to tell us'

As they returned to the panel, the programme began once more.

(O) Now, you already know quite a lot… that the messaging part of "togethering" uses brain pattern transfer and works through all humans and animals whether they are part of your trust circles or not and that these individuals have no idea they are performing messenger services. When you ask a "togethering" question, the request spreads out like a giant web involving many, many people,

searching their memories for clues as to who might hold the answer, gradually homing in on all those able to add detail and value. It is impossible for people to detect when a "togethering" session is in operation, even if they are actually involved. And this works in the blink of an eye, no matter how many people are included and regardless of how many "togethering" sessions are in play.

'WOW! Is that possible?' exclaimed Bill 'It's incredible. If the Google and Internet guys knew about it, they'd surrender straight away. It must be faster than the speed of light.'

'Better keep it to yourself, Bill,' said Sally, winking to the others.

***(O)** The next thing we need to tell you about is the lasting and permanent effect of "togethering". You can of course use it to ask mundane or trivial questions, but that's a terrible waste, not exactly a misuse as such, but not exactly purposeful either. When you ask a purposeful question, a slight indication of your "purposefulness" is lodged in the memories of those attempting to answer the question as the message is received, responded to, or simply passed on.*

The more of these questions you ask, the stronger your "purposefulness indication" becomes. Your "trust quotient" then grows in value, and you become increasingly trusted in the world as a whole. However, a mundane question has the opposite effect. Through asking purposeful questions, you will touch millions of people and although you may never meet them, the level of support they will give you in times of need will appear almost magical. Never underestimate the depth of value and joy this support will bring.

A most important aspect is what we call the "truth factor", and it relates to the individual who knows the answer to a particular question. If that person is holding a lie or deceit and is purposely trying to hide a truth from others, with "togethering" the truth is always returned. It should be pointed out that the person responding to an information request is never identified. Also, the truth, sadly, is not always provided. It is only revealed when the person asking the question has strong purposefulness and trust indications. There are some evil people in the world who will almost never provide a truthful response. It is not that they tell an untruth, they just give no response at all. This means that only someone with extraordinarily high purposefulness and trust indications will be guaranteed to receive a truthful response.

'Jo, that confirms it, the proof we were looking for. That's how you found the "grot spot" cinema site irregularities,' said Fred. 'It was obviously nothing to do with your Google searches.'

'You may well be right,' agreed Jo. 'After all, we found no trace in my browser history of where the information came from.'

(O) More importantly, if a person knowingly tells any verbal untruths, intent on covering up an essential truth, then that person's trust quotient is always automatically reduced. A reduction in trust quotient will reduce an individual's ability to use the "togethering" capability either in part or completely.

'Oh dear,' sighed Fred, 'I hope that little white lies don't count otherwise we're in serious trouble.'

(O) Another important aspect of "togethering" concerns alarm signals. If any of your trust circle or family or friends ever find themselves in trouble, under threat or in a stressful situation, then you will know about it almost immediately. In severe cases, you might even see the situation as if you are actually there, watching it unfurl through the eyes of your friend. In this case, the messaging aspects of "togethering" are immediately magnified, shifted into hyper mode by the shock of the situation. It can be disturbing when you receive such alarms but stay calm, and all will be well.

One of the wonders of "togethering" is its impact on health and wellbeing. Once part of "togethering", you will find that you will be much healthier. Minor ailments will disappear and muscle, bone and tissue damage will heal more rapidly. You will be happier, less stressed, able to solve problems faster and see solutions more quickly. The collaboration and sharing aspects make life much more interesting, satisfying and enjoyable.

You will inevitably be drawn back to nature and the environment. Knowledge of beautiful cliff walks by the sea, walks through parks and beautiful places will become enticing and incredibly rewarding. Animals will become friendly towards you, and some may even attempt to communicate with you. Over time, as your trust increases, all creatures will be only too happy to help you in any way they can.

'I hate to say it,' said Bill, 'but this is already happening. Jo, your hay fever seems to have vanished. Sally, your calf muscle damage has healed quicker than anyone expected. Fred, you had no claustrophobia when we were underground. And the squirrel at the boule competition certainly seemed to know you too, Jo.'

'And the speed with which you solved my mum's impossible Sudoku puzzle was astonishing, Jo,' said Fred, 'especially considering how useless you used to be.'

'Well, I wasn't that bad,' replied Jo, giving Fred a dig in the ribs.

(O) We have debated long and hard about giving you another important piece of information but decided that now might not be the right time. It relates to an event that you might find quite unnerving so we are giving it to you in a locked fashion. We will release it to you when you need it most. It will provide you with a greater understanding of one of life's most important mechanisms. You will need to be strong when the time comes.

That's enough for now. Come back soon, there is still so much we need to tell you. Jo, you and your friends are making fantastic progress. Your pursuit of Jake and his dreadful gang is courageous, even more so because no one else appears to be brave enough to confront them. It is just what we would expect from you, and you are clearly enjoying the challenge as we knew you would.

Take care. Bye for now.

The four friends dashed back through to the entryway in Fred's garden, arriving at the house in time for a late afternoon sandwich lunch. It was only then that Fred began to ponder on the final words from the Ancients. 'That was a strange expression, wasn't it?'

'What was?' asked Sally.

'Well, the bit about our involvement with Jake. Doesn't it strike you as odd?' asked Fred. 'First of all, they appeared to know all about it. Then they used the words, "enjoying the challenge", then added, "as we knew you would". It's almost as if they'd planned it.'

'Don't be daft, Fred,' said Jo. 'We'd found Jake and his gang a week before we found the Ancients. You're not making any sense.'

'Maybe,' admitted Fred, 'but the Ancients are pretty careful with their words. It's just surprising, that's all I'm suggesting.'

The four of them sat quietly finishing off their lunch, but Jo's thoughts were now going into overdrive. 'Perhaps Fred has a point. It's true the four of us had wanted something exciting to do. But the idea of tracking Jake had started before we discovered the Ancients. Yet, when I think about it, it was only half an hour after Fred and I were standing directly over the entryway, even though we had no idea it was there at the time, discussing the best position for the shed in his garden. Was it possible the Ancients were aware of us even then and had somehow planted this idea in our minds? But how would they even know about Jake and his ugly gang? No, this is too ridiculous, just nonsense, simply impossible, surely.'

They had just finished tidying away the lunch things when Fred's mum appeared. 'We've had a productive session and have carefully planned out our questions for tonight's Council Meeting. It will be interesting to see how they respond. It's not going to be fun for the councillors, but we have to get to the bottom of it. The local taxpayers need to know, and it's time that the Council understood the importance of transparency. They cannot be allowed to carry on like this if they want us to continue voting for them. Have you lot had a good time? What have you been up to?'

'Oh, not a lot' responded Fred, breezily. 'We had our paper aeroplane competition in the park and then went for a stroll over the Common to watch a bit of cricket practice.' Keeping his fingers tightly crossed behind his back, Fred hoped that this little white lie would not dent his trust quotient, though he was not at all sure what it was or if he really had one yet.

'Well, why don't you all come back here this evening, while we're out at the meeting?' suggested Fred's mum. 'We've a few new DVDs you could watch, or you could come along to the meeting?'

'Thank you very much,' said Jo, politely 'but I think we'd perhaps rather watch a film if that's OK?' They all agreed that their own meeting was a better idea. They had a great deal of planning to complete if they were going to successfully expose Jake and his gang let alone stand any chance of winning the mini-drone event.

Chapter 15

Birds to the Rescue

Later that evening the doorbell rang three times and soon Jo, Sally and Bill had joined Fred at his home.

'We have a lot to discuss this evening,' said Fred. 'Now, I have selected the Mamma Mia DVD. We've all seen it many times, so we don't need to play it again. Let's concentrate on our master plan. Our parents left fifteen minutes ago for their showdown with the Council, so we have a couple of hours to work on it, maybe more.'

'OK. Shall I summarize where we're at so far?' chipped in Sally.

'A quick aside,' said Fred. 'Jo, are we on for Scotney Castle tomorrow to help your grandmother? It could be fun, couldn't it?'

'Absolutely,' said Jo. 'Let's meet at 10.30am at my house?'

Sally continued, 'Now, where was I? Oh yes. We need to assess the feasibility of us participating in the mini drone competition and see how we can build thirty planes and equip them all with Bill's computer chips, and find the money for a new super radio controller. We also need thirty tiny spy-like cameras, and Bill will need to write the software to identify movement on the ground and develop an imaging system so that the MIGHT guys can focus in on any particular area of activity. My view is that it's not a practical proposition without thousands of pounds and several extra months.'

They all gawped at Sally, so assertive and confident. Gone was the uncertainty and worrying nature so often on display. They had to admire her ability to sum up the situation with such clarity. Her chess-like decision making had vastly improved and was now apparent in her real life too. Where had this new Sally come from?

Bill was about to speak when he was interrupted by a sudden tapping on the window, tap tap tap, taap, taap, taap, tap tap tap.

'What's that?' exclaimed Fred. To his astonishment, there was a rook sitting on the window sill, tapping away on the window. It did it again, tap tap tap, taap, taap, taap, tap tap tap.

'Hey, that's Morse Code, and it's spelling out S-O-S,' said Bill.

(O) Listen carefully, Jo, watch the rook, and let your mind clear.

'Wow,' said Jo, 'I've just had a message from the... the Ancients. They're telling me to tune in to the rook, somehow.'

Jo concentrated, opened her mind and unbelievably started to communicate with the rook, with some sort of brain pattern transfer.

'Hi, Jo. Yesterday, in the park, you asked for help to track Jake and his band of crooks. The squirrels called us down, and well, we think you noticed us but probably didn't realize we were listening to you all, using "togethering". Anyway, we received mental images from you of this gang of hooligans, and me and my rook mates called in our pigeon and starling friends and we flew off to find out what they were up to. They have mostly been at the old cinema site but now they have gone to the Civic Centre where some of your parents went earlier. If you concentrate hard, I'll send you an image, and you can see them arriving... There we go. Did you receive it?'

'Yes, I did. How did that work? Somehow you've given the gang a red outline and our parents a blue one. That's fantastic.'

'It's easy. We do it all the time when we share threat situations. Anyway, we wanted to tell you as we're worried; Jake and his mates are bad news, big trouble, and dangerous. We've seen them before, up to their dirty tricks. We'll keep you up to date with whatever else we might see. By the way, we are thoroughly enjoying this. It is thousands of years since we were last able to have this human interaction and share these tasks. You and your friends should know that we are happy to do more, much more. By the way, we loved helping with the model planes on the Common, it was great fun.'

'Thank you so much, and please pass on our thanks to all your, er, bird buddies and your squirrel friends,' replied Jo, hardly able to believe she was communicating with a rook.

'Wow, I can't believe my eyes or my ears,' said Bill. 'Not only are you chatting to a rook, but we are all seeing and hearing the messages at the same time. This "togethering" stuff is remarkable.'

'We'd better warn your parents,' said Sally. 'It'll be a disaster. The meeting could get really nasty, and they'll be right in the middle of it. Come on, let's go.' Sally stood up and almost ran for the door.

'Hang on,' said Jo. 'There'll be lots of people there, and they can look after themselves – my dad did judo when he was a boy, hope he hasn't forgotten it. There's little we can do and we'd only get in the way. And how would we explain that we knew what was about to happen? We can hardly say a rook told us. So, where were we?'

'Well, I was about to describe how we might build the thirty planes,' continued Bill, going deeper into the technology of chips, circuit boards and programming complexity. He was so engrossed that he failed to notice three pairs of eyes gradually glaze over.

Jo was wrestling with a way to politely interrupt Bill's monolog when she felt a searing pain shoot through her head.

'Oww... no!' yelled Jo. 'It's... it's my mum. I can see it. It's happening now. There all outside the Civic Centre, the meeting is over, but there's shouting and shoving going on. Jake and that great big ugly guy are confronting our parents. Jake is prodding my mum, threatening her, yelling and swearing. Dad's trying to intervene, but he's being yanked back and held in a vice like grip by Jake's enormous buddy. Jake's pushed her to the ground. Oh, my poor mum. Now Jake is bending over her, about to punch her. Wow, a bird has flown right into his ear. He's looking up. Birds are everywhere, flying around him, flapping their wings in his face. He's standing up, flailing his arms, trying to get the birds away. Now Jake and his buddy are running. The birds are chasing them and pecking them. That was amazing, incredible. The birds were helping, trying to protect my mum. I've never seen anything like it.'

Sally was terrified. 'Jo, is your mum all right? Can she move?'

'Dad's helping her up. Jake shouted that they should keep their noses out of the cinema site business. He said it has nothing to do with them and if they're caught snooping around, there would be real trouble. Thank goodness the birds intervened. I must go. I need to be home when they get back and make sure Mum hasn't been hurt. I'm sorry we didn't reach any decisions about our mini drone strategy but I do have the beginnings of an idea that I think you'll like. Hopefully, we can chat more tomorrow.'

As Jo left, so did the rook. He and his buddies had done a brilliant job, but there was more work to do and not a moment to lose.

Chapter 16

A Close Encounter

The following day's Scotney visit was delayed as animated discussions were underway at Jo's house following the events of the previous evening. Undeterred by Jake's threats and bullying, Jo's mother was more determined than ever to confront the Council and hoped the headline in the Daily Post would stir things up. She still could not understand why Jake Grunt had arrived at the Council meeting with pockets full of bird seed.

<u>Heated Debate and Damning Accusations.</u>
<u>[Abby Newsome]</u>
Last night's open Council meeting dissolved into angry scenes when local taxpayers charged the councillors with a cover-up relating to the old cinema site redevelopment, acquisition, and regeneration programme. There were also damning accusations aimed at both the owners of the site and the Council for allowing such an important part of the town to fall into rack and ruin over the past ten years, so much so that it is now known locally as the "grot spot". Council denials were criticised when they refused to share negotiation reports and committee decisions.

Local businessman, Jake Grunt, awarded the job of site demolition, declined to comment on contractual terms. However, he was anything but tight-lipped afterwards and was seen bullying local residents.

Jo and Fred's parents privately agreed that far more information was required if they were to present indisputable proof of any misdemeanours being hidden from the public.

Fred's mother sighed, 'We've made reasonable progress so far but digging out the dirt from carefully buried documents is proving troublesome. We definitely need some assistance with this, someone with tenacious Googling skills. If you could prize Jo away from her pals, just for a day or two, we might make some serious progress.'

Jo's mum replied, 'I'll have a word with her, but everyone wants her to get involved in things just now. They're off to Scotney shortly, aren't they Gran, to see if they can unscramble the robberies?'

As the parents paused briefly for coffee, Jo, Fred, Sally and Bill scrambled into Jo's grandmother's car and off they went. 'Sorry guys,' she said, 'we're late so we're going to my favourite pub, the "Hop Pickers Arms", close to Scotney, for an early lunch.'

'Sounds good to us,' said Bill, licking his lips, thinking of bacon sandwiches. Fred winked, liking Bill's train of thought too.

'Guys,' murmured Jo, *'I don't want Gran to hear this. Last night when my parents arrived home, I asked them how the Council meeting went. They said they had made some progress but needed more tangible proof of the goings-on. No mention of any trouble.'*

'They're obviously trying not to worry you,' said Fred. *'At least it's out in the open now, thanks to Abby's article. It was front page news today. We really must arrange that meeting with her soon.'*

'We obviously need to help your parents gather the proof they are looking for,' added Sally. *'We need to look into it all anyway if we are going to bring all Jake's devious criminal activities to light.'*

The silent chat carried on for the next twenty minutes, trying to formulate a plan until the car pulled into the pub car park.

'Well, we're here kids. I didn't realize my dodgy driving would stun you into complete silence,' laughed Gran.

'Oh, sorry Gran,' said Jo, 'I guess we were wondering how things could be stolen from Scotney, when it's like Fort Knox in there.'

As they sat down and ordered their food and soft drinks, Jo's grandmother explained in more detail what they knew so far. 'There have been three thefts to-date, including several valuable paintings, some silverware, pottery, a rug and even some bedding. The total value is about £25,000. The locks have been changed and all the windows are secured with bolts too. Someone could have climbed up the drainpipes to the roof, but there is no clear way into the house from up there. The police have examined the ground immediately around the house but have found no footprints. So far the police have no answers or clues. As far as everyone at Scotney is concerned, we're just paying a visit as part of a school policing project. I'll show you around. Mrs. Pennymore, the house manager, is happy for you to be there, but you're not to get in the way of the visitors.'

Ten minutes later their lunch arrived and they turned their conversation to recent holidays. Although everyone seemed fully engaged in this conversation, another private chat was also on the go.

Jo commented, *'This is beginning to sound very much like an inside job. All the visitors are counted in and counted out, so there's no chance of someone remaining hidden inside when the house closes. Even if they did manage to hide, they couldn't have carried the stuff out, certainly not large items like the rug. The police have searched everywhere and found nothing. It's all very strange.'*

Fred agreed, *'I suppose once inside they could throw things out of a window to an accomplice below, but there was no trace of any footprints outside. It's a real mystery.'*

Sally said, *'Perhaps it's a disgruntled employee or a thief acting as a volunteer.'*

Jo disagreed. *'That's unlikely, they are all so trustworthy. They've been volunteering for years.'*

'Ideally, we need to stay hidden inside the house and see what happens,' added Bill, *'but then we could be waiting there for days.'*

Sally, increasingly the voice of reason, piped up, *'Today we need to have our eyes open and see if anything looks amiss, anything the police might not have noticed. Ohhhh no! Guys ... don't look round. You'll never guess who has come into the pub. This is awful.'*

Jake had just walked in with Gertrude and Grant, the hulk of a man from the aeroplane competition, and another rather unkempt-looking fellow. 'Jorik, come here. Give me the parcel. You carry the drinks. Barge your way to the front. Use your elbows if you have to.'

They muscled their way to the bar and pushed people aside. When the other customers complained, Jake gave them an extra shove and barked at them for supposedly waiting in the wrong place. The bartender was too petrified to argue; he knew Jake of old.

Jo, Fred, Bill and Sally looked at each other, Jo silently exclaiming, *'Did you see that? How does he get away with it? What is he even doing here? Here we are in a pub which borders the Scotney Castle estate, and Jake turns up. Coincidence or not?'*

Jake grabbed a table in another bar area at the opposite end to where they were sitting. Sally followed their movements out of the corner of her eye. *'I don't like this one little bit. The last thing we want is to get into an argument with them, especially with your grandmother being here. Since we've finished our lunch, I think we'd better make an exit soon before they spot us.'*

'I'll give Gran a nudge, suggest we might be running out of time. I could point at my watch perhaps, but that might be a bit rude so ...'

'Right, time to go,' said Gran a moment later, oblivious to the trouble they could be in if they stayed much longer.

'Whoa, did she hear us?' asked Sally.

'No, I don't think so,' said Jo. *'She's just keen to get going.'*

Gran said, 'Thank you for joining me. It's not often that I get to go out with four lively and talkative youngsters.' With that, they headed for the door, but their escape had not gone entirely unnoticed.

'You see those kids over there with that white-haired old granny of a woman?' said Gertrude with a mouth full of crisps. 'Well, the boy with the long black hair and pimply face is Bill, you know, I pointed him out to you in the Pantiles the other day. It was his planes we stole for the aero competition. Two of the others are the brats of the people you were arguing with outside the Civic Centre last night. Those kids are always around when they shouldn't be. That girl with the ugly red hair aggravated our dog in the Pantiles a couple of days ago. It's time we put the frighteners on them, good and proper.'

Jake leered, dribbling at the thought of all the violence he could dish out. 'Hell yeah, I recognize 'em, especially her with the flaming mop. We keep seeing them down in the Pantiles, meddling oiks. We've already taken care of one of the parents, haven't we Grant? And we're gonna put the fear of God into the granddad too. Those kids ain't gonna be smiling for long. It's time to sort that kid Bill out. You kids can deal with that too. Find out where he lives and get everything he's got, hardware, software, the lot. Do your worst.'

Oblivious to these conversations, Jo's gran and the four friends had exited the pub. Standing on the balustrade at the side of the patio eating area were two magpies, but they weren't waiting to gobble up any leftover crumbs from the day's lunches. As Jo walked past one of the magpies turned its head and winked at her. At that point, she knew the birds were anything but hungry, hearing reassuring words in her head, *'We're on the case.'*

Chapter 17

Investigating Thefts

Ten minutes later, Gran pulled into the car park at Scotney Castle. At the admissions desk, they all went through under the guise of a school policing project, investigating unsolved crimes. She guided them through the house with her usual family history spiel.

Sally was to take plenty of photos for checking observations later. Gran told them of the old castle and its moat built in the 1300s. She explained how the new house was constructed using stone quarried from the garden, and sited on higher ground far from the water.

On reaching the kitchen, Gran smiled, 'Let's meet up later when you've brought the robbers to justice. Oh, this is Puss-Puss the house cat and resident mouse catcher. No mouse is safe in her territory.'

Sally focussed her camera, with Puss-Puss in her element, a tiny smile appearing between her whiskers if you knew where to look.

The four friends wandered around the house several times, checking doors and windows and various cupboards, but to no avail. After a final fruitless look, they settled back in the kitchen.

All the while, Puss-Puss had been following, keeping a safe distance, keen to see what they were up to. Eventually, she leapt up onto the kitchen table, purring vigorously, but getting quite frustrated at the failure of these kids to read her body language.

Fred sighed, 'I can't believe it. We've found nothing. Let's have one last look. The thieves must have left some kind of trace.'

Puss-Puss, annoyed at being deserted and ignored, dashed off in hot pursuit, meowing like anything as if protesting, 'Wait for me.'

They examined every inch of the entrance hall, even craning their necks to peer up inside the chimney. They examined the study then on into the library. Puss-Puss leaped up on to the bookshelves, gently brushing her tail over each book; not a speck of dust to be seen.

Jo and the others searched, shrugged, gave up and repeated the exercise in the garden room and on into the dining room. The huge dining table was laid up as if a superb meal was ready to be eaten.

'We can't just give up,' sighed Sally, 'where else can we look?'

Puss-Puss was disappointed. She could tell that her new friends were about to leave and she'd be alone in the house until those horrible thieves turned up again. She had watched them come and go, often at her peril as they would always kick at her if she got too close. Although she knew exactly what her four new friends were looking for, she really did not want to put their lives at risk. On the other hand, she knew they might help. 'I'll just have to show them, can't wait any longer,' she decided.

With that, Puss-Puss approached a beautifully carved wall panel and rolled around in front of it. The kids just stood there and laughed 'No, don't do that,' Puss-Puss thought, 'how stupid can you be?' She jumped up and started leaping at the wall. *'Stop messing around and look at what I'm trying to show you!'* she meowed.

'What was that, who said that?' asked Jo, only to see confused looks from the other three, who'd heard nothing.

Puss-Puss tried again, meowing much louder this time. *'Look at the oval carving and the cheeks of the two small figurines in the middle of the wall panel behind me, near the fireplace. Push the left cheek, then the right cheek, then the oval in the centre.'*

Mystified but trying to follow Puss-Puss' instructions, Jo approached the wall panel, 'This is crazy,' she thought. 'First, it was the squirrel, then the rooks, and now Puss-Puss is talking to me.'

Jo waited until the volunteer in the dining room moved away and then pressed the three carved areas as indicated. The wall panel flipped open, leaving just enough space to climb through.

'Oh no, here we go again,' sighed Bill.

They all squeezed in after him as he fumbled for his phone torch. Fred closed the panel behind them, and Puss-Puss leapt through too.

Behind the panel it was snug, to say the least. Counting twenty steps downwards, the four of them struggled sideways, hesitating as the narrow staircase opened into a small arched brick cellar.

'We are not the first to explore here,' said Jo. 'Look at all the footprints in the dusty floor.'

'And look at all these old beer casks, must be thirty or more,' said Bill, trying unsuccessfully to lift one. 'They must still be full.'

'It's amazing that they've survived so long,' added Sally.

'Obviously the National Trust doesn't know the cellar exists.'

'Look,' said Fred, 'there's two missing, circles with no dust.'

Puss-Puss bounded on, and Jo followed, pointing out an archway on the left-hand side and a narrow tunnel ahead sloping gently downhill. 'Let's see where this goes. It's the only obvious exit.'

After fifty yards they hit a dead end, encased in stone blocks of different sizes. Bill shone his phone torch around but apart from a stone seat to one side, there was no obvious way forward.

Sally sat down on the seat. 'This is the end of the road, maybe this is some kind of bolthole or hiding place. What next?'

As Puss-Puss jumped up onto her lap, Fred sat down beside her. To their surprise, a moment later, the front of the seat jolted downwards, and a large stone at the end of the wall rotated outwards.

'Wow,' cried Fred, rushing to look, 'there's a sheer drop here.'

As Jo looked out too, they found themselves three-quarters of the way up a cliff edge in the quarry garden, with no obvious way down.

Puss-Puss could stand it no longer and quickly jumped down a series of slightly projecting rocks. *'You guys are useless. Follow my lead. Honestly, what would you do without me?'*

'Well if she can do it perhaps we can too,' suggested Fred. He then pressed his face tightly against the rocky wall and slowly made his way down, gently feeling for footholds and handholds as he went.

Before long, he was at the bottom, 'It's not as tricky as it looks.'

One by one, they followed Fred. Once safely on the ground the large stone slowly closed, hiding the tunnel entrance once more.

'Hmmm, that's all well and good but what now?' asked Jo.

Puss-Puss meowed. They turned to join her on the steps leading up out of the quarry garden as a squirrel jumped out of a nearby tree and shook its tail at them. Jo couldn't be sure, but she thought she heard Puss-Puss say, *'See you later, Alligator.'* Before they could give the obvious reply, Puss-Puss ran off, her task completed.

After a few yards, the squirrel dashed off and a chirpy-looking magpie appeared, and guided them down to the moat, past the old castle and into the garden growing in what was now the folly remains of the old connected house. The magpie tweeted loudly, before flying away, leaving the friends at a complete loss once again.

'Good ruin' said Bill, wondering why they had been stupid enough to follow the movements of animals that dash randomly around these gardens all the time.

Then two more squirrels appeared from nowhere and climbed what had once been an internal chimney stack of the old house. After twenty feet they jumped, landing on two carved animal heads jutting from the stonework. Suddenly, both heads tipped downwards, acting as levers, and a large stone rotated out from the chimney base.

'No,' sighed Bill, 'not more underground treks.'

'Come on,' yelled Sally, 'this is great fun. The more, the merrier.' Descending thirty steps down a stone staircase, they entered a tunnel with constant drips of water and muddy puddles to negotiate.

'This part is much older, nowhere near as solid or well built,' said Bill. 'You know, this could be the priest's hole that let the occupants flee from French invaders back in the 1300s. I bet it's where Father Blount hid from the Justices back in the1500s too.'

'Gosh, where did that torrent of history come from?' teased Sally.

'Well, I knew we were coming here, so I checked out Google. I was looking for floor plans, but I got hooked on the history. Besides, can't have you thinking I'm just a geeky computer nerd,' smiled Bill.

After twenty minutes of slow, soggy progress, they came to another set of stone steps going up. Reaching the top, Sally put her full weight on what looked like a new wooden trap door, but nothing shifted. With Fred's help, their combined effort pushed the door silently upwards. The hinges had clearly been recently oiled.

Scuttling through, they found themselves in an area surrounded by trees. Brambles had evidently been cleared not so long ago. Sally snapped a couple of photos then opened Google maps to find out where they'd emerged. The telltale blue blob fell right in the middle of Kilndown Forest, a quarter of a mile from their earlier pub lunch.

Fred muttered, 'You're right Bill. It probably was an escape route for the occupants of the old castle. We must have come under the moat and the river. No wonder it was so wet down there.'

'C'mon, let's follow this path,' suggested Jo. 'You can just about see where people have been walking on the grass. Careful though, we don't want to bump into whoever's been trampling through here.'

They'd barely gone 100 yards when they heard voices. Tip-toeing through the trees, they were shocked by what they saw as they peered through the bushes. Pitched amongst the trees were three large tents and four men with rifles, deep in discussion. Huddled nearby were another twenty or so people, including men and women, some old, some young, and at least five or six children.

Making sure the flash was off, Sally took another photo. *'I think we should go before they see us and we get caught.'*

'No, not yet,' said Fred, *'we need to know what's going on here.'*

Fred edged nearer, as close as he dared get without risking being seen. *'Look, over there, those two beer casks either side of the entrance to that tent. These guys have obviously been partying too. But I need to get even closer to hear what's going on.'*

Jo grabbed his arm, *'Hang on,'* she said and pointed up in the tree where several birds seemed to be watching. *'I can hear what's going on. Those birds must be passing on the conversation, listen.'*

'Yes, we were expecting all these illegal immigrants to be moved tonight but there's been aggravation at the cinema site. It's too risky to do it today. I met Jake earlier in the pub and handed over the usual drugs package. He said that they'll be using the cinema basement area for the next few weeks to house the eight pickpocket kids. The older teenage girls are going straight to London as part of Jake's fashion business. The old guys are assembling the kit planes in a disused basement area next to the railway station before moving on to their domestic slave duties in London and Birmingham.

I know it's cutting things fine as we have to move this lot out before the new batch arrive tomorrow, but there's not much we can do right now. Hopefully, the boat will be late into Rye Harbour after offloading them from the container ship. It's so tight getting these deliveries every three days, but we have to make the best of it. Jake pays bloody well, and the ale is fantastic. So far no one seems to be aware of us here. We're good here for the time being as the police have no idea how we're getting in to steal those items from Scotney.'

'We've heard more than enough. Jake is far worse than we ever imagined. He's evil and he's got to be stopped. Let's go,' said Jo.

They turned around but Bill missed his footing and trod on a thick dry twig. They all froze, wincing at the loud crack that followed.

'What's that?' said one of the guys. 'Jed, quick, go take a look.'

Jed lifted his rifle and headed towards the kids, as yet unaware of their presence. Suddenly two rooks took off right in front of him, followed by a rush of squirrels scattering in different directions.

'It's OK Jorik,' said Jed, keen to rejoin his mates, 'just the wildlife messing about, no one there.'

Holding their breath, Jo, Fred, Sally and Bill trod gently forwards, eyes firmly fixed on the ground this time.

'That guy giving the orders, Jorik, he was in the pub, the scruffy one with Jake at the bar,' said Jo. *'So, we now have more names to add to our list of Jake's gang members, and we know far more about his devious businesses. It's appalling what he's up to.'*

Once back out at the old castle they made their way up to the Manor House, looking as though they'd just completed a regular tour of the grounds. A volunteer at the entrance called out to them as they were passing. 'Hey kids, I didn't see you sneak out earlier, how did you do that? Anyway, your grandmother was looking for you about ten minutes ago. She went to check if you were at the café.'

'Oh thanks,' called Jo, 'we'd better get moving.'

As they walked off, they saw Puss-Puss sitting to one side, almost smiling with a definite twinkle in her eye. *'So glad you could join my tour today guys. Hope you can appreciate what's been going on here. We must put an end to all the midnight interruptions. I can't begin to tell you how much I've loved chatting with you. Mother was right. She said this would happen one day. See you soon, hopefully.'*

'It was an absolute pleasure Puss-Puss and thank you so much for your help and, of course, your patience,' replied Jo.

Arriving outside the café, they found Gran. Fred had a quick word with the others. *'Let's not tell her or the police what we've discovered until we know how best to deal with it. We can't risk Jake and his gang escaping with just a slapped wrist or a telling off.'*

'Hi, I've been looking everywhere for you,' said Gran. 'Did you find any clues?' Seeing their long faces, she added, 'Ah well, you can't have made less progress than the police. I suggest we head home as I made a chocolate gateau yesterday. Knowing you lot, I suspect you can easily demolish it.' They all nodded enthusiastically.

Going home, Jo's grandmother was delighted that the kids were no longer frightened of her driving as they were laughing the whole way. She had no idea that a silent conversation was underway as the friends tried to piece together what they'd seen and what to do next.

Chapter 18

Jo's Mum Goes Missing

Jo's grandmother pulled into her driveway. 'You go around the back. The side gate should be open. You'll find Gramps in his shed, busy inventing something. I'll bring the tea and cake out shortly.'

As they entered the garden, Bill could hardly believe his eyes. 'What is all this?'

All around the edge of the garden path, on both sides, were metal poles about eight feet high and three feet apart. On each pole was fixed what looked like a large black ball about two feet in diameter and constructed from a dozen or so interconnected segments.

'It's a long story,' explained Jo, 'but Gramps is a bit crazy, always building something, usually to do with energy supplies that don't harm the environment. These black balls are heavy and made of copper on the outside. As the sun shines on them, the segment that is facing the sun expands. This forces the ball up the pole and twists it at the same time, bringing another area to face the sun. As days and weeks go by, all the balls eventually reach the top of their poles. Gramps calls the whole ingenious setup his "Gravity Power Station".

His favourite joke is that his invention of "GPS" was first, long before the satellite navigation system came into being. Anyway, as electricity is required the balls are allowed to fall slowly down the poles, each one turning a generator inside. Gramps says that his electricity bills are almost zero since he built it. Isn't that brilliant?'

'It certainly is,' replied Bill, but where is he? I'd love to chat with him about his inventions. It's all fascinating.'

'Well there's more,' pointed out Jo. 'Those are his earlier solar concentrators, and that's a solar steam engine. That tree over there is an artificial energy tree, his latest idea. He'll explain it as it's very complicated. It generates electricity from the sun, wind, and rain.'

'Wow! And that looks like his workshop, the old shed over there. He won't mind if I pop in will he?' Without waiting for a response,

Bill trotted over and opened the workshop door.

They all followed him in, but there was no sign of Gramps. 'Incredible, just look at this. There are electric motors, circuit boards, processor chips and tiny batteries everywhere. Looks like a museum for old computers too. I didn't know he was into all this stuff.'

'Yes, well, Gramps has spent almost his entire life as a computer boffin,' explained Jo. 'He told us that in his early days computers could easily fill a house or two and yet were not as powerful as our mobile phones today. How daft is that?'

'Hey guys, look, two really old wooden tennis rackets and old silver trophies hanging on the wall,' said Sally. 'It says they were mixed doubles champions, three years in a row, over forty years ago. Your Gran and Gramps must have been good players in their day.'

'Oh they were, but they don't play much now. They just have an occasional knock about in the park to keep fit,' added Jo.

'Don't forget his ping-pong. There's his old bat on the shelf over there, lots of badges and shields,' pointed out Fred.

'And paintings too. These watercolours aren't bad,' said Sally.

'Well, he likes to dabble but he has so many interests that he can never concentrate on his art for more than an hour or so.'

At that moment, Gran came out through the patio doors with a tray of tea and large slices of chocolate gateau. 'See what you think of this. Gramps has left a note saying he's just popped out to briefly, but I've saved plenty of cake for him too. He shouldn't be long.'

The delicious cake disappeared rapidly. The four friends thanked Gran for a terrific day, licking their fingers as they went. Gramps did not return but Bill was assured he could come and chat anytime.

As they walked off, Fred said, 'Right, we a need a plan for Scotney and we must find out what Jake is up to regarding the farmer with the vineyard. Once that becomes clear, we can plan how best to expose everything he's up to in a way that doesn't appear to involve us. We need to stay hidden on the sidelines. I've a nasty feeling that danger levels are about to erupt and go sky high.'

Back at Fred's house, the four friends were surprised to find Jo's dad sitting with Fred's parents, all three clearly agitated. Jo's father turned to her, 'I'm sure there's nothing to worry about but your mum hasn't returned home from shopping, and she should have been back a couple of hours ago. She may have met a friend of course, but she'd usually call if she's running late and she's not answering her mobile. I've been phoning around, but none of her usual crowd has seen her. She has been taking photos of the demolition of the cinema site every couple of days, and I'm worried she might have gone there. Her camera is missing, and the cinema site is on her shopping route. There's no way she would have resisted the chance of a few more photos to add to her monitoring activity. We were all curious because there's been little progress since the fire. They're still using the asbestos excuse, but we know that was completed months ago.'

'Dad, you should have called earlier, we could easily have come back from Scotney sooner,' said Jo, clearly distressed. 'We'll go right out and look for her, come on guys, let's go.'

'Hang on Jo,' said her dad, putting his arm around her. 'Don't go rushing off without a plan, that's not like you. If she's not back within the next hour I'll call the police.'

Jo sat down, anxious and frustrated. Phasing out of the conversation around her, she reached out for a solution, using "togethering" to ask the difficult questions. She soon found out that there had been no reported problems at the cinema site, and her mother was not on any hospital lists. There had been no traffic accidents, no problems with the trains, no trouble in the pubs or anywhere else. Her mother's diary showed nothing, no pilates, yoga or gym classes, and no choir rehearsals.

'Dad,' she insisted, 'we can't sit here doing nothing. I don't see how the police can help. It can't be a coincidence that something like this has happened after the Council meeting last night, and all that threatening behaviour. I think we should start our own search. We'll go down to the Pantiles and see if she's been in any of the cafés. I'll have my phone with me if you need me. Call me if she turns up.'

Jo's dad sighed. He knew there was no point trying to persuade his daughter not to go once she had made her mind up. Following Jo's lead, Fred, Sally and Bill were already halfway out the door when Bill's phone vibrated. He held it up to his ear. 'Oh no! Has anyone been hurt? I'll be right back, see you in 10 minutes.'

'I'm sorry,' said Bill, 'but I've got to go. My mum's come home to find the house in a terrible state. We've been burgled. They've taken the TV, my dad's new iPad, and who knows what else. They've completely trashed the place, paint thrown over the walls.'

With that Bill rushed out the door, with Sally in hot pursuit, 'Wait for me Bill, I'm coming too. I'm sorry Jo, keep us updated. Hopefully, we'll see you tomorrow, and everything will be all right.'

Before Jo and Fred could get out the door, another phone rang – Jo recognized her dad's ringtone. They waited, listening. From the conversation, it sounded like Jo's grandmother. Trying to calm her down, he said, 'There is nothing to worry...' He was interrupted. 'Well you stay there and take care of him. No, she hasn't come home yet. We are attempting to find her. I'll call you back soon.'

'That was Gran. I phoned her a few minutes ago to see if your mother was there. Now Gramps has just got home and isn't feeling too well. Apparently, he got knocked over by a couple of cyclists. One of them ploughed into him as he was crossing the road by Hoopers. They didn't even have the decency to stop and see if he was all right. He was using the pedestrian crossing too. He wasn't hurt apart from some nasty bruises on his legs. There's nothing broken, but he's understandably shocked and shaken. I'm sure Gramps will be fine,' he said, trying to reassure Jo, who was now hesitating at the door.

'Why does everything happen at once?' asked Jo. 'We'll call in on Gramps when we've sussed out the Pantiles, and cheer him up.'

Fred and Jo peered into every café and shop, asking everyone about Jo's mum, but no one had seen her. They even went into the pubs and bars but drew a blank there too.

'I think we should go and check out the cinema site, just in case,' said Fred, 'though I know your dad wouldn't approve. We can call in on your grandad on the way.'

Jo's grandad was a little better but still lying down. Her grandmother was quite worried, but the doctor was on his way. 'Your mum hasn't turned up yet has she? No? Well, I haven't told Gramps about it yet as I don't want to increase his stress levels.'

When Jo and Fred reached the cinema site it was still boarded up and almost impossible to get a decent look inside. While they were there, they received a text from Bill saying that all his computer stuff had been taken including his backups. Luckily he'd attached another backup memory stick to his key ring, which held copies of all versions of his software, including the most recent. Although he was not close to applying for a patent, he thought he could use that if necessary to prove that the software being used by Jake's company was really his. Luckily his latest prototype plane was still hanging in the shed where the latest coat of paint was drying.

Scouring the outside of the cinema site, Fred found several cracks in the top of the hoarding which he could just about peer over by standing on tip toes. As far as he could tell there was no sign of any activity and indeed no sign of fallen rubble or Jo's mum.

'I don't think she's here unless she's inside somewhere, but there's no way she would try and climb over these boards,' said Jo. Before giving up, she took one last look around the site perimeter. 'What's that over in the corner, a heap of white stuff?'

'Oh, horrible. Two dead pigeons surrounded by a host of feathers,' said Jo, tears welling up. 'I'll bury them in the garden at home. Can't leave them here like that. Have you got a plastic bag?'

'No,' replied Fred, 'but there are several lying on the ground.' He tutted, as he went off to pick one up. 'Filthy litterbugs.'

As Jo bent down and scooped up the two bodies, gathering up all the feathers, she sensed something solid, 'What's this?' She brushed the feathers aside. 'Oh no, it's a camera! It looks like my mum's. She must have been here. She'd never leave it behind.' Jo burst into tears.

Fred was about to say something but decided to keep his thoughts to himself. It was obvious that whoever had grabbed Jo's mother was dangerous. It wasn't hard to figure out who was probably behind it.

They raced home to pass on the terrible news but stopped when they saw an ambulance outside Jo's grandmother's house and two paramedics supporting her grandad out into the waiting ambulance.

'He deteriorated just after you left,' said Gran. 'They think he might have a blood clot in his leg. They say it's not too serious provided they can get him to the hospital quickly. They've given him an injection to thin the blood. I'm going with him. I've phoned your dad to tell him and I'll call again when I have more news.'

Jo's dad was back home when they got there. Clearly, the news about the camera was the last thing he needed to hear. 'Well I have no option now, I'm going to ring the police.'

Jo replied, 'I agree, I can't think of any other reason for dropping her camera and not coming home, and not telling us where she is. It all happened outside the cinema site. It cannot be a coincidence.'

'Pass me the phone Jo, there's no point in wasting any more time.

Where is the camera though, let me check it is hers first.' Jo passed it over. Her dad was hoping to see what pictures she had taken but was surprised when no images appeared. He opened the bottom and was shocked to see that the SD card was missing. 'There's the proof, she didn't drop the camera - it was discarded by whoever grabbed her.'

'So, how do we prove to the police that it is her camera?' pointed out Fred, without wishing to increase anxiety levels further. 'I guess the police could do a fingerprint test, but then we've probably all touched it too. Will the police be interested? They may prefer not to act until she's been missing for at least twenty-four hours.'

'I know, we can't force them to do anything,' said Jo's dad, exasperated and extremely anxious. 'And we have no way of finding where she's been taken and we can't just sit here doing nothing. Surely we must notify them and at least show the police the camera.'

As Jo's dad started dialling, Fred heard the letterbox flap open and went to the front door to find an unaddressed envelope lying on the floor. He opened it and dashed back to Jo's dad, grabbing the phone from his hand to cancel the call.

'What are you doing?' asked Jo's father, somewhat horrified. Then Fred thrust the note into his hand. He read it, all colour draining from his face. Without saying a word, he passed it to Jo.

We have your wife. You were warned not to interfere and you ignored us. You and your idiot friends must stop pursuing your vendetta against the cinema site and its funding. If not, or should you notify the police, then you will never see her again. Do as you're told and your wife will be returned, unharmed, in two week's time, at which point various contracts will have been signed, and you'll be unable to do anything about it. So, it's in your hands, you know the score.

Giving Jo and her dad some space to digest the letter, Fred returned home. He explained everything to his parents and they agreed to pause their challenge with the Council. Fred doubted Jo would turn up tomorrow given the day's events. He could not help but worry about her, her granddad, and about Bill and his family too. How had today gone so terribly wrong?

Chapter 19

A Rescue Plan

The following morning Fred, Sally and Bill were sitting in the Pantiles, but Jo was nowhere to be seen. They'd settled in the area often used for boule competitions and the summer art fairs.

'I didn't like to call for her,' said Fred. 'She and her dad have so much on their minds. And Bill, how are things after your burglary?'

'Well, the place is a mess. The police have dusted for fingerprints but only found ours. The insurers came this morning. We gave them a list of things that have been taken but apart from the TV and dad's iPad it was all my techy stuff. The glaziers are there now replacing the smashed window and the cleaners are in this afternoon. The decorators are repainting the walls tomorrow. It's all so disruptive. I've no idea how I'm going to recover all the hardware I've lost.'

'That's awful, so sorry Bill. And we still have the vineyard farmer's problem to sort out. We could cycle out there now. It's only five or six miles, and it would be excellent exercise.' said Sally.

'Am I hearing correctly? Since when did you volunteer to do exercise? Anyway, that's a really good idea,' agreed Fred, 'but let's give Jo another half hour or so, in case she turns up.'

Though not wishing to appear lazy, Bill asked, 'Why can't Jo use her "togethering" skills to find out the farmer's problem with Jake, rather than us pedalling all that way, up all those hills?'

'It's a pity Jo hasn't passed on more of her skills to us,' said Sally. 'Maybe we're inadequate in some way. Perhaps we need to be more like her, though how we should change is difficult to know.'

'You could be right. If we think carefully, we can probably work it out,' said Fred. 'We know she loves animals and spends hours volunteering at the animal sanctuary. She has always been a proper vegetarian. She doesn't eat fish or any animal producs, just the occasional ice cream I suppose. She does lots of other charity work and is always putting herself out to help others. If she could see and avoid every ant on the pavement, we know she would.'

'Yeah, she's pretty special I agree,' said Bill, 'not that I have a, err, um, a thing for her or anything, um, if you know what I mean.'

'Honestly, would we blame you if you had, Bill?' added Sally, snapping slightly. She was immensely glad that no "togethering" was in play at that moment to reveal her true feelings on the matter.

Fred carried on. 'The environment is vital to her, and she spends hours analysing the climate statistics. She thinks most world governments just pay lip service to it, despite recent international agreements. They have little real interest in reducing carbon dioxide and other emissions, despite rising sea levels and the health risk to billions of people. She can't understand how governments can be so blind. Regional flooding is getting more frequent and widespread, the costs of insurance are sky-rocketing and, as Jo would point out, the disastrous effects on wildlife barely get a mention...'

Pausing for breath, he resumed where he left off. 'She's never happy just doing the easy things in life and always pushes herself beyond her comfort zone. She's a leader, though doesn't actually realize it. She never forces her argument, hardly even raises her voice, but seems to just gently bring people along with her. We've seen it in the Student Debates, she's brilliant. And, what's more...'

'You are absolutely right,' interrupted Sally. 'Have you ever watched Prime Ministers' Question Time on TV? It's like verbal gladiators in an arena, and this is supposed to be democracy. The MPs on both sides are appallingly, booing, hissing, shouting, and it's even worse now that it's being televised. It's just about point scoring. No one ever listens to the questions, let alone answers them. They need someone like Jo to make them see sense, show them how to discuss things calmly but openly until they reach a conclusion that's right for the whole country, not just their own parties. Honestly, they wonder why we all think so little of politicians! Half of their ideas are impractical, and that's with all their vastly overpaid advisors too. I know a lot of them do great work in their own communities, but don't get me started on their expenses fiasco, that was shameful.'

'Wow,' said Bill, 'that really struck a nerve. Where did that come from? You could almost be Jo. You're right, though, it desperately needs changing, but how do you change anything without joining in? Guess that's your lifetime challenge sorted,' he joked. 'You're right about the environment, though. We had that brief discussion last week about wind turbines and solar panels? Obviously, wind turbines are far better than oil and gas from a pollution perspective, but they do destroy the beauty of the countryside. It is far better to have them out at sea, out of view, though costly to maintain, of course. So often they're stationary whenever you see them. And on so many cold and foggy winter days there's no wind either, so they stand there idle, producing no electricity whatsoever, just when it's needed.'

Bill hardly paused before he was off again. 'I'm surprised we don't do far more with wave energy and tidal flows to effectively harness the wind and the moon's gravitational gift to us. I suppose it all needs significant investment and more experimentation to get the technology right. I think those photovoltaic solar panels have real potential, especially as prices are coming down all the time. But I do think it would be better to put them on rooftops than ruin swathes of open fields. Apparently, the next version will look just like regular roof tiles so they can cover entire roofs and will look far better and generate more too. Either way, electricity storage from renewables is still quite difficult to do at an acceptable cost, though battery technology is improving all the time. I think the Government's needs to do far more to demonstrate support for micro-generation. I wonder why Gramps' Gravity Power Station hasn't been taken up - surely it's just perfect. I bet he hasn't told anyone else about it.'

'Wow, listen to you, added Sally. 'I hate to say it, but we all seem to be getting a huge chunk of Jo's passion and enthusiasm suddenly. And we appear to be discussing things we've hardly spoken about before. Where did we suddenly get all the knowledge and understanding from? What's happening to us?'

Meanwhile, Fred was still going, apparently off in his own little world, almost oblivious to Bill and Sally's conversation. 'And Jo always encourages people, is always positive, rarely negative, and she's a superb team player, believes in collaboration and sharing. She's so sporty, loves cycling, swimming, tennis, netball and even distance running. Good job she's not a sprinter as she came last in the 100 metres recently. And she knows how to relax too. She always has her nose in a book and loves films. She always sees the best in people, never judges a book by its cover. Have you noticed what a lovely friendly face she has, and such a beautiful smile? She...'

'Ah, here she comes now, almost running,' interrupted Sally, grinning and raising her eyebrows at Bill. 'Don't worry Fred, your secret is safe with us. Quick, let's change the subject.'

Jo arrived, almost gasping for breath. 'So sorry I'm late, but Dad's in a state over mum so I couldn't get away. And then we went to visit Grandad in hospital. He now has cramp-like pains in his right leg which they're trying to sort out. They think it might be Deep Vein Thrombosis, but at least he's in the right place. Anyway, I haven't told Dad yet but I know where Mum is.'

Jo took a deep breath. 'They've got her on the Common, near Wellington Rocks, in that derelict house. Most people don't even know it's there, deep in the woods; been uninhabited for years.'

'Well let's go and get her,' rushed Bill.

'I wish, but it's not that easy,' explained Jo. 'I tried asking "togethering" questions and got more than I bargained for. She's locked in a basement room, behind bars. It's one of those jail-like places you see in old westerns. And there's only one way down. Three armed men are guarding her. They are all key players in Jake's gang, and their names are Zolt, Zonk, and Grilch. They're the ones we've been following. To make matters worse, she's been sedated. We can't call the police as we were warned against it in the letter. And if we did, they'd want to know how I found out. This "togethering" thing is fantastic but it does create its own problems.'

In a moment of chess-like logic, Sally had a strategy to impress even the CIA. 'We'll create a distraction to divert two guards then knock out the third one. Then we get a key to the prison door, and one for the bars, or break them down. We'll grab your mum, escape, then run like hell so they can't catch us. What do you think?'

'Well,' said Bill, 'that's it in a nutshell. But, I think we need just a tiny bit more detail, like how do we distract them, who's strong enough to knock the third one out, and how do we find the keys, or break down doors and bars? I know Jo has a lot of new talents, but I'm not sure super human strength is one of them.'

'Isn't that what I just said?' said Sally, bemused.

'Sort of, I guess,' replied Bill, with a cheeky grin. 'It's not the detailed logic you need to write a computer program, but it's a start.'

'Ha ha, who's a geeky face?' retorted Sally, while secretly agreeing with everything Bill had pointed out.

'How about this?' asked Jo, suggesting a much more detailed plan. Thirty minutes later, they all agreed. 'I'll sort everything out my end if you can do your bits. Let's leave it at that and we'll meet up on the west side of Wellington Rocks, 6am tomorrow morning?'

Sally, Bill and Fred nodded; keen to sort out their tasks and get them underway. Sally paused slightly not knowing whether to ask or not. 'It's the summer chess championships for all the schools in the Tunbridge Wells district this afternoon, and I'm wondering whether to enter or not. I'll probably go out in round one as usual, but if I could at least get through to the last sixteen, I might finally get into the school team with a bit of luck. What do you think?'

'Go for it,' said Fred. 'We know how much you love the game.'

'And we could come and watch if you like,' added Bill.

'Oh, no,' said Sally, 'I hate it when people watch my every move. I get so nervous and end up making really silly mistakes.'

'You should definitely enter and beat some of those boys,' said Jo, smiling, but trying hard to forget the challenges of tomorrow.

They could tell that Jo needed time to herself. As they got up and walked away, Jo closed her eyes, her brain working overtime. How was she going to pull this off without anyone getting hurt?

Gentle melodic words seemed to enter her mind, massaging her troubled thoughts and reassuring her. Calmness seemed to spread through her, releasing the tension she had been feeling. She could even hear the sound of the bees going about their business and the flap of wings as a butterfly drifted by. As something landed gently beside her on the seat, she opened her eyes. A squirrel was sitting, facing her, the same one she had enjoyed meeting during the boule competition. Then words started streaming into her mind.

'Hi Jo, it's me, Squidge. You do know we can help, don't you? I overheard your idea to rescue your mum, it's a brilliant plan, but I think we might be able to improve it. Would you like to hear it?'

'Of course I would,' said Jo. They chatted for another few minutes, until Squidge jumped back into the tree, climbing up to the lowest branch where a magpie was perched. A few moments later, after what looked like some kind of exchange, the bird flew off.

Jo stood up and headed home to meet her dad. Together they drove back to the hospital to visit Gramps.

Chapter 20

Prison

Later that evening, Zolt, an enormous bulk of a man and one of Jake's closest mates, trundled down the stairs of the old ruin on the Common. He unlocked the basement door and shone his rather feeble torch in to find Jo's mother awake but groggy, trying to hold on to one of the rusty steel bars in her crumbling prison.

She was dishevelled but relatively OK given the way she'd been grabbed from the cinema site and bundled into the back of a dirty old VW Camper Van. They'd thrown a towel over her head and injected her and she'd passed out. She could remember nothing.

As Zolt moved closer to the bars, Jo's mother recoiled at the stench of his breath. She tried to force out her question, desperate to know why she was being kept in this awful place.

Zolt said absolutely nothing – what was this mumbling woman trying to say? He pushed the tray towards her, littered with a few stale biscuits, a tiny bit of cheese which had seen better days, and a mucky glass of cloudy lemonade, though the fizz had long since departed. Jo's mother knew not to touch the food but was so thirsty she took a sip of the drink. Gulping the rest down she fell back onto the cold, damp mattress, feeling terribly woozy again all of a sudden.

'That'll teach you,' muttered Zolt. 'Keep your nose out of our business in future. That should knock you out for at least another 10 hours.' With that, he stomped out, slamming the door shut behind him before locking it with an enormous key, which seemed to have its own dedicated pocket in his oversized moth eaten leather jacket.

If he'd had an inkling of what was about to happen, he might not have been so quick to storm off. He joined his brother, Zonk, upstairs and their other gang member, Grilch, and threw himself back into his chair. Their guns were strewn on a makeshift table along with a dozen large beers and a small mountain of tortilla chips.

An old rusty barbeque was sitting in the fireplace, still dripping with the animal fats of several weeks' worth of dinners. They now sat there staring at their mobiles, playing games and swigging their beers, interrupted only by the odd indecipherable grunt or groan.

All three of them were dressed head to toe in black, broken only by their greasy dark hair and pock-marked faces. They were well over six feet tall and despite their terrible diet were built of solid muscle. It was now dark outside, and a solitary candle spluttered on the table. They were fed up with being stuck in this hole in the middle of nowhere. Their shift was ending in the morning when Jake was taking over, albeit only for an hour or two.

Outside, hundreds of animals were going about their business in the dark as they always did. The birds would usually be settling in their nests for a good night's sleep, but tonight there were many clusters of magpies and blackbirds stationing themselves along the branches of trees surrounding the derelict property. The animals seemed more focused than usual, moving with coordination and speed, especially an unusually large family of rats who'd had a long trek after receiving a request from a magpie visitor that morning.

Downstairs Jo's mum continued to sleep, giving her some relief from the oppression of her dungeon. Dark and damp, with holes dotted all over the walls, this wasn't a space you'd want to linger in.

A tiny amount of soil dropped through one of the holes about five feet above the floor. The same thing happened in several other places just a few feet away. Peeking through the first hole appeared an ant, who hesitated briefly to look around, apparently checking directions. As she scampered off, she seemed to be leading a whole line of her buddies, all pouring out through the holes. They proceeded to run down the wall and across the ground as fast as their legs could carry them, seven or eight streams heading straight towards Jo's mum.

As they reached the rusty old bars, they changed direction and ran up the bars, gathering around the lock area. They circled it for a while, before running off and going back out through other holes in the wall. It was an incredible sight as there must have been millions of them, a never-ending and growing army of ants.

Without a magnifying glass, it was almost impossible to understand what they were up to but these ingenious ants were on a mission of vital importance and were loving it. It was thousands of years since the last request, and now they were busy once more.

They'd waited several hours to build up their supplies, and now they could wait no longer. They were relieving themselves on the rusty old bars. Even though their urine smelt strong, their task could only be completed in the allotted time with lots of them working together. Collaboration and teamwork was the name of the game, as always, the only way to guarantee a successful outcome, whatever the task.

The door of the prison was another challenge. It was made of solid English oak. This was going to be a major problem, one that the ants could not possibly tackle in their lifetime, let alone a few hours.

By three o'clock in the morning, Zolt and Zonk were fast asleep, snoring in an alcohol-induced slumber. Grilch was only just about awake, vaguely keeping up his allocated guard slot. Just as he felt his eyelids closing, a tapping sound came from the door... tap, tap... then another... tap, tap. What was it? It couldn't have been tree branches, there was no wind to speak of that evening... tap... tap... tap.

Now wide awake, Grilch grabbed his gun, walked over to the door and wrenched it open. There was no one there. He looked around, stepped outside and looked again, shining his torch this way and that, still no one to be seen. He stepped back inside, closed the door, put his gun down and sat comfortably in his chair.

An hour later the same thing happened. The first time this had occurred, unbeknown to Grilch, two squirrels, Squidge and his sister Squeeel, had dashed inside, grabbing the opportunity while he was lumbering around outside. They'd spent the last hour casing the joint.

This time, while Grilch was outside, Squidge jumped up onto Zolt's seat and started to gently tease out a filthy handkerchief from his pocket, revealing what looked like a giant key. Suddenly, Zolt snorted at the critical moment, and with eyelids flickering he shifted his position. Luckily he didn't look down and soon nodded off again.

Squidge, who had kept perfectly still, turned his attention back to the handkerchief, gently tugging the corner until it slid right out, bringing the key with it, and falling noiselessly onto the old and grotty seat cushion. Grabbing the middle of the key in his mouth, Squidge jumped down to the floor where his sister was waiting. Between the two of them, they scampered down the stairs to the prison where Jo's mother was sleeping.

Using all their energy, they pulled themselves up the door. With a bit of a tussle, Squeeel managed to insert the key into the lock. They desperately tried to turn the key but nothing happened, it wouldn't budge. They simply couldn't get enough pressure.

The two squirrels looked at each other in dismay. *'This isn't going to do it,'* said Squidge, *'we need more leverage.'*

'You're right,' said Squeeel, *'but I know just the thing. Stay here.'*

Squeeel took a deep breath and dashed back upstairs. Checking all was quiet, she crept towards the rusty barbeque where she'd seen a long metal skewer earlier. She grabbed it in her mouth and was just about to take it downstairs when Grilch came back in through the door, closing it behind him. Squeeel stayed stock still then she seemed to screw up her eyes and nod. She waited.

A few seconds later, there was another tap, tap, tap at the door. The magpie immediately flew off. Grilch turned around and yanked the door open. In the time it took to peer outside again, Squeeel was off, skewer in her mouth, carefully avoiding anything that could get in her way or make a noise and disappeared down the stairs.

The two squirrels managed to manoeuvre the skewer into the hole at the end of the key, pushed it through as far as it would go and then leapt on the end of it. Their combined weight and the added leverage of the skewer turned the key, making a loud click. This thankfully seemed to coincide with Grilch returning and falling into his chair.

After a few moments of keeping perfectly still, just in case, Squeeel eased the skewer out. Squidge then pulled the key from the lock, and they headed back upstairs. They waited some time until Grilch's eyes had closed, his head lolling forward, and then, between the two of them, quietly lifted the key back onto Zolt's chair. This was as far as they dared go as getting it back into his jacket pocket was far too risky. Finally, Squeeel carefully carried the skewer over to the barbeque, gently placing it on the floor close by. For now, their work was done. All they could do was sit and wait patiently for the next stage of the plan to be put into operation.

'So far, so good,' said Squeeel. *'Well done brother.'*

'You too Sis. At least we can have a rest now. It was quite a walk here from the Pantiles, further than I'd remembered,' said Squidge.

Chapter 21

A Shock for the Jailers

It was 6am and Zolt and Zonk were just waking up. Grilch was exhausted but desperate for a pee. As he rushed out the door, he was followed by the two squirrels, also keen to leave but for quite a different reason. They knew the main event was about to begin.

Ignoring Grilch, Zolt stretched out, knocking the key onto the floor as he did so. Thinking nothing of it, he reached down, swept it up with the handkerchief and put both back in his pocket.

Meanwhile, Jo, Fred, Sally and Bill had met up on the other side of Wellington Rocks. 'I don't like this,' said Sally. 'This is the most frightening thing I've ever done. If we're seen by these ghastly monsters, they'll eat us for breakfast.'

'She's right,' added Bill, feeling extremely nervous, 'and they'd spit out our bones like pips from a grape. Surely we should have got the police to surround the place and charge in, all guns blazing.'

'No, Jo's right, this is the only safe way,' said Fred. 'If we did it your way, Bill, we'd have bodies everywhere, including Jo's mum.'

They had come fully prepared after Jo had advised them of the revised plan the previous evening. Sally had food and drink in her bag. Fred carried a small torch with a new battery, a catapult, and his pocket was full of tiny stones. Bill was holding a coil of rope that he thought might come in useful. Jo had nothing, just a strong desire to rescue her mother, desperately hoping she was fit and well.

'This is it, let's go,' said Jo. She had hardly slept a wink that night, hoping against hope that they were not making a terrible mistake.

Grilch had located their latrine area - a deep hole in the ground about twenty yards away. He unzipped his trousers and the relief swept over him, totally unaware of what was happening behind him.

The previous evening, Squidge, now standing a few feet behind Grilch, had bitten through a piece of rope from the covers of the nearby cricket pitch. Now, as Grilch zipped his trousers back up, a beautiful emerald green butterfly fluttered past his nose and landed on a branch above. As Grilch looked up, distracted, Squidge leapt at Grilch's legs and ran around them twice, tying them loosely together. The other end of the rope was wrapped around a tree further behind.

Squidge put his paw to his mouth and blew a high pitched whistle only squirrels can hear. Five more squirrel cousins appeared out of nowhere. They joined Squidge, grabbed hold of the loose end of the rope and leant back, just like a tug of war team. The fox was ready and he jumped at Grilch from behind, pushing him in the rear. At the same time, a very familiar rook flew into the back of his head and he lost his balance. Grilch tried to step forward, but his feet remained anchored to the ground.

As he was diving headfirst into the quagmire of filth, Squidge and his cousins released the rope from their grasp, after all, drowning Grilch had never been part of the plan. Spluttering and shocked, Grilch floundered around, trying desperately to find his feet. Finally, he succeeded but every time he attempted to haul himself to more pleasant smelling air, his hands were pecked by birds or nipped by rats. He did not dare to open his mouth to scream. It was bad enough diving head first into such a mess, let alone swallowing it.

Squidge sent a silent message to Jo who told the others, 'Our friends have done it, can you believe it? They're such fantastic creatures. So, one down, two to go. Let's move in.'

After ten minutes or so, Zonk shouted, 'Where on earth has Grilch gone? I'll go and find him.'

'Better take your gun just in case,' said Zolt.

Zonk rushed out of the door. He glanced over towards the latrine area but, seeing nothing, he searched around the derelict building. Hearing a slight rustling in the trees nearby, on the other side of some bushes, Zonk laughed, 'I knew you would not tolerate that latrine any longer. Hang on I'll join you, it's been a long night.'

As he stepped through the bushes he looked around, confused, no sign of Grilch anywhere. Beginning to think he'd made a mistake, he turned to go back. Suddenly, all around him, things were moving. It was like a horror movie. Scores of rats were leaping at his legs, nipping him, birds flapping their wings in his face, pecking every inch they could reach. He fell to the ground, passing out in shock.

'Come on Sally, quick, help me drag him over there.' They each grabbed an arm and hauled him over to a well hidden tree. Then they used the rope to tie his wrists together, around the tree trunk.

'Bill, give me your handkerchief, and I'll gag him while you tie his legs together,' said Sally. 'That should keep him quiet. And I'll throw his gun into the bushes.'

'Jo, it's done, two out of three, one to go,' communicated Sally without saying a word. *'We're good for the final stage. Ready?'*

It was time to get Zolt out of the derelict building. He was the only one keeping them from Jo's mum. They also knew that Zolt was the worst one, truly evil. He'd take them all down given half a chance. This was going to be difficult, but they couldn't stop now.

A greenfinch landed gently on the decaying window frame of the derelict building. Taking care to avoid all the jagged remnants of glass sticking out after years of neglect, it peered inside. The poor thing nearly fell off its perch when it smelt the greasy fat on the barbeque. Zolt was boiling a kettle on a gas Primus stove and had prepared three grimy coffee cups. He poured in the hot water then shovelled five spoonfuls of sugar into each one. The stench of curdled milk was too awful even for him.

'Where are those idiots?' he muttered, his temper rising. He wrenched the door open and yelled, 'Come and get your coffees before I spit in them!' Remembering where he was, he retreated quickly inside, not wanting to attract the attention of any early risers on their morning walk across the Common.

This was just the moment the greenfinch had been waiting for, and she sent an urgent message to the fox, *'Go for it Foxy, your second task, it's urgent. Hope you're ready.'*

Zolt looked puzzled. Something was wrong. He grabbed his rifle and opened the door again, scanning the surroundings. The birds were singing as usual, and he could hear the hum of the early morning commuters on the nearby roads. He stepped out of the doorway, and almost slipped over. He'd trodden in a huge pile of poo that was now encasing his shoe, emitting a pungent, acrid stink.

'Damn foxes, been saving yourself for me have you?' he grunted. He stood his rifle against the wall and walked over to the bushes, trying to remove the muck by rubbing his shoes over the grass.

He was so focused on his shoes that he completely failed to notice the events behind him. Squidge was in action once more, stuffing acorns down the gun barrel, which his magpie friend then pecked at like mad to make sure they were well and truly rammed in.

The many rats who'd abandoned their morning routine at the railway station (a guaranteed breakfast spot) had positioned themselves in the trees facing the front door. Seizing their opportunity, five of them scuttled quickly into the ruined house, fighting vomit as they too were hit by the stench of the fatty residues on the old barbeque. Keeping their cool, they each found a hiding nook and lay there, awaiting their next cue for action.

Bill and Sally had positioned themselves twenty yards away behind a tree, and Bill started groaning loudly, 'Hellpp,' trying to mimic the tones of Zonk and Grilch. He repeated it twice more. Zolt heard the cry then heard it again and again. He ran back, grabbed his rifle and headed to where the noise was coming from.

Unknown to Zolt, the spiders had also been busy that night, spinning the largest web they'd ever created. Zolt was a huge guy, with massive shoulders and tree trunk thighs, but he absolutely hated spiders, no matter how tiny. You can imagine his reaction when he ran head first into this enormous web. Floundering around, he frantically tried to pull the sticky bits of web from his mouth, nose and ears, inadvertently tossing and dropping his rifle as he did so.

As the gun flew towards the ground, it caught on a nearby branch, where a stubby twig got stuck in the trigger guard. There was a sound of a gunshot, and a split second later, Zolt felt a searing pain in his calf. A fragment of steel from the exploding gun barrel had shot straight through his trouser leg. Little blood was drawn, but he'd had a hefty clip to his calf and was more than a little shocked.

Unfortunately, another steel fragment had ricocheted off the side of the tree that Bill and Sally were standing by. A shower of tiny wood splinters had shot out, catching Bill in his left arm. Both Bill and Zolt yelled out at exactly the same time giving an unholy echo. Bill tried to pull the tiny splinters out but to no avail. Zolt looked at his leg, shocked that so little visible damage could cause such pain.

Then he heard a rustling in the bushes as Bill and Sally ran off, trying to lure him further away. Zolt looked down at the remains of the rifle, kicking it in frustration as he realized the barrel had somehow split into pieces. The rustling had unnerved him, but he knew instinctively that he should get back to his prisoner.

Meanwhile, Jo and Fred had dashed into the ruined house, avoided the fox poo, and hurried down the stairs. Jo eased open the prison door, nodding to Fred, 'Squidge and Squeeel have unlocked it, just like they promised.' She stepped inside. 'Quick, Fred, the torch.'

Only then could they see Jo's mum, lying on a mattress. Fred yanked at the bars. 'Harder,' said Jo, 'let me help.' They both heaved together. On the third pull, there was a grating sound as first one bar broke, then another. Finally, the lock broke, and the door opened.

'I can hardly believe it,' said Fred, 'the ants have succeeded too.'

They rushed in, 'She's out for the count,' said Jo, 'we'll have to carry her out, you take one arm, and I'll take the other.'

They grabbed her, as gently as they could. Although she was quite slim, she was a dead weight, and they were acutely aware that they were on borrowed time. It was hard to manoeuvre her out of the door, but they did their best, hurrying up the narrow staircase and out into the living area. They were halfway across the room when a warning arrived from Sally, *'Hurry, he's coming! Get out, quick!'*

At that moment, Zolt jumped through the front door. Jo and Fred stopped dead in their tracks. Zolt took a step forward, 'I know you, seen you before, down in the Pantiles. Ghastly red hair. You ain't going nowhere; pesky little busy bodies. Three for the price of one. Boy, am I gonna have fun with you lot.'

He took another step forward. Jo and Fred inched back, keeping a tight grip on Jo's mum. Zolt took another pace, cornering them back to the staircase. He was about to shove them down the stairs when two rats ran to his trousers and vanished, one up each trouser leg. The other rats, the backup squad, were ready, just in case.

Now, Zolt hated spiders, but positively detested rats. As he felt movement inside his trousers, he knew what was coming. He could imagine their teeny sharp teeth gnawing their way up and he couldn't bear it. He plunged both his hands down, desperate to protect his groin area. One rat was a fraction slow and failed to reach its target.

Sadly for Zolt the other one was fast, like lightning, and knew exactly where it was heading. Not a pleasant task for the best of rats but it was a dirty job and he had to do it. Zolt yelled out in agony, frantically trying to undo his trouser belt. Pulling his trousers down, he wrestled with the beast before wrenching it away, bending over and clutching his groin area in agony. Thankfully the rat escaped unharmed after directing a few more nips at Zolt's clenched fist.

Jo and Fred tightened their hold on Jo's mum and marched as quickly as they possibly could, stepping carefully out through the door, back the way they'd come. Approaching the edge of Wellington Rocks, Bill and Sally joined them and they rushed onwards. A rapid "togethering" conversation brought them all up to date with the escape and the magnificent part played by all their animal friends. This was stopped short by the sound of lumbering footsteps from behind. Zolt, red-faced, was hot on their heels.

'We can't carry on over the Common, we're too slow. We'll be out in the open, he'll see us, and he's still faster than we are,' said a petrified Sally. 'Bill's hurt, his arm got punctured by splinters when Zolt's gun exploded and metal bits hit the tree we were hiding by.'

'We need to hide,' said Fred, 'quickly, over this way.'

They scrambled behind the nearest rock, still struggling with Jo's unconscious mum. 'He'll know where we've gone when he can't see us,' pointed out Bill. 'He'll come straight back here.'

They watched as Zolt lurched past, partly doubled up in pain and swearing under his breath. He stopped and looked all around, before retracing his steps. He knew that Jake was due in half an hour, and he was not going to be happy at this turn of affairs, not happy at all.

'Mmmmmmmm, ohhhhhhh, where am I?' slurred Jo's mum.

'Oh, no,' said Jo, 'that's all we need, she's coming round, she'll give us away.' And she shoved her hand over her mother's mouth.

(O) Relax Jo, no need to panic. Try and get your mum up to the very top. More help is on its way.

'Right, we need to get Mum up to the topmost rock, don't ask me why but the Ancients have just told me to go there, they say help is on its way. Come on guys, give me a hand.'

They started to cajole Jo's semi-conscious mother up the rocks, Jo lifting and pulling and Sally and Fred pushing from behind. All the children make it look so easy when they are playing on the rocks, but when someone is after you, it suddenly seems so difficult.

Bill was hurting too, though he tried not to show it. Seeing his pained expression, Jo reached down to help tug him up too but inadvertently grabbed his wounded arm. Bill's face creased up and he was about to yell when a strange tingling sensation enveloped his injury, and all the pain seemed to fade away. Their combined strength yanked Bill up beside her, and with renewed effort, they started making real progress with Jo's mum. But as they got closer to the highest rock, Zolt started to climb too. Jo looked around, desperately searching for the help the Ancients had promised.

Then a rush of wind threatened to throw them all off balance. Nearly a dozen magpies and blackbirds swooped upon Zolt, trying to dislodge him. But Zolt was determined. Despite the nagging pain in his groin, he knew that things would get infinitely worse if Jo's mum was not safely back behind bars when Jake arrived. Batting the birds away, he continued to climb, drawing ever closer to the top. Fred took out his catapult and fired down a volley of stones, but it made little difference. Zolt was closing in, more focussed than ever before.

Jo, Fred, Sally and Bill could go no further. They stood, shaking, at the top, clinging on to Jo's mum. They had nowhere to go. As they sat Jo's mum gently down, Jo put her hands on the rock to steady herself. Zolt was one rock away. They could almost smell his sweat.

As Zolt's hands and head appeared over the rock edge, he leered at them, triumphantly. Five horrified faces looked on. They glanced at each other, desperately searching for the Ancients.

Fred was about to stamp on Zolt's hands and kick him in the face to push him off the rocks altogether. Somehow he seemed incapable of taking such drastic action, as if some force was holding him back.

They watched, terrified, as Zolt's face grew larger, his shoulders heaving his body up towards them. Suddenly, the leer gave way to a look of absolute disbelief. The centre of the rock right in front of him momentarily dissolved and with it the five people on it. He blinked. The rock was solid once more, but his targets had completely vanished. Zolt could not believe his eyes.

He scrambled up and bent down to examine the surface. It was normal, heavily weathered, but with millions of little lines, dots and squiggles, a bit of graffiti. He stamped on it but nothing shifted. It was solid rock. He could not remotely fathom what had happened.

Dejected, he slid down off the rocks and headed back to the ruined house. Jake would not believe a word of it.

Chapter 22

Bemused, Bothered and Bewildered

Zolt was totally mystified. How was he going to explain it? Those four pesky kids had apparently rescued this dreadful woman from right under their noses. He had to think of an entirely plausible cast iron excuse. He still had no idea where Zonk and Grilch were. Still in shock, Zolt lumbered back to the derelict building.

Meanwhile, Sally, Fred, Bill and Jo were equally bemused. Jo's mum was still only functioning at about thirteen percent brain capacity and had no idea whether she was coming or going.

'What the hell happened?' gasped Fred. 'One moment we were practically done for and the next we're here.'

Part of the rock they'd been standing on seemed to have floated away beneath their feet so quickly that, for a brief moment, they were in freefall, completely weightless. The rock appeared to lose its structure and solidity, and they sank through it as if it were made of custard. As they fell, they seemed to push the atoms of the rock to one side which squelched back together above them as they passed by. After a second or two they found themselves on solid ground once more. Zolt might have been in a state of shock, but that was nothing compared to what they were feeling.

Bill looked around him, marvelling at the engineering, deep in thought. *'This is incredible, vastly superior to anything known today. Everything seems to be a perfect fit, allowing for all possible temperature changes, all coefficients of expansion and any surface deterioration even over thousands of years. And yet it looks entirely natural, just like rock, but then how did we pass through it like that?'*

Sally smiled, *'You're the techy guy, so what's the answer?'*

Now standing, they gently eased Jo's mum up. Looking around, it began to dawn on them where they were, standing at the very top of the spiral stalagmite-stalactite staircase, back in the cavern of the Ancients. The view over the cavern was incredible, but the most impressive feature was the bannister. It was nearly three feet wide, perfectly smooth and slightly concave in shape.

Sally looked down at it, another grin appearing. 'Those Ancients really knew how to enjoy themselves. Come on,' she said, and with that she jumped on the bannister and was off, gathering speed as she continued down the spiral, much like a helter-skelter. At some point, she hit a constant speed, not too fast, not too slow. Surprisingly neither her clothes nor her legs suffered from the friction of the descent. As she approached the end, she slowed and jumped off. Seeing her success, the others followed, first Bill, then Jo. Fred waited, carefully lifting Jo's mum up onto the bannister, making sure she was properly aligned before giving her a gentle nudge. Once he was sure she was moving smoothly, he jumped on.

Jo's mum was almost singing, 'Wooondeeeerful, again, again, another ride.' Laughing, Jo and Bill helped her off the slide, resting her into Jo's arms, with Fred arriving to lend a hand too.

As they made their way towards the exit from the cavern, Jo sensed a message from the Ancients.

(O) Congratulations team, that was brilliant. Now make sure you send a text to the police to pick up those gangsters. Boy did we enjoy that, didn't realize that modern life could be so much fun. Those guys really got what they deserved. You'd better get your mum out of here quickly, Jo, before she realizes what's going on. Take her up out of the bookshop entryway. The bookshop doesn't open until later but hopefully, Bill knows how to disable the alarm and open the front door. You can then get into a café and pretend you found your mum wandering aimlessly in the Pantiles.

While you are on the way, Jo, we need to tell you about another important dimension of "togethering", one that can be used to influence people and even cause them to completely change their attitudes and opinions. To be able to do this, you must have an incredibly high trust quotient and an extraordinary purposefulness status. You can then ask what might be called a leading question, one that suggests a particular point of view.

While such a question will not automatically change views and perceptions, it will always make people stop, think and closely examine their arguments in a more open minded and carefully considered way. Only their subconscious minds will know that their views and perceptions are being queried and challenged in this way. You must be aware, though, Jo, that if your question is not based on the highest principles, then your trust status can be drastically reduced, potentially even permanently undermined.

Anyway, enough of that, time for you to get your mother to the Pantiles. She'll soon be fully conscious of what is going on.

Taking the advice of the Ancients, they made their way up the long narrow spiral staircase to the opening wall in the bookshop. They'd expected it to be a real struggle climbing all that way, while supporting Jo's mum, but it was rapid and seemed almost effortless. Maybe they were getting fitter somehow.

Bill did indeed know how to work the bookshop's alarm system and took care not to set it off as they emerged. Making their way to the Choco Shop, they sat down, relieved that it opened early enough to satisfy those too lazy to organize their own breakfasts at home. They ordered tea, coffee and toast, and Jo called her dad to tell him they'd found her mum after coming to the Pantiles early to help the bookshop owner. With enormous relief, he set out to join them, while Bill sent an anonymous email to the police about the vagrants on the Common and where to find them.

'Sorry I grabbed your injured arm just now, Bill, back up on the rocks,' said Jo. 'Let me see how bad it is.'

Bill pulled up his sleeve but was astonished to find no splinters, or cuts anywhere. 'Eh? It was there, honestly. It was really painful, and I could hardly lift my arm at all until you yanked it. It gave me quite a shock I can tell you but then oddly painless,' he said, looking quite shamefaced. 'It certainly feels fine now.'

'He was telling the truth,' added Sally, attempting to come to Bill's rescue. 'I saw the splinters with my own eyes. Look there's still several stuck in his shirt material.'

'Well,' said Fred, 'maybe the splinters were dragged out through friction with the banister as you came down the slide.'

Jo's mum was starting to come round, and a torrent of questions soon began. 'What's happened? Where am I? Where have I been? I remember a jail and bars and some really horrible men. Then I had a silly dream of being on a very long slide. What's going on?'

'Slow down, Mum, one question at a time. You were kidnapped, but somehow you escaped, and we found you wandering aimlessly down here. You've obviously been drugged and had terrible nightmares,' said Jo, her fingers tightly crossed behind her back.

At that moment Jo's dad ran over, completely out of breath. There were hugs and kisses, and his relief was obvious. 'I'll never let you out on your own ever again. I'll always look after you, I'll, I'll, I'll...'

'Don't be daft,' said Jo's mum, starting to feel more like herself again. 'Things are starting to come back to me. I was taking photos of the cinema site, and suddenly it all went black. I must have dropped my camera, oh no, the evidence! It's all gone. I've lost it.'

'No you haven't, your earlier photos are all backed up on the laptop at home. We only lost the ones you took on the day,' replied Jo's dad. 'Jo found the camera next to the cinema site, sadly minus its memory card. We can only think that guy Jake grabbed you, and took it. So, where were they keeping you? How did you get away?'

'Well, I don't really know, it's all a bit of a blur... hopefully I'll remember once the shock eases off.'

Bill, Jo, Sally and Fred kept silent through this, although more than glances were flying back and forth between them.

'Look,' said Jo's dad, putting a supporting arm around his wife, 'I need to tell you about your father, Gramps, he's in hospital. He got knocked over by some cyclists, and he's not well. Let's get you home and cleaned up and then we'll go and visit him together.'

***

In the meantime, Jake had arrived early for his handover meeting with Zolt and was furious, having a heated argument. Jake had re-examined the bars of the jail. He knew they were slightly rusty, but he could not understand how they had deteriorated so rapidly. '... and you failed to lock the prison door too. You are utterly useless.'

Zolt had prepared his defence. He took a deep breath, 'We did lock it, and I had the key in my pocket the whole time. How they opened the door, I don't know. Breaking the steel bars like that is another mystery. We couldn't do anything. There were six guys with Kalashnikovs. We were outnumbered, outgunned, and they moved like lightning, real pros. I've never seen anything like it. They lured Zonk and Grilch outside and incapacitated them, then threw some sort of stun grenade in here. I still haven't found the other two.'

Jake was mad, his plans unravelling before his eyes. He desperately tried to make sense of things. 'Who could these guys be? That woman's partner must have access to more resources than I gave him credit for. Could there be some other group trying to muscle in on my patch? We know there's competition for the solar farm and that idiot vineyard farmer might have called in some heavies. Or could it be one of our competitors in the mini drone project? But how would they know about this little exercise? Is someone's double-crossing me...'

Jake got out his gun, his finger tightening on the trigger as he moved purposefully towards Zolt, who was now sweating and shaking uncontrollably. There was only one way out of this...

'Stop, wait! I'm lying. I didn't think you'd believe what actually happened. The truth is, it was those damn kids, from the Pantiles, the girl with the violent red hair and nasty, threatening green eyes. I don't know how they did it, but I nearly had 'em. Then these rats ran up my trouser, and, well, they got away, but I chased them up to the rocks and, somehow, they just vanished into thin air, in front of me.'

Jake kept his finger firmly on the trigger, squeezing it more tightly. 'That's the biggest load of rubbish I've ever heard.'

He could so easily end things for Zolt, right then and there, in a split second. How could four pathetic little kids get past his three best men and vanish? No, this was nonsensical. Zolt was lying through his teeth. He squeezed the trigger harder. Then he heard the police sirens, growing louder, seemingly closing in on all sides.

Jake looked around, stuffed his gun into his pocket and shouted to Zolt. 'Last chance you useless piece of filth, you're going to help me deal with the vineyard farmer, but I'm warning you, fail me again, and you'll be kicking up daisies with your brother and his mate.'

Luckily they knew the Common like the back of their hands and escaped through the trees with no difficulty. Zonk and Grilch were not so lucky. The police found them exactly where they'd been told and took them in for questioning. Once they'd been cleaned up and checked by the police doctor, the interrogation started, but the police could not take a word they were saying seriously. Two big thugs brought down by a bunch of birds and animals, what a load of nonsense. Apparently, some inter-gang warfare was involved, but they did not have enough to charge them and reluctantly let them go..

Back in the Pantiles, Jo and her parents started to head for home. They waited briefly as a family of squirrels ran past with Squidge and Squeeel leading the way, Squeeel winking at Jo and Squidge giving her the thumbs up. Jo gave them the biggest smile she could muster, her eyes full of gratitude for these loyal furry friends.

Fred, Sally and Bill were left behind, excited but relieved about the success of their operation. 'I was sure it was going to be a disaster,' said Sally. 'It was frightening but I really enjoyed it, once we got going. It was a brilliant plan. So, what's next?'

'Well,' said Fred, 'I've got a shed to put together, fancy helping?'

'I'd almost forgotten about that with everything else going on,' muttered Bill. 'We were half expecting you to suggest cycling over to Mark Cross to see what's happening with the vineyard farmer. But it's a long way, so many hills to go up. It would be exhausting, and we've already had quite a lot of excitement for one day.'

'Well, we could, it's a lovely day after all,' said Fred. 'On the other hand, if you were to help me out with the shed, we could think through our plans at the same time. Then perhaps we could all go to the vineyard tomorrow or the day after? Perhaps some challenging DIY would be good for us?'

'Perfect,' sighed Bill, not happy about a long tiring bike ride, 'and Jo could come too, might take her mind off the worries at home.'

'You boys have completely forgotten, haven't you?' asked Sally.

'Er, what, it's not your birthday is it, surely?' muttered Fred.

'No, you really are useless sometimes,' said Sally.

'Oh, it completely slipped my mind,' said Bill. 'It was the chess championships yesterday. Did you get through the first round?'

'Yes,' said Sally, 'and the second and third. You won't believe it, but I'm the new Tunbridge Wells Schools Chess champion. It was one of those timed events where you hit the clock once you've made your move. The boys were not happy bunnies I can tell you. I just seemed to see all the moves in my mind's eye, clear as day. And I wasn't nervous even when everyone was watching in the final.'

'Well, that's brilliant! Well done,' said Fred.

'I knew you'd do it one of these days. Must have been all the advice we gave you,' said Bill with a huge grin.

'Ha ha, if only,' said Sally. 'Now, let's go build that shed.'

Chapter 23

Hiding a Secret

The three friends were standing in Fred's garden looking at the site for the shed. Only Jo was missing, though they hoped she'd be along later when her mother had fully recovered from her ordeal.

'So,' explained Fred, 'I've levelled the area, built a brick surround and checked all the measurements against the summerhouse. We are now ready to prepare the base by pouring in the sand/cement mix and laying the concrete slabs.'

Bill was worried. 'It's not a tiny shed. It's much larger; a lot of work. Perhaps the cycle ride was a better option after all.'

'Sorry, but Mum convinced Dad that a summerhouse would be much more useful. It has a wooden terrace, so my parents will be able to enjoy the early morning sun, and even have breakfast outside, as if they're in Greece or the South of France. The advantage is that we can cut a hole in the terrace and fit it flush around the entryway. Then the Water Company can get into the drain if it needs to.'

'Ha ha, that's a good one,' laughed Bill. 'I forgot, your dad still doesn't know that it has nothing to do with water, does he?'

'Er, no,' said Fred. 'Shall we make a start, see how we get on?'

The work was exhausting on such a warm day. Bill and Sally prepared the sand/cement base, and Fred checked it was all level then he carried the concrete slabs over and laid them carefully in place.

Sally was impressed. 'How do you have the strength to lift those slabs, Fred. It's tiring watching you. Must be your sports training.'

'Yes, you should join me. You and Bill would be very welcome.'

Four hours later the whole base area was finished and they sat in the sun enjoying a break while the cement solidified properly. Then Jo turned up. 'I've come to help. Mum's had a shower, a short nap and managed to eat a good lunch. She is much brighter. My parents have now gone to visit Gramps. So, what's next, what can I do?'

'We're done for the day,' said Bill. 'I'm totally exhausted, it's been incredibly hard work. The cycle ride would have been easier.'

'You could come back tomorrow and help me finish this off,' said Fred. 'Then we can start ending Jake's activities once and for all.'

***

The following morning they were ready to go, although Jo was late having visited her grandad in hospital.

'How are you feeling today, any aches and pains?' asked Fred knowing what a punishing time they'd had the previous day.

'No, surprisingly we're both fit and well,' said Sally stretching her arms in anticipation. 'Ready Bill?'

Under Fred's direction, they began bolting together the components of the summerhouse. It was well into the afternoon before they were ready to lay the decking which Fred cut neatly around the entryway, giving a lovely curved finish.

There was one last test. They first made sure no-one was looking, then Jo put her hand on the entryway, opening it as before. Fred climbed down, closed the entryway, then immediately reopened it and climbed out, waiting briefly for it to close of its own accord.

'Well guys, I could see the whole garden from down there, it works a treat. That's a job well done. I can't thank you enough,' said Fred. 'I'll print your DIY certificates when I get a moment.'

'No probs,' said Jo, 'but before we break, we need to decide what to do about Jake and his fight with the vineyard farmer.'

'Can't you use "togethering" to check it out?' suggested Bill.

'Yes, but all I know is that Jake is trying to force the farmer to sell his vineyard and has threatened him if he doesn't. The farmer is nervous. His wine recently won a major award, and he's now making a small profit. He thinks Jake is going to bulldoze the vines, but he can hardly stand guard with a shotgun all night, can he?'

'Let's cycle out there tomorrow,' suggested Jo. 'We have an excuse as my parents are organizing a wedding anniversary party and we need to check out his vines. They need to be organic because insecticides kill all sorts of insect life, while the right mix of microscopic beasts will look after the vines on their own.'

Sally chuckled, seeing Jo's concerns about the environment shining through once more. 'So, let's meet up here tomorrow at, say, 10am with our bikes. Come on Bill, let's go.'

Fred and Jo waved them off, before having a quick chat

themselves. 'Fred, after leaving you yesterday I've asked hundreds of "togethering" questions, trying to get to the bottom of everything that's been going on. It could be really dangerous if we carry on. Just look at what happened to my mum. Incidentally, had you noticed the similarity between the descriptions of the cyclists who knocked Gramps over, and those young guys on motorbikes who stole the components from Bill's planes from under the tree on the Common?'

'Yes, I had. And it is dangerous, but we can't stop now, can we?'

'No, but we need to expose what Jake's up to while protecting everyone at the same time. The trouble is, it's all very much more involved than we'd realized. Let me explain…'

'Hang on Jo, shouldn't we involve the others in this conversation as they need to be aware of all this too.

'You're right, let's use "togethering". You try it, call them up.'

'I'll give it a go,' smiled Fred. *'Hi Bill, Sally, can you hear us?'*

'Course we can,' indicated Bill.

'Me too,' chipped in Sally. *'Carry on, we're all ears.'*

Jo continued. *'So we now know some of what Jake is involved in; the cinema site, the bank robberies, the mini-drones, solar energy, the vineyard, people trafficking, drug smuggling, stealing from Scotney Castle, and the modelling agency business. The people trafficking is more than just a modern slave trade as many of them end up working in Jake's commercial cleaning operation, which already has contracts with several of the UK's largest business companies. The drug smuggling and dealing is a sophisticated operation ruining many lives and he's also selling the stuff locally. The modelling agency business is decidedly dodgy too. Blackmail is rife as a result of many of his activities.'*

'So, Jake, it turns out, is a much cleverer guy than we give him credit for,' said Fred.

Jo went on. *'Now, the fire at the cinema should have been put out faster than it was and that was a diversion for the bank robbery, so, there could be a connection between Jake and either the fire or the police departments. Jake can't be funding all these activities from his own filthy pockets. I reckon he must have a wealthy crime lord supporting him, pulling his strings. We've got to find who is involved and put them permanently out of business too. Sadly not all my "togethering" questions are being answered. Jake is blocking them.'*

'How have you managed to get all this info then?' asked Fred.

'Well, Jake can block my questions at the moment because my "trust" status is not yet high enough to infiltrate the "need to know" barriers he's created in his evil mind. I have to ask many more purposeful questions to raise my status, and this I have been working on. Luckily, Jake has had to involve many people in his operations, so there are others who know important details. They might be corrupted by Jake's money but they're not as strong minded as Jake, and so they're not blocking me in the same way.'

'I think I understand,' replied Fred, *'How long will it be before your trust levels are robust enough to break Jake's barriers?'*

'I don't know,' answered Jo, *'but I sense that I'm getting close. I'm feeling more confident, stronger, getting more effective in asking the questions. And I'm constantly receiving some kind of positive feedback or encouragement, though I know that sounds ridiculous.'*

The familiar voice of Fred's dad broke into their world, dragging them back into reality, their "togethering" conversation vanishing in a puff of sound. 'Hi guys, how's it going?'

Fred replied, 'Check out the summerhouse! We had lots of help from Bill and Sally too, they did a huge amount of the donkey work.'

'Wow, you've done amazingly well. Jo, I hear that you found your mum yesterday morning, just wandering around the Pantiles? Good job you all happened to be down there so early. How is she?'

'She's very confused, but then she was drugged, so I guess that's not surprising. I'm sure she'll be OK soon. We were just helping Bill down in the bookshop, tidying up the place before the owner arrived to open up. Then we saw her outside.' Jo kept her fingers tightly crossed behind her back as yet another white lie slipped out.

'Gosh, that was lucky. Anyway, here's a little thank you for your hard work with the summerhouse,' said Fred's dad, handing them a big bunch of film vouchers for showings at the Trinity Theatre over the next few months. 'I can't wait to start filling the shed up with all that stuff I've been hoarding in the garage.'

'No, don't worry Dad. Jo and I can do that,' said Fred. 'You're far too busy, and we're just on holiday with nothing better to do.'

Chapter 24

Frazzled Vines

Next morning there was a clattering of bikes outside Fred's house as Bill and Sally rushed to get there first. Then Jo turned up ready to go. Adjusting her helmet, Sally asked, 'Who knows the route?'

'It's all good,' replied Bill. 'I've looked up Mark Cross on Google Maps and printed it out and it's relatively straight forward.'

'Something tells me we won't need the map,' laughed Jo, looking up to the sky. 'We seem to have our own SatNav, operating a bit closer to earth.' There, circling above, was a large bird, apparently waiting for them to set off.

'Do we all have water and snacks 'cos it's looking like a warm day? I've packed several chocolate and granola bars,' said Fred.

'And I've a couple of bananas and some apples,' joined in Jo. 'It's the slightly healthier option.'

'Surprise, surprise, we've brought fruit and chocolate bars and orange juice too,' added Bill. 'Come on, let's go. It's only six miles and beautiful countryside with some brilliant hills to climb. We've been up since 7am and we've already done a forty-five minute run through the town, including three laps of Dunorlan Park. Good eh?'

Jo and Fred gawped in amazement at Bill and Sally's transformation into fitness fanatics and had to quickly jump on their bikes and chase after their friends, who'd set off at top speed.

The cycle ride was indeed just over six miles, and they reached the turning to their destination in little over half an hour, despite both Bill and Sally complaining that they weren't peddling fast enough. They had not needed to check the map as their friendly guide above didn't let them down once. Finally, they turned right and followed the track to the vineyard, half a mile further on, where they met their guide chirping over the sign, "Mayden Vineyard".

They cycled in and parked their bikes down the side of a large barn. They shoved the huge door and it groaned its way open. Inside it was clad with rack upon rack of wine bottles. Then another door creaked open and the farmer walked in.

Seeing four eager young faces, he said, 'Hi kids, sorry but I've had to cancel the holiday jobs while I sort out a few problems.'

'No, it's not that,' said Jo. 'We're doing some research for my parents. They're planning a small party. They saw you at the Farmers Market and read about your success in that competition recently.'

'That's kind, but I'm afraid I can't possibly let you taste the wine. I don't think you're old enough and I can't risk losing my licence.'

'No, no,' laughed Jo, 'we just wanted to check that your organic statement means organic, you know, really organic.'

The farmer was a little put out until he realized they were genuinely interested. He spent an hour showing them around and explaining everything from planting and tending the vines right up to the bottling process. Finally, he said, 'You sure you're not interested in jobs, you know, once I get the business problem sorted?'

'We might be,' said Fred, 'but what's the problem, can we help?'

'I wish, but it's too complicated. I don't mean to be rude, but I've got to sort it myself. However, I can tell you more about this place, how we chose the grapes we use, how it became a vineyard, and ...'

The farmer carried on and the kids kept interrupting with practical questions despite being deep in their own parallel conversation.

'Guys,' said Jo, *'I've just asked some very specific "togethering" questions, ones that only he could answer even though he doesn't realize it. He's had the vineyard for five years but has only just made a small profit. He's invested everything, but his bank has refused to lend him more and yesterday they cancelled his overdraft. Others are apparently interested in buying the site, supported by the bank, even though they'll rip up the vines for a new business. He doesn't know what, but I now do. It's all linked to a lucrative solar farm project.'*

'But that's not fair,' said Sally, 'how can a bank do that?'

'I asked him the same thing. He says that's just what the banks have lowered themselves to, anything for a quick profit. They lost any desire to help the little people long ago. Now it's all about big business, big profit, big bonuses and wealthy shareholders.'

'Look,' said the farmer, 'take these three bottles home and if your parents like it, come back, and I'll give them a good discount.'

They were about to go when several squawking blackbirds landed on the roof above. 'Oh, it's the birds, they're unhappy because we're netting the vines to keep them out, otherwise they'd eat everything.'

At that moment, they heard a vehicle draw up outside and two doors slamming shut. The farmer peered out then turned back. 'Quick kids, go into the back office, keep quiet and stay out of sight.'

Who should walk into the barn but Jake and Zolt. With the office door slightly ajar, the kids could hear the angry conversation. 'I told you I am not selling. I've invested too much to pull out now.'

'I'm warning you, this is your last chance to sell. It's a rock bottom price, but it's better than nothing,' sneered Jake.

'I'm not selling. Even if I did decide to, I know I'd get a much better price than you're offering,' said the farmer, raising his voice.

'Zolt, do it!' ordered Jake.

'Brilliant,' said Zolt, an evil grin spreading across his ugly face.

As Zolt walked out door, Jake grabbed the farmer, 'You will sell, and at my price or I'll burn your vines down, and your barn. This land is perfect with its vast south facing acreage. I can install a thousand solar panels and make a fortune. It'll still be a farm but a solar farm, quite ironic eh? You sell, or it burns, your decision.'

With that, he dragged the farmer outside. Zolt was walking along the first row of vines, pouring something from a container.

'Come on guys, quietly, back into the shop,' whispered Jo. 'Jake and Zolt are at it again, and we need to see what's happening.'

As they peered cautiously out through the shop window, they saw Zolt pull out his cigarette lighter, and a row of vines turned to ash.

'Jake can't bully him like that,' whispered Jo. 'We must help.'

'What can we do?' replied Fred. 'If Jake and Zolt see us, we'll be dead meat. After we rescued your mum we must be top of their hit list. It's not as if we have anything to frighten them off with. We can't exactly throw stones at them or call in the cavalry, can we?'

'This is awful,' squeaked Jo, 'I can't bear to do nothing. Surely we could *help*, attack them with wine bottles or something?'

Jake hurled the farmer to the ground. The frightened birds flew off into the nearby woodland, now screeching like mad. 'If you haven't signed this property over to me in three days time, I'll burn it down, whether you're here or not. These papers had better be signed when we come back.' Jake threw an envelope at the farmer's face.

Piercing the air at that very moment came the sound of tearing bracken as two angry wild boars broke through the trees, charging wildly towards them. Jake and Zolt could hardly believe their eyes. They turned and ran for their car, making it in the nick of time.

Jake started the engine, confident his new Porsche would pull away, forgetting about the gravel. The boars rammed the rear of the Porsche, smashing the lights and denting the bodywork. The tyres finally gripped and the car disappeared in a cloud of stones and dust.

Jo dashed out to help the farmer to his feet as the boars trotted calmly away and melted into the woods from whence they came.

'My goodness. Where did those wild beasts come from? I've never seen them here before,' exclaimed the farmer, brushing himself off. 'Well, that's it. I guess I'll have to sell now.'

Jo was exasperated, 'You can't let them get away with it. We have to stand up to people like that, and, and we'll help you.'

'Ha ha,' laughed the farmer. 'I don't mean to be disrespectful but what can four young kids do? When they come back, there'll be more of them, and they'll be armed. Sadly, it's game over.'

Jo thought for a minute, the others listening in. 'I've an idea. It may not work, but it will give Jake a real slap in the face. If he can feel a fraction of the pain that he inflicts on others, it'll be worth it.'

With that, Jo proceeded to explain her plan. The farmer listened in, somewhat amazed, 'How did you come up with that? I mean, I didn't even know you an hour or so ago. You had no idea about vineyards, had no inkling of the problems here, had no idea who these terrible people are or what they are up to. Yet in a split second you come up with an extraordinary plan that might, and I mean might, just work. For some reason I trust you too. If by some miracle it succeeds then your parents can have as much of my wine as they like. There's a lot to do in three days though. Where do we start?'

Fred smiled, 'Well, I think we could all do with a cup of tea, you more than the rest of us I'm sure.'

They sat down in the small farmhouse, drinking tea and sharing their fruit and granola bars with cheese and biscuits the farmer had thrown in. The farmer passed Jake's papers over to Sally. With the plan decided, the four friends got up to leave. They wheeled their bikes over the gravel and waved back at the smiling farmer; no flying gravel chips, no foul language, just a shared sense of determination.

Chapter 25

Gramps

The following morning, Jo helped Fred move his dad's stuff from the garage into the new summerhouse. Other than some light lifting and simple shelf construction, there was nothing too taxing for the brain.

This was just what Jo needed, time to ask the many hundreds of purposeful "togethering" questions taking shape in her mind. Some were linked to the showdown at the vineyard, others directed at every aspect of Jake's criminal life. These were interspersed with questions to the doctors and nurses concerning her grandfather's progress.

Jo and her parents had spent the previous evening in hospital with her grandfather. His condition was getting worse. While the Heparin injection had eased the Deep Vein Thrombosis, the improvement had not lasted. They'd sat with him until midnight exchanging a few words now and again. When he finally dozed off, Jo was sent home to get some sleep. The doctors continued to check him periodically and nurses took his vital signs every hour. However, at 6am, they realized he was slipping into a coma. By 8am, he was on life support.

Jo loved her grandfather dearly. He had always been wonderful to her. He and her grandmother lived close by. They'd read books to her throughout her early childhood and enjoyed walks together, always asking her questions like, 'What do you think of this? Is that the right thing to do? Why/why not? What would you do if…?' There was always something challenging to think about. Her parents were fantastic too. She'd always been encouraged to ask questions, about everything and by listening to her parents' carefully considered answers she'd learnt how to construct well-reasoned arguments too.

Yet, here she was now, feeling she had taken all of this for granted. She knew a lot about her granddad but there was so much more she had little idea about. Jo was is no doubt that everyone has to do their bit to leave the world a better place than when they arrived, and to strive to help others, especially those less fortunate.

There was so much pain in the world, pointless wars, and needless cruelty to other humans, animals and the wider environment. There was so much greed and corruption, so much unfairness, intolerance and inequality. What did her grandad think of all this? She made a promise that as soon as he was out of hospital, she'd start asking him the big questions, and the little ones too, and write everything down.

They were about to break for lunch when Jo started feeling dizzy. 'I feel a bit weak and wobbly, I'll just grab a banana if that's OK?'

'Of course, I'll get it. Relax, have a rest,' said Fred, anxiously.

Jo sat down, the lack of sleep and the events of the last couple of weeks catching up with her. As she leaned back, a bright blue flash ripped through her head. It was shocking, terrifying. She had no idea what was happening. The world, her world, closed in on her, everything dark, before a sudden brightness almost blinded her.

A million images, sounds, words and phrases were speeding through her mind. What were they? Where were they coming from? She couldn't quite grasp them. They were out of focus, out of reach. Yet they seemed familiar and friendly. Could they be memories, she wondered, thousands of memories? Why was she getting them now? Each one seemed loaded with emotions and feelings, getting stronger and stronger, almost overwhelmingly so. Before she could begin to make sense of it all, everything stopped. The world fell quiet.

She opened her eyes, and it struck her. They were her grandfather's memories. She was suddenly elated. "Togethering" had answered all her questions at once. But why not wait until she could ask her grandfather directly? As the answer dawned on her, her eyes welled up, and her elation turned to fear, and then horror.

'Nnnnnoooooooooooooo,' she cried. 'It can't be. It mustn't be.' But somehow she knew it was. In that moment, her grandfather had slipped away, and she had not been there, had not even said goodbye.

She was in a terrible state, sobbing uncontrollably, silently wishing it away. 'Don't let it be true. It's not meant to happen this way. He's too young. He's too wonderful. I love him too much. We need him in our lives, *Hhhheeeeeeeeeeellllllpppppppp!*'

As Fred came out carrying a banana and a glass of water, he was horrified to see Jo in floods of tears, 'What is it Jo, what's wrong?'

Jo sobbed, hardly able to speak, 'It's Grandad. I think he's gone. I had this terrible flash of memories, all crashing in front of me. Sorry,

I, I, I, need to go, find out what's happened.'

At that moment, Jo's phone rang. It was her mother. 'Jo, I have to tell you something. It's your grandfather. His condition deteriorated, and a few minutes ago his heart stopped, all his vital signs indicated the worst; a flat line, a continuous beep. The doctor and nurses rushed in and put the defibrilating paddles close to his heart. But then, before they could do anything, his eyes opened, just like that, and he smiled. His heart was beating again, restored, as if nothing had happened. He looked at us and asked after you, saying he couldn't go, there was still too much he needed to tell you.'

'The doctors are dumbfounded. His DVT has completely vanished and he keeps saying how hungry he is. He's just got himself up and is getting dressed. He seems more vibrant than he has for a very long time, it's quite extraordinary. The doctors are insisting on doing further tests to check he's OK, but he's adamant that he wants to discharge himself and go home right now. Jo, can you come home too? He really needs to see you. We won't be long.'

'Of course I can,' gasped Jo, crying and smiling at the same time, a wave of relief almost tipping her over.

Fred was smiling too, 'I can read your mind. You got it wrong didn't you? He's OK, isn't he? It was just a random premonition.'

'He is,' replied Jo, happier than she'd ever been, even if still thoroughly confused about what had happened to her moments before the call. 'I must go. I need to see him.'

As Jo walked up the road, a now familiar voice entered her head.

(O) Hi, Jo, we're very sorry you had to go through that. We said it would be difficult, but you've just experienced one of the astonishing properties of life, or rather death. We couldn't tell you beforehand because you would never have understood. So now, while you're walking, let us try to explain what has just happened.

First, whenever you meet someone that you trust and have a genuine affection for, information is exchanged. There is the usual knowledge you gain through conversation, body language, facial expressions, tone of voice, for example, but other information is exchanged too. The more you trust someone, the more you care and love someone, the deeper the information that passes between you. It is shared at every meeting, every phone call, but, of course, those involved know absolutely nothing about it. This information includes knowledge, history, experience, memories, feelings and all manner of emotions. However, none of this information can be accessed or retrieved because it remains hidden, secret, safely locked away.

Now, when someone dies, there is a massive transfer of energy, a magical spark, generated at the very last instance of life. That spark is a message, and it contains a key, one that travels around the world using "togethering" links. As it travels, it recognizes all those extra special people and unlocks all that secret information. This spark, like a vivid blue flash, is generated by absolutely everyone at the same precise moment at the end of their days.

The problem is that this spark is a powerful "togethering" message. It can only be recognized and processed by people with "togethering" capabilities. Just now, you received this spark from your grandad, the key to unlock all that unselfish information that he has been passing to you all these years. At this moment of time, you know everything possible about your grandad, everything he has wanted you to know. Sadly, or perhaps happily on this occasion, that information is already being relocked and removed from your memory because your grandfather recovered, against all the odds.

So, this brings us to the second point... how did he recover so quickly and so fully? Over the last few days, you have issued many purposeful questions, stronger questions than we have seen before, and thousands of them. As a result, your trust quotient and purposefulness status has risen to significant heights. You have already reached millions of people, and they have recognized your trust status. You have gained millions of friends and millions of trusted contacts as a result. When you cried out for help just now, you sent a "help" request out into your "togethering" world. Every single friend within that world, humans and animals, unknowingly, understood the depth of your concern and all had a single desire, to support and help you. They all responded immediately.

Each and every one of them sent you a tiny portion of their energy. You focused that energy on your grandad, targeting it on his recovery. This powerful beam of energy invaded his body, searching for sick components, attempting to rectify each in turn. His body reacted in the only way it could. It was a truly wondrous result. We've experienced it ourselves before, on very rare occasions. So now, Jo, you can finally begin to understand why establishing high purposefulness and trust quotients is so incredibly rewarding. You might find that your grandad has some very special words to share with you. Listen carefully, treasure everything he has to say.

Jo arrived home almost an hour before her parents and grandparents, as they'd been kept waiting while the discharge papers were completed and signed. She could not get her mind off what had happened and was even beginning to think she had imagined everything. This whole thing about the Ancients was too impossible for words. Had she really saved her grandad? It was just so hard to believe. How could something like "togethering" actually exist, let alone have such miraculous capabilities?

She found her mind wandering to all of the ways that she and her friends seemed to be getting better, healthier and fitter. Her hay fever had almost disappeared, and Fred was not suffering from claustrophobia anymore. Her sudden ability to understand foreign languages was too incredible for words. Sudoku puzzles and challenging mathematical equations seemed to sort themselves out just by looking at them. The way Bill's arm had recovered was strange; the splinters had somehow removed themselves. Sally and Bill were running, cycling, getting fitter by the day, determined to improve their physical wellbeing and actually enjoying it in the process. Sally had surprised everyone and won the chess tournament too. All four of them seemed to have more energy, more determination, thinking situations through so much more carefully, logically and thoroughly. Was this all through the power of "togethering"? Jo could not think of any other plausible explanation.

Her thoughts were interrupted by the front door opening. Jo rushed to her granddad and nearly bowled him over as she gave him the strongest hug he'd ever had. Silent words passed between them, *'Jo. You saved my life. I can't thank you enough. We have so much to talk about, once I get the hang of this "togethering" thing.'*

Jo hugged him more tightly than ever, utterly flabbergasted. She could not believe what was going on, her head bursting as she tried to comprehend the pure wonder of "togethering".

Chapter 26

Delaying Tactics

The next morning, Jo's family gathered around the kitchen table for breakfast. Her grandparents had stayed the night as everyone wanted to make sure Jo's grandad remained fit and well, each still fearful of a relapse. Thankfully, quite the opposite was apparent. He was up and showered before anyone else, raring to go.

Everyone was chatty, buoyed by the almost miraculous events of the previous day. Unbeknown to the rest of the family, a silent conversation was also underway between Jo and her grandad throughout breakfast. In just a few seconds, Jo had revealed to her grandad everything that had happened over the past couple of weeks.

'Jo, are we really having this "togethering" conversation or am I imagining the whole thing? Look, this scheme of yours with the vineyard owner, I want to help.'

'Don't be silly,' admonished Jo. *'You've only just left the hospital and, I don't want to sound ageist but aren't you a little mature for something like this?'* She was not sure of the best way to phrase it.

'I might have agreed with you a few days ago,' said Gramps, *'but honestly I feel great, and I want to help, seriously. For a start, I can drive, and these things always need a getaway driver. Also, your parents' party is going to be a fancy dress affair and I'm going as a policeman and Gran as a nurse. We've already hired the costumes and mightn't they come in handy in some way?'*

Jo thought for a moment, processing the idea, then a smile crept over her face. *'Gramps, that might actually fit in extremely well.'*

Jo's mum was looking at Jo and her granddad, wondering what was going on. 'What are you two smiling at?'

Thinking rapidly, Jo replied, 'It's just that I told Grandad about us finding you down in the Pantiles after your escape from the kidnappers, when you were having those crazy visions. I know it was awful, but it's hard not to see the funny side in hindsight.'

'Amusing was it?' responded Jo's mum, pretending to be angry but breaking into a smile when she looked at the pair of them trying to suppress a laugh. 'It was all quite ludicrous now that I think about it. The police thought I was crazy too but were too polite to say so.'

The next two days were incredibly busy. Before they knew it, their date with Jake at the vineyard had arrived. Fred, Bill, Sally and Gramps were with Jo who was raising issues with the plan. 'We're as prepared as we can be but we don't want Jake to turn up with his whole gang. We'll be in trouble if there's more than two of them. Also, we don't want Jake to arrive in the Porsche but it's been repaired after the damage inflicted by the wild boars. We need him uncomfortable, on edge, embarrassed even. Now, we know how much money he'll have with him because it's set out in that legal transfer document, assuming he keeps his word. Jake has an appointment with his bank manager this morning, so that's encouraging. OK, I think we've got everything covered. Gramps, do you agree we're ready to go?' Grandad nodded, no words needed.

***

Jake got up early, showered, shaved and pulled his new suit from the wardrobe. It seemed like a good day to display a £1000 suit to the world for the first time, show everyone exactly who was boss. After a full English breakfast, taking care not to dribble egg yolk down his tie, he sorted out the paperwork, reached for his jacket, and rang Zolt to confirm that he'd swing by shortly as the Porsche was ready to go.

It had been repaired the previous day, although the garage hated it when Jake turned up. He'd always appear at short notice, demanding they drop everything else. He was unbelievably rude but paid incredibly well and in cash too. None of his vehicles were insured. Insurance was slow and expensive. He wanted things sorted immediately and without questions asked. He was still furious about the wild boars. Today he'd more than get his own back.

His first appointment was at the bank for the £25,000 deposit. He was still chuckling at the bargain he'd made, £250,000 for the entire vineyard estate. Probably less than 25 percent of what it was really worth. Still, 25 had always been his lucky number.

As he slammed the door behind him, he was watched by a magpie perched on the guttering high above the front door. Half a dozen pigeons were there too, all chatting feverishly amongst themselves, although Jake was too focused on the day ahead to notice them. Jo received a "togethering" message from her feathered friends.

She called out to the others to warn them that "the day" had begun and phase one of the plan was underway. Then she issued a special instruction to her avian friends, *'He's too early for his appointment. Please slow him down, make him late. If he's in the Porsche, use the deviation plan. Thank you, as always!'*

Jo knew that Jake was due to see the bank manager at 11am. It was in the manager's diary and his secretary was easy to retrieve information from. Hopefully, Jake would be frustrated and angry by the time he got there, and deeply disappointed shortly afterwards.

Jake climbed into the Porsche and started the engine. He pressed the remote control button to open the gates at the end of the drive. Nothing happened. He turned the engine off, climbed back outside, and pointed the remote at the gate, pressing "open" repeatedly. The gate was usually silent, but now he heard a strange clicking noise.

Had he paid more attention to his surroundings when he'd climbed into the driver's seat, he might have noticed a pair of squirrels scurrying away. They had been on duty, each armed with a hazelnut, waiting for the perfect moment to race up to the gate, where they had carefully dropped the nuts into the opening and closing mechanisms on either side, and disappeared.

Jake reached the gate. Peering into the mechanism, he could see what was wrong. A few choice words later, he cursed the local children, opened the garage doors and rummaged around until he found a screwdriver long enough to push the nuts out.

To the dismay of the squirrels, their handiwork was quickly undone. As Jake returned the screwdriver to the garage, the squirrels sent another message to Jo, who immediately responded, *'Shame about the nuts but great thinking. Please try again.'*

At this point, the magpie winked at the pigeons, indicating Plan B, and they took off. They circled once then swooped right down over the car. As Jake emerged from the garage, he stopped short. His once gleaming Porsche was now covered with more than a small amount of toxic bird poo. It was splattered all along the roof, the rear window, the windscreen and the boot. He could not believe his eyes.

There was no way he was going to pull up outside the bank with his Porsche in this state. He stormed back into the garage, cussing and swearing. He quickly found the hose and proceeded to wash the car off as best he could. Pigeon poo can be exceedingly sticky at the best of times, and the previous evening's supper was a perfect choice, whatever it was. Unfortunately for Jake, the water from the hose was not going to shift this treacly mess. As Jake scrabbled around the car with a sponge and lashings of car shampoo, his smart new suit was beginning to look somewhat soggy around the edges.

The magpie reported in again, *'Oh, Jo, it was a joy to behold. The pigeons have performed magnificently as I'm sure you can imagine!'*

'Great work, but we still need more of a delay and we really don't want the Porsche to turn up. If there's anything you can do to put it out of action without putting yourselves at risk, please have a go.'

While Jake replaced the hose and locked the garage door, he missed the next episode entirely. The squirrels had moved to Plan C. They scampered to the car and placed nails, each two inches long, against the front tyres. They'd grabbed them from a tin on the top of the workbench in Jake's garage while he'd been distracted with the hose. As Jake got back in the car, they retreated and waited.

Jake started the Porsche, opened the gate, and off he went, closing the gate behind him. Fifty yards later, his near side tyre hissed and sagged. Feeling the thumping of the wheel, Jake was beside himself. Why a puncture today of all days! Despite the flat tyre, he rapidly reversed the car, remembering to open the gate, ignoring any extra damage he might be doing to his masterpiece of car design.

Jake pulled out his mobile and called Zolt. 'Zolt, get over here fast, my car is going nowhere, tyre's punctured. Everything's against me this morning. I'm going to be late, very late. But don't you dare turn up in that revolting old camper van.'

'Sorry, guv, but it's all I've got. Do you want me to steal something posher?' replied Zolt, somewhat miffed at Jake's dismissive description of his loyal vehicle, still running after 300,000 miles and more years than he cared to remember.

'Damn it!! Just get your rust bucket over here Zolt. Why can't I hear the engine running already? Hurry up! Don't forget the crate of empty wine bottles. We need to look authentic wandering around the vineyard. You'd better not be in your greasy mechanic's overall either, and don't you dare bring those useless, ugly mates of yours.'

Chapter 27

Aggro at the Bank

Zolt arrived twenty minutes later, in a cloud of smoking exhaust and a grumbling engine. 'Sorry Jake, I couldn't start the damn thing.'

Jo smiled as she received another message from her friends in the sky, *'Only two of them, so far. Shiny Porsche disabled. Filthy VW Camper Van on its way. Mission accomplished.'*

Jake grabbed his Samsonite briefcase and a carrier bag but hesitated about getting inside the van. It really was in the most disgusting state. What would it do to his very expensive new suit? Realizing he had no other option he reluctantly cleared the rubbish off the seat and spread his handkerchief out before sitting down. Ten minutes later Zolt dropped Jake off, stopping just a few minutes walk away from the bank. Jake certainly did not want to be seen getting out of an aged, smoking, smelly, dirty old Camper Van.

Approaching the bank, he passed a tree full of starlings, making a dreadful racket. Mindful of his earlier episode with the pigeons and his Porsche, he was careful to walk around the tree, not under it.

Finally, Jake entered the bank, carrying just the large Sainsbury's bag-for-life, padded out with newspapers. He hoped that no-one would suspect that he would later be carrying a significant amount of cash in something so flimsy. Why he was worried about being mugged, he had no idea. He almost kicked himself at the thought. No one would dare mess with him after all. He demanded to see the manager. He did have an appointment, and he was very late, but the manager was expecting him.

A few minutes later an official came over to him. 'Sorry Sir, but it will be at least forty minutes as there are two or three clients already in the diary and waiting. You really should have been here earlier.'

Jake started to rant, 'This is simply not good enough. I'm one of your best customers, and the manager knew I was coming and...' At that point, he broke off. Noticing someone walking out of the manager's office, he dashed towards the office door.

'Oi! Stop! Come back! You can't go in there yet, you were late and missed your appointment, others are waiting.'

Jake stormed into the office, slammed the door, and squared up in front of the manager who was standing by the window, trying in vain to swat a recent onslaught of flies that had appeared as if out of nowhere. They had been irritating him for the last thirty minutes, continually trying to get at his coffee and long awaited doughnut.

'Greg, I'm late, had car problems, I won't keep you long but I need it now, the cash, and then I'll get out of your hair.' Jake always used the manager's first name. It was a form of intimidation and disrespect, something that gave Jake great pleasure.

Greg turned around. He was pretty fed up with Jake. Everything was always urgent. Jake was a nasty piece of work, certainly no gentleman, with the patience of a flea. On the other hand, he brought an enormous number of highly profitable transactions to the bank, helping him to meet his targets and guaranteeing that all-important annual bonus, quite a substantial one at that. However, Greg knew that Jake was involved in money laundering and this was something he'd not been feeling entirely happy about, at least not recently.

He could be in a lot of trouble if the Financial Services Authority found out about it. Perhaps now was the time to put a stop to it. Over the last couple of days, in particular, he'd been plagued with doubt, all sorts of questions going round and round inside his head. He could hear the words even now, *'Are you happy to destroy a successful business like the vineyard, just for your own bonus? What will you do if the FSA finds out about the money laundering? Do you really want to do business with a crook like Jake? How many other unlawful requests is he likely to demand of you in the future? What will you do if Head Office finds out about it?'*

He had no idea why these doubts were suddenly plaguing him now when he'd been playing this game for nearly twenty years without a hint of remorse, but he and other colleagues involved with Jake's activities had really been feeling jittery. Of course, poor Greg and his colleagues had no idea that Jo had been deliberately planting these doubts and concerns in their minds over the past few days. Similarly, Jake had no idea that Jo had questioned whether a Sainsbury's bag might be more secure than a briefcase as surely no-one would ever carry huge sums of money in something so flimsy.

'I'm s- s- s- sorry Jake, but we've had a change of policy. We can't lend you this kind of money anymore, it's not an acceptable risk,' he stuttered.

'WHAT? What nonsense is this, what kind of policy? Who the bloody hell do you think you are all of sudden? Policy change? Whose idea was that? Some jumped-up little squirt of a strategist in the back office somewhere I suppose. It's absolute nonsense, and you know it.' Jake smashed his fist on the manager's desk. 'Get me that money Greg, and get it NOW, or this is going to end in tears.'

Greg stood his ground. His entire body was shaking, but he could not, would not change his mind now, 'Sorry Jake, I c- c- c- can't. As I said before, we've had a review of all our accounts and we c- c- cannot lend you this money. I'm s- s- sorry, but that's the last word on the subject.'

'Sorry? SORRY? The last word? The **last word** is it? We'll see who has the last word here. You're a fool, Greg, an absolutely imbecile. You clearly don't know who you're dealing with.'

Jake took out his mobile, dialled up, and shouted down the phone. 'Your branch manager has decided to turn down my loan request at the very last minute. Sort it, NOW, or it's the end of our arrangement.' With that, he stood glaring at the manager, eyeballing him. If he'd had lasers for eyes, Greg would be dead in a second, completely frazzled, just like the vines.

In less than 10 seconds, Greg's phone rang. He answered it, 'BUT... BUT... BUT... OK, OK, I hear you. No, I d- d- don't agree but clearly I have no choice. Of course, I want to keep my j- j- job. Yes, YES SIR, yes OK, I get it, now, fine. I'll see to it right away. Yes, yes, I KNOW, I understand, **SIR**.'

Greg put the phone down and immediately picked it up again, pressing button five. 'Greg here, get me the £25K please, yes, now, I know, I know, but hurry.'

Jake snarled, 'I warned you, next time you'll lose your job, and more. Don't ever think about pulling a stunt like that again in the future, got it?'

Greg's deputy entered with the money in a bag, all packaged tightly together. He did not look at Greg and certainly was not going to make eye contact with Jake. Silently placing the money on Greg's desk, he quickly walked out again without looking back.

Jake grabbed his Sainsbury's bag, chucked the newspapers all over the floor, and then stuffed the money inside instead.

'You'll need to sign this loan agreement and cash withdrawal slip, in t- t- triplicate,' muttered Greg, now unable to look Jake in the eye, and unable to face himself in the mirror again for a very long time.

Smirking to himself, Jake signed the forms, left two copies for the bank and dropped the other in his bag. He stuffed a couple of the newspaper scraps back in and walked out with a swagger. When he'd grabbed the Sainsbury's bag instead of his briefcase, he'd failed to realize how ridiculous he'd look, strutting around in a smart suit, albeit a bit soggy, with a scruffy-looking bag-for-life at his side.

When he exited the bank, a "togethering" message was sent from one of the fly survivors in the manager's office to a starling perched in the tree just outside. This was passed on through various people before arriving at a pigeon, a blackbird, and then finally reaching Jo at the vineyard. *'Jake has just left the bank. He is carrying the money in a Sainsbury's bag, and looks ridiculous.'*

Jake strolled out of the bank, down the road, turned the corner and climbed back into the rusty, smoking camper van, nestling the Sainsbury's bag full of bank notes into his lap. 'Hang on a moment while I transfer this loot into my Samsonite briefcase. Whatever was I thinking? It'll be safer there, and it looks smarter, more professional.' He hurriedly shook the packs of notes into his case and grabbed the loan agreement, missing the withdrawal chitty buried underneath. Lodging the case under his seat, he threw the Sainsbury's bag behind him, adding to the mountain of rubbish in the back of the van. 'Right, let's go.'

Jo called out to everyone, 'My suggestions to those in the bank to reconsider their loan to Jake almost succeeded but failed at the last hurdle I'm afraid. He's on his way. He'll be here in twenty minutes. The second stage of the plan is now in operation, so it's time to get into position. This could be tricky, timing is everything. We've done our rehearsal. Good luck everyone, and thank you in advance.'

Chapter 28

The Con

Everything was in place. They knew what time Jake would arrive at the vineyard, as he would not hang about given his desperation to finalize his exploitation of Sam. They also knew about Sam's next-door neighbour who was collected each day by ambulance for her routine kidney dialysis session. Tying the two together was integral to the plan. Although they had achieved the seemingly impossible in delaying Jake, the ambulance had arrived early. Jo knew they would need to delay its departure if the plan was to remain intact.

Over the last couple of days, Sally had worked wonders. She had managed to replicate the legal document that Jake had previously thrown at Sam. It was almost identical. The paper was perfect; the right colour, size, and weight. The typed words had an identical font, size, spacing and dark navy blue colour. She had recreated an exact copy of the law firm's logo, and had matched the colours precisely. Cleverly, she had reused the original page containing Jake's signature, witnessed by his solicitor, and Sam's signature had been added and witnessed by Ben, the bookshop owner. However, a few key words had been changed. These would be hard to spot unless carefully read; a task Jake would find far too boring.

Meanwhile, Bill had been sent on a difficult paper-sourcing mission. Finding the best paper to replicate the original was challenging since this particular type of paper was hard to come by. Printing was exceedingly difficult. It was tricky to find a way of printing the metallic strip that ran through the £50 note he was copying, together with the ultraviolet feature and the hologram, not to mention the Queen's head watermark and micro-lettering. Anyway, he knew it only had to pass initial muster and must not be too perfect. He had printed sheets of them, front and back before cutting them into strips. Finally, he packaged them together. It was a neat and tidy job and barely detectable without close inspection.

Fred had been creating some stickers to add to Gramps' white Ford Focus. Clad in his fancy dress costume, Gramps had darkened his bushy eyebrows to make himself look considerably younger. Bill had also concocted some interesting adhesive tape to add to the mix.

'Right, I'm told they've just passed the left turning to Wadhurst. Sally, tell Sam it's time to go and light the straw bales,' directed Jo.

As Sally passed the message on to Sam, he grinned, striking a match to the straw bales outside the barn. Soon, there were plumes of smoke billowing into the air.

Zolt was distracted. A warning light of some sort was glowing on the dashboard of his ancient vehicle. He knew the warning lights were as unreliable as the rest of the clapped out mechanics in his vehicle, but the constant flickering was disconcerting nonetheless. The steering wheel was loose and extremely wobbly. How the van was still moving was a miracle in itself. Zolt was almost certain that it was his own willpower that kept it on the road.

Jake found the whole experience made him nervous and jittery. 'This is a monstrosity. How you can drive it is unbelievable. You've got a queue of cars behind you, it's embarrassing beyond belief.'

Jake glanced up through the dirty windscreen, 'Have you noticed the millions of damn birds flying about these days? They're everywhere. It must be a migration thing. They're up there now circling around, ghastly creatures. Pity I didn't bring my shotgun.'

'They've just reached the pub in Mark Cross apparently,' said Jo, *'but the ambulance is leaving. We must delay it for a moment or two if we can.'*

As the words left Jo's mind, a cow ambled into the lane just where the ambulance would soon be waiting to enter the main road.

Behind the ambulance, about fifty yards further back, Fred was adding his stickers to Gramps' car, transforming it to an image of a police car. Just behind that, Bill had strung his tape across the lane, effectively closing it off. Gramps, wearing his police uniform, was standing to the side, remaining slightly out of view. He was carrying a leather case with an envelope peeping out of it, the one that Jake had left with Sam a couple of days earlier. Now though, thanks to Sally's handiwork, the envelope was badly singed and burnt around the edges. Thankfully the ambulance driver was too preoccupied trying to get out of the lane to notice the activity behind him.

Jake and Zolt were half a mile away from the vineyard turning when Jake looked up, startled, 'That's a lot of smoke, where is it coming from? I don't suppose, no... no, it can't be! I told you that on no account should your ugly mates do anything until after our visit. What did you tell 'em to do, burn it down, you flamin' idiot?'

Zolt spluttered, 'N, n, nothing, I, I, I told 'em to wait. I, I said we'd tell 'em if it was necessary, that's all, nothing else, honest guv.'

As Zolt drove up to the vineyard lane entrance, the cow wandered off, nodding its head in Jo's direction, where she was waiting out of sight behind a tree. Zolt was indicating right, about to turn, when he had to slam on the feeble brakes as the ambulance emerged from the lane directly in front of him. 'Bloody hell,' muttered Jake, 'if your boys have done what I think they have, I'm really gonna kill 'em.'

As the ambulance drove off, Zolt entered the lane only to find it blocked off by police tape 50 yards away, where a policeman was standing next to a police car. Jake snarled angrily at Zolt, 'Stop here, don't get too close. They're bound to wonder about the state of this thing. Come on, park up. Bring a crate of empties. We need to get past this police idiot; show him we're at the farmhouse on business.'

They climbed out of the camper van, and Jake put the Samsonite case on his seat. He tried to slam his door but, of course, the thing would not shut. 'No, leave it,' winced Zolt, 'or you'll pull it completely off its hinges. It's very delicate, needs a gentle touch.'

Jake scowled, giving the door an extra kick for good measure, and they both walked towards the police officer.

Jo's grandad looked up, 'Sorry sir you can't stop 'ere. There's a major fire at the vineyard. The owner's been taken to hospital.'

'That's terrible,' pretended Jake. 'I was supposed to have a meeting with him today. I wanted to order some of his fabulous wine and return some empty bottles. I hope he's gonna be all right.'

'Seriously ill, I'm afraid sir, badly burnt. He may not make it. But the paramedics have done a great job. That new hospital in Pembury will sort him out. The fire is out, but there's a lot of smouldering timber. Everything's been completely destroyed except the wine store. There's a fire brigade team down there and a police forensic squad. You'll have to come back another time, can't be blocking the lane. More police are on their way so move along now please.'

Jake and Zolt were about to go when Jake thought he noticed an envelope, his envelope, sticking out of the police officer's leather case. Unsure how best to approach it, he said, 'Oh, by the way, I was expecting a written quotation today. Did that go up in smoke too?'

'I imagine so sir. Oh, although actually, when the ambulance arrived they found the owner almost unconscious on the gravel outside. He was clutching this letter, muttering something about getting it collected.' Gramps took out the badly singed envelope, looked at the addressee and asked, 'What's your name, Sir?'

Jake replied, truthfully for once, 'Jake Grunt.'

The policeman said, 'Ah well, this is for you then, Sir, though not sure it's gonna be much use to you now. Can I see some ID, please?'

Jake dug out his wallet and passed over his driving licence. Gramps looked at it closely and said, 'Well Sir, look at this, you need to drive more carefully in future as I see you have nine points on your licence. Bit risky for the rest of the country's drivers isn't it? Anyway, if I could ask you to sign here, you can have the document. And take the empties back home, can't leave them here.'

Jo's grandad had done an utterly superb job of occupying and distracting Jake and Zolt. While all of this was going on, Fred had scrambled out from behind a hedge and into the open door of the camper van carrying two bags, one empty, the other carrying several magazines. He could not immediately see a Sainsbury's bag-for-life but found the Samsonite case on the passenger seat and was amazed to find it unlocked. He opened it, tipped all the money into one bag, replacing the notes from the case with magazines from his other bag. He closed the case and quietly retreated to join Jo behind a tree.

'Whew, that was a bit bloomin' nerve-racking,' whispered Fred, his heart pounding and sweat dripping down his forehead.

Meanwhile, Jake could not believe his luck as he climbed back into the passenger seat putting the Samsonite case on his lap. Zolt gently nudged and levered the door back into place. 'Sorry, it often catches like that.' Zolt reversed out of the lane and headed back down the road towards Tunbridge Wells.

Returning his attention to the blackened envelope, he could not believe his eyes when he took out the document. He gave it a cursory scan and saw the farmer's signatures. 'My God, we must have really terrified the guy. Not only has he signed the transfer of the vineyard over to me but he's also signed to confirm receipt of the £25K cash deposit. I'm £25K better off without even trying. A useless idiot like that doesn't deserve to be in charge of all that land anyway.'

Trying his luck, Zolt smirked, 'Do I get a bonus now then guv?'

'You flamin' well don't. You ain't done nothing,' scoffed Jake.

Zolt drove on, wrestling with the gears and continually pumping the breaks to slow down at bends. He was getting increasingly sick of Jake. 'Well, at least my boys have saved you a clearance job if they did burn down the barn. Surely that deserves something.'

'Don't be an idiot. If they've killed the vineyard owner, or the police discover it was arson, there's gonna be hell to pay. Just make sure they lie low for a while. I'm sick of clearing up their mistakes. Right, pull up outside the law firm. I need to pass this agreement to the solicitor. Then you can drop me home. I've got to get my Porsche puncture repaired.' Zolt parked up in silence, still quietly fuming.

Jake's solicitor was busy with a client, so he gave the papers to the secretary. He left the office, a broad smile on his face, thinking of all the money he'd saved. No doubt the vineyard owner would kick up a major fuss but the law is the law, and he did not have a leg to stand on, assuming he had not already kicked the bucket of course.

Back at the vineyard, they waited for an hour or so to make sure everything was safe before moving the so-called police tape further down the lane to the entrance of the vineyard itself, a necessary precaution in case Jake returned. The burnt straw bale remains were cleared up and the coloured stickers removed from Gramps' Ford Focus. Everything was more or less back to normal.

'Right,' said Jo, 'the Stage Two Plan has possibly been completed successfully, but I don't want to speak too soon.' They all had a little chuckle, relieved, to say the least. 'How come you weren't in the theatre Gramps? That was an excellent performance you just put on.'

They laughed as Gramps winked, 'How do you know I wasn't?'

'OK team,' said Jo, 'it's time for Stage Three of the plan. Let's go!' The four friends piled into Gramps' car, each silently thanking their fantastic little helpers in the sky and on the land. They knew they could not have done it without them.

Sam was nervous. This stage was crucial, and he knew he had to remain fully alert to keep safe until the mission was completed.

Chapter 29

The Double Whammy

Jake was dropped off outside his home, glad to get out of Zolt's stinking vehicle. Zolt drove off in a stuttering cloud of black smoke, hoping to make it home before the engine seized up altogether.

Clutching his Samsonite case, Jake went straight up to his office and phoned for a car mechanic to come and repair the puncture. He placed the case carefully inside his safe, closed it, twiddled the combination, and pulled across the painting he used to conceal the safe door. Then he settled down to make some important phone calls.

Meanwhile, back in Gramps' car, Fred was looking through the bag of money. He'd never seen so many real notes in one place before. 'Wow, this real £25K looks almost as good as Bill's counterfeit stuff, are you sure we can't keep it?'

Soon back at Jo's house, they tipped the money onto the kitchen table. 'Look,' said Sally, 'he's an idiot, he's left the withdrawal chitty in the case too so we won't need the one I forged.'

'Even better,' said Jo. 'Now let's replace these packs with Bill's counterfeit notes. We'll put some of the real notes at the top and bottom of each pack to make it look authentic and put it in a Sainsbury's "bag-for-life". I'll write a note for the charity shop.'

'What shall we do with the rest of the real money?' asked Sally.

Jo thought for a moment and then replied, 'We'll give that to Sam. There must be £20K there. That should compensate him for his dreadful bank not giving him the loan he requested.'

They placed the withdrawal slip under the first row of money packs, as if it had been mislaid. They added Jo's note on top, sellotaped the bag shut, then strolled up to the British Heart Foundation charity shop, located next to the Great Hall.

When no-one was looking, they snuck the bag into the collections area where several people were sorting out other donated items. Hoping they'd gone unnoticed, they crossed the road to make three calls from one of the few public phone boxes still in operation.

The first call was to the Heart shop itself. Bill put on his deepest voice trying to imitate Jake, 'Afternoon. I've just left a generous anonymous cash donation inside the collections area. Please make sure it's found before it gets mislaid. It's in a Sainsbury's bag.'

The second call was to Abby at the Daily Post newspaper. Again, Bill used his best deep voice to make sure she did not recognize him. 'Quick, get over to the Heart shop between Hoopers and the Great Hall. Something is happening there that you won't want to miss.'

The third call was very similar, contacting the BBC Local TV studio also located nearby in the Great Hall.

'Well done Bill, you should be in the theatre too,' said Gramps.

'Let's stay here in front of the railway station. We've a good view of the Charity shop from here without getting too close,' said Jo.

Three minutes later a huge cry echoed from the shop premises. This was captured by Abby, who arrived in the nick of time, closely followed by the BBC reporter and camera man. What looked like chaos ensued, as people came rushing in and out of the shop, all very excited. Eventually, Fred and Bill walked over to see what was happening. Two young ladies came out giggling and smiling.

When Fred asked what the commotion was about, one replied, 'It's a miracle. An enormous donation has been left for the Charity, thousands of pounds. They're counting it now. They were worried it was the proceeds of one of those recent robberies, but no, it's come straight from the bank, still in the bank wrappers. And there's a withdrawal slip too, so they're trying to contact the donor right now.'

Fred turned and gave a thumbs-up sign to the others. 'Well done guys,' said Gramps, 'I think we've done it, it's time to go.'

At that moment Abby came out of the shop, notebook in hand. Hi, it's Bill isn't it? From the Common. The aero expert?

'Yes, hi. We were just passing. What's all the commotion about?'

'Well, I've misjudged Mr Grunt. He's just made a very generous donation. Sorry Bill, can't stop now, need to get my report written.'

Bill ran to catch the others up. Back at Jo's house, they tuned in to the local BBC news. The donation was the only thing on air, with TV footage inside and outside the Heart shop. They could clearly see themselves in the crowd. 'We're on TV,' squealed an excited Bill.

'Oh dear,' said Jo, identifying a minor flaw in their plan.

Now Jake was still in his office doing his paperwork when his phone rang. It was his solicitor. 'Oh, hi,' said Jake, 'you got the document then? Don't tell me you've dealt with it already?'

'Errrrm, Jake, did you read it? As in, did you read it through thoroughly?' asked his solicitor, somewhat tentatively.

'I could see it was all signed and witnessed,' replied Jake. 'Why?'

'I hate to tell you,' said the solicitor, pausing slightly, 'but you have just purchased ten years of visiting rights to the "hide" on the edge of the forest by the vineyard for the princely sum of £25,000. This is not the document I gave you, just a brilliant forgery, same paper, ink and logo. You have been tricked, and I can see no way out of it. You had signed the document in my presence, and I had countersigned it, and they've reused the original signature page.'

'What? It can't be.' Jake hesitated, deep in thought. 'Besides, I still have the money in my safe. I'm going right back to sort that pesky vineyard owner out. It won't just be his barn and house burning down, I'll smash up his wine store, see how he likes that. That's if the last fire hasn't already finished him off.' Jake could hear beeping, another caller trying to get through, but he ignored it.

'Jake, be careful what you say on the phone. You never know what's being bugged these days. I'll put my bill in the post.'

Now Jake may have appeared calm on the phone, but he was furious. How could the vineyard owner have conjured up such an ingenious plan? He must have been helped, but by whom. Well, he was in for it this time. As Jake stood up to go, the local TV news caught his eye. The camera was focused on Tunbridge Wells. Curious, Jake turned to watch as the camera zoomed into the Heart shop. Turning up the volume, all colour drained from his face. 'A £25K donation has been found in a Sainsbury's bag in the British Heart Foundation charity shop.' Jake was more than a little confused, particularly as he heard his own name and company mentioned.

'The donation, initially anonymous, appears to be a philanthropic gesture from a leading local businessmen, Jake Grunt of Grunt Technology Solutions. Efforts are underway to locate him so that the British Heart Foundation Charity can thank him in person. This will make a massive difference to their charitable works, and they cannot thank him enough for his heartfelt gift… sorry, no pun intended!'

Listening to the laughing reporter, Jake was totally bemused.

What was going on? Why would they be thanking him? Slowly, it dawned on him. As he scrambled to open the safe, his phone rang again. 'Is that Jake? Yes? We can't thank you enough for...'

'Stop,' Jake cried, 'it's not meant, I mean...' He was going to say it was a huge mistake, that the money had been mercilessly stolen from him, but he realized he had not reported it, so he said the first thing that entered his mind. 'It was supposed to be anonymous, and now the whole damn world knows. I've a good mind to ask for it back! No, no, you keep it, but I don't want any more calls and certainly no interviews. Is that absolutely clear?'

He slammed down the phone, stormed over to the safe, slid the picture back and entered the combination. As the safe door swung open, he grabbed the Samsonite case and opened it up. Horrified, he looked down to see piles of model aircraft magazines and comics, glossy pages galore but not a penny in sight.

Disgusted, he kicked the magazines across the floor and hurled the case at the wall. What the hell was going on? No one ever messes with Jake Grunt. Well, no one would again, that's for sure.

Three hours later, Jake's horrible offspring arrived home. Grant shouted up the stairs, 'Dad, Jake, what's going on? We've been teased something stupid by all our mates. They're all sayin' you've given to charity. Did you? After all you've said about those 'orrible good-for-nothing charities, Jake, did you? Where are you? You used to spit in their general direction. You goin' soft in your old age?'

They hurtled into Jake's study, albeit confused to see the door open when it was usually closed and off limits. Almost as quickly as they flew in, they reeled backwards, shocked to see Jake sprawled out on the sofa, his arm curled around an empty bottle of whisky. Jake was comatose, drunk as a skunk.

Looking from each other back to Jake, they knew they did not want to be here when he woke up. They'd go and stay with friends tonight, well not exactly friends, but kids who would not dare send them away. They were Jake's children after all.

The following morning Jake had a thumping headache. After scrabbling around for Nurofen he opened the morning's Daily Post and promptly blew a fuse. He grabbed his phone and summoned Zolt, who arrived bang on time, fearful of the repercussions after yesterday's debacle. He'd read the local rag too, but even he could not have anticipated Jake's rage. 'Have you seen these dreadful headlines and pictures? Zolt, look closely and tell me what you see.'

The headlines were not what Jake had expected. True, he felt sick about losing the money but at least thought the whole affair would have done something for his reputation. How wrong could he be?

<u>**Heart Felt or Heartless, You Decide**</u>
<u>[Abby Newsome]</u>

Jake Grunt of Grunt Technology Solutions Ltd gives huge £25K philanthropic donation to the British Heart Foundation Charity. When contacted by the Charity, he argued that he'd wanted to remain anonymous, claiming that the bank chitty used to identify him had been left with the donation in error.

However, subsequent events indicate this grand gesture was, in fact, an underhand cold-hearted marketing stunt. When the Heart shop manager tried to deposit the funds, the bank rejected much of the money as counterfeit.

The solicitor for Grunt Technology Solutions has denied any impropriety and confirmed the funds came directly from the bank. The bank said the money was carefully checked both on arrival from head office and when issued from its vaults. The police are now investigating what appears to be a significant case of fraud. The solicitor has assured the Charity his client will honour the donation while the police investigations continue.

Jake looked set to explode. 'Not only have I been cheated out of the vineyard but now I've given £25K to a charity! Jake Grunt has been seen to do charity! And it now looks as if I've got to give them another £25K which is utter madness. What is all this nonsense doing to my reputation?! Where's the original money gone? And what can I possibly do about it with a police investigation underway and a load of aggro at the bank? It's been a nightmare from start to finish. Who's behind this Zolt? I'll tell you who. The photos Zolt, look!'

Zolt examined the double page spread in the newspaper, 'Well it certainly attracted a lot of attention.'

'No, not that you idiot. Look! It's those four pesky kids,' pointed out Jake. 'The same four kids who were in the pub out near Scotney the other day. The same four kids I keep seeing down in the Pantiles.

Now Zolt, tell me, what are they doing there?'

'Just passersby, enjoying a commotion.' Zolt strained to focus his eyes on the picture. 'Wait. It's the horrible red-headed girl. The same kids who rescued that woman we had in the ruin on the Common!'

'Wooaaah,' said Jake, snatching back the paper to look more closely himself, 'and take a look at that older guy standing next to them. He looks familiar. Isn't he….? No, no, he can't be, surely? But he is, he's the damn policeman from yesterday, outside the vineyard. Wait a minute. Where's last week's paper? It's here somewhere. Which day was it?' Jake started throwing back copies of The Post onto the floor behind him. 'Here it is. Look at that, it's that girl's nasty old grandad. Our kids knocked him over with their bikes, on purpose. He ended up in hospital. How did he get out so soon?'

A few minutes later, the penny dropped. 'I thought that guy was a bit old and the police were running low on recruits but, no, he wasn't a policeman at all. We've been well and truly conned, by four little kids, a stupid old pensioner, and the vineyard owner.'

Jake was fuming. 'One of those brats has my £25K, and I WILL get it back. Plus, look, there's nothing in the papers about a fire at the vineyard. Surely that would have had some coverage especially if there had been a significant fire and a life in danger? I bet that pesky Sam isn't even in hospital, but then what was the ambulance doing there? How did they do that, and how did they get the police car? They can't possibly be alone in this. Someone else is involved. We've got to work this out. No one dupes me and gets away with it.'

'So where's my apology?' asked Zolt. 'My boys were telling the truth. They'd done nothing and been nowhere near the place.'

'Well,' mused Jake, ignoring Zolt's last remark, 'I gotta be real careful until I identify who's behind this. I bet that guy Sam is gonna be well guarded out there for the time being and there's no way I'm gonna stick my head in that noose. The police will be everywhere. They're probably waiting for me. It's a trap, that's what it is. '

Jake sprang into action, 'Right, sort out these kids. Follow 'em, track 'em, for as long as it takes. They'll lead us to whoever is funding and supporting them. Get your boys on to it, pronto, BUT, do it quietly, lurking in the shadows. Use my kids, Grant and Gertrude. Why are you still standing here? Go find those damn kids.'

Chapter 30

The Hunt Begins

At the crack of dawn the following morning, Jake and Zolt could be found having a full English breakfast in a little café by the station entrance in Mount Pleasant, the town's main shopping street. It was all Jake could do to stop himself looking over the road at the charity shop where yesterday's fiasco had embarrassed him so severely. Grant and Gertrude were sat beside them, shovelling in a very similar breakfast but with additional portions of bacon and baked beans. Gertrude's dog, Zorog, was tied up to a drainpipe outside, growling at anyone who got within six feet of him. Zorog had had a bad night unable to sleep in the drafty log store he was forced into each night.

'Zolt, you must follow those kids wherever they go today,' muttered Jake, spitting a half chewed sausage in Zolt's face as tomato ketchup dribbled down his chin.

'Dad, you've got ketch...' began Grant.

'Shut up you little oick,' interrupted Jake, 'can't you see I'm talking?' He was not going to let his whining offspring ruin his favourite greasy meal of the day. He carried on speaking, spraying sloppy egg yolk in Gertrude's direction as he did so.

Ignoring his daughter's displeasure, Jake continued issuing commands to Zolt, 'Take Grant and Gertrude and that mutt of a dog with you and don't let them out of your sight. I want a report every thirty minutes, by text only, don't ring. Now push off, all of you. I want to know exactly where they go and who they see.'

'But Dad, we haven't finished our breakfast yet,' moaned Grant.

Cut short by the alarmingly evil look in his dad's eyes, Grant abruptly stood up and left the cafe with the others. They grabbed Zorog's lead and pulled him along behind them while he tried desperately to bite as many taxi drivers' legs as he could reach. When they arrived at the corner of Chapel Place and Mount Sion at the bottom of the old High Street, Zolt turned to the kids, 'You go to

Madeira Park and find those little buggers. I'm going into this café to finish off my breakfast. They do great coffee and buttery pastries. Call me when you see 'em, don't lose them.'

'But you're supposed to come with us and not let us out of your sight,' sniggered Gertrude.

'If you think I'm going anywhere with you two and your dog you've gotta be kidding,' said Zolt. 'Now push off, go on, vamoose.'

***

Meanwhile, the team had assembled at Jo's house. Bill and Sally came rushing in, hot and sweaty, after another five-mile run.

'You really are serious aren't you, with all this training? What are you up to and why such a change of heart?' asked Jo.

'We don't understand it either, but we're feeling much fitter than we were,' replied Sally. 'Look, Bill has had a haircut too and he's washing it nearly every day. Just look at his skin, most of his spots have vanished. He's looking almost handsome, don't you think?'

'Well, I wouldn't go that far,' laughed Fred, 'but now you mention it, you are both looking much healthier.'

Sally smiled, pleased that her training regime was making a difference. Jo's grandad was happy too and could not quite believe he was now part of the team.

'Well,' said Jo, 'I think that went pretty well, far better than we could have imagined. Sam is absolutely delighted and is delivering twenty bottles of his best wine to my dad today for his upcoming party, as promised. Sam has also said that if we'd like holiday jobs with him, he'd be only too delighted to have us. We are going to give him the £20K when he gets here. That should enable him to progress his vineyard plans and hopefully remove all the stress he's been under with the bank. Our watchers, the birds and all the other fantastic animals, are still keeping a close eye on Jake and we have more creatures supporting Sam at the vineyard, just in case.'

Bill added, 'We seem to have scuppered Jake for the time being, but things are going to get more dangerous from here on in.'

Fred chipped in, 'I imagine all hell will be let loose at the bank, especially with the police investigation into the counterfeit money. That's a brilliant outcome too, an added bonus. But Jake won't just sit back and take it. He'll be demanding answers from his motley crew and he'll be after revenge, so we need to watch our backs.'

'Definitely. What fun, though?' said Sally. 'Gramps, you loved every moment of it, didn't you? You seem to have a new lease of life. Ooh, I forgot to tell you. Bill and I have done it, last night, the "togethering" thing, sending silent messages to each other, it just sort of happened, and without your involvement, Jo. We hadn't planned it, but it was fantastic, wasn't it Bill?'

Bill agreed, 'Yes, it was about three in the morning. I suddenly woke up thinking about radio controlled drones, planning my next upgrade. Then Sally butted in completely out of nowhere. We had what seemed like a lengthy discussion though it wasn't more than a few seconds really. Then I realized I could ask much wider questions, a bit like Googling, only without a laptop or wifi, and it all worked. We seem to have progressed, apparently now into a deeper part of your trust circle Jo. It's brilliant, thank you so much.'

'It's nothing to do with me,' said Jo. 'I don't control it, as far as I know. It's all about you, what you think and feel and do. So that's great. It will be interesting to see it develop and who else joins in.'

Gramps had a surprise too. 'Jo, sorry, but Gran now knows everything. The same thing happened to us. She was upstairs pottering about, and I was in the kitchen making my favourite bread and butter pudding, when she silently spoke to me, querying my recipe. It was quite a shock at the time. She came straight downstairs and asked what had happened. Then we experimented with more "togethering" banter, and she just loves it. Eventually, I told her everything we've been up to. She was outraged at first, furious that we'd left her out. She said she would have loved being involved, and could easily have worn her nurse's uniform out at the vineyard, which would have added more authenticity. She was particularly angry about the visit to Scotney and would have loved to have joined you wandering through the secret tunnels and chatting to Puss-Puss, though she has forgiven you all for talking silently while she was chatting over lunch in the pub.'

Jo was very relieved as she had not enjoyed keeping secrets from her gran. The Ancients were right, her trust circle was beginning to grow, albeit slowly, but this sort of thing was bound to take time. 'Now we need to decide what to do next. We can't do everything at once, and we still don't have a master plan, but then that's hardly surprising given the effort that went into the vineyard confrontation.

We might have created a breather for ourselves for now, but probably not for long. Jake is not going to take this lying down, and if he puts two and two together, he might just realize what's happened, which could bring more trouble on us all.'

Fred replied, 'Well, I don't see how he can connect us to what happened at the vineyard and the charity shop. He surely wouldn't believe that four kids like us could cause such havoc to his plans?'

'No, maybe not, but…'

(O) Hi, Jo, sorry to break into your meeting, but now seems the right time to have another chat. You need to start planning the rest of your campaigns against Jake and his evil band of buddies. The vineyard escapade was absolutely brilliant, and we desperately wanted to be there with you to experience it all first hand. Sadly we have a great deal of other stuff to do, but maybe next time. You all seem to be growing in confidence, with Jake proving to be the perfect foe, just as we'd hoped. Now, there are the Scotney robberies to sort out. May we suggest that you meet us in your favourite café in the Pantiles. It's always been one of our favourite places too though it's very different from our day. See you shortly.

Everyone in the room seemed to have received the same message. Gramps was disappointed, 'Sorry but I'm afraid we can't make it as we have a tennis match to play, got to keep fit you know, but you go ahead, we'll meet up later.'

'Jo, they're at it again, did you notice?' asked Fred. 'I'm absolutely convinced now. The Ancients have yet again implied that our confrontation with Jake is all their doing.'

'I'm beginning to think you may be right, Fred, but why, and more importantly, how? Anyway, they're waiting for us, so we'd better be off. Let's go,' said Jo, 'unless you need the loo first, Bill?'

'No, that's another thing,' said Bill, 'because I'm doing all this exercise and eating fruit and lots of other healthy food, my need to go to the loo frequently, has almost entirely cured itself. I can't believe how much better I feel. So, yes, let's go.'

Chapter 31

Zorog Interferes and Marge Intervenes

The four friends were having a lively discussion while sitting in their favourite café in the Pantiles. At least that's what everyone around them thought. In reality, they were "togethering" with the Ancients and planning how to resolve the crisis at Scotney Castle, which still had the police dumbfounded. An hour later they decided to check on Jo's grandparents and their tennis match. They started to walk back via Chapel Place, a pedestrian link between the Pantiles and the High Street that was full of old and interesting shops.

Now, everyone knows dogs are superb at detecting different human smells, or maybe it was something else, but Jo suddenly received an urgent warning. *'Hi Jo, it's me Zorog. I know you're nearby. Grant and Gertrude are sitting outside the Italian Coffee shop on the corner. My lead is tied to the leg of Gertrude's chair. They walked down your street twice, looking for you, but got bored and are now waiting for Zolt who is in the café stuffing his face. They're out to get you, so beware.'*

'Oh hi Zorog, great to hear from you, and thanks for the warning,' said Jo. *'Are you happy to cause a little mayhem for us?'*

'You bet. What have you in mind?' replied Zorog.

Jo quickly explained. They were just twenty yards away when Grant noticed them. He quickly stood up, about to dash in and grab Zolt, but thought better of it. As the four teenagers strolled past the coffee shop, they could see Zolt inside, tucking into a pastry.

Zolt looked out of the window, almost choking on his apple cake as he saw them, spraying crumbs all over the poor customers on the next table; a bad habit he'd inherited from Jake. Jo gave him a cheeky wave and then ran off laughing. Jake accidentally hit the "send" button on his mobile, now misinforming Jake that the ghastly kids were still at home closely watched by Grant and Gertrude.

He stormed out of the café, and that's when it happened. Seeing

Grant get to his feet, Zorog had already moved to the other side of the café door ready for his manoeuvre. As Zolt came charging out, Zorog took another step and planted all four feet firmly on the ground, imitating an elephant. Zolt had absolutely no chance of seeing the dog lead straighten and stiffen across the doorway and went head over heels, knocking Grant's feet from under him, the two of them left sprawling on the ground. As Zolt's feet snagged the lead it tugged Gertrude's seat forward, tipping her over the back.

'Let's double back down Frog Lane,' said Fred. 'I bet Zolt will be expecting us to go straight home. If we hurry, we'll lose him.'

Zolt was dazed. He staggered up but his four targets were nowhere to be seen. Seeing Grant and Gertrude struggling to get to their feet he lent them a hand, knowing his actions were certain to get reported to Jake later on. They tried to give chase up Mount Sion but were held back by more stubborn behaviour from Zorog. Only the café owner's irate yells and shaking fists sent them on their way.

After twenty minutes and another three times around Madeira Park, they lost heart and gave up. Zolt was fuming. These two kids could never be trusted to do anything properly, and the dog was a disaster. What to tell Jake? He could hardly admit to leaving the job to the useless pair, and he was getting increasingly fed up with being outsmarted by four young kids.

The four teenagers crossed the busy road by Hoopers and were walking towards the entry to the park, unaware of the events taking place behind them. Six pigeons had flown down and landed on the pavement four or five yards back. They were hopping, jumping and flapping their wings to keep up, pecking the ground as they went.

'Those kids must be dropping breadcrumbs as they walk,' one shopper was heard to say.

Just then, who should emerge from Carluccio's Italian restaurant, but Jake. He was chatting to a lady friend, both seemingly oblivious to the rest of the world. What was more disconcerting was the half smile on Jake's face, a rare occurrence of late. The lady in question was the new bank manager, brought in to replace the one who had brought the bank into disrepute. This was only her second day on the job since being transferred at short notice by the regional director. Jake had spent the last couple of hours charming her over lunch.

Looking down the road, Jake stopped short as he saw the

teenagers approaching. He grabbed his phone from his pocket to see if Zolt had been in touch, but there was nothing new since Zolt's earlier assurance that the targets were still somewhere in Madeira Park. Either the kids had escaped unnoticed or someone was lying.

Jake was furious. How could Zolt and his own offspring be so unbelievably useless? Realizing confrontation would be pointless, he just about managed to refrain from lashing out. He grabbed the lady bank manager's arm and pulled her towards the window, feigning interest in the Italian goodies on sale in the deli linked to the restaurant. While he relaxed as the kids walked past without seeing him, he was disgusted by his cowardly reaction. 'This has got to stop,' he thought. 'How can I be this unnerved by four ghastly kids?'

Jake did not realize that Jo and the others had seen him too but had decided to try and wind him up a little. They would avoid the park entrance and walk on but completely ignore him. This put the onus on Jake to do something, should he dare.

As they carried on up the hill, Fred commented silently, *'That was interesting. Jake clearly saw us, seemed all set to react, but then rapidly backed off.'*

'You're right,' agreed Jo, *'but it's a perfect opportunity to embarrass him if only we could think of a way.'*

They had not walked more than a couple of yards beyond Jake when his phone rang. He excused himself to his lady friend, explaining that it was a call he could not miss. Zolt must have a good reason to phone rather than text as he'd been instructed. As he answered the call, one of the pigeons that had been following behind was very brave indeed. It took off and flew directly at Jake, swooped in and grabbed the phone, as if it were a large slice of bread. Nonplussed as to what had just happened, Jake looked quizzically at his new friend, assuming she was a playing a joke on him. Her expression suggested otherwise and she was pointing upwards.

Following her gaze, Jake was shocked to see his phone flying away from him when the pigeon swooped back down and gently dropped the phone right in front of Sally. Oblivious to the pigeon's brave effort, Sally just heard the phone land on the pavement and assumed someone must have dropped it. She picked it up, keen to get it back to its rightful owner. As she and the others looked to see who might have dropped it, they saw Jake rushing towards them.

'Give it 'ere,' he yelled, 'now!' He was red in the face and fuming. Fearful of what he planned to do to Sally, Bill immediately stepped in front of her, almost adopting an oriental defensive fighting position, his hands ready for action. Other people on the street had also stopped at this point, unsure what was going on.

'No, we'll give it back to its owner,' stated Fred firmly, 'once we know who has dropped it.' He looked at the other passersby expecting one of them to say, 'It's mine.'

'It is my damn phone, give it back, now, revolting kids,' shouted Jake, aware that his anger was spiralling almost out of control.

Within a second, a rather large woman stepped forward from the growing crowd of spectators. She must have been all of six feet tall, with a solid build, and carrying several large shopping bags. She stopped Jake in his tracks. 'There is no reason to shout like that. That was rude. You should be ashamed of yourself. Whatever is this town coming to? These youngsters are only trying to help. We all heard them say they wanted to return the item to its owner, and so did you, unless you are deaf as well as objectionable? Prove you're the owner, and the item is yours, otherwise please step aside.'

Jake had never ever been spoken to like this before, least of all by this revolting busy-body, and he was completely taken aback. 'Well it is my phone, and I was in the middle of a call when a damn pigeon grabbed it out of my hand and flew off with it.'

The lady laughed. 'That's the stupidest story I've ever heard.'

In fact, everyone was laughing, except Jake, who was both angry and mortified, 'It is my phone, and this is the number.' He shouted it out, then added, 'Go on. Check it. I haven't got all day.'

Sally had no way of knowing, gave him the benefit of doubt, and put it in Jake's outstretched hand, almost feeling sorry for him.

'Well?' said the large lady. 'A nice thank you to these four very kind and sensible youngsters, wouldn't go amiss.'

Jake mumbled a few unintelligible words and turned back, but his lady friend had vanished. He walked off grumbling to himself. 'Those kids, I hate them, and those birds. Everywhere I go, they're there, causing me grief. Damn pesky birds, damn pesky kids!'

'Thank you so much,' said Jo to their new super tall lady friend.

'I'm only too pleased to help. My name is Marge and I can't stand overbearing businessmen. They think they can be rude to everyone just because they're wearing overpriced suits and have large bank accounts. That was great fun. Pity the pigeon didn't drop the phone from higher up! Thank you all. See you around.'

'Well that was confusing, disturbing, and amusing all at the same time,' said Bill. 'Jake is going to hate us even more now, though.'

'Bill, what was that Kung Foo fighting action all about? Where did you learn that?' asked Fred, somewhat amazed.

'I don't know. It came out of nowhere. I suddenly had this inner energy and Sally needed protection. It didn't look silly did it?'

'Absolutely not, very brave,' smiled Sally, briefly reaching out to take Bill's hand, but stopping quickly before anyone noticed.

As the four pals arrived at Calverley Park a few minutes later, the annual rapid mixed doubles tennis competition was in play on the new grass court in front of the cafe. There was a huge crowd watching but not a sound to be heard. As they approached the court, Bill felt a tap on his shoulder. 'Hi Bill, hi Sally, I thought it was you,' whispered Abby from the Daily Post.

'Hi Abby, great to see you again.' said Bill quietly. 'Let me introduce you to Jo and Fred, our best mates.' They all shook hands.

Abby added, 'It's the final. These two older guys are playing quite well even with their ancient wooden racquets. But they're losing five games to love against a much younger couple in their twenties who are hitting the ball incredibly hard. There have been a few dubious line calls against them too.'

'Oh dear, that's not fair,' said Jo. 'They're my grandparents, team Gran & Gramps. I'd really like to *help* but there's not much I can do from here.'

'Well, they've attracted lots of attention,' said Abby. 'Oh, look, a magpie has just flown in and is sitting just behind the umpire, almost on his shoulder, though the umpire doesn't seem to have noticed.'

Ten minutes later it was match point to the youngsters. The game was nearly over. With both his opponents volleying at the net, Gramps produced a beautiful topspin backhand lob that landed an inch inside the baseline. The umpire began to shout, '**ou...**' when a strange thing happened.

What no one knew was that a sparrow hawk was circling high overhead looking down on the game. He'd been on duty watching over Jo and her friends just like the magpie. The magpie had heard

Jo's "togethering" request to *help*, and asked the hawk to use his brilliant eye sight to monitor the ball and report his findings. When he had reported back that Gramps' lop shot was in, the magpie went into action and had nipped the umpires ear. The opposing team were now running to the net to claim their win thinking the umpire had called **'out'**.

Knowing that everyone was watching, the umpire realised he wouldn't get away with another dubious call at such a critical moment. **'Sorry guys, I yelled "OW", not "OUT", as I think I've been stung by a wasp. Its 40:15, still Match Point.'**

From that moment on, Gran and Gramps began to play wonderful flawless tennis and unbelievably they clawed their way right back into the game. Their teamwork and concentration was simply exquisite. Their opponents began to argue amongst themselves and they blamed each other as the errors crept into their play. Twenty minutes later, as the tie break reached a conclusion, the shoe was on the other foot.

'6 games all, 5 points to 6. Championship Point to the oldies.'
The umpire bit his lip. He hadn't said "oldies" out loud had he?

Gran served the ball, but Gramps at the net was clearly in trouble. The leather grip on his racquet came adrift, making it hard to hold. It was the longest rally so far, no one able to finish it. Twenty-five shots later, Gran put up a desperate lob as she struggled to return a shot deep to the baseline. Gramps was at the net watching the ball soar high over his head. The opponent moved in closer. The ball was accelerating rapidly towards him, confirming the laws of gravity. He leapt into the air and launching a furious attack. The contact was exquisite, the trajectory perfect, guaranteed to land within six inches of the baseline. What if Gramps could stick his racket in the way as the ball shot over his head? Impossible; human reactions were simply not able to compute the correct position within such a minuscule time frame. He did the next best thing. He threw his racquet instead. But he knew the rules. If the racquet left his hand, it wouldn't count.

In a flash of inspiration, he grabbed the loose end of the grip, letting the racquet spin of its own accord as the grip unravelled. The racquet reached the perfect spot in time and space. There was a clash of molecular entities too numerous to describe. The ball smashed into the spinning racquet frame, splintering the ancient wood. But such was the force of the collision that the ball went whizzing back the way it came, scorching into the corner of the court, untouchable.

Their opponents were numbed, shocked beyond belief. The umpire stared, squinted, then nodded, satisfied but utterly mystified. The ball was in. Gramps had won the point, and still had a tenuous hold of the racquet that would sadly never be used again. Its spinning motion had first unravelled then continued to spin and wind itself up again. Gramps was left holding a handle and very little else.

'Game, Set and Match. Team Gran & Gramps. Champions.'

There was a huge roar of approval, and Abby could be seen snapping away with her camera. As the cup was presented, Jo's grandparents gave high praise to their beaten opponents, offering words of admiration and encouragement.

Jo laughed, whispering to Fred, 'The Ancients always come up trumps when you need them.'

(O) Sorry guys, nothing to do with us. Your grandparents achieved their win entirely on their own merits. Never forget the importance of teamwork, helping each other to do the best you can, accepting that mistakes can happen but trying to learn from them. In this case, your grandparents may have used "togethering" to speed their communication, but communication lies at the heart of teamwork, however it's achieved.

Moments later, Gran held out their trophy. 'We haven't won one of these in a very long time. Not sure how we did it because they were by far the better players, truth be told,'

'Right, let's get home and change out of our sweaty tennis clobber,' said Gramps. 'It's time to plan our showdown with the town's drug dealers. Jo, this is going to be a fascinating.'

Chapter 32

Community Courage

The following morning the Daily Post made them all chuckle.

Retirees Smash Tennis Favourites
[Abby Newsome]

Age appears to be no barrier when it comes to winning at tennis. Team Gran & Gramps came from behind to smash the much younger favourites and win the Annual Mixed Doubles Challenge. Their skill, concentration and teamwork proved a winning formula and provided a positive message to all retirees to get out there, have fun and keep fit. Well done, Champions, Gran & Gramps.

The previous evening, Jo, Sally, Bill and Fred had enjoyed a lengthy discussion with Jo's grandparents, gradually formulating a plan to put the town's drug dealers out of action. They had been putting the final details together when Jo was interrupted.

(O) Hi Jo, you'll need help in trapping the drug dealers. Ask your grandmother to recruit some friends. You won't be disappointed.

Jo was delighted to receive such advice though she did not fully understand the significance at the time. She repeated the message to her grandmother, who made a number of phone calls to her friends from her University of the 3rd Age Walking Group and her Yoga class. All were eager to help and excited about the new challenge.

They wondered what to call themselves. They knew the group would need to be strong-minded, brave, courageous and determined if it was going to resolve the drug dealing problem. They also realized that, if successful, this might be the first of many similar activities. They almost settled on "**Courageous Communities of**

Tunbridge Wells", hoping to replace the well-known but rather tired "**Disgusted of Tunbridge Wells**" label. Jo felt this might be a little long-winded and made an alternative suggestion, 'How about shortening it to "**Courageous Communities**", or even just "**CoCo**"?'

'That's definitely an improvement,' nodded Fred, 'but you're nuts if you think a name is really going to make the task any easier.'

'That's it!' cried Jo. 'Fred, you're a genius. We should call the group the "**CoCoNuts**"! What do you think?' Everyone agreed, enjoying this new identity. Sally took it one step further, applying her artistic talents to hastily make a set of membership cards.

The following morning the first CoCoNuts recruits were meeting up for the first time in a cafe in the town centre. Jo's grandmother introduced Jo to the full group of CoCoNuts ladies. Jo was quite surprised when she saw who was there, 'Hi Marge, it is you isn't it? You helped us out yesterday, outside Carluccio's.'

'I did indeed, with that terribly arrogant man who'd dropped his phone. What an enormous fuss about nothing. Well, fancy meeting you again so soon,' said Marge with a smile. 'You seem to have arranged some more fun for us, we can hardly wait.'

Jo went through all the details of the plan to rid the town of its drug dealers. 'As you can see,' she explained, 'it is dangerous stuff. And we could do with a few more members. Can I ask you all to contact your friends and neighbours and see if they might be willing to help. We all know that the police have made very little progress and it has reached the point where it is vital that we rid the town of these pests. Let's all meet up tomorrow at Gran's house, confirm our numbers and get ready for action.'

Back at Jo's grandparents' house, the following day, it was all systems go. With many more locals wanting to join in the fun and rid the town of its troublemakers, the CoCoNuts were in full flow. Ably directed by Gran and Marge, they quickly produced a mission statement, behavioural guidelines, roles and responsibilities, membership cards, and an action plan in meticulous detail.

They were yet to understand what had triggered this avalanche of interest in being involved. Even Jo had no idea that asking a few simple "togethering" questions could elicit such a response. *'Would you like to help your community? Do you wish to turn around the lives of trouble-makers in the town? Do you want to love and protect your community? Would you like to help your community to be a fantastic place to live?'*

These questions and more had rippled through the minds of many of the local residents and, without fully realizing it, most began examining their feelings and opinions on the matter with a far more open mind than usual. The result was remarkable and showed the community in a surprisingly fair, constructive and determined light. Jo had also received another interesting message.

(O) Hi Jo. This new group of yours, the CoCoNuts, is just an incredible achievement. You don't know it yet, but it is going to succeed where everyone else has failed. It's amazing how creative you and your friends have become since your involvement with Jake. We knew a target like this was all that was needed. The world will never be the same again. Just you wait and see.

Jo smiled. She just loved receiving these messages even if it was all in her imagination. But there was that clue once more that this might all be part of a grand plan engineered by the Ancients.

Things were going really well now. Abby at The Daily Post had offered to resource the immediate CoCoNuts coordination activities, even giving Bill and Sally full access to their computers to create a new website, courageouscommunities.com which mapped on to coconutseverywhere.com.

Over the next two days plans were finalized for the drug bust and focus was transferred to resolving the Scotney Castle thefts. This was to be a double assault on two of Jake's activities designed to give him two monstrous headaches at the same time. Although ongoing news coverage of the crimes taking place at Scotney was boosting tourist visits to the castle, the crooks needed to be exposed. After much discussion, Gran was tasked with seeking agreement from the management of Scotney Castle, the National Trust, to proceed.

Jo's job was to help her grandmother by asking some carefully selected "togethering" questions that would smooth the way for such a discussion. She also made a call to Abby at the Daily Post, who was delighted to hear from her, especially since their recent meetings had significantly boosted the newspaper's sales. They had a lengthy conversation, and Abby was only too happy to encourage Jake's participation in the exercise. A late call to the police was scheduled for the next morning, hopefully leaving them little time to respond.

Jake, meanwhile, was getting increasingly twitchy. His plans seemed to be leaking. Those horrible kids knew where they'd been holding the girl's mother, and about his plans for the vineyard. He decided to have his house, particularly his office, scanned for bugs. Nothing had been found. He'd even ordered a search of the woods behind his house in case eavesdropping equipment had been planted, but again nothing was identified. 'Not that it would have picked anything up anyway,' Jake muttered. 'Too many bloody birds chirping and squawking away in those woods these days. God knows where they've all come from.' In desperation, Jake had also checked his car and Zorog's kennel, but he'd drawn a blank.

Racking his brains, he tried to think if he could have been followed. He could recall those four troublesome kids being close by in the Pantiles, but not close enough. They were occasionally on the same street but always too far away to hear any conversations. Perhaps that smart kid Bill had invented a real Harry Potter invisibility cloak, as if such a thing could ever exist. He knew Zolt, Zonk, and Grilch would never drop him in it, too scared by half.

Still trying to work things out, he grew increasingly frustrated at the constant twitter of birdsong around him. 'Can't a man get a moment's peace around here?' Suddenly, it came to him, a flash of recognition, sheer genius. It was the birds. Not real birds, of course, that would be ridiculous, but radio-controlled model birds. Yes, of course, battery operated birds, and loads of them, taking surveillance shifts according to their battery power. That must be it. His Russian computer expert had discovered an in-built capability for this sort of refuelling feature in Bill's stolen planes.

'Hmmm,' he mused, 'these bird planes must have a listening device too, maybe even a built-in miniature camera. My God, that kid Bill really was a clever little so-and-so. Jake sniggered, proud of himself for getting to the bottom of it all. Now he just had to work out how to get hold of Bill's latest technology. It could save him a fortune and would outstrip the one his Russian expert was working on by far. Smiling to himself he poured a large measure of whisky, a little reward and celebration for his ingenuity.

Chapter 33

The Carrot

The next day Jake woke up earlier than usual, desperate to steal Bill's new bird drone technology. He sat down to eat his full English breakfast, dutifully prepared each morning by his wife. He opened the Daily Post newspaper, scanned the front page, then dribbled fried egg down his chin and onto his shirt as a headline grabbed his eye.

Auction of Constable Painting
[Abby Newsome]
This evening at 8pm, an auction of the recently discovered painting by Constable, "Reflections at Scotney Castle", is to be held at the Victorian Country Mansion in the Scotney grounds, a short walk up from the castle where the painting was created.

This follows a recent TV programme describing in detail how the work of art was discovered, verified and validated. Bids are expected to exceed its £5 million price tag.

A private company, "Art Protection Engine" has been employed to provide extensive security both inside and outside the auction room. A full search of the premises will take place with sniffer dogs immediately before the champagne reception. Attendees are limited to just the 25 on the invitation list.

All thoughts of Bill's drone technology drained from Jake's mind. If the painting was going to fetch £5M, then he could expect to fence it for at least £3M with no questions asked. The police had no idea about the tunnel into the Scotney dining room, so getting into the house would be child's play. The challenge would be locating the painting's exact position, grabbing it and making an escape without being seen. One thing was troubling him. 'Why hasn't my police informant tipped me off? What's going on?'

Jake dialled a private mobile number. The response was

immediate. 'At your desk again? Doesn't anyone go out on the beat these days? Seen the front page of the Post? Why didn't you call?'

'Oh, the auction at Scotney? The National Trust only requested our help half an hour ago, and we are struggling to get the necessary resources together. Apparently, it's all been very hush-hush until this newspaper article went public. The National Trust is furious. Jake, steer well clear of this. APE are real professionals, using state of the art technology. They're the bees' knees in this type of security apparently. I wouldn't start any monkey business with them.'

'That's for me to decide. Let me down again and there'll be hell to pay. Just watch your step.' Jake cut the call, his anger rising.

Jake's brain was on overtime. His desire for the painting was becoming an obsession. Google quickly brought up images and the floor plan for the Scotney Mansion. He started, thinking aloud. 'The auction won't be in the entrance hall which leaves the library, dining room or study. The study has comfortable furnishings and tasteful décor but would be a tight squeeze for twenty-five people. The dining room has a massive table, too heavy to move. It has to be the library. Therefore they'll choose the entrance hall for refreshments, handing out champagne flutes as the moneyed idiots arrive. Those fools will go crazy when they discover the painting is trash.' Jake cackled, all thoughts of previous fiascos were long forgotten.

'Now, the bidders won't be allowed to examine the artwork beforehand because a TV programme has already revealed all the technical procedures undertaken to prove its legitimacy. The painting will be kept under wraps until the last moment, raising the tension.'

Jake knew there were risks with the devious plan he was formulating. Could he rely on his men in Kilndown Forest to do the job properly or was this a job he had to do himself? Much as he hated entrusting this kind of operation to his useless crew, he had no choice. He couldn't risk it himself, or could he?

Jake sent his gang at Kilndown a secure coded email, 'Dear Mum, hope you're well, see you at the usual place for lunch at noon, love Jake xxx.' No one knew that Jake's mother had died in childbirth. She took one look at Jake, saw pure evil, and withered away.

While Jake drove off to meet his gang, Jo's team was busy preparing a defence. They'd had no proof yet that Jake had taken the bait, but the usual observers were peering down from above, looking for signs of his intentions. They assumed that Jake would make a play for the painting, it was simply too tempting given his knowledge of the secret entrance to the dining room. This might provide an opportunity to grab Jake and finally have him sent to prison, ending the suffering that Jake inflicted daily on so many people.

Everyone was busy. Gran had been in touch with Scotney's house manager, Mrs. Pennymore, whom she knew well from her volunteering. Considering she was usually somewhat severe, she agreed to their request quite quickly. Of course, she had no idea that Jo had already planted the idea in her mind with a "togethering" question. *'Wouldn't it be an excellent advertisement for Scotney if the auction of a valuable work of art were to be held there? It would reach the national press and thousands of visitors would flock there.'*

Gramps was getting kitted up to look like a wealthy guest in a smart dinner jacket and bow tie. Gran was Mrs. Pennymore's assistant. Sam from the vineyard had given his delivery truck a makeover, which was now labelled as "Art Protection Engine". Ben from the bookshop had joined in too. It was the least he could do after all of Bill's hard work in the shop. This temporary organization now had a growing number of employees, and most were dressed in new overalls with "APE" written in large letters on their backs.

Marge was the manager, responsible for catering and drinks. Anna, the Big Issue seller, was overjoyed to take on the role of waitress, handing out champagne to arriving big-wigs. Abby would be the Press representative, ready to record whatever might transpire.

School friend, Sandra, felt honoured to be asked to help find two more dogs to join her dog, Chaser, as sniffer dogs and knew just where to find them. Up the road in The Grove Park were two giant black Newfoundland dogs that were familiar to everyone living nearby. Not only were they beautiful specimens, but they were widely known for their loyalty, strength and calmness. As luck would have it, both dogs were having their lunchtime walk around the park when Jo and Sandra caught up with the owners who were chatting together on a bench. Jo explained what was needed, but the owners didn't think their wonderfully intelligent dogs could pretend to be sniffer dogs given the little time left to train them.

'If I can persuade both of your beautiful creatures to come over and sniff Sandra's bag at the click of my fingers, then bark SOS in

Morse code, will you let us borrow them for the evening?' asked Jo.

The two guys looked at each other, 'Well, we guess so,' said one, smiling, 'but I don't believe you'll do it, even though they are highly intelligent animals. It would save us the evening's walk and we could even go to The Compasses for a pint instead. Go on, give it a try!'

Jo sent a few "togethering" words to the two big black dogs. *'Hopefully, you heard all that? So, please, I'm going to click my fingers now, if you'd like to come and help, you know what to do.'*

The two owners were astounded, as was Sandra, when both Newfoundlands lumbered over to Sandra's bag just as Jo clicked her fingers, before each began to bark in Morse code. 'That was incredible,' said the second owner, 'so here are the dogs' leads. Don't forget to give them supper. We'll be in the pub if you need us.'

Jo and Sandra walked away with the beautiful dogs, passing by the corner of the park in front of a house with a gigantic teddy bear clearly visible in the upstairs window. Jo knew for sure that it could not have happened, but she could have sworn that it waved at her.

Meanwhile, Bill was busy with his new prototype model aircraft made of balsa wood. He carefully lifted it out of its box and in seconds had attached the wings to the fuselage. He had painted it to look like a magpie and it was very quiet with its electric motor.

'But I thought all your stuff had been stolen in that burglary the other day,' queried Sally. 'So where did all this come from?'

'Ah yes, well, my dad was brilliant,' replied Bill. 'He lent me the money in advance of the insurance claim, so I was able to buy all the required electronic bits and pieces. They missed the plane during the robbery because it was in the garden shed being painted. My latest software was safely backed up, so it's taken no time to reconstruct everything. I've improved it a lot too, so let's see how it goes.'

He launched the plane in Fred's garden, taking care to avoid the surrounding trees. He controlled it carefully until it was circling above, then placed the controller gently on the ground.

'Won't it crash if you're not controlling it?' asked Sally, worried that another disaster was in the making.

'No,' replied Bill, 'the plane has a GPS chip. When I press this button on the controller, the plane goes into autopilot mode and uses its position at that precise moment as a reference point to circle around. I can change the radius of the circle at any time.'

'That is super impressive,' said Fred.

'So, we can use it at Scotney as a security backup,' said Bill.

'But what good would it actually do?' asked Sally.

'Well,' replied Bill, 'watch this.' He took out his mobile phone, typed in a short text message and pressed send. Then he held out his phone for everyone to see. Images of nearby gardens were flashing up on the screen, a different picture appearing every few seconds.

'How have you done that?' asked Sally in disbelief.

'Well,' replied Bill, 'it's all very simple really. Fixed inside the plane there's another mobile phone looking down through a small hole in the fuselage. When it received my text it started sending photos back to my phone here. The pictures aren't great quality and it would obviously work much better with the latest phones and using a 4G network. Anyway, I'm currently developing an app that continually compares the two most recent images. It searches for minor differences between the two, then tries to work out the position, size, and shape of those items and how far they might have moved. It can currently identify nearly twenty different things like cars or people or animals, but in my next release, it will be 200. I then superimpose all this on a Google map to make it easy to see. It needs more work as it's tricky stuff to program, but it's a start.'

'That's fantastic and incredible,' encouraged Fred. 'Do you really think we could test it at Scotney this evening?'

'Absolutely,' said Bill, 'but what we really want is for Jake to see it and plan to steal it to use in the next MIGHT mini drone trial. You see, he won't know that I can secretly take control of it at any time using my phone, so he'll never win the mini drone competition.'

Bill brought his plane back to earth, packed it carefully away in its box, and he, Sally and Fred walked up the road to Jo's house where a small gathering was taking place.

'What have you found there?' asked Gran, seeing Jo and Sandra arrive with the two beautiful black dogs.

'These are our extra sniffer dogs,' replied Sandra, 'aren't they wonderful? We've borrowed them for the evening.'

'Great work,' said Gran. 'Right team, Let's get changed into our uniforms, then it'll be time to go and get set up at Scotney.'

Chapter 34

The Auction

With the equipment packed in the car, the team were all set to go when Jo received a "togethering" message from the magpies, which she quickly passed on. 'Apparently Jake is at the pub in Kilndown again chatting to that guy Jorik from the tent village in the forest. Our spies have caught a few words: "art, famous, TV, money, auction, Scotney". It's game on. Jake seems to have taken the bait.'

Half an hour later Gran arrived at the Mansion with Jo, Fred and Bill. Marge arrived having picked up Anna and Gramps. Sam came in his delivery truck five minutes later with Ben, Sandra, and the three dogs. Puss-Puss was overjoyed and rushed over to have a friendly chat with Chaser and her two enormous friends. Sam, Ben, and the teenagers looked very smart in their navy blue overalls with "APE" written in large letters on their backs. Mrs. Pennymore shook hands with everyone, delighted that people had started to turn up.

Unexpectedly, six police drove up, in two cars, sending gravel flying in a needlessly over-exuberant arrival. A figure in his black uniform stepped out of the first car. 'I'm Inspector Grabham. Where's the boss of "APE"?' he asked, getting straight to the point.

As Sam walked over, they shook hands. 'I don't know if you were expecting us but our Chief Constable was adamant we should be here to support you. We're a bit thin on the ground as we had no advance notice. I hear you are experts in this field, but we're here as extra backup in case things go awry. I need to meet your personnel.'

'Of course,' replied Sam, using his best efforts to diffuse the gruff attitude of the Inspector, 'but I think there's been a misunderstanding. You see this is not a real auction and there is no valuable artwork here. This is a carefully staged plot to catch the thieves who have been stealing from the Mansion. As your guys have yet to catch the thieves, we've been requested to put a stop to the robberies once and for all. We suspect this "carrot" will be too good for the crooks to miss and we'll grab them the moment they appear.'

'That is the most ludicrous idea I've ever come across. Who in their right minds conjured up such a thing?'

'We did. It may not be on page 25 of your handbook for catching elusive robbers, so you're welcome to leave. However, if you insist on staying then please tell your men to remain in the shadows. Under no circumstances are they to intervene without the nod from us.'

'Are you serious? No crook would be stupid enough to fall for this. This smells like a complete fiasco, so we'll stay, but I need to assess the strengths and weaknesses of your team.'

'Of course,' replied Sam. 'This is Ben, my most senior officer with over twenty years experience in museums around the world. He's never lost a single item and has caught many would-be art thieves red-handed.' His fingers were tightly crossed behind his back, fully aware he was delivering an enormous lie.

He continued, 'Marge, she's as tough as they come, acting as the Catering and Drinks Manager. She can stop thieves in their tracks just by looking at them. That's Anna, our karate expert, tonight's drinks waitress. Tell your men to beware as Anna can break bones with a flick of her wrist. Our sniffer dog team controller is Sandra.'

'You must be joking! She's only a child, and those dozy creatures look nothing like sniffer dogs. They'd be better curled up in front of a roaring log fire and keeping someone's slippers warm. There's no way they're capable of smelling out a villain, let alone catching one.'

The Inspector was quickly corrected as the three dogs looked up and started circling him. They did not harm him but merely closed in, buffeting and taunting him a little. Chaser suddenly leapt up onto the back of one of the big black dogs and tugged a handkerchief out of the policeman's pocket containing three very inviting chocolate bars.

'That's enough boys and girls,' called out Sandra. The three dogs immediately retreated and sat down in a line, putting their paws out to offer the chocolate bars, still untouched. No-one knew that Jo had been instructing the dogs with a series of "togethering" messages.

'That was totally uncalled for,' exclaimed Inspector Grabham, straightening up his uniform. 'At least they didn't eat my supper.'

'Well,' smiled Jo, 'these intelligent animals just wanted to show you what they're made of and what sensitive noses they have. Perhaps you'll be less quick to judge on first appearances next time.'

'I, I, I'm sorry,' said the Inspector, 'and who exactly are you?'

Ben butted in. 'My Art Protection Engine team, of course. Kindly refrain from underestimating them as quickly as you did the dogs.'

'But they're only kids, for heaven's sake. They've no chance against dangerous thieves! This is nonsense. Our Chief Constable was right, we might just save the situation after all.'

'That's quite enough of that,' said Marge, decisively. 'These young people are worth a thousand of your men as you will shortly discover. Now don't just stand there Inspector. Deploy your guys where you must, and let's see what they are made of.'

Inspector Grabham was red in the face. He'd never been spoken to like that before, but it was pointless arguing. He had been given a thankless task and that was it. He sent his team off with their walkie-talkies to check the grounds, soon reporting back that all was clear. But Jo felt uneasy. Jake was definitely nearby and the painting was ready, tempting him, sitting on its easel. It was wrapped in brown paper for protection and covered with a golden drape.

The police did a final check following Sandra's sniffer dogs who continued their act, sniffed the air, and moved on. The sooner they could complete their pretend job, the sooner they'd get their favourite supper of meaty chunks topped with crunchy bone treats.

Abby from the Daily Post had also arrived and her car was searched thoroughly just in case she was smuggling someone in. This Inspector trusted no-one. Abby was delighted when she'd received Jo's late call the previous evening with all the auction details and even more thrilled to be invited to Scotney to record the events.

Once Mrs. Pennymore realized who she was, she was keen to be introduced, hoping to get a mention in Abby's write-up the following day, maybe even a photo or two. 'Would you like to take a few pictures of the Constable before the auction begins?'

Abby had been well primed and knew that Mrs. Pennymore would never have agreed to this evening's activity had she known what was really going on. 'Yes please. It would be great to photograph the library and the entrance hall, but I think they're hoping to keep the painting under wraps until the very last moment.'

Anna moved a small table in front of the door that led from the entrance hall into the garden room. The door was to be kept closed as they did not want Jake to see an empty entrance hall. Anna lifted several bottles of Prosecco from a freezer bag and on to the table plus two dozen champagne flutes, adding some realism to the scene.

Mrs. Pennymore, well into her seventies and wearing strong pebble spectacles, requested that they lock the door from the entrance hall into the library, ensuring the wealthy guests would see the lovely study en route to the library. 'Anna, please move the tall vase of flowers in front of the door too.'

Anna did as she was asked before handing Mrs. Pennymore a large glass of Prosecco.

'Thank you, dear. That's very kind of you. It's my favourite drink you know, I just love the lively bubbles.'

Gramps was strutting his stuff in his dinner jacket and bow tie, giving a perfect imitation of a multimillionaire, thinking to himself, *'I could easily become accustomed to this lifestyle. Hmmm, if only.'*

'Enough of that, dear,' said Gran, wagging her finger at him.

Mrs. Pennymore was dressed up to the nines and waiting for the guests to arrive, still blissfully unaware of a critical part of the evening's entertainment.

Just before 7pm, Jake made his move. He quickly reviewed the possible auction arrangements, and issued clear instructions to his gang. 'They will have opened up access to the gravel driveway by the Mansion front entrance as there's no way these uppity millionaires are going to walk from the visitors' car park. The library is the likely room to use as it's a suitable size. Now, imagine we are going in through the secret panel in the dining room. The door to the left leads to the small dining room which then leads to the kitchen, but we can forget about that as it's highly unlikely anyone will be there, though keep an eye on it just in case. The door to the far right leads into the garden room, so go through there, then straight ahead into the library. Jorik, you must go first and check that all's clear. At that point, you should see the painting, and you must grab it while your mate then swaps it for our forgery. Then bring the original straight back to me as I will be waiting behind the secret panel. Now, is that all understood? Absolutely no deviations from the plan will be tolerated. Let's go.'

At last a conversation overheard and relayed. Jo passed it on, silently, *'They're moving. They're on their way. Let's do it!'*

By 7:10 Puss-Puss was ready for the tasks she had to perform.

Sandra was with the three dogs just outside the front door, patting them, thanking them for their excellent and thorough work.

At 7:15 Inspector Grabham and three of his men were in the entrance hall, bored, certain it was all a terrible waste of time.

At 7:20 Sally was outside the front door. She turned on the first digital recording at the highest volume. She had spent the morning at Sainsbury's car park recording the sounds of cars arriving and car doors slamming. Tuning into these familiar sounds, Mrs. Pennymore beamed, 'Ooh, I think I can hear our guests arriving, this is exciting.'

At 7:30 Bill launched his plane outside and set its flight pattern around the house, checking to ensure images were being received.

At 7:35 Fred started his recording. He had spent lunchtime in the Old Opera House pub with Gramps, recording people drinking and chatting. Anna opened another bottle of Prosecco, poured a glass for Gramps and topped up Mrs. Pennymore. She became over excited, clinking glasses with millionaire Gramps and causing both to spill in her enthusiasm. 'Oops, sorry, but here's to a successful evening Mr. Gramps. I hope you have your chequebook handy. Clever getting here so promptly. The early bird catches the worm and all that.'

At 7:45 Sally turned off her recording and moved inside. There was no way she was going to miss the action unfolding.

At 7.50 Fred turned down the volume of his recording, replacing it with one by Gramps announcing that the auction would start in 10 minutes at 8pm in the library. Mrs. Pennymore added, 'Oooh, I can hardly wait, but our guests are taking a long time to park their cars.'

At 7:51 Fred restarted his original recording. The chatting and clink of wine glasses could be heard once more. Mrs. Pennymore had her glass filled up yet again, now chatting non-stop to Gramps.

Anyone watching from outside the Mansion would have seen the whole thing was a charade. Those listening from the inside, however, could easily have been persuaded that an excited group of wealthy individuals were drinking champagne, and about to attend an auction in which a vast amount of money was to be exchanged for a very important and highly valuable Constable painting.

Chapter 35

Theft

Three men had already reached the quarry. They'd come through the tunnel from Kilndown Woods, under the moat, and exited via the chimney base of the old castle. They'd stepped carefully through the trees, avoiding the path, moving only when they were sure that no one was nearby. They could hear distant noises of cars arriving and car doors slamming so they knew that the gathering was under way.

They were about to climb the wall of rock in the quarry and open the entrance into the second tunnel when they heard a walkie-talkie close by. They hid once more. As the policeman walked away, they made another move only to hear a slight buzzing sound above, sending them back into the shadows.

Jake peered out from the tree he was hiding behind and looked up. He saw what he first thought might be a bird but then he realized it was a model aeroplane circling above. He cursed. He knew what it was. But what was it doing here? His earlier idea, his bugging theory, that the plane must look like a bird, was correct. He knew this drone would be incredibly useful, maybe more so than the painting. No, it would just have to wait. He could not miss this chance to grab a valuable artwork. It would give him financial freedom after all.

The men waited a few more seconds for the drone to pass by, then climbed the concealed steps to the rock door and entered the tunnel. At about 7.40pm they arrived behind the secret panel in the dining room. Jake could hear the clink of champagne glasses and excited chatter. He smirked at the thought of their later disappointment. When he heard Gramps announce the start of the auction, he knew the time had come. He had just ten minutes to complete his mission.

Unknown to Jake, Puss-Puss was sitting on the other side of the secret panel. With her acute hearing, she could detect the smallest intake of breath and knew immediately when they'd arrived. Galvanised into action, she decided that as well as a "togethering" warning to Jo, she would put on her own little show. She scampered out of the dining room, through the small garden lobby area, into the library, past the picture on its easel, through the study, and out into the entrance hall. There, she meowed like mad in front everyone, before dashing back to her station.

'They've arrived,' said Jo. 'The thieves are here and waiting for the right moment to steal the painting.'

Inspector Grabham laughed, 'Don't be ridiculous. There is absolutely no way they could have got in here. I told you this whole idea would be a total waste of time. The place is surrounded. My men would have reported in if they'd seen anything. Cats run in and out and meow all the time. It's nothing new, for heaven's sake.'

He could not understand what the Chief Constable had been thinking, sending them down here. There was no way a thief could get past his men and steal the painting. Even if they did, how could four kids and this ridiculous amateur team do anything about it? By now he'd dismissed the whole exercise as a complete shambles.

Moments later, a loud crashing sound reverberated through from the library.

Jake had been smart. He'd looked up the details of the painting on the Daily Post website. He knew exactly what its dimensions were. He'd found a picture with a similar sized frame in an antique shop in town. He had also printed off a copy of the painting and stuck it over the painting he had acquired. He thought this was a hilarious idea. The bidders would get such a shock when it was unveiled. Little did he know that Jo had also gone through the exact same process.

The painting itself was not a Constable anyway. Gramps attended art classes at the Adult Education Centre and had spent several hours searching through Google images to find something that looked right. He had merely printed out a copy of the picture on high quality paper and then carefully painted over the original artist's signature. He was slightly embarrassed to be taking on the role of an art forger but knew it was for a good cause. An image of his modified painting had been sent to Abby for inclusion in the newspaper's website.

Puss-Puss watched as events unfolded. First, Jorik emerged from behind the wall panel in the dining room. He looked around. He'd been there before several times, and he knew the layout well even without Jake's instructions. The door on his left leading into the small dining room was closed. He'd been told not to worry about it, so he did not. Deviations from the plan were punishable after all. He peeped into the garden room and stepped through the doorway. Luckily the door on his right, back into the entrance hall, was closed so no-one would see him from there. He bent down to peer through the keyhole, but all he saw was a table with bottles of champagne and wine glasses completely blurring his view. He suddenly felt very thirsty but immediately dismissed the idea from his thoughts.

The door ahead of him, into the library was ajar. He approached and peered through. There was no one there. He crept in and checked the door to his right, also leading to the entrance hall, but all he could see through the keyhole were flowers. As he turned around, he spied what had to be the "Constable" positioned on its easel ahead of him, with chairs neatly lined up in rows. He waved back to his mate who came out through the panel carrying the fake painting and was now waiting impatiently in the doorway of the garden room.

But Jake had taken a big gamble. He had entered the dining room through the secret panel and grabbed the fake from Jorik's mate, then pointed for the guy to stand guard over by the doorway leading to the small dining room. This was not part of the plan. Jake had intended to stay hidden behind the panel, but in situations like this when his adrenalin got the better of him, he just could not help himself. He wanted to be part of the action. He now moved quickly to stand behind Jorik, who was blissfully ignorant of the switch in personnel.

Puss-Puss did not know whether to do it now or to wait. She knew from her mouse hunting training that it was better to wait for precisely the right moment. But she wanted her revenge. She still had bruises. A timely "togethering" message came through from Jo, *'Don't rush, take your time.'* So she held back before creeping slowly forward, ready to pounce.

The fake painting was heavy. It had a very solid frame. It had been hard work carting it all the way from the forest. Jorik's mate had really struggled with it and was secretly amused when Jake snatched it from him and began to realize how cumbersome it was.

Jorik quickly peered around the library door into the study, enormously relieved that it was empty too. Thankfully his brain had somehow failed to register that there was no one guarding the "Constable". He could hear the celebrations in the entrance hall next door, the anticipation, and could feel the champagne bubbles trickling deliciously down his throat. But he was extremely nervous. One false move and they could be caught out at any moment.

He stepped back into the library and turned around. Ahead of him, he could see the easel and painting beckoning him. With Jake close behind, he yanked the gold drape off. Jake was surprised and disappointed not to see the painting in all its glory but assumed it was probably all part of the build-up, the excitement, leaving it carefully wrapped in brown paper, possibly to protect it.

As Jorik snatched the painting off its easel, Jake quickly replaced it with the fake one he was carrying and threw the drape back over to cover it. Then Jake turned, grabbed the original from Jorik, swivelled on his heel and rushed off, heading back via the garden room to the dining room where he could make a safe exit out through the secret panel. Jorik was bemused. What had happened? Why had Jake not stayed behind the wall panel as planned? Alas, in his confusion he hesitated for a fraction of a second longer than he should have.

Puss-Puss had not expected to be confronted by three ugly men. She was not sure which one to go for. Jake had surprised her as he rushed past with the brown paper package. She was left with only one option. She launched herself at Jorik as he was the cause of most of her bruises. She had not realized quite how high she could leap.

Jorik had never had a snarling cat in his face before. He was surprised, then terrified. He fell back, trying to escape the outstretched claws aiming for his ears, and the open mouth about to snap around his nose. The cat appeared three times bigger than he had remembered. He fell further back, right into the easel. The easel clattered to the floor, the picture fell, he fell, Puss-Puss fell, all culminating in the loud crashing sound that had been heard by Jo and the police in the entrance hall on the other side of the study door,.

Inspector Grabham looked at Jo. Jo looked quizzically back and raised her eyebrows saying, 'Shouldn't you do something about it?'

Chapter 36

Caught

Galvanised into action, the Inspector and two of his men rushed through the study to the library. What they saw in front of them was a surprise; the easel and painting lying on the floor. Puss-Puss had seen them out of the corner of her eye and had jumped off Jorik to scurry away and hide. Jorik, still petrified, leapt up and rushed back through to the garden room, trying to escape and catch up with Jake.

'Quick, follow me,' yelled the Inspector to his men. They dashed through the library and into the garden room where they could see Jorik desperately trying to open the dining room door, but Jake had slammed it hard behind him and it had stuck fast. Jorik had no option but to exit the garden room via the reception hall knowing full well it would be crowded with people. He had completely forgotten about the table and champagne bottles on the other side of the door.

Meanwhile, Jake was rapidly making his escape. Despite his size and the weight of the hefty painting, he had already stepped through the secret wall panel in the dining room, closed it behind him, and nearly fallen down the narrow steps to the cellar below. Jorik's mate was still on guard at the far end doorway. He'd heard the commotion and was shocked to see Jake vanish through the secret wall panel.

Inspector Grabham had seen Jorik change direction and gave chase, yelling at his men to check the dining room. Moments later, Jorik's mate was grabbed and handcuffed.

Meanwhile Jorik, having flung the door open in front of him, had crashed into the table on the other side. Many of the bottles and wine glasses shattered as they hit the floor. But Jorik had momentum, and he leapt over the upended table and straight through the reception hall. If he was surprised there were so few guests, he did not show it.

In his mad rush he barely noticed Sally standing in his way but caught her arm, spinning her like a top. Somehow Sally kept her balance, quite a feat for someone who considered herself more than a little clumsy. Her arms flew out, but her rapid rotation caused her spectacles to go flying, landing on the floor right in front of Jorik.

It was not his fault entirely, but his foot hit the ground a split second after the spectacles, and he crushed the lenses and frame into smithereens, adding them into the mass of broken glass from the Prosecco bottles and wine glasses.

Stumbling on, Jorik almost made it to the front door, but his legs became heavy and immobile, and he fell to the floor. Gramps' rugby tackle would have earned him the highest respect from England's national team had they had the pleasure of seeing it. Marge was now sitting on Joric, high-fiving Gramps at the same time.

Moments later Inspector Grabham stepped through into the hall, saying, 'Couldn't get through, that damn table was in the way, and there are shards of broken glass and champagne everywhere. Sorry, but while the painting is OK, the thief got away.'

'No he didn't, Inspector,' called Marge from outside. 'Honestly, do we always have to do your job for you?'

The Inspector was very embarrassed, but had nothing but praise for everyone when he realized what had taken place. Jorik was quickly cuffed and he and his mate were lead away. Jo and Fred were watching carefully as the two prisoners passed by.

'But... they're... the wrong...,' blurted out Fred, 'it... was JJJa...'

'What did you say?' said the Inspector, turning to Fred. 'There was no-one else. OK I was sceptical about the whole operation, but I have to admit that you were right and I was wrong. I don't often eat humble pie, so, well done. We finally have the Scotney thieves. The Chief Constable should be congratulated for, well, everything.'

Jo made a move to enter the study, but her route was barred by a burly policeman. 'Sorry,' said Inspector Grabham, 'but we need to take photos and gather forensic evidence. You should go home and rest up after all the excitement. We've got the culprits. We've no idea how those two got in there, but at least we've grabbed them.'

'But, but...' stuttered Jo.

'Don't argue with me, young lady, we know what we are doing. Now, all of you go home, you were a great help, but it's all over.'

Gran tried to intervene, 'You don't understand, Inspector, you need to listen to these kids otherwise...'

The Inspector gave her a stern stare and said, 'That's quite enough, Madame, it's getting late, we can do everything from here, now please, take these kids home, thank you!'

'But the painting,' pointed out Fred, 'it's ours, and we'd like it back, the frame cost us a small fortune.'

The Inspector said, 'You'll get it back tomorrow, go home.'

'Wait, I've got to find my specs,' said Sally. 'They were thrown off and trodden on by that idiot. I'm as blind as a bat without them.'

'Let me help,' added Fred, 'though whether we'll find them amongst all this broken glass, I very much doubt.'

Fred was crouching down, peering everywhere, reluctant to kneel amongst the glass fragments and Prosecco puddles. 'I'm sorry, Sally, this is hopeless. I can't find anything. You'll have to buy a new pair.'

'Let me see,' responded Sally, looking closely at the floor. 'Ah, I thought so, here they are, well, at least the crushed remains. That guy really did have big feet didn't he?'

'But how can you see all those tiny bits and pieces, when I can't and I've got perfect eyesight?' asked Fred, somewhat astounded.

Sally stood up, looked left, then right, and spotted Bill. She saw him more clearly than she ever had before and peered straight into his eyes. 'Bill, you really are better looking than I remember, almost handsome. That spin I had seems to have completely corrected my eyesight. Perhaps every cloud does have a silver lining.'

'Wow,' said Bill, staring into her eyes and somewhat lost for words, 'without your glasses you look fantas...'

Fred coughed. He hated to spoil their moment. 'Come on you two, time to get everything packed away and tidied up.'

'Oh, my plane,' exclaimed Bill. He dashed outside with his pals in hot pursuit. His plane was still circling around the house, so he sent a text to turn off the camera, picked up his transmitter and brought the plane into a perfect landing. Bill looked at his phone. It was full of photos gathered from the circling aircraft. One was particularly interesting. It showed a shadowy figure climbing down the wall in the quarry carrying a large object under his arm.

'Look at this,' said Bill. He passed his phone around. 'Guess who this is? Look, what do you imagine he might be carrying?'

'It can only be one person, Jake,' said Fred, 'The inspector said nothing was missing, yet that looks just the right shape for our painting. What's going on? Where is Puss-Puss, we need to chat.'

Puss-Puss was saying goodbye to her doggy friends outside. As they padded off with Sandra, she received the "togethering" request to reveal all. Shortly after, Jo and the others brought Abby up to date with the latest findings. Things had not gone entirely to plan since Jake had escaped once more. Still, Abby had a brilliant story to tell her readers the following morning. She agreed to enhance the ending to further irritate Jake and rub salt into his wounds.

Ignoring the Inspector's instructions to go home, they helped tidy the place up, sweeping the broken glass away and mopping up the last dregs of Prosecco from the floor. Mrs. Pennymore was utterly confused about the awful ending to the evening. It was such a disappointment after what was supposed to be one of the most high-profile evenings she'd been involved with at Scotney. She perked up when Marge handed over two intact bottles of Prosecco and was even more delighted that Abby was planning to put her picture in the Daily Post the next day. The dogs climbed into the back of Sam's truck, each ready for their promised banquet back at Jo's grandparent's house before being led home.

Jo called over to the others, and they huddled together well away from the twitching ears of the police. 'Is everything set for this evening?' she asked them.

'It certainly is,' replied Marge. 'The response was fantastic, so many friends wanted to help and join in the fun. Our CoCoNuts membership has soared over the last day or so. Everyone is ready, and they know their allotted tasks. They are raring to go despite the dangers. Your plan is just brilliant! I really don't know how you kids come up with such great ideas. We won't let you down.'

'We have some last minute calls to make to people we know in the police force,' added Gran, 'so there is absolutely no way they can avoid any involvement in the drug bust. This Inspector Grumpy, sorry Grabham, is going to be really upset when he realizes how much more work he still has to do tonight.'

'I don't know how my editor is going to feel about me hogging the front page with two stories tomorrow,' laughed Abby.

'Inspector? They're going. The kids, and the rest of them, the APEs. They've all been whispering over there. They purposely moved away so we couldn't hear what they were saying and they're laughing about something. I don't like it,' mused one of his men.

'Hmmm, it does seem fishy. We weren't able to identify these thieves with all our resources, and they've grabbed them in less than an hour. It was a nonsensical plan that worked perfectly, highly suspicious. Things never ever work out this well in real life. Something else is going on here, and I don't like it one little bit. Four young kids, an organization called "APE" and sniffer dogs that have no reputation for smelling. It's like something out of a movie. We need to follow these guys closely. There's more to this than meets the eye and I don't like secrets, one little bit. Still, I suppose the Chief Constable will be a happy bunny, that's something.'

***

Meanwhile, Jake had reached the quarry exit and was climbing down the wall. He'd heard the drone pass overhead and looked up, no longer caring if he'd been seen or not. Though he was sorry to have deserted Jorik and his mate, they'd known the risks. He crept back the way he'd come and out into the middle of Kilndown Forest. The painting was getting incredibly heavy and his arms were nearly dropping off when he finally arrived back at his Porsche which he'd left it in the Hop Pickers Arms pub car park. Placing the work of art in the boot, he fought off the desperate temptation to nip inside for a quick and much-needed pint.

Once home, he propped the painting up against the wall on a table near the desk in his office, poured himself a delicious malt whiskey and pondered the removal of the brown wrapping paper, salivating as he imagined his £3M reward. This would kick his jittery sponsors into touch. Taking a pair of scissors from his desk, Jake smiled in anticipation. What a wonderful moment this was. He turned the painting around to face the wall, not wanting to damage it, and carefully made two diagonal slits along the brown paper at the rear of the frame. He lifted the painting up and gently let the brown paper fall off. Then he closed his eyes and turned the masterpiece around before opening his eyes once more.

He looked, blinked, looked away, blinked again, and then refocused. His brain could not process what his eyes were telling him. He was surprised and confused. It was the wrong painting. He had somehow brought his own fake picture back. How on earth...? But no, he had been there, he had seen it happen. He had put his own fake painting on the easel after Jorik has removed the real one. He had then turned around and grabbed the masterpiece from Jorik.

He re-played the whole thing through his mind. Then he'd run. There was no way the picture could have been switched back. He had never relinquished it. He looked again, more carefully this time. The frame was similar. It was the same picture as the one he'd printed off earlier, but was it? He reached out and touched it. No, it was better, had stronger definition, thicker, high-quality paper. He grabbed it and ripped it off. He was about to crunch it up and throw it in the bin in a fit of anger when he saw words printed on the back.

'We know who you are. We know what you are up to. We know about everything. We are coming to get you!'

'What on earth?' muttered Jake, astonished. 'How could the police have known? Perhaps my spy on the inside has been turned. No, impossible, I know too much about him, the blackmail is too powerful. Plus, the police would never leave a message like that. But then where did it come from, and who would write it?'

He pondered, racking his brain. Ever so slowly it dawned on him as he recounted the events of the day. 'The drone, of course, it had to be that damn kid and his pesky mates, it was those four meddling brats again! But how? How did they know? How did they find out? They must be reading my mind, but how? There must be a logical answer. I really am gonna kill those kids and their entire families.'

As he grabbed for a whisky bottle, his brain cells started to vibrate, getting increasingly agitated. The problems were mounting up, and more quickly than he thought feasible. He did not like problems unless he was causing them. He rarely had a problem he could not solve, one way or another. He'd figure out an answer, he always did. He had to get his plan back on track. He'd been devising it for so long there was no way he was not going to succeed.

Working his way through glass after glass of whisky, a solution started to materialise, with each idea modifying itself and improving to produce a better, nastier, more evil plan. As he reached the end of the bottle, he reached for the next, and the lights gradually dimmed. The sparks went out as he fell headlong into a whisky-fuelled sleep. 'Hopefully... this is all just a... dream, an appalling... dream, tomorrow will be... good, tomorrow will bring me £3M...' His eyelids fluttered and closed, and his own personal nightmare began.

Chapter 37

Front Page Disaster

Jake was surrounded by snow, with lightning flashing down in front of his closed eyelids. Why he was lying outside in his pyjamas on cold, sodden grass, half buried in snow, he could not understand. A squirrel was trying to prise open his left eyelid, looking for life, while a blackbird sang into his right ear, both trying to bring life back into his seemingly dead body. With one eyelid open, he saw what looked like a fox trying to brush the snow off him with its tale.

'Whaaaat is it?' mumbled Jake in a groggy almost delirious state.

But he was not outside, nor was he cold or wet in his pyjamas. There was no squirrel and no blackbird, just Grant poking him in the eye, and Gertrude shouting in his ear and thumping his back. There were no other creatures just his own irritating offspring who ran off as soon as they saw him slowly re-enter the land of the living.

Craning his neck, he realized he was lying on the couch in his study in the clothes he'd had on yesterday. Then he remembered yesterday's turn of events. Gingerly, head thumping, he looked at the floor. There was his newly acquired masterpiece, now slightly crumpled. He'd expected to hear the sound of gold coins falling noisily into his piggy bank. Alas, such hopes were now futile and his mood immediately changed from bad to worse.

Peeking back through the door of the study, Gertude called, 'Jake?' She never called him Dad, never had, never would. 'You said you'd come with us to the Common today. You know, it's the practice for the music festival competition tomorrow, we're performing, you know, our rock group, "The Blast".'

'Yeah, you promised,' whined Grant, his head also appearing around the door. 'There's gonna be well over thirty bands playin', you promised, you said we'd win, get the trophy, you know, riggin' the votin' like you always do. We're being picked up in ten minutes by Zolt in his clapped-out camper van. We're already late, so he's gonna collect all our equipment and the other band members too.'

'Oh, damn,' muttered Jake, still staring at the forgery. 'You'll have to go on your own. I've got bigger fish to fry, need to get on with it right away. I've got serious planning to do.'

'That's not fair, you never keep your promises, we'd be better off without you, we hate you,' whined Gertrude, 'and what you doin' buyin' paintings? You know nuffink about 'em, and that one's 'orrible anyway, you're out of you mind. We're going.' Jake ignored them, already thinking about the tasks ahead.

Twenty minutes later Jake was in the kitchen after having a hot and cold shower hoping to shake out the cotton wool proliferating inside his head. He was eating the biggest full English breakfast he'd ever had, knowing his body needed every calorie to rejuvenate his energy flows. He was on his fifth sausage, covered in ketchup, when his wife pushed the Daily Post under his nose. Suddenly, bits of chewed sausage and egg splattered all over the wall ten feet away. Seeing the news, he thought he was dying a second time.

Thieves Captured in Outrageous Sting
[Abby Newsome]

Yesterday evening a joint operation by the police and the private security firm "Art Protection Engine" (APE) prevented a fiendishly clever theft of a recently discovered Constable painting being auctioned at Scotney Castle. Due to a spate of recent thefts from Scotney, a fake was planted one hour before the actual auction hoping to entice the thieves into action.

Despite a thorough search of the house and gardens, the thieves had managed to hide inside the chimney in the dining room, well out of reach of the sniffer dogs, before the Mansion closed its doors for the day. The National Trust House Manager, Mrs. Pennymore, was dismayed at how her stringent control of visitor arrivals and departures had gone awry on this occasion.

The thieves were caught red handed having been surprised by the house cat, Puss-Puss. If it had not been for the courage of several APE employees, all members of the CoCoNuts organization, one of the villains might have escaped as he tried to dash through the entrance hall, smashing Champagne bottles and wine glasses in his desperate attempt to avoid capture.

The police would like to offer their sincere thanks to APE for the part they played in the operation, especially Gramps for his rugby tackle on the villain and Marge for detaining him.

Mrs. Pennymore offered high praise for the four young teenagers who came up with the plan. She said, 'While this was an audacious scheme, devised and executed brilliantly by these fantastic young people, it was a frightening and stressful ordeal, and the outcome could easily have been detrimental to the house itself. All in all, it was a very mischievous prank indeed and one that should never be repeated again, not in my Scotney Castle.'

The auction was, however, a great success and was completed one hour later when the painting finally sold for £10M to a buyer who wishes to remain anonymous.

Jake just could not believe his eyes. Time and again he had to shake his head to regain focus. 'What the... what, what, what...?' were the only words his voice box and lips were able to frame.

He simply could not understand it. He'd heard the cars arrive. He'd listened to the chat and laughter. He'd heard the clinking of Champagne glasses. Everything was perfect, just as he had imagined, just as he had expected. But somehow he'd been conned, duped. The whole thing was an immensely clever sting operation.

When he looked at the newspaper photos, he was horrified. The smiling faces of the four kids he hated most in the whole world were there. They had cooked the whole thing up. That ugly old guy, Gramps was there too. Then he saw the picture of that horrible woman, Marge. When he saw the vineyard owner Sam, he knew. They were trying to put him out of business, permanently.

'No one challenges me,' he said to himself, spitting out yet more of his breakfast. 'No one beats me or spoils my plans. How dare they? They've had it now.' A surge of energy ripped through his body, completely revitalising him. There was no way he was going to lose this epic battle with his enemies, those four meddling kids.

Jake was momentarily in another world. His wife was keen to see what had attracted Jake's attention in the newspaper. Courageously she reached over and was about to borrow it when Jake snatched it away. He had just seen the small headline further down.

Local Drug Cartel Curtailed
[Abby Newsome]

Last night, over 300 members of the Community Courage group of Tunbridge Wells, known as the CoCoNuts, smashed a local drug cartel that had been causing growing concern and disruption in Tunbridge Wells over the last eighteen months.

Members of the group, mainly pensioners, came out in force to the pubs and clubs of the town. These included several hotspots where little progress had been made by the police in curtailing the highly lucrative business. The CoCoNuts interrupted and blocked transactions that were taking place, forcing the drug dealers to leave many premises empty handed.

Clubs and bars tried to prevent the pensioners from entering their premises, worried about overcrowding and upheaval for regular customers. But, the sheer force of numbers overwhelmed bouncers who were left mentally if not physically scarred.

Every single bar order taken was for either orange squash or tap water causing profit margins to plummet.

As the drug dealers were forced to flee for more lucrative locations, the police were waiting. In what was a well-coordinated operation, the police made over forty arrests and the dealers are now being interrogated to give their supplier details.

The CoCoNuts have been highly praised by the police, council officials and by hospital staff as A&E numbers have tumbled.

'This is a disaster!!!' yelled Jake. 'Those damn women, those damn pensioners! I bet it was her, Marge, that horrible woman I argued with outside Carluccio's. She's behind all of this. She's the ring leader of the CoCoNuts. She ought to be arrested herself. Her and those ghastly people opposing the cinema site funding. They're all in it together. Probably with those damn kids too. They started it, they're at the heart of this fiasco, and whoever is funding them.'

His wife, who had seen Jake's tantrums before, said, 'Calm down Jake, take it easy, these problems are never as bad as you make out.'

'You stupid woman,' he snapped, 'you've no idea.' With that, he chucked his breakfast on the floor and stormed back to his office.

Back at his desk, he logged on to his communications website, mushroomhuntingforidiotchefs.com. This was a front, a website with a £1000 per annum registration fee that was intended to put anyone off from subscribing (for those undeterred by the site's ridiculous name). The site was, of course, hosted back in Russia, but the communication links were complex, travelling umpteen times around the world through many countries and many other websites also doing anything but what their URLs pretended.

The site had at least a hundred different types of mushroom, one for each drug dealer who had to give a daily sales figure. Dealers who failed to comply by 6am were at risk of being removed, in more ways than one. This had never happened before, until now.

Jake was horrified to see that at least forty of his contacts had failed to enter data that morning. At this point he knew he was in trouble, not because he might be identified – he worked through distributors, so none of the dealers knew him – but he would now have to replace these with new contacts. This would require time and effort, neither of which he could afford right now. He would have to increase his sales volume in London as a temporary measure.

Jake grabbed his secure phone and dialled his man in the police. 'Why the hell didn't you tell me what was going on last night? You've nearly ruined me, you damn idiot.'

'I called you several times, but you didn't answer. Where were you? You vanish off the planet then it's too late to do anything. Don't blame me. At least you stayed clear of Scotney, so, well done.'

Jake was fuming. He hung up and dialled Zolt's number. No answer. He tried again but still no reply. He was getting angry. When Zolt finally rang back, he let rip. 'Where have you been you imbecile? I told you to always be at the end of a phone. Have you seen today's press? Why didn't you say anything? You're useless.'

'Er, sorry Guv, I've just dropped off your lovely kids, Grant and Gertrude, and their buddies, and their music kit, to the Common for their rehearsals. They're brilliant, you know, they'll probably win.'

'How many times have I told you not to mollycoddle those dreadful teenagers of mine. They can carry their own guitars and amps in future, I don't care how heavy it all is. Of course they're gonna win, they can't lose, I've seen to that, as I always do. Now get your backside down to our bar in the Pantiles, immediately. Bring Zonk and Grilch with you. We have serious aggravation to cause.'

Chapter 38

Confession

Meanwhile, Jo and her three friends were heading towards the Common, keen to see the stage being set up and the sound system checks for the music event the following day.

'Have your grandparents recovered from yesterday's fun and games at Scotney?' asked Sally.

'Oh, they loved it,' replied Jo, 'and the report in the Daily Post this morning.'

'And the drug bust was incredible too. Pity we weren't allowed to join in after all our hard work planning it,' said Fred.

'They're all meeting up in the Pantiles for a celebratory coffee and cake later this morning,' said Jo. 'Sam and Marge are joining them too, and they'll try and drag Ben away from his bookshop if they can. Even Anna and Abby are hoping to be there. We should amble down there later too, especially if there's free cake on offer.'

'I don't believe it,' said Fred, wincing, 'what a dreadful noise. It can only be "The Blast". I wouldn't want to be any closer.'

'Look, there's a stall going up over there? The banner says "Vera's Veggie Delights". Let's go and investigate,' said Fred.

'Hi Vera, can we lend a hand putting the stall up?' asked Jo.

'Oh, hi kids. Well, there's not much more to do. If you'd like to set up my seating area outside, I can finish off the inside.'

They quickly set up several tables, organized the seating and that's when Jo received her message.

(O) Hi guys, you need to know that Jake has been giving his gang a real talking to, back in the Pantiles. You'd better listen to this. The entire conversation of Jake and his men has been remembered and recorded by all the birds, animals and thousands of insects nearby, each taking a tiny section that they won't forget. Jake has hardly stopped ranting for nearly ten minutes. The creatures are ready for the

replay, all knowing their precise position in the sequence. Are you ready? You'll see it in your mind's eye. Watch and listen carefully.

The replay began, Jake's voice coming through loud and clear.

'You useless idiots have been a fat lot of help to me lately. You think you're hard, only too willing to hand out terrible physical punishments. You think you're smart, capable of out-thinking anyone, except me of course. Well, I've never ever come across such a useless group of pathetic wimps in all my life. Those four pesky kids continue to put a spanner into the works of everything I do, and they are all still alive and breathing. You have failed me miserably. Think I'm being unfair? Well let's go over recent events a bit more carefully, shall we?

It all started when we stole those three planes - well done, that's the one simple task you've completed, though actually, my kids did that. We just about managed to steal the cash machines and, fair play, that was good, clever, a rare moment of satisfaction.

Since then, all you've done is to let me down. Those horrible kids and the girl with the shocking red hair and evil green eyes have...'

Jo and her friends listened carefully as Jake rambled his way through all the upsets that had confronted him, finally reaching the end.

'..... So now to the latest fiasco with those damn CoCoNuts again. They somehow cottoned on to our drug dealing in the town and I've lost 50% of my dealers, in just one night. Tell me how this has been allowed to happen? Who blew the whistle? You've been doing the deliveries, so clearly one of you is to blame. I've a good mind to bury you all in concrete! If I had any building projects on the go, I would. So, tell me how are you going to rectify this abysmal state of affairs?'

'Well,' replied Zolt, nodding and agreeing with Zonk and Grilch, 'we all have our illegal firearms and when we see those four revolting kids, we're gonna obliterate 'em, shoot 'em dead and be done with it.'

'Perfect,' replied Jake. 'But don't shoot that lanky-haired Bill just yet. We need his latest technology. It was there at Scotney yesterday, circling overhead. My kids missed it when they raided his house. They're still so damn useless. By all means rough Bill up until he tells us what we need to know, but we need him in one piece for now.'

As the replay ended, Jo and her friends continued their own rapid "togethering" conversation.

'Jeeez, I don't like the sound of that one little bit,' exclaimed Fred.

'Tell me about it,' replied Bill. *'If only we could somehow transpose that recorded conversation onto a DVD, then the police would arrest Jake and his gang, problem solved.'*

'But that's not very likely, is it? Besides, you're safe for now, they don't intend to bump you off yet, just a bit of "roughing up", whatever that means, sounds pleasant huh?' said Sally, wryly.

'Ha ha, don't worry though, you'll be quite safe as you can all line up behind me, see, problem solved,' Bill joked.

Jo interrupted, *'Come on you two, please try and be serious for once. So, Jake and his gang are down in the Pantiles and I'm worried as that's where Gramps and the others are going to celebrate last night's successful operations. I think I'll set up a little protection just in case. In the meantime we'd better tune back into Vera.'*

'Vera, we're on our way. See you tomorrow,' called Jo.

'OK, and thanks for that. Good luck with the music festival. I know you are a million times better than the group playing now, it's painful to the ears. Do come back again tomorrow, I'm sure you boys will enjoy my recipes too.'

As they moved away, two policemen strolled into view pausing briefly to watch Vera struggling to adjust her advertising banner.

(O) It's us again Jo. Just thought you ought to know that two policemen have been tracking you since you left home. They were at Scotney with you yesterday.

'We got that message too,' said Fred. 'Don't look round. We need to find out why they're following us and not Jake.'

At that moment the "The Blast" session ended and the four of them strolled nonchalantly past the practice area heading for the rocks.

Grant looked up and saw them as he was packing his guitar away. 'Bloody hell, it's them, those meddling excuses for teenagers, the ones our dad hates, and us too. Quick Gertrude, pack your stuff up and let's follow 'em and shake 'em up before tomorrow's concert. We can leave our stuff here, no-one's stupid enough to steal from us. I'll phone Jake, and tell 'im we're tracking the ghastly girl and her ugly mates.'

Minutes later, Sally, Fred, Bill, and Jo were standing on the top of Wellington Rocks, enjoying the view. They could see Grant and

Gertrude rushing towards them, Grant desperately trying to chat on the phone. They had both picked up stones, ready for a fight, and entirely unaware of the two policemen closing in behind them. Grant launched a pathetic throw and the stone merely bounced off the lower rocks. Gertrude made a far better shot, her stone whistling past Sally's ear.

'Oi, stop that you hooligans!' yelled the first policeman, after blowing his whistle.

Jake's offspring turned around, surprised to see the police so close, as their ammunition was man-handled away from them.

'We weren't doin' nuffink, honest guv, just playin' games, they're school buddies of ours, feeble and useless as kittens, just a bit of target practice, need to toughen 'em up,' said Grant trying to wriggle free.

'It looked pretty vicious to us. We're going to arrest you for disturbing the peace if those four youngsters make a complaint.'

The two policemen looked up, but there was not a soul to be seen. The surface of the topmost rock, where Jo and her team had been standing, had momentarily dissolved and they were well on their way down the banister in the centre of the magnificent cavern underneath.

'Well, they ain't complained, Officer, they just vanished into thin air,' said Gertrude, full of ego and contempt. 'Think you'd better let us go. You ain't got a leg to stand on.'

Sadly she was right on this occasion. She and her brother dashed off, with Grant attempting another urgent call to his dad. 'It's no good Jake, the police interrupted us just as we were about to finish 'em geezers off for good. Now they've done their vanishing trick again. Don't you start on me, you never turned up to hear our practice session, you're the useless one. Don't shout. I hear you. We'll have a final search up 'ere, if we have to. You don't need to come. Then we're gonna walk down to the Pantiles and join you. We want compensation. We'll break a few windows and key a few cars on the way, don't you worry, that's the one thing you did train us for. You'd better be here tomorrow though, the concert is gonna be great. It's absolutely your last chance!'

Chapter 39

Stalling for Time

Back in the Pantiles, Jake, Zolt, Zonk and Grilch sat down once more at their table. 'No need to gulp your beers down guys,' said Jake. 'That was Grant. The damn police have got in the way again and allowed those creepy kids to escape once more. Can you believe it?'

As they adjusted their seats, Jake's frown turned into a smile. 'I always say there's a golden shadow to every black cloud. Look who's arriving at the next café. It's those grandparents of that ugly girl with the flamin' red hair, the vineyard owner, and that wicked woman Marge. They were all at Scotney last night, their pictures are in today's local rag. We should bump 'em all off, including the four pesky kids, but we need the skinny one, Bill, alive.'

Back on the Common, the police officer and his mate circled the rocks then called in. 'Sorry Inspector Grabham, we lost them. They escaped into the trees while we were sorting out another altercation.'

'How can you possibly lose four kids? You're no better than admin clerks. You obviously need more training, so meet me in the Pantiles and you can sort out any hooligans there.

After Jake's earlier rant, his gang should have been shaking in their boots, but his string of ugly words just floated past them while they each planned how to recover their evil reputations. They were now imagining the permanent removal of Jo's trouble making support group. Jake finally lost his patience. 'Let's do it!'

As Jake and his gang leapt to their feet they were met by a rush of wasps and bluebottles, triggered by Jo's urgent request for protection insurance. Unfortunately, Zolt had a cigarette lighter in his pocket and started wafting the flame around. The wasps and bluebottles had to fly off but not before stinging Grilch painfully on the neck.

The next line of protection, the pigeons, were already airborne and lined up but had to abort their flight plan at the last minute. Jake had subconsciously detected their dive bomb positioning and ushered his men back under the safety of the column-lined walkway.

Just as Anna and Abby arrived and sat down to chat, the four familiar characters in black approached. Sam flinched as he saw them out of the corner of his eye. Gramps, Gran, and Marge looked up, any brave thoughts of being CoCoNuts quickly drained away.

'What a pleasant little gathering. Not so happy now, are we?' sneered Jake. 'Over there, the lot of you, down the steps to the kitchenware shop. Now, move further to the right, go on, under the balcony of the old jewellery shop. Do it.' Jake waved his gun at them then hastily put it back inside his jacket.

Jake was beginning to show a smidgen of intelligence. He had given himself four avenues of escape; back past the Chalybeate spring, into the Corn Exchange, back out past the boule court, or out by the side of the Brasserie restaurant to the main road.

'So, guys,' said Jake, 'I'll make this absolutely clear, in words of one syllable, since some of you are pathetic pensioners. Tell me what I need to know or it's goodbye to the Pantiles forever. First, where are your ghastly kids? Second, who is funding them? Thirdly, which of you is masterminding everything?'

Jake's voice rose. 'Is it you, loud mouth Marge? Speak up, I haven't got all day. Or maybe it's you, Granny. You might be cleverer than you look though I doubt it. What's under that grey hair I wonder? Let's have a look. Give me the knife Zonk.'

Words suddenly filled Gran's head, and her eyes looked left then right searching for the source.

(O) It's OK Gran, help is on the way. String them along for as long as you can. Make them angry too if possible.

Gran could not believe she was hearing from the Ancients. Suddenly her mouth began to move. 'It's true. I am the boss. I'm Gran, not Granny, so use my proper title in future. I have masterminded everything and provided the financial muscle from the £10M I won on the lottery last year.'

Gramps and Marge looked at Gran with a mixture of incredulity and awe. She was such a brave person.

'Gramps,' said Gran, *'I've been told to prolong this as long as possible, make them agitated and annoyed. I'm doing the best I can.'*

Jake roared with laughter. 'What absolute nonsense. You must think I'm a real idiot trying to feed me lines like that.'

Marge took over. 'Gran is only trying to save us. If she'd actually won the lottery you don't seriously believe she'd still be living in Tunbridge Wells, do you? She would have moved to the South of France, or Greece, or sunny Australia. Though actually, maybe just Sandbanks in Dorset – it is so beautiful down there, gorgeous sandy beaches, and it is always sunny, only ever rains at the night, and...'

'Shut up you stupid woman,' said Jake, spitting everywhere. 'I've had enough of your drivel, always poking your nose in where it doesn't belong. I hate you as much as those stinky kids.'

'Truth is, I feel sorry for you,' replied Marge. 'You need to open your eyes. I'm the boss of this group. We have been targeting your miserable gang for weeks now. We will bring you down, you know that. I gave Bill the money for his drones because he is destined to become one of the greatest engineers and inventors the world has ever seen. I inherited millions from my father who made his money by marketing those high quality black leather jackets you're all currently wearing, though I've seen them on far better bodies...'

'Bumptious and still talking the hind legs off a donkey,' replied Jake. 'Well, not sure you'll be doing much "bringing down" from here on, Mrs so-called "Big Boss". You've thrown away your last chance, like a candle in the wind, never knowing who to...'

Gramps was acutely aware that their situation was deteriorating. He stepped forward, bringing his face close to Jake's nose. 'Lovely poetic phrasing, Jake. That's the only thing you're any good at, although it sounded vaguely familiar, and like everything you do, it was stolen from someone else. The truth is, Jake, I am the real boss, the true brains behind everything. The kids have been acting, trying to protect me. Do you really think I ended up in hospital after your two children thought they'd knocked me down on their bikes? I had to practically jump in front of them. I helped our team vanish up on the Common when you kidnapped my daughter, Jo's mother. I was the policeman at the vineyard when we conned you out of your down payment and gave the counterfeit notes to the charity shop. I was behind the statue in the library at Scotney, and I switched the painting when your mate Jorik briefly put it down to get a better grip. I funded brilliant Bill and his drone development, drawing on my early years as a computer scientist...'

'You bumbling old fool,' replied Jake, 'you don't honestly expect me to believe such drivel do you? I know my kids dumped you into the road and you were lucky not to die in the hospital. Who knows how you survived that one. There was no statue in the library at Scotney. Your whole story is a pack of creative lies. So...'

'Jake,' interrupted Gramps, 'you don't want to do this. If I press this button on my car key holder, two things will happen. First, a laser with four beams will flash out and blind you all, it's my latest invention. Secondly, our four young friends will be here in less than a second and you and your pathetic excuse for a gang will be obliterated. Right, so you want the horrible painful truth. Our young friends really are the brains and the muscle behind all the unbelievable embarrassments that have surrounded you. How does it feel, Jake, to know you've been out-smarted and humiliated by four young teenagers? You'll never live it down. Wave the white flag now, Jake. Give in. It will be better for you that way, believe me.'

'Oh Gramps,' laughed Jake, 'you just get better and better. Go on, do your worst. Press that button on your car key holder and let's see what happens. A four-pronged laser attack? Pigs might fly! You're a crazy nonsensical crackpot. My guess is that a key will simply jump out of the end, but go on, let's watch it happen.'

Jake nodded to Grilch, Zolt and Zonk. All four of them pulled out their guns, pointing them at Sam, Marge, Gran, Gramps, Anna, and Abby. They took a step backwards, improving their aim.

'Press the button **now** Gramps,' said Jake with a broad, crazy smile, as if possessed. 'Go on, **do it!**'

Gramps pointed his laser car key invention at Jake. Then he silently screamed, *'Heeeeellllpppppppp.'* 'I'm going to count down from five. You were warned. I've told you what will happen. I do hope you've all got adequate health insurance, you're gonna need every penny of it. Five... Four.... Thrree..... Twwwooo.......' The words and the pauses between the numbers were getting longer and longer. Gramps did not quite know why. 'Ooooonnnneee...... Zzzzeeeerrrrooooooo.......' With that, Gramps pressed the button.

Chapter 40

Back in Time

The key snapped out of its holder. All was quiet for a second or two. Everyone was focused on the car key held out in Gramps' hand. They waited for the explosion of blinding searing light, not a soul daring to blink. Jake looked at Gramps, Gramps looked at Jake. They both looked down at the key. No laser light flashed, nothing ripped through the eyes of the attackers. Not a flicker. Just a key.

Jake's expression changed as he slowly shook his head and sneered, 'What a fool you are.' Zolt, Zonk, and Grilch grinned, and all four of them began to squeeze the triggers of their guns.

At that moment, the world seemed to enter a trance, as if the earth's rotation was slowing to a standstill. There were just a few people around, at the far end of the Pantiles. To Gramps and the others, they appeared completely frozen, some walkers poised on one leg, others sporting strange facial expressions, captured mid-sentence, mid-word. Time stood still. Whether this actually took place is hard to tell. Einstein would have been shocked to realize his famous formula had failed to predict the possibility of such a reality.

***

Meanwhile back in the cavern, Jo and her friends slid off the central helter-skelter and began to make their way to the exit point but were suddenly brought to an abrupt stop. In front of them a wide stretch of wall spanning several archways and their enclosed panels began to flicker and glow, as did the floor beneath their feet. Seconds later a life-size view of the Pantiles appeared before them as if they had somehow been transported outside into the real world. Then the cavern floor seemed to change and became a pavement of stone slabs, just like the real thing. And, although they were standing motionless, their feet started to slide across the pavement as they were drawn along to their favourite cafe. I was a strange feeling being bystanders. They could see themselves sitting and chatting as

Fred appeared, breathless, dashing to join them. The vision, if that's what it was, seemed to be a recording of that day a couple of weeks ago when Fred arrived late for their meeting in the Pantiles, when they were determined to keep tabs on Jake and his men.

Then something even more remarkable happened. As they watched, a figure from the next table rose up. It was the beautiful woman, the Ancient with the auburn red hair and green eyes. She began to move towards them, walking out from the image, the recording, or whatever it was they were watching. Sally tentatively tried to reach out, to test the air and the surroundings, but it was impossible to tell if this was a real person or just an incredible three-dimensional hologram.

Then, as the woman smiled and beckoned them to follow her, all the archways and panels around the outside edge of the cavern came to life, one after the other. Moments later the whole cavern, floor to ceiling, glowed and became not just a magnificent domed cinema screen but whole new virtual reality. The four teenagers were transported into another world and taken back to the days of long ago, twenty thousand years, maybe more. As they followed their guide, she spoke to them, constantly looking their way. In front of them, right in the centre, where the spiral staircase once stood, appeared a glorious image of towering rocks, flowers and hanging gardens.

(O) Hi Jo, Sally, Bill and Fred, we're sorry to bring you down here again while you were having fun checking out the Common ready for the music festival. It is a fantastic view from the top of Wellington Rocks. As you can see before you, the rocks were even better in our day, standing so high up, much like a massive pyramid of proud boulders, and dominating the surrounding countryside; a genuinely beautiful place. We used the shape and structure to plant gardens with flowers cascading down over rocky ledges, creating tiny terraces and hanging gardens. We would often gather here in the afternoons and evenings, facing the sun, chatting and singing with all our bird and animal friends. They are here now, so come with me, let's join them, they've been waiting to meet you.

What astonished Jo, Fred, Bill and Sally most was that all the animals and their Ancient friends seemed to know them by name, chatting as if they had known them forever. There was laughter and joy, and music with wonderful harmonies they had never heard before.

'I've just shaken hands with a beaver,' said Fred.

'And that breeze,' said Bill, 'it's so fresh, energising my lungs.'

'And the fragrance of all these magnificent flowers,' said Sally.

'And the bird song is so beautiful. Is this is how the world once was?' said Jo. 'It's simply magnificent.'

(O) Keen to make the most of such a beautiful spot, we made a pact amongst ourselves, agreeing that regardless of our important work, we would always spare at least one day to take this time out. We divided our days into periods of seven, and we called this very special day our sun-day, when the inner warmth generated by these wondrous happy moments would revitalise us and give us the determination and courage needed for our mission.

Alas, we see now that our "hanging gardens" are long gone, and many of our beautiful terraces are buried well below the vegetation that has sprung forth over the thousands of intervening years.

Now, after yesterday's successes, things are about to get quite dangerous. Jake won't take any of this lying down. You need to be prepared for severe acts of retaliation. Jake is angrier than you've ever seen him before. The recorded conversation with his gang was a testimony to that. This is good though as angry people don't think with their brains, they think with their, er, well, it doesn't matter, but the outcome is that they make terrible mistakes very quickly, without thinking through the repercussions and likely outcomes.

'Mmm,' muttered Fred, 'they're right, we've really got to be on the lookout now. We can't afford to take chances.'

'No, we can't,' agreed Jo. 'We need to take good care of Gramps, Gran, and the others. They're all targets now, high on Jake's hit list.'

(O) You have been superb at scuppering so many of Jake's devious money making schemes, just as we'd hoped and planned, but, unfortunately, he's now really out for your blood. Don't let that put you off or distract you from your objectives because we have

ways and means of providing rather unusual and surprising protection. There are many more aspects of "togethering" that will help you, though you may not be quite ready to fully understand them just yet. Don't forget that no matter what else they're doing, the animals and birds will always be on hand to intervene if necessary.

Now, guys, we brought you down here for a reason. It's time we told you a little more about us, where we've come from, what our beautiful island was like. We'll tell you about the mistakes we made, how we recovered and put things right. You need to know how we discovered the importance of the environment and nature, how we nearly ruined everything. We'll tell you about our technology too as you've only seen a tiny part of it so far. We'll also tell you about many more incredible and unbelievable aspects of "togethering", including how we first discovered it and how it never seems to stop evolving, providing dramatic and wonderful improvements to the lives of those it embraces.

'This is going to be fascinating,' said Fred. 'I can't wait to hear what they know about the universe and how light and gravity all work, not forgetting the tiny stuff, you know, the particles that make up matter and anti-matter, if there really is such a thing.'

'I'm keen to hear about their techy stuff,' said Bill. 'Did they have computers and drones and things like that?'

'I'd really like to hear far more about their arrival here,' said Sally, 'and how they lived in these beautiful caverns.'

'I want to know all about them,' smiled Jo, 'and what they've been doing for the past twenty thousand years. More importantly, where are they now? Why choose us, why me? And what happens next?'

(O) That's certainly a lot of questions. We will, of course, tell you everything in good time. Let's start by answering Sally, that's the easiest place to begin. Have a look at this.

Almost immediately the rocks and hanging gardens vanished and the cavern became a sea shore and another world appeared. Suddenly there they were, all four friends, side by side with the ancients, back in time, experiencing every moment of the Ancients' arrival.

They were physically on board the beautiful boats, chatting to the crew members as they drifted through the mist before entering the bright morning sunlight. Ahead of them, they could see a magnificent whale as it turned and drifted alongside. They each put a hand over the side to pat the whale affectionately, feeling its skin and showing sincere gratitude for all its hard work in bringing them safely to their destination. As their boat drifted onwards and ground gently on the beach, gangplanks rolled forward at the front making it easy for them and the crew members to reach the beach.

They marvelled at the sight of the sandy shore and began to wonder where it was that the boats of the Ancients had actually landed so long ago. Jo was convinced that it would have been near Rye on the south coast, somewhere between Winchelsea and Camber. Why she should think this she had no idea.

The departure of the whales and dolphins was a sad moment after being at sea together for so many weeks, but they suddenly found they were leading the singing of the Ancients and tapping their feet to the beat of the whales as they slapped their tails on the sea, saying their goodbyes. Watching the birds dance on the back of the whales made them all laugh too.

The arrival of the animals, fish, and butterflies, brought by the birds and eagles, was a remarkable moment of sheer pleasure, especially as they'd all dissolved into laughter, sharing some joke or other. The four friends found that tears were rolling down their faces they were laughing so much, though later they were unable to recall either the joke or the punch line.

They loved the miracle of the fish helping to float and push so many containers up the river. Again, Jo sensed for some reason it was the River Rother, though its size and direction had almost certainly changed many times over such a lengthy period. Just watching so many teams of animals pushing and lifting containers through trees and forests with such determination was a joy to behold, especially over the last few miles after leaving the assistance of the river behind. Once again, they seemed to be fully involved, helping to carry a large container, almost feeling the weight of it but finding new strength to make light of the task.

The cheerfulness of these people as they made their way to their new home was captivating, and their relationship with all the creatures was a memory they would never forget. The music and singing of the Ancients and the magnificent creatures at the end of the journey filled their hearts with joy. They knew those feelings would remain with them forever.

There were, of course, profoundly disturbing emotions as they relived the massive earthquake and eruptions that destroyed the Ancient's homeland and prematurely ended the lives of so many people and creatures. As the experience came to an end, they each took a deep breath, trying to process the many visions tumbling through their minds.

(O) Now, we would like to take you on a much longer journey. We will show you our lives before "togethering" and step forward through the centuries so you can see how we discovered and embraced "togethering" and shared it with all the people of our land. You see...

...Whoa, sorry to interrupt but we have an emergency! Jo, your grandparents and friends have just arrived at the Pantiles hoping to celebrate yesterday evening's successes over Jake. But they haven't noticed that Jake is close by. He is absolutely gunning for them. Go quickly now! They desperately need your help. There's not a second to lose.

Chapter 41

Face to Face

In an instant, the "togethering" session ended. Jo, Fred, Bill, and Sally rushed off faster than they'd ever run before. Somehow the long flight of steps from the cavern up to the bookshop felt like a downhill run. They were too focused on their mission to realize, let alone wonder, why the climb that should have taken nearly ten minutes was completed in only seconds. That the entryway and the secret entrance into the book shop opened automatically, they hardly noticed. If they'd had time to think about it, they might have come to the conclusion that Ancient engineering was to credit or that the magic of "togethering" was behind it once again.

As they dashed past the bookshelves into the shop itself, Jo grabbed a thick heavy book, and the others did too. Yet the reason for doing so seemed neither strange nor utterly ridiculous at the time.

As they zoomed through the shop, Jo yelled, 'Ben, we really need your help if you can spare a moment, the others are in trouble.'

Then they were flying through the doorway, out into the Pantiles, now a far more dangerous place than ever before. Without thinking, they each lobbed their books high into the air, stumbling as they did so but quickly regaining their balance and rushing on.

That's when they heard Gramps say, '... One.... Zero.......' and saw the car key leap out of its holder. At that moment, they might well have seen four fingers squeeze down on a trigger, but they did not as this was the real world and they did not have X-ray vision. They did not need such superhuman powers as they had something far greater, infinitely more valuable. They had "togethering".

Jake and his cronies were entirely focused, almost shaking with anticipation as they drew closer to wiping out the support team of their detested teenage enemies. They would not be distracted. They were killers, killers in black, after all. Little did they realize this focus was soon to be their undoing. Just when they needed a little flexibility in their lives, they did not have it. They should have looked up, but they did not. Gramps, on the other hand, could see what was about to happen out of his peripheral vision. Thankfully, Jake failed to notice the flicker of a smile appear on Gramps' face.

The four books, having risen to their highest point, were now on their way down, driven by gravity, gathering speed, and not entirely on their own. They had not been thrown in what you might call a perfect trajectory. After all, who stumbles at high speed out of a book shop doorway and achieves a perfect aim? The books were probably nearly thirty feet in the air, jettisoned there in an action similar to that of an ancient trebuchet. But, at their highest point, four rooks had appeared out of nowhere, with brilliant style and coordination.

They'd heard Gramps' cry of *'Heeellllppp,'* as had all the creatures nearby, and they were ready. Such in-depth critical pre-planning of every conceivable eventuality might be entirely unknown in the human world, but it was commonplace in the "togethering" world of Earth's animal kingdom. Each rook flew in like a rocket, pounced on a book and adjusted its direction and flight path, giving it an urgent shove, increasing its speed by a factor of ten.

The books were now homing in, precisely on target. The squeezed triggers finally reached their limit. Their hammers snapped shut, each striking the cap end of a bullet, just where the gunpowder was waiting to ignite and expand with maximum ferocity. Four explosions later and each bullet went speeding down its own short barrel aimed at one of four hearts. Anna would need a second shot from Zolt, Abby another from Jake. Alas for Jake and his evil cronies, they were about to suffer another huge embarrassment.

The books, now with vastly magnified momentum, landed precisely on their gun-barrel targets, instantly forcing them downwards. Three bullets finally escaped but ricocheted off the pavement sending sharp fragments of stone flicking onto the legs of the three men in black. A fourth bullet went right through Jake's left shoe narrowly missing his big toe but breaking a toenail so long it should have been chopped by a chiropodist long ago. His toe would be sore for several weeks as a valuable reminder of supreme folly.

Jake glanced down, a painful look piercing his eyes, perhaps more of a surprise than anything else. He looked up and across at Gramps. Gramps looked back at him, shrugged his shoulders and raised his eyebrows saying, 'I tried to warn you.'

Jake was about to raise his gun again when he heard a shout from behind, 'Jake, look, you want us? We're over here.'

Jake turned around and saw Jo and the others rushing off in different directions. 'There they are! Forget this lot, get those kids! Follow 'em, chase 'em, shoot 'em.'

Jake and his men set off in hot pursuit, dancing and limping slightly as they went. Ben shouted to Gramps and the others, trying to stop them from chasing after the crooks. He ushered them inside the Choco Shop for a cup of hot chocolate to quieten their nerves. Abby was frantically jotting down everything unfolding before her, though whether her readers would believe a word of the distressing and ugly confrontation, let alone the flying books, she had no idea.

Five minutes later Jo, Fred, Bill and Sally had given their chasers the slip. They had appeared supremely fit, disappearing like shadows in the night, leaving Jake and his gang wondering what they were up against. Jo and her friends regrouped and re-entered the Pantiles via the Corn Exchange, looking carefully in every direction. It was pointless to run away. That would only delay the inevitable. The problem had to be sorted, right now. They had achieved their objective of distracting Jake and saving the others.

Creeping up the steps and turning left past the bandstand, they stood silently in the centre of the tree-lined boule area. For the first time in several weeks, a few spots of rain could be felt. They looked up to see birds in all the trees and on all the buildings nearby. Yet strangely, there was not a sound to be heard. It was as if they were all holding their breath, just waiting.

Jake, Zolt, Zonk and Grilch re-entered the Pantiles at the other end by the Chalybeate Spring, outmanoeuvred and outsmarted once again. They walked on, two on the upper pavement, two on the lower, peering this way and that, searching, desperately trying to regain a vague sense of control. It did not take long for them to spot their teenage targets. Jake looked up to see a huge flock of starlings alight on a tree in front of him. He hated birds, and his ears failed to notify his brain that this time, bird song was entirely absent.

It was like an old western. The kids stood still, side by side, just a foot or two apart, their arms hanging loosely by their sides. The men in black approached, their guns now pointing in just one direction.

There was no-one else about as the earlier gunshots had frightened everyone away. Jake pointed his gun up into the trees, sending thousands of birds flying into the air with a pervasive squawking noise that, strangely, was vaguely familiar to Jo and the others, even though it was last heard nearly twenty thousand years ago.

Jake must have known the police would be on their way. Gunshots are unusual in this part of the world. Inspector Grabham had been joined by his two men, and they were there too, no more than fifty yards behind Jo and her pals.

Now, police are intelligent people on the whole, and they know all about rain clouds, a rare nugget of knowledge remaining with them from primary school days. There had to be a point where rain started, and rain ended. They might also have realized how peculiar it was to see only one small rain cloud, positioned directly overhead in front of them, set against an otherwise bright sunny blue sky. They were standing in the dry but ahead there appeared a somewhat blurry picture. Through a wall of mist, they could just about see the four teenagers they had lost contact with on the Common. They were worried about their safety, having been alerted to the previous gunshots, and moved towards them, cautiously.

Jake was confused too. Aware of a few drops of rain, he could not understand why his targets were slightly unclear, with dark shadows appearing further behind them. Unwilling to lose this opportunity, he did not dwell on. It was now or never. He'd never get a better chance. He and his three gang members lifted their guns and aimed directly at Jo and her friends.

Suddenly, from high above came a massive fluttering of wings as thousands of birds took up their positions. Jake and his men were briefly distracted. When they looked back, their targets had moved slightly to the side, just a foot or two and certainly no more. The dark shadows were now slightly larger than before. The rain ahead of them was heavier, blurring the outlines even more. It was like a flash flood, a wall of water, unfolding before their eyes. They adjusted their aim minutely, pressed the triggers and fired.

From high above, the cause of the sudden rain storm was evident. The cloud had a diameter of about 100 yards, possibly less. There was almost no wind, so the rain was falling vertically with no deflection. Amazingly, the birds had formed a cone-shaped funnel in the sky, flying in circles, wider at the top, narrower near the ground. They were flapping their wings as fast as they could, pushing the rain drops inwards. The smaller birds, robins, starlings and tits were in the top layers, thousands and thousands of them. Below that, in the middle tier, flew the middle-sized birds, mainly blackbirds, and pigeons, combining the raindrops and pushing them further towards the centre. Finally, in the lowest layer, closer to the ground, came the larger stronger birds. They were mainly magpies and rooks, flying in tighter circles still; enjoying every second of their high-speed task as they created a continuous downward flow of water. Only a few hundred birds were positioned in the very centre of the cone, making opposite movements, driving the water droplets outwards, ensuring that a central core was completely dry. All this avian motion had concentrated the rain into a circular curtain, no more than an inch thick, four yards in diameter, surrounding the teenagers.

Jake and his men were highly trained shooters, and they were spot on with their shots. Sadly for them, there had been just enough rain to act as a refraction device, as if looking at an object on the floor of a swimming pool, where the object is never quite where your eyes think it might be. Now, the police had moved closer behind the kids they had been following, completely ignorant as to what was taking place, their dark uniforms looking like shadows from a distance through the murky mist.

Once more the world seemed to decelerate, mirroring the slow motion effect perceived during times of high stress and great concentration. Jo, Fred, Bill, and Sally saw the bullets come bursting through the curtain of rain, scattering water droplets in all directions. They did not move, try as they might. Their eyes followed the bullets as they approached head on, drifting along in slow motion. Every bone in Jo's body was trembling, every muscle tensed, trying desperately to dissipate the rising panic.

Jo's first thought was that they were going to be hit, they were about to die. Her blue spark was preparing to pass its lifelong information on to much-loved friends and family, at least to all those in her "togethering" circle of trust. Yet, almost as quickly as the spark had arrived, it spluttered out. Jo knew then that she must have a guardian to be so incredibly lucky, maybe an angel, or perhaps something infinitely stronger. The bullets regained their normal speed as they continued on their journey, flashing between Jo and her pals, missing them entirely, even if only by the narrowest of margins.

Fred and Bill were finally on the move, jumping instinctively sideways to cover Jo and Sally and protect them. Their brave intentions were a natural reaction but clearly too late, delayed simply through lack of time. Even the birds above had stopped their frantic wing flapping motion, either frightened by the gunshots or perhaps aware that their work was done.

As the bullets passed by, the curtain of rain vanished altogether, the cloud passing over. Jo and her friends could now clearly see Jake and his murderous companions, their guns still pointing towards them. Jake and his gang could see Jo and her pals too, the two boys now standing directly in front of the girls. The kids heard screams from behind them and turned to see where they'd come from.

Their shock and horror were almost too great to witness. Although they had miraculously escaped the bullets, it looked as though the police standing some yards behind them had not been so fortunate. Without any thought for their own safety, completely oblivious to the risk of another round of shots, they turned to rush back as they watched the three police officers fall to the ground.

By now Jake and his guys could see what had happened. They lowered their guns. They had missed all four of their targets. How was that possible? Worse still, they had shot the policemen in broad daylight. As evil as they were, this was something they had never done before. 'NOooo, how did we do that?' yelled Jake, hardly able to believe his eyes. He did not like the police, but he had never been so stupid as to hurt them directly like this. 'Right guys, let's scarper and lie low for a while. No, wait, the kids, this could be our very last chance to put a stop to their meddling.'

Jake was confused, stay, and be caught, leave, and lose the targets he was desperate to finish off. 'This is it. Just one more shot. Come on guys, do your worst with these pesky kids and then go. Shoot!'

Chapter 42

Justice

As Jake's gang raised their guns one last time, Jo's animal friends sprang into action. As the guns moved, eight squirrels, four teams of two, leapt from the branches, and thousands of birds were already reaching the limits of their gravity-induced dive.

The squirrels got there first and they have incredibly sharp teeth, exercised through gnawing nuts all day long. Fingers wrapped around guns present a prime target for further honing. On this occasion, the skin was never going to last long as the first four squirrels pounced. To hear grown adults scream is not pleasant but from these four evil men, it was almost too good to be true.

Human ears are also a superb target for an eagle-eyed squirrel. Four more squirrels landed with the precision that NASA would have been proud of, each with their claws outstretched. The gunmen tried in vain to wrestle the squirrels away using their one remaining good hand, but the squirrels were not to be deterred. They had a job to do, and they did not do things by halves.

As four guns clattered to the ground, Jake and his buddies moved back a few steps, tearing at the tiny creatures in a desperate effort to rid themselves of the attacking monsters. Satisfied their work was done, the squirrels leapt away, back up into the trees for cover.

The boss squirrel, Squidge, sent a "togethering" message, *'We're all clear guys, over to you.'*

The reply, *'Message received and understood, we're on our way,'* was really unnecessary, just the polite thing to say.

By now, the birds had reached their terminal velocity. The weight of their bodies in their downward dive could increase no more due to the resistance of the air below them. Thousands of birds were soaring down from the sky, each accurately positioned along four perfectly aligned flight paths. They had one last manoeuvre to perform and closed in, resembling something that Jake had earlier sworn was an absolute impossibility. They swooped down around and under the trees in one of the most beautiful demonstrations nature has ever seen. Their targets could not have escaped even if they'd wanted to, assuming they had the slightest inkling of what was to come.

As each bird reached an exact pre-calculated delivery point, it unloaded a parting gift. Jake had only a few milliseconds to glance upwards. Only then did he realize how easy it was to be wrong, to utter familiar phrases without fully understanding the fallacy behind the words. Out of the corner of his eye, he saw four giant creatures flying straight for him. He had just enough time for one last thought, 'Pigs? Flying? That can't be right. It's impossible, surely?'

Jake and his gang had always been known as the "Men in Black", and proud of it, but a new name soon seemed more fitting. With each gang member now receiving at least a thousand "deposits" in the space of only a few seconds, they began to resemble four Greek statues carved out of a single block of pure white limestone. Such was the thickness of the coating and the rapid-setting nature of these deposits, any kind of motion or escape was impossible. It would take a torrential rainstorm or more to dissolve this new coating of natural cement and free the occupants from their statuesque positions.

Jake had apparently failed to fully comprehend his predicament. His three buddies heard a muffled command, 'Go, guys, go. Plan 25, you know, minimum twenty-five days in hiding. Go. Go. Go.' Alas, none of them were in any position to respond.

Meanwhile, Jo and her friends were examining the police who were lying unconscious on the ground behind them.

'Jo,' yelled Sally, 'this one has a horrible flesh wound in the leg.'

'Jo,' screamed Bill, 'it's Inspector Grabham, he's down.'

'Jo,' cried Fred, 'this one isn't breathing. There's blood everywhere. It's horrendous. The bullet's gone right through his heart.'

'I'm here Fred, let me see. Oh, poor man, that's terrible.'

(O) You can do it, Jo, you've done it once before. You did it for Gramps. Remember the focus and do it again. Concentrate, bring your mind and energy to the wound and call on your many millions of trusted friends and supporters.

'Fred, I don't know if I can do it, it's too late, look at him.'

'You can do it, Jo. Take a deep breath and do as the Ancients instructed. Let me help if I can.' Fred unbuttoned the man's jacket and shirt, trying hard not to think about what he was doing. He had no option but to wipe the blood from his fingers on the officer's shirt.

Jo concentrated intently as a tiny chunk of her own energy was transferred into the policeman's chest. What followed was like an avalanche, with an unbelievable rush of healing health energy arriving from all around the world, donated by billions of humans, animals, birds and insects, each determined to help, targeting their efforts towards the recovery of this mortally wounded police officer.

They watched. Suddenly the wound began to glow white before emitting an incandescent pale blue light. Then it faded away, leaving no trace of a scar, just a slight pinking of the skin. The blood stains on the shirt and jacket also began to vibrate and shake themselves into nothingness. One moment they were bright red, the next, they'd completely vanished. The officer coughed, slowly regaining consciousness as Fred and Jo carried him to a nearby bench. The other two officers were still unconscious. Satisfied that the first officer had stabilised, Jo and Fred carried the second officer to the bench, and Jo repeated the exercise, though the effort required to repair the leg injury was trivial by comparison.

Jo then joined Bill to examine Inspector Grabham, who was still out cold. 'There's nothing wrong,' mused Jo, 'except an enormous bump on his head. Perhaps he fell and hit his head on this bench.'

'He'll have a dreadful headache when he comes round,' said Bill.

There was a scurrying along the ground beside them as eight squirrels pushed and tugged four guns into the designated delivery zone. *'Thanks, Squeeel, that'll do nicely,'* said Jo.

'We should go and check Gramps and the others are OK, ideally before the police realize what's been going on,' suggested Fred.

'Look,' exclaimed Sally. 'Where did these statues come from? We were obviously too preoccupied to notice them earlier. They're pretty good carvings aren't they?'

'Probably part of the art fair starting here soon,' said Bill. 'And Jake and his gang have vanished. The cowards have done a runner.'

None of the kids heard the muffled cry coming from the statues as they turned to leave. As they passed the Choco Shop, Ben saw them and leapt out through the café door to bring them inside.

'You got away then kids?' asked Gran. 'We knew you would. That was madness, very frightening indeed. Thank you for diverting them away from us like that. They were about to shoot us, can you believe it? What nasty men.'

'They seem to have gone now, there's no sign of them anywhere. Thought we heard a few more shots in the distance,' lied Jo, fingers crossed once more.'

Abby looked at the four youngsters, knowing them well enough to recognize when she was not hearing the full truth. Bill winked at her and she smiled back, certain that the full details would shortly be revealed.

***

'Ooooh, what happened?' groaned the Inspector, his consciousness returning. He hauled himself up onto the bench.

'I really don't know. I was in excruciating pain, thought I'd been shot in the leg. I could almost see the bullets coming slowly towards me but then passed out with no real idea of what happened.'

'Me too. I thought I was having a heart attack,' said the other one.

'I thought I heard shots so I threw myself backwards,' said the Inspector, holding his head. 'One moment we seemed to be closing in on the kids, now I'm on the ground looking up at you two.'

'Well, that's a huge bump you have on your head. It's a beauty. You could win a prize with that.'

'Hmmmm, yeah, right, thanks,' he mumbled, holding his head. 'And what a state we're in, completely dishevelled, and your shirt is unbuttoned and ripped. What has happened to us?'

All three stood up slowly, brushing themselves down and tidying themselves up. They could not go about looking scruffy; the police had to adhere to a strict dress code and standards.

'Come on, let's go, we need to find those kids again, and get some answers,' said the Inspector.

'Hang on, what's this, by the bin?'

'It's a pile of guns, four of them,' said Inspector Grabham, 'and,' he added, sniffing the barrels, 'they have all been recently fired.'

They gathered them up, put them in transparent evidence bags, and walked slowly back past the four new statues, giving them nothing but a passing glance. On hearing sounds of laughter emanating from the Choco Shop they went in to see what all the merriment was about.

'Hi, Inspector Grabham isn't it? What can we do for you?' asked Gramps, who was sitting closest to the door.

'Oh, you lot again, all together once more, I see. Time for tea is it? Or is that just a cover for some kind of secret meeting? I need to ask these four kids what they were doing outside in the rain just now? Why they were playing with guns, and I mean real guns, not replicas? What exactly is going on?'

'Don't know what you mean, Inspector,' lied Jo yet again, severely worried about the diluting effect such behaviour might have on her trust status. 'We've been in here since before the rain came.'

'Don't you lie to me young lady,' he retorted. 'We saw you, we were right behind you! You were outside, standing in a line in the rain, and there were gunshots, bullets flying everywhere.'

'Inspector!' exclaimed Marge. 'Please. We received enough of your abuse yesterday evening at Scotney when all we were doing was helping you do your job. What's going on? Why are you after these youngsters, harassing them? Just feel their clothes. Are they wet? No. Are they even damp? No. Now please get on with your job of hunting down criminals and kindly leave us alone to enjoy our well-earned tea and cakes. Thank you.'

'Yes, well, it appears you have a point, they are completely dry. There's something very odd going on here and I will get to the bottom of it. Shooting in the Pantiles. This is most unusual, and here you all are, right in the thick of it. It can't be mere coincidence.'

Marge frowned, 'Inspector, maybe you need to tell us what's going on. You barge in here looking like death warmed up. Your uniforms have seen better days, they're scruffy and moth-eaten, full of holes. That's a very nasty bump on your head too. You look like you've been fighting a war? You're quite incoherent too. Maybe you're suffering from concussion? You seem more than a little exhausted too if you don't mind my saying.'

'Oh it's nothing, the swelling will soon go down. I've had far worse knocks I can assure you.'

Marge carried on. 'You were involved with the drug bust late last night, weren't you? I saw you handcuffing some of those drug dealers. We were there too, though not the kids of course. The action has been all over the news this morning, great result, well done.'

'Yes, we were, last night. It was very late indeed, early hours of the morning actually. We got called out at a moment's notice, missed supper entirely, but a positive result at least. And, now I think about it, I remember seeing some of you lot there too. You didn't have your APE uniforms on or your posh DJs. You were part of that cocoa group that stirred up all the trouble. Trying to do our job for us, again! Well, you don't know what you're letting yourselves in for. Besides, we can't have two groups fighting crime and antisocial behaviour. You should leave us to get on with these things. The Chief Constable is planning to have you nut cases outlawed.'

'He'll never do it,' said Marge politely but firmly. 'We're here to stay. The CoCoNuts are on a roll, doing many of the tasks that your lot either don't want to do, can't do, or aren't resourced for. Yesterday's two events prove that we can work together to good effect so you'd better educate your Chief Constable or you could all be out of work. With the CoCoNuts mushrooming as they are, some might even start asking why we need you. You'll be left just playing with your toys and having fun in those high-speed car chases.'

'Well, you might have a point there. I was incredibly impressed with how your team reacted and responded last night. It was a joy to behold the way you closed down those bars and pubs and ejected those drug dealers. How you found them doing business in alleyways and car parks was quite astonishing. The planning that went into it was remarkable. The degree of sophisticated communications required to co-ordinate everything was quite something. So, maybe you're right, we can learn a thing or two from you choconuts or whatever you call yourselves.'

Jo and her three friends, including Gran and Gramps, smiled inwardly. There was simply no way they could possibly explain about the role of the owls and the other night-time creatures that had been busy checking out every neighbourhood for drug related activity. Inspector Grabham would not believe a word about "togethering" or the Ancients, even if they were allowed to tell him.

'Well,' replied the Inspector, 'I look forward to our next challenge then. Perhaps this is the start of something new and wonderful. See you all very soon, no doubt.'

With that, the police departed, though Inspector Grabham had a nagging feeling that he had been deflected, having completely failed to get to the bottom of the day's events. On returning to his office later that day, he would eventually write two reports. The first would describe the shootings, entitled the "Pantiles Predicament", and would be the most challenging case study ever created, designed to underpin all future police investigative training. The second report would, in years to come, be hailed as a masterpiece in public/police collaboration, though Inspector Grabham would never remember writing a word of it. His recommendations would become widely recognized as the "Pantiles Prophecy", for which he would receive an MBE on his eventual retirement.

The police left the café, and who should appear but Grant and Gertrude strolling towards them, their dog Zorog in tow. Inspector Grabham called out, 'Not here to stir up more trouble I hope?'

'We're not doin' nuffink!' replied Gertrude. 'Why you always pickin' on us? We're just looking for some friends, but they're not 'ere, so we'll be on our way.' With that, she tugged at Zorog's lead to yank him away, but not before the smiling dog had cocked his leg and relieved himself all over the legs and feet of the new white statues. The police followed them closely, ushering them away before they could cause any mayhem.

Moments later Gramps and the others left the café too. 'We're heading home guys. See you at the music festival tomorrow.'

'I'll be there too,' said Abby. 'I just know it's going to be another great story. I can't wait.'

They all walked away, leaving Jo, Fred, Bill and Sally to mull over the events of the day. They sat down outside and ordered ice creams, well Bill did, for all of them, somewhat pleased with himself for getting their choices perfectly correct, without even asking.

Chapter 43

And So...

(O) Well done guys. That was a terrifying experience and more dangerous than we might ever have imagined. Amazingly you came through it without a scratch. And nicely handled with the police, Jo, so glad you were able to sort out their injuries without them having a clue as to the horrors they had been through.

You made it back to the Pantiles in the nick of time. Lobbing those massive books at Jake and his gang was a master stroke, and the added impetus provided by the rooks, without doubt saved the lives of Gran, Gramps and all your friends.

How the birds managed to create that curtain of rain water to spoil the aim of Jake and his men is something no one will ever believe. Then the way your squirrel mates and bird buddies were able to intervene and put Jake and his cronies out of action at such a critical and dangerous moment, when they were about to fire their guns a second time, was truly magnificent. It was all a magical demonstration of how "togethering" has the ability to resolve so many tricky situations.

We've had a marvellous few weeks, enjoyed it immensely, and you have achieved so much. It has been great fun though perhaps a little frightening at times. We hope you have enjoyed your brief introduction to the power of "togethering", though so far we've hardly scratched the surface of its capabilities. You will soon find that you are able to reach out, tackling problems and topics that have immensely greater importance in the grand scheme of things.

We were so incredibly lucky to detect your presence, Jo, all those years ago. Waiting for the right moment to intervene and encourage you to join us, has not been easy, but we knew we had to bide our time and watch you develop. You were just a few weeks old when your mother introduced you to Fred, and he was only a couple of days older himself. You were babies back then, both making strange gurgling noises and lying on a rug on the grass out in Fred's garden, close to our buried entryway where our special blue flowers were growing. We knew the time had finally come, recently, when you and Fred's family were discussing the position of their new garden shed. Luckily you were receptive to our suggestion for its location, and we knew that sooner or later you would unearth the entryway. We were even more delighted when you took onboard the idea of following Jake and doing battle with him and his not so merry men.

'I knew it, and they've finally admitted it,' said Fred. 'They've been behind everything we've been up to. They planned it and engineered the whole thing. But I still don't understand why they've picked you Jo, or why they've let the three of us tag along.'

(O) So, why have we chosen you, Jo? Perhaps now is the moment to explain the qualities we have been desperately searching for. Fred summed it up a week or so ago when your friends were waiting for you in the Pantiles the day after your mother's kidnapping.

'Oh no, surely they are not going to repeat all that are they?' mumbled Fred, turning away from Jo's questioning glare, desperately hoping to avoid another embarrassing moment.

(O) To begin with, care for all human and animal life and its welfare is of paramount importance. This implies a kind and caring nature and always being ready to help others whenever possible. Just as important is a love of the environment and everything in it, keeping it pure and healthy for all Earth's magnificent life forms.

Taking control of yourself, being responsible for your actions, not relying on others, is vital too. A strong, determined approach to life, never giving up, and doing the difficult things, not just what is easy, is another characteristic. And keeping to the rules of life, defined deep in your DNA, means always trying to do what you know to be right.

An appetite for learning and sharing knowledge is absolutely essential. In our world, information and knowledge are freely available, and shared with everyone, whether rich or poor, young or old, black or white, male or female. This is the primary building block of "togethering". We are great believers in collaboration, and as we work together to gain information and turn it into new knowledge, then everyone gets to share it too. As all four of you know by now, you have only to ask a question, and the answer will be found and returned in the blink of an eye.

It's what people do with knowledge and how they apply it that makes it valuable. We believe that imagination and creativity are the life blood of the future. Being innovative and inventive and able to imagine a future that benefits everyone, is the only way mankind will make real and lasting progress. We've been there and proved it.

'They're right,' said Fred. 'If everyone has the same base of knowledge then everyone has a chance to achieve something useful. A level playing field means equal opportunities for all.'

(O) So, Jo, you are the one we have been searching for. We found you in the nick of time, because your world is in grave danger.

We are not talking about any physical confrontation like an asteroid collision, a solar flare, or an alien invasion. Things like this are out of our hands; almost impossible to manage or control.

It's true that your people have made great strides forward in science, technology, health, and education, but you've made a nasty mess of nearly everything else.

Sadly, global warming has been horribly accelerated by your mindless over use of fossil fuels, and this has resulted in millions of human and animal deaths from rising sea waters, violent weather storms, and excessive pollution. Such negligence is hard to forgive.

Even worse is the treatment of the animal kingdom. In the wild you have encroached on their territories, taken their water, destroyed their forests, and allowed them to be killed even in the safety of their own reserves. The pollution of the seas with chemicals, plastics, sewerage, oil and other foul liquids is a disaster of immense proportions, destroying the habitat of some of the planet's most wonderful creatures.

The way you farm animals for their meat to support an ever growing human population crowding out the planet is abhorrent. It leaves these creatures with no pleasure in life, no life whatsoever. It's a horror that your world today should be utterly ashamed of.

Unbelievably it is the appalling way you humans treat each other that is the greatest failure of all.

'Oh dear! Not sure I wanted to hear all that', said Bill. 'Not exactly a high pass mark, two out of ten if we're lucky.'

'No, not pleasant words at all,' said Sally. 'We're quite good at the geeky stuff but terrible in the kindness and caring category.'

'They are only telling it how it is,' added Jo. 'There is so much pain in the world, so much bullying and inequality, everywhere you look. I guess it's time to face up to reality. The Ancients are right, but on the other hand, we see love and caring attitudes too, especially in families, hospitals and charities. And there are so many people giving their time to volunteer and help others. So the good things are there; they just need to break through so that one day our leaders and governments will finally see sense, work together, and start doing the right things for people, not always focusing on power and profit. Let their hearts rule their heads for once.'

(O) We arrived here twenty thousand years ago on our mission. It was the most important and challenging task that mankind has ever been entrusted with. We brought with us our gift to help with the mission, and that gift is "togethering". We believe we have shared it wisely. Now, Jo, it is over to you. You are ready to take on the responsibilities entrusted into your hands. You are the last hope. We tried this once before, long ago, but fell at the final hurdle. We won't make the same mistake again.

See you back in the cavern tomorrow morning before the music festival. We still have much to tell you.

'What are they talking about?' asked Fred. 'What exactly is "The Mission"?'

'Yes, I'd like to know too,' said Bill.

'And why us, why you Jo?' questioned Sally.

(O) Now, this is for your ears only, Jo. As we've already said, we did indeed set you up to oppose Jake and bring an end to his criminal activities and evil behaviour. Put simply, it has been a training exercise, but in reality it has been vastly more than that.

This has all been designed to introduce you to "togethering" and help you to understand and test out some of its capabilities. You have proved yourself in every way, and now you are almost ready. The full truth is that our gift to the world is in two parts. The first part is 'togethering". The second part, Jo, is ... you.

This is what our Mission is all about. It's time we shared it with you......

So, as you can see, it is an enormous challenge, full of fearful danger and frightening consequences. Greater than anything mankind could possibly imagine. This is why you need us every bit as much as we need you.

'I wish I knew,' answered Jo to her friends, her fingers crossed tightly behind her back as yet another white lie slipped out. She paused for a moment, her mind working overtime, desperately trying to understand the secret message that clearly only she had received.

They ate their ice creams, all the while wondering what the future might hold. What was the grave danger the Ancients had spoken of, and how could they do anything about it? They were just four teenagers. How could it possibly be their responsibility?

But in the last couple of weeks, they had changed, all four of them. Their confidence levels had grown enormously. Sally was now more self-assured, no longer uncertain and always ready to question and critique things, examining alternative actions and outcomes more carefully. Her chess had improved dramatically too, seeing her moves and counter-moves so clearly in her mind's eye. More than anything, she loved seeing the world with fresh, sharper eyes now that she no longer needed to wear glasses.

They all seemed fitter, healthier, happier and more at ease with the world. Both Sally and Bill felt stronger and full of energy, and they loved their exercises and daily runs in the park. Bill seemed a changed person too with good clear skin and healthy hair. He even had some muscles to show, helped by his new training programme and healthy diet.

Fred was still the same old Fred on the outside, but inside he felt different. He had no fears and knew he would always be there for his friends and anyone who needed support and assistance.

All four of them felt older and wiser than before and vastly more knowledgeable, able to concentrate with greater focus, less distraction, each thinking more deeply to help each other solve tricky issues and problems. They were beginning to get a strong sense of what was right with the world and, importantly, what was wrong.

If they were surprised by these changes and the strength of positive feelings that now embraced them they did not show it. Inside, however, they had a burning desire to share these qualities with everyone they met, knowing that patience was the key and that only "togethering" would know when the right time had come.

As for Jo, she suddenly knew *exactly who* she was and precisely why *she was* here. Nothing was going to *deter her from achieving* the goals that she was now seeing so clearly before her. In her mind, in just a few seconds, she had already formulated a detailed and demanding plan. She knew precisely how she and her *growing circle* of trust were going to tackle things left unspoken *by the Ancients.*

Jo knew that she had her family and three remarkable friends to help her. She had a circle of trust that was increasing by the day, creating a peaceful following of like-minded individuals by her side, throughout the world. Of course, she also had her helpers, her growing band of creatures in every corner of the planet, excited beyond belief to have rekindled this positive human relationship, desperate to forge a better place for all living things.

Then there were the Ancients, with her every step of the way, whoever they were, wherever they might be. They had given her "The Mission" and the means to carry it out. They had given her the gift of "togethering".

'I don't know if you realized it or not, Jo,' said Fred, 'but you were flickering in and out of "togethering" just then with your thoughts. We caught a few words, and we're ready for "The Mission", whatever it is. We are with you, no matter what.'

(O) And we heard it all too, Jo. We've known from the very beginning that you are the one, the only person who can do what has to be done. We will be with you, side by side, every step of the way, together.

As they walked towards the end of the Pantiles, they heard a roll of what sounded like thunder. Another torrential rainstorm was brewing. Once again the rain was tightly focused in just one small area, and that pressure slowly began to dissolve the four statues behind them.

Excited by the challenge of the music concert the next day, and anticipating a wonderful debrief by the Ancients, the four friends got ready to head home, oblivious to the fate of the slowly dissolving statues. They could not quite believe what was happening to them, how incredibly lucky they were to be part of the Ancients' world of "togethering". It was indeed a magical gift, and they knew their lives were about to be changed forever.

'You boys were very brave throwing yourselves in front of us just now, when the bullets were flying towards us,' said Jo smiling.

'Yes, you were,' teased Sally, a big grin crossing her face, 'even if your reactions were a bit on the slow side.'

The birds, squirrels, and thousands of tiny creatures nearby watched and smiled. The stories had been passed down from generation to generation for thousands and thousands of years. They knew that finally the world was poised for the most remarkable and important change in its history. The messages had been sent, far and wide, to all corners of the planet and to every creature alive or being born. They too knew that Jo was the one they had all been waiting for. This was the world's last opportunity, its only chance. They would do everything in their power to make sure it ended well.

Two squirrels watched them as they walked past. *'Squidge,'* said Squeeel, *'it's finally happening, at long last, just as they said it would. Isn't she wonderful?'*

'Yes, it's hard to believe,' replied Squidge, *'and yes, she most certainly is. The best friend we, and the world, could ever have.'*

As a family of butterflies fluttered gently by, a warm glow engulfed the teenagers as Jo took Fred's hand and Sally held Bill's. Their smiles showed they were honoured and happy to take forward the challenge being handed to them by the Ancients. Whatever it was, they were ready. They would do it. Together.

Author's Note

Did the Ancients really arrive on the shores of Southern England twenty thousand years ago? **Jo, Fred, Bill and Sally seem convinced that they did.**
Does the magnificent domed cavern with its beautiful arches cut out of stalagmites and stalactites really exist under the Common in Tunbridge Wells? **Jo and her friends know that it does.**
Is the magical gift of 'togethering' real and have the brains of Jo and her best friends really been enhanced by it? **How else could this story exist? It is way beyond the imaginings of any author.**
Does the Pantiles exist in Tunbridge Wells and is it as delightful and historic as the book suggests? **You'd better believe it.**
Does Wellington Rocks exist on the Common and is it possible to climb to the top? **Of course, we've all done it.**
Is there a derelict house hidden amongst the trees on the Common? **Maybe you just need to look harder.**
Is there a derelict cinema site in the heart of Tunbridge Wells known as the 'grot spot'? **Yes, though it has now been demolished.**
Are there any misdemeanors surrounding the cinema site and its refurbishment? **Certainly not, but it makes a great story line.**
Are Jake Grunt and his ghastly business associates real? **Of course not. We're talking Royal Tunbridge Wells here!**
Is there a vineyard near Tunbridge Wells? **Yes, more than one.**
Did John Constable really paint a picture in the beautiful grounds of Scotney Castle? **It is a perfect place to paint as any artist will tell you. So maybe Constable did too.**
Do tunnels exist under the Scotney Mansion and can they be accessed by a secret wall panel in the dining room? **Ask The National Trust, though some secrets are worth keeping!**
Are the CoCoNuts really a force to be reckoned with, righting wrongs and about to spread like wildfire? **Just you wait and see.**
What is The Mission and why is it the most challenging and fearful of any human endeavour ever undertaken? Why is Jo the only person on the planet capable of completing it? **All will be revealed ... one day ... soon ... get ready ... we'll do it ... together.**

Acknowledgements

This book would never have been completed without the encouragement of some very special people. They mostly know who they are including Ruth, Stephen, Sandy, Phil, Emma, Peter, John, Dennis, Charlotte and Moira. John from Dorset even read it while on holiday. Kevin from Essex provided much advice on shock and awe, and so much more. Mike from East Sussex found the anonymous manuscript in his porch and still found the time to read it and give great feedback. Without Sarah it would never have been written. She even gave up her Sunday evenings to go through it time after time after time. Immense thanks to all of you. Are you ready for book two?

Printed in Great Britain
by Amazon